He felt as if someone had thrust something sharp through his chest...

So beautiful! Instead of facing the terrifying notion that a St. Eyre had fallen in love with a woman who ran a crew of smugglers, he lifted her face up to his and slowly fastened his mouth on hers.

He slid the peignoir over Megaera's shoulders, and the costly garment fell to the floor unheeded in a crumpled heap. Meg's sigh, her half-parted lips, made him tremble with desire. Softly, under his breath, Philip began to moan . . .

"I love you. I want you. Love me . . ."

OTHER BOOKS BY
ROBERTA GELLIS

Alinor
Bond of Blood
The Dragon and the Rose
Gillianne
Joanna
Knight's Honor
Rhirannon
Roselynde
The Sword and the Swan
Siren Song
The English Heiress

The Cornish Heiress

Roberta Gellis

A DELL BOOK

Published by
Dell Publishing Co., Inc.
1 Dag Hammarskjold Plaza
New York, New York 10017

Produced by Book Creations, Inc.
Lyle Kenyon Engel, Executive Producer

Dell ® TM 681510, Dell Publishing Co., Inc.

ISBN: 0-440-11515-9

Printed in the United States of America
First printing—October 1981

The
Cornish Heiress

Chapter 1

"Have you given Philip money to pay his debts again, Leonie?" Roger St. Eyre asked his wife.

Leonie raised her golden eyes to her husband's bright blue ones. "*Sacré bleu,*" she sighed, "please do not be angry with him, Roger. It does not mean anything to me—you know that. It was not that he feared to go to you. It is only—I cannot bear to see him so unhappy. He did not ask me. He does not even know—"

"I know that," Roger said, kissing her fondly and sitting down beside her. "How do you think I found out? Philip came to thank me, and to tell me—very stiff and proper—that it was not necessary. He had his own plan for settling, he said. I just told him that I hadn't known he was in debt again."

"Stiff and proper?" Leonie repeated anxiously. "Is he still angry because you would not buy him a commission, Roger?"

"No. He may be a fool, but not that much of a one. He did as I suggested and looked into the matter more carefully. Besides, I didn't say I *wouldn't* buy him a commission. I said I didn't think the life would suit him and pointed out that he was just as likely to be sent to the Indies or ordered to guard one of the damn palaces as to be involved in the war with France. He went out to prove me wrong—and found out I was right."

"Do you think he will wish to enter the navy now?" Leonie asked fearfully.

"No." Roger smiled. "The navy is not a service a person can enter as an adult. Besides, Philip knows that life is even more rigid and restricted than the army." Roger paused and his mouth hardened. "God in heaven, I will never forgive myself. I should have strangled Solange a week after she gave birth to him. Dead thirteen years, her curse still lingers."

Leonie did not answer that. She never uttered any criticism of her husband's first wife, although she often felt she would have killed Solange with her bare hands had she not been dead already. Roger was right. The scars Solange had inflicted on her husband and her son, though healed, still deformed them. Solange had ignored Philip as an infant, and later had tried to use him to manipulate Roger. The only reason Philip was not totally ruined was that Roger had given him the warmth and tenderness, the unvarying affection that made him a whole person.

To save his own sanity, Roger had yielded to Solange in her insistence on surrounding Philip completely with French servants. It did not seem important to him that the child spoke French far better than English. He was bilingual himself and assumed Philip would drop the French for English when he started school. He was more concerned with his son's character, and he talked to him a great deal about the need to reason out what was right rather than blindly do what a feared—or even a loved—authority ordered.

Roger was thinking of Solange when he was so insistent that Philip reason rather than obey. However, the habit of independent thinking, encouraged by Roger himself always listening to his son and explaining why a thing must be done, was naturally carried beyond his mother's influence. Innocently, Roger had taught Philip to resist the urge to "be like everyone else," because that was the excuse Solange used most often to explain her gambling and extravagance. He never meant, of course, that Philip should resist when what "everyone else" was doing was good and sensible, and, in general, Philip did understand that. However, the habit of sticking by his guns unless there was a good reason not to had wider repercussions than Roger ever dreamed.

These began quite early. When Philip went to school and the boys called him "Frenchy," he blacked their eyes to prove he was a good Englishman rather than change his patterns of speech. In fact, the pressure of his peers and his teachers made him cling passionately to his accent and to speaking French by preference. The problem eventually grew so acute that the headmaster referred it to Philip's father.

After soothing the headmaster, who was greatly incensed by the flouting of his authority and not at all in sympathy with Roger's notion that he should have given Philip a *reason* for speaking English rather than simply ordering him to do so and beating him when he refused, Roger interviewed his son.

"It does no harm," Philip said stubbornly. "It is *my* way of speaking."

Roger could not help chuckling. "It certainly did no good to Lord Erne's eye or to Lord Kevern's nose, not to speak of the Honorable Elliot's loose teeth."

Philip had cast a flickering glance at his father. What he saw made him grin cheerfully. "Perce and Harry did not mind, and they were not Elliot's *front* teeth, sir. They were the side ones that had to come out anyway. Really, sir, I do not see why the headmaster made such a fuss. The other fellows only wanted to be sure I was not a sissy. We are all friends now."

"Well, there are less destructive ways of proving

your manhood," Roger felt obliged to say, but the
reprimand was rather spoiled by the twinkle in his
eyes and the golden guinea he pressed into his son's
hand. Then he grew more serious. "But I do not like
rudeness, Philip, and it is *very* rude to chatter in a
language others around you don't understand or have
difficulty understanding. Certainly I don't insist that
you speak English exactly as the others do, but I hope
you will be sufficiently a gentleman in the future to
match your manner and speech to your company."

The arrested look on the boy's face—cruel rudeness
was one of the devices his mother had used both on
him and, in front of his face, on his father—showed
Roger he had made his point, and he said no more.
A good reason was usually enough to set Philip on the
right path. He was a remarkably intelligent child. To
a degree Roger was right. There was no more trouble
about language. Although Philip never lost his accent
and French continued to be the language he spoke by
preference, he soon switched back and forth between
English and French without thought, responding
automatically to the tongue in which he was addressed.

However, Roger had long ago stopped worrying
about Philip's speech. He was an extremely, a compul-
sively, just person. "It is not fair to blame Solange
completely," he said. "I had more influence on Philip.
My lectures on reason sank in a little too far, I suppose."

Leonie could not restrain a little giggle at that
understatement. She suppressed it as quickly as she
could, but her eyes danced. "*Eh bien,* but once Philippe got to Oxford he was much better," she comforted as gravely as she could. "He saw the reasons for
the rules and was quite—ah, *ma foi*—most of the time
he stayed out of trouble." Then the laughter died out
of her face and her big golden eyes looked haunted.
"But his hatred for the French—that is my fault. I—"

Roger put his arms around his wife and kissed her.

"You have done him only good, my love. You always knew just how to deal with him."

"But I never corrected him," she murmured. "I let him get into all kinds of mischief. I even joined him. You were often angry—"

"Never angry, Leonie." Roger smiled at her. "Sometimes exasperated, but never angry. Anyway," he added briskly, "you were right. You could stop him from doing anything really dangerous or bad just with that *'Mais, Philippe, non!'* where all my lectures—and reasons—would have been useless."

"Yes, in little things, but in this . . . Oh, Roger, you can make me talk of something different, but it is my hatred of the French that Philippe has absorbed. I tried not to—but . . ."

"Don't be silly, Leonie. You don't hate the French, you're half French yourself. I don't think he hates them either. He's just young. He wants to be a hero."

"*Bien sûr*, but it is more than that. When the war was declared in 1793, Philippe did not care. Your stepmother told me. He was worried about you, but once you were back he showed no interest in the war. I know that because all he talked of was his school—the games and sports. It was only after he started to ask me what had happened to my family that he began to talk of the 'iniquities' of the French."

Roger shrugged. "Then it is my fault. I told him more than you ever did. All you said was that it was dull and uncomfortable to be in prison."

"But he is very sensitive, that Philippe, and *very* clever. He read inside me. . . . He saw. . . ."

She shuddered and Roger held her closer. Neither of them talked of the real horrors of Leonie's imprisonment, of how she had been brutally raped by several men, of her mother and brother dying in the filthy cellar where they had been confined, of her f being shot and killed during their escape. Roge that she was right, that despite her light, s fusal to discuss those dreadful months, Philip had drawn his own conclusions. Philip adored Leonie. He would very likely wish to revenge her hurts. However, that was something Roger would never admit. He would not, if he could prevent it, permit Leonie to blame herself for what could not be helped.

"Nonsense," he said briskly. "He never said a word about joining the army all the time he was at Oxford. He talked himself into 'hatred' in those damned debating societies. I wish they had improved his English instead of fixing the horrors of 'republicanism' in his mind. And then the 'peace' nearly drove him insane."

Diverted momentarily, Leonie giggled again. "You were no better, raving on and on about Cornwallis accepting terms that were only fitting for a 'defeated nation' and taking worse losses at the conference table than he had in the American colonies. Humiliating, you said."

"I still think so." Roger's blue eyes flashed vividly. "And then Bonaparte violated every provision, and screamed bloody murder when we would not evacuate Malta." He shrugged again. "It was that, I suppose, that really set Philip off. I should have held my tongue. It was when war was declared again that he first said he wanted a commission. Perhaps I should just have purchased it and let—"

"No!" Leonie exclaimed. "He would have ended up in Court-Martial. Besides, Philippe admitted he was wrong. I know he was furious at first, but he was very glad to make up the quarrel when you sent for him."

"Yes," Roger sighed, "but things aren't really much better. He's never sober, and I'm afraid he's developing a taste for gaming that will end in disaster. And then I had to be so stupid as to suggest buying him a seat in Parliament."

Leonie squeezed her husband's hand sympathetically, but there was little she could say. That suggestion had been very unwise. It only produced another

THE CORNISH HEIRESS 15

violent quarrel in which Philip, quite justly, accused his father of violating his principles out of affection. It was true, but Leonie knew Roger hated to see his son turning to the usual opiates of a young man with money—wine, women, and gambling.

"I'm at my wits' end," Roger admitted. "There's nothing to do but let him run his course."

Roger had traveled the same road himself after his first marriage turned sour, so he had not criticized his son's excesses. He had not even remonstrated with Philip when he outran his very generous allowance, but had paid the debts presented without a word of blame. The second time Roger had said only, "Draw it a little milder, Philip. You look like hell."

Because self-disgust and guilt do not breed patience in the young, this gentle reproof had sent Philip back to his own chambers in a black rage, which expanded into another round of wild parties and all-night gambling sessions. It was fortunate that Philip was either a lucky or a skillful gambler. Men had been known to gamble away their entire fortunes in a night. The Duchess of Devonshire was reputed to have lost £50,000 in one session at the tables. Philip's excesses were not of that magnitude. Nonetheless, he was soon in debt again.

He had said nothing to his father this time, resolved to find his own solution to the problem he had created. At another time Roger would have noticed that his son was more than usually disturbed. This time he did not. For one thing, he had become accustomed to seeing Philip miserable and sullen; for another, he was extraordinarily busy. When it became apparent that the war would be resumed, Roger had been asked to act as a consultant on French affairs to Lord Hawkesbury, the Foreign Minister.

It was thus Leonie who had noticed that her ste~ was more than ordinarily depressed. Thinki~ could avoid another confrontation between f?

son, Leonie had deposited a large sum in Philip's account, telling his banker (who was hers also) to deny he knew where the money came from. Fortunately for the banker, Philip had never thought to ask. When he found his account unnaturally swollen, he had assumed his father had tried to spare him the embarrassment of asking for money yet again. Philip had found this generosity even more acutely painful, and Roger's prompt and surprised denial—which made it plain that his stepmother had been the culprit—caused him even greater anguish.

"I will not touch it," he had raged. "Leonie has no right—"

At which point Roger's long patience had snapped and he had gotten to his feet so quickly that the chair he had been sitting on crashed to the floor. "If you say one word or do one thing to hurt Leonie," he roared, "I will give you the hiding you have well deserved for these past six months. Now get the devil out of here! Take yourself and your petty vapors down to Dymchurch and stay there until you can say 'Thank you' to your stepmother with becoming gratitude. And don't show either of us that sullen face again. *Get out!*"

Roger's lips tightened as he thought of the scene, and Leonie relaxed her grip on his hand and sighed. "He was angry about the money. No, he was quite right to be angry. I see now it was a stupid thing to do. I did not think—only that a young man would be careless and take it gladly and say nothing. I should have realized he is too much like you—too honest. I will tell him I am sorry when he comes today. You know he stops in almost every day."

"You will do nothing of the sort," Roger said sharply. "Nasty, ungrateful whelp that he is. And don't think he's angry with *you*—because he won't come today. I sent him off to Dymchurch with a flea in his ear."

Leonie said nothing for a moment, looking down at

her hand held tight in her husband's clasp. In some ways she knew Philip better than Roger did. She understood his fury. It was the natural outlet for a child's frustration, but Philip was no child. Leonie understood that he would be sickened by his own behavior as soon as he recognized it. In retribution he would meekly pay his debts and stay at his father's estate until he was released—but that was no solution to the problem. In fact, it would only make it worse.

"We must do something," she said in a constricted voice. "If he felt he were part of a real effort in the war, he would be willing to take orders. Why cannot one join the navy as a man? Philippe knows well how to sail. All summer he is in that boat of his, and he used to go with Pierre. Do they not need men who know how to sail?" Her beautiful eyes dimmed. "I would be afraid for him, *bien sûr*, but—but I am growing afraid more and more of what will happen if he does not find—find—whatever it is for which he seeks."

"I, too," Roger agreed, "but the navy is not the answer."

"Pierre!" Leonie exclaimed suddenly. In her desperate attempt to find a solution, she suggested Roger should ask Pierre Restoir to tell Philip he needed help aboard the *Bonne Lucie*. Pierre was a Breton smuggler, an old friend of Roger's, who had been responsible for getting Roger and Leonie out of France in the days when the guillotine was claiming its daily victims. He had saved their lives; perhaps, Leonie was thinking, he could save Philip's.

"I can't go to Pierre," Roger replied. "Don't think I haven't considered it myself. The trouble is that if Pierre gets caught he'd only be interned as a prisoner of war—and I could probably get him paroled into my custody. If Philip got caught, they'd hang him as a traitor. Well, maybe I could save him from that, but he'd be ruined for good, Leonie."

Still, the idea lingered in Roger's mind. Although

Pierre was nearly sixty now, and a rich man from the years of successful smuggling, he still engaged with enthusiasm in his illegal trade. He had weathered the Terror by moving his base of operations to the Low Countries, and during those years he and Roger met frequently. Though Pierre was not a spy, he would bring Roger what information he heard, particularly any new word of French ship movements. When the Netherlands was overrun by the French, Pierre returned to his native Brittany and from there succeeded in making contact with a smuggling gang in Cornwall.

During the Peace of Amiens, Pierre had visited Roger and Leonie once or twice just for the pleasure of seeing them. He told them he had made a most satisfactory connection in Cornwall with, believe it or not, a woman. "She drives a devilish bargain," Pierre had complained, shaking his head at the paring of a profit he did not in the least need but felt obliged to make as large as possible on principle. However, she was honest, he insisted, which was more than two other groups he had dealt with before. Roger had choked over the word "honest" in connection with smuggling, but he did not argue. He knew what Pierre meant. Smuggling was illegal, but if you did not overcharge and fulfilled your commitments as to quantity and quality, it was not, in Pierre's opinion, dishonest.

Since the renewal of the war Roger had not seen his friend, but he knew where to reach him. West of Penzance on the rocky Cornish coast was an alehouse called The Mousehole. There messages could be left, as they had once been left at the Soft Berth in Kingsdown. The trouble was that The Mousehole was three hundred miles from London rather than about seventy. If it had not been for that, Roger thought as he made his way to his legal chambers the next morning, he would have been inclined at least to ask Pierre's advice. He *was* at his wits' end regarding what to do about Philip.

* * *

When Roger arrived at his office on the morning of October 8, he found a message requesting that he call in at the Foreign Office at eleven o'clock. Roger looked at it blankly and then told his clerk to cancel his appointments from ten-thirty on, unless he could handle the problem himself. Actually, Roger was somewhat relieved. His mind was so full of Philip that he doubted he would have been much good to either a legal or a political client.

The meeting at the Foreign Office, on the other hand, would probably not require any serious thought. Lord Hawkesbury liked to hear himself talk, but he liked an audience too. There would probably be a group among whom Roger would be lost. By and large Lord Hawkesbury's ideas were harmless, so Roger did not feel obliged to do or say anything beyond a nod now and again. He was somewhat surprised, therefore, to find his lordship alone and to be waved to a seat on the opposite side of his desk.

"I am given to understand that you know France and the French very well," Hawkesbury began.

"I have done business with them for many years," Roger replied cautiously. "Both of my wives were born in France. I have visited many times and from 1791 through 1794 I lived in France. Whether that means I know France and the French, I am not sure."

"You know that Bonaparte was assembling a fleet at Boulogne to invade England just before the peace, and that work was resumed on that fleet with enormous energy when war was declared again." Hawkesbury touched a file of papers. "Some of the information seems to have come from you, but we have other information that implies that work on that fleet was never completely discontinued."

"I do not believe the latter can be true," Roger remarked. "A friend—the one from whom I obtained the other information you mentioned and, er, whose name

I prefer not to give, told me that the craft already built were lying unprotected and were decaying from neglect. This was some time in May, shortly after the declaration of war. I have no reason to disbelieve him, as we have been friends for nearly thirty years and he has risked his life for mine more than once."

Hawkesbury looked at him. "Yet a man may do things for his country that he would consider below mention on a personal level."

"You mean he might have lied for the sake of *la belle France?*" Roger smiled. "No, he is not French and does not love any government at all. He regards governments as useless and oppressive organizations designed solely for the enrichment of those who govern."

Lord Hawkesbury sputtered with indignation, and Roger had to fight an urge to laugh aloud. Often since he had become a member of Parliament he had found himself in agreement with Pierre. However, there was no sense in offending Lord Hawkesbury, who was personally an honest man if not a brilliant one and who, for once, really seemed to need and want information.

"Do you mean, St. Eyre, that you do not think a fleet is building at Boulogne?"

"Not at all. I am sure one is being built now. During the peace, I renewed many of my old contacts, and I have reason to believe Bonaparte is obsessed with the notion of invading England. There might be some reason, however, for wanting us to think the work was more forward than it is in reality."

"Were your French contacts reliable?"

"Oh, yes," Roger said dryly. "One of them was a cousin of Joseph Fouché, who is—as much as any man could ever be—in his confidence."

Hawkesbury pursed his lips thoughtfully. Joseph Fouché, like the astute Talleyrand, had managed to survive the Terror, keep his balance *and* his influence through the unstable Directories, and was one of those involved in the coup d'état that had placed Bonaparte in power. Unlike others who had done favors for the First Consul, Fouché was neither imprisoned nor exiled. In fact, as head of the Ministry of Police, it was on his advice that others were removed, temporarily or permanently, from circulation. He seemed to be suffering a brief eclipse, dating from 1802, which was when Roger had met him again on a very short visit to France, but there was considerable evidence that Bonaparte still listened quite closely to that efficient and totally unfeeling gentleman. Everyone assumed that Fouché would soon be back in office.

"Can you still reach this man?"

"No, Maître Fouché died quite suddenly a few months after my visit, but even if he were alive I would not try. Maître Fouché was an old friend and a fellow barrister, but he was also a loyal Frenchman and would have told nothing, even if he knew anything to tell, which I doubt. His daughter is still alive, but being Fouché's cousin would be no protection to her. If anything, it would be a danger. If Joseph learned his cousin had contact with the English, he would throw her to the wolves in a moment—provided, of course, he thought it would do him some good."

"I see." Hawkesbury frowned. "That is not much help. We have a problem that I hoped you could solve. Receiving intelligence from France is not difficult. There are many émigrés who profess themselves eager to serve England as their adopted country. However, since the amnesty Bonaparte offered, it is growing more and more difficult to determine which of our agents are loyal. Furthermore, those whose loyalty cannot be doubted, like poor Jacques d'Ursine, are so bitter that their opinions cannot be trusted. If one were to believe Jacques, Bonaparte must drink babies' blood, have twenty million men under arms, and be capable of appearing in five places at once."

"I have heard him," Roger said dryly. He did not like Jacques d'Ursine, who suffered too much from self-pity for his taste, and he did not think it wise to have a monomaniac around the Foreign Office, even if the man's mania was enmity to Bonaparte. However, d'Ursine was Hawkesbury's personal secretary, and it was none of Roger's business whom he chose to employ.

Hawkesbury shook his head. "Yes, poor Jacques. Well, what with one thing and another, it is almost impossible to weed out what is true from what is deliberately planted—like the information that hundreds of seaworthy craft are ready for launching at Boulogne."

"My dear Lord Hawkesbury," Roger exclaimed, "that may be true, for all I know, although it sounds unlikely. My information is from May. I have no idea how quickly such ships could be repaired and built if sufficient men and materials were available."

"Neither do we," Hawkesbury said wryly. "That is, we have most contradictory reports as to what is happening. Unfortunately, until we are sure how forward the enterprise is, more of our ships of the line than the Admiralty likes are committed to the Channel."

He passed across the desk from the file under his hand a copy of a report from Lord Keith, Commander in Chief in the North Sea, on which some lines were heavily marked. Roger read: "A fleet or squadron may get out of Brest unperceived and watch for an opportunity for running up to the Downs or Margate roads, in which case it might be superior to our squadron long enough to cover the landing of any extent of force from the opposite coast."

"You spoke of a friend who seems to have knowledge of the condition of the fleet at Boulogne," Hawkesbury said when he saw that Roger had read the marked passage. "Do you think—"

"He is not in that area any longer," Roger interrupted, "and he is not the kind one can pay to spy. He would tell me if he knew, but I doubt he would be willing to interrupt his business to find out. Nor could I reach him quickly or surely. His English base is on the Cornish coast, but," Roger smiled ruefully, "I'm afraid his business is quite illegal—"

"I gathered as much from your reluctance to use his name or give any other particulars," Hawkesbury said with dissatisfaction, then sighed. "Do you have *any* suggestion as to how we could check on this matter?"

All the time they had been talking Philip lay heavily at the back of Roger's mind. When Lord Hawkesbury brought up the subject of Pierre acting as a spy, the two things clicked together. Pierre would not be bothered with deliberately gathering information, but he could be relied upon to carry Philip into France and back again to England. In fact, he would do much more for Philip. He would doubtless be willing to introduce him to the whole chain of smugglers and corrupt officials with whom he was connected, and he would protect him in any way possible.

Roger looked across at Lord Hawkesbury and bit his lip. "I am not sure," he said slowly. "I do have an idea, but I—I am very reluctant . . . It is my son, you see—"

"Your son? My dear St. Eyre, how could a young Englishman gather information in France? He would be betrayed by his speech and manners—"

"Not Philip," Roger interrupted. "You may believe me when I say he can pass as French easily. He will not even have the problem that your émigré spies have. Their accent is aristocratic. Philip's is pure Parisian and a bit coarse, since it comes mostly from his servants. However, I am not sure he will be willing and—and I am not sure, my lord, that *I* am willing to broach the matter to him. It is very likely that if he is caught, he will be executed out of hand. Bonaparte is not as particular as we are to observe the niceties."

Lord Hawkesbury made no answer to that for a moment and then rose to pull a bell rope that would

summon a footman. Seating himself again, he drew a
sheet of blank paper toward him. "I am writing to see
if Mr. Addington will receive us," he remarked to
Roger as he scrawled the request. "I think he can better convince you of the urgency of the situation. I can
understand your feelings, St. Eyre. This is not the same
as agreeing that a son enter one of the services. Any
particular ship or army unit might never see action at
all, whereas in this case you, personally, would be sending your son into great peril. It is my opinion that we
must ask this sacrifice of you, but let us hear what Mr.
Addington has to say."

In fact, although Addington confirmed the great necessity for accurate information and went so far as to
summon the Secretary for War, who further confirmed
this opinion and added other details, it was far more
the memory of Philip's face and behavior over the past
months that convinced Roger. It was true Philip might
be caught and killed, but Roger trusted his son's
brains and "Frenchness" and Pierre's help. Pierre had
never been caught, and he would watch over Philip as
carefully as if he were his own son. Most significant of
all, Roger felt that if he could not soon find something
Philip could do—that Philip felt was worth doing—his
son would sink deeper and deeper into self-destructive
habits until he would, perhaps, be better off dead.

Tentatively Roger agreed to put the question to
Philip and, torn first by one fear and then another,
decided to post out to Dymchurch House that very day.
He could not bear to face Leonie and tell her what he
had done. If Philip refused, as he had refused every
other suggestion Roger had made concerning ways to
occupy himself, Leonie would not need to be worried.
He sent a note to tell her he was going to Dymchurch
to speak to Philip, promised he would not quarrel
with his son again, and said he would be home the
following evening.

There was no trouble in traveling. The road from

London to Dover had many posting houses with excellent teams of horses for hire. In his eagerness to leave, Roger had not even wanted to wait while his own phaeton was brought round from the house. Besides, he was afraid he might find Leonie in the carriage if he sent for it. His wife was highly intelligent and not the most docile and biddable woman in the world. She would certainly suspect that something more was going on than he had told her. Ordinarily Leonie would never interfere between Roger and Philip, but in view of their less than amicable parting, she might feel any discussion between them would be improved in civility by her presence. Thus, Roger hired a post chaise.

He was very sorry before they had covered half the distance. There was no fault to be found with the progress they were making, but without the necessity of driving himself, Roger had nothing to do but think. He began to wonder whether he was lying to himself, whether he was sending Philip off to be killed because he was so selfish that he didn't want to put up with his son's bad temper. By nine-thirty, when the chaise drawn by the last team of smoking horses came up the long drive and stopped in front of Dymchurch House, Roger would have turned around and started back to London if he had not known that the horses and postillion were too done up for another stage.

The condition in which he found Philip rapidly reversed the opinion of himself as a deliberate murderer on which he had been brooding during the long drive. Philip was not dead drunk, but he certainly was not sober and he looked like death warmed over.

"Could you not trust me to come here?" he asked belligerently as soon as Roger walked in.

"I have something serious to talk to you about," Roger said, ignoring his son's remark. "Are you sober enough to listen?"

"Now what have I done?" Philip snarled.

"Nothing sensible for months, if you want the

truth," Roger snapped, "but I have a proposition to make to you. There is a piece of work for which you are suited. It is not nice work, and it is very dangerous, but it will be of infinite benefit to our nation if you can stay alive long enough to do it."

"I thought you had given up discovering petty tail-chasing occupations . . ." Philip began, but his voice drifted off as the pain and fatigue on his father's face finally pierced through the alcoholic fog in his brain.

"Do you want to wait until morning?" Roger asked.

"No." Philip got to his feet, wavering only slightly. "Give me twenty minutes, sir, and I will be ready for you."

Chapter 2

The twenty-four sturdy ponies strung together made surprisingly little noise as they trotted docilely down beside the narrow stream toward the sea. The path was well defined, but that did not bother the lead rider. People from the village were encouraged to beach their boats in the cove and eke out their thin crops by fishing. There were plenty of reasons for a path to be trodden flat leading to Lamorna Cove. The reason the ponies' hooves were muffled was to keep the sound of steel striking stone from echoing off the naked cliffs that rose on each side of the narrow valley the stream had cut.

That sound might have been what betrayed to a revenue cutter the smugglers who had used Treen Cove, or it might have been an information laid. That was what the gang had thought, and it had led to murder; but the gang had been broken, although about half of its members and its leader had escaped. Since the war had started up again, there were fewer customs men around; they and their ships had more important duties than watching for a boatload of wine and brandy that would not pay duty. On the other hand, naval patrols were frequent, and sound

carries a long distance over water. It would be stupid
to take the chance that such sounds as ponies trotting
through the night should be heard and reported.
Many things were said of the new leader who had
reorganized the scattered smugglers, but never that she
was stupid.

The ponies emerged into the open area of the cove.
Shadows stirred in the darkest place against the cliffs,
resolved themselves into men who came forward and
led the ponies into the concealment they had come
from. The lead rider dismounted, and from the end of
the string of ponies a giant trotted forward to loom
over the small, slender woman. The breeches she wore
were no attempt to conceal her sex, merely a conces-
sion to the security of riding astride.

If any of the men looked at her with sexual interest,
he did so only from the concealment of the dark. One
man had been knocked senseless for making a suggestive remark; another had an arm broken for touching
her. Now all were very careful.

The giant made a soft, gobbling noise, and the
woman turned to him and took the lantern he handed
her. Kneeling, she struck flint, lighted a spill from the
tinder, and lit the lamp. There was only a faint back-
glow, for three sides were blackened and dark wings,
which the woman had opened when she lit the lantern,
shielded the front. It would not be possible to see the
light anywhere but from a ship on a direct line from
the cove. The little light that reflected upward and
from a scratch or two in the blackened surfaces was
blocked by the woman's body.

In that dim light her features were remarkably fine.
Close examination would have showed her eyes to be
a quite astonishing violet color, distinctive and unmistakable, but no one in the smuggling group ever got
very close. In the dark her eyes looked black at a few
feet. A straight nose, just barely tip-tilted, and an adorable full-lipped mouth were made less appetizing by

streaks and smudges of dirt and a mass of tangled, stringy, seemingly filthy red hair. Occasionally the cleverer men wondered why Red Meg stayed so coarse and dirty. She must be making plenty of money on the smuggling lay, but she hadn't changed her clothes—or, apparently, washed her face—in the year they had known her. Such thoughts, when they came, were usually suppressed quickly. Red Meg didn't like questions —and the dummy made sure none were asked.

Almost as soon as the lantern was directed seaward a light flashed back from beyond the low breakers. It went out, then flashed twice, then once again. Red Meg worked the wings of the lantern in some response pattern. The men did not bother watching. The pattern from the ship seemed to change each time, and probably the reply changed also. There was no chance of slumming that arch doxy. She was up in every suit. There was no sense in it anyway. She paid fair. It was just the fact that she was a woman that some resented —that and that she was dead set against any trouble in the local villages. No robbery or fooling with the women except on order—and there was never an order for those things, only once or twice for a burning.

There was another flicker of light from the sea. This time only one short blink. Red Meg turned her head toward the men waiting in the shadow and said, "Go."

They hurried forward and began to run the villagers' small boats into the water. If there was sun the next day, the boats would be dry and the villagers would never know they had been used. If there was no sun, damp might well linger in the bottoms of the boats. However, no one would remark on it, just as no one would turn a head or get out of bed to look when the ponies passed through the town, as they sometimes did. It was much, much safer to notice nothing. Curiosity resulted in inexplicable damage to one's crops, in a house burnt to the ground.

The squire's daughter, Mrs. Edward Devoran, had

made good the loss, but there was no guarantee that she would do it again, and thus it was an adequate warning for them all. Next time it might be a killing, and even Mrs. Devoran would not be able to cure that. So when the soft thud of many hooves passed in the night, those with windows by the bed turned their faces to the blank wall. There had been some angry muttering before acceptance was forced on them, but it was no distaste for smuggling that caused it. Quite the contrary. The men from the village were angry because they were never employed in the lucrative work.

As time passed the villagers grew resigned, particularly since a few coins were periodically found in the boats left in the cove. It was better to profit from the smuggling that way. Mrs. Devoran was kind, but she was a great stickler for obeying the law, and she hated smugglers. This wasn't surprising, because it was rumored that a smuggler had shot and killed her husband. The village women looked at each other whenever the subject of the late Edward Devoran came up. He was surely no loss to his wife, whether or not she knew it.

Oddly enough, Red Meg was thinking almost identical thoughts to those of the village women. She thought of Edward every time she came out to meet Pierre's ship. Edward's death and the events that followed it had restored Megaera Devoran's faith in God. She grinned in the dark when she thought of the vicar's horror if he knew the source of both her faith and her generous contributions to St. Buryan's. But really, seven years as Edward's wife had just about made an atheist of Megaera; she had had to become Red Meg to believe again.

It hadn't been too easy to believe in the goodness of God before that, either. After her mother had died, her father had disintegrated rapidly. He had never been a strong person; he was sweet and kind but always sadly addicted to the bottle and the gaming table. Lady Bolliet had ruled her husband, and her daughter was also strong-willed, but Megaera had been too young to take control when her mother died.

Then, somewhere, Lord Bolliet had met Edward Devoran and fallen so deeply in debt to him by gambling that he could not pay. How the two men had come to the conclusion that Megaera's hand in marriage would clear the debt, she never discovered. When she asked her father, he burst into tears; when she asked Edward, he laughed. Now, Megaera knew, she should simply have refused, but then she had been only fifteen. With her father weeping and babbling of ruin, utter ruin, and Edward, handsome and soft-spoken, assuring her that it was her beauty that had driven him to using such underhanded methods, Megaera had agreed to the marriage.

She had lived to regret it bitterly. Within weeks of the ceremony Edward was after the servant girls. When Megaera, not so much hurt as outraged, had told him in no uncertain terms that he was to leave the girls alone, he had tried to beat her. He had learned swiftly not to do that. Megaera had defended herself with furniture, teeth, and nails. Edward had ended more bruised than she. Then, to enforce the lesson, she had set John on him. He had been beaten so soundly by the giant deaf-mute that he was in bed for several weeks. He had no recourse because he had already made himself so obnoxious to everyone in the house that with one voice they would have perjured themselves about the cause of his injuries.

That had ended any open contest and any marital relationship between Edward and Megaera. Unfortunately Edward was clever and Megaera was innocent; Edward had his revenge. Over the next five years he had encouraged his father-in-law's weaknesses. Lord Bolliet sank deeper and deeper into alcoholism. Megaera did what she could, but it was impossible to

watch her father day and night, and she could not
bear to set a keeper over him; in spite of everything
she loved him. That, and not recognizing Edward's
part in her father's decay, was a serious mistake. Somehow, over the years, Edward had forced or deceived
Lord Bolliet into mortgaging his properties. By the
time Megaera discovered what was going on, the debt
was very large compared to the value of the lands.

Over the next two years she had paid the interest
and a bit of the capital by selling her mother's jewels.
There was no need to set a watch on her father to be
sure he signed no more papers. No banker or even
usurer would lend a penny more on the Bolliet estates.
Megaera pared expenses to the bone, but there was no
way to pay off the debt out of income. She watched
her resources dwindle with helpless terror. There
would soon come a time when she and her father
would be thrust penniless out of their home.

Naturally enough, the first restriction on expenses
was the allowance that had been paid Edward. Nor
could he take anything from the house to sell or pawn.
All the servants watched him eagerly, and he knew
Megaera would either set John on him again or would
go further and endure the scandal of accusing her husband of stealing, for the advantage of being rid of him.
The only reason his presence was suffered at all was
that he had not destroyed Lord Bolliet's notes of hand,
as he had promised he would when Megaera married
him. If he were pushed out, he threatened, he would
present those to be paid—and he had arranged them
to look like legal debts rather than gambling losses.

Ever inventive, Edward discovered a new way to
turn a dishonest penny. He made contact with a group
of smugglers. This was not difficult, as he had been an
avid customer for duty-free brandy for some time. Edward himself drank only socially and seldom enough
to interfere with the devious workings of his brain;
however, he had fed his father-in-law's desire for obliv-

ion until the profit in it ended. Now he offered to arrange direct deliveries to the houses of the gentry for a split in the profit.

Although Edward did not know it, Black Bart was not a man who could be overawed by his new "partner's" exalted connection. Edward collected the price of the wine and brandy Black Bart delivered, and the split was not honest. It took a little time for Black Bart to discover this. He had his own blind spots. Most of his men and the local farmers were so afraid of him that they would not dream of cheating him. It was several months before he realized that Edward did not share the caution of his other employees. When he did discover it, his action was direct. He shot Edward dead.

In fact, Bart was glad of the excuse Edward had offered. He had been considering getting rid of his partner for a week or two. Once Edward had established the delivery route, he was really unnecessary to the scheme. Unfortunately for Black Bart, he and Edward had very similar things in mind; Edward, however, acted less directly. Feeling that Black Bart was unnecessary now that he knew the "French" smuggler, Edward had betrayed the group to the customs officers. Only a few hours after his own death a raid on the barn, in which the smugglers had gathered to divide and distribute the cargo Pierre had delivered, gave Edward a posthumous revenge.

The revenge was not complete because his murderer escaped only slightly wounded. Not realizing at first that the most important malefactor had slipped through their hands, the customs men rounded up about half the men and all the cargo and were quite content. Then Edward's body was discovered. Soon there was no doubt of either the reason for his death or who had committed the crime. A search was instituted for Black Bart, but it was rather cursory. It was assumed that he would be very far out of the district or hidden in one of the numerous caves in the area, of which an adequate examination was impossible and very dangerous.

This assumption did not take into consideration the fact that the wound Bart had sustained, although not deadly, was in a spot that made both walking and riding very painful. In addition, he hated the caves. They generated in him a nameless terror that could reduce him to a whimpering jelly. This combination forced him into an abandoned hut about halfway between Bolliet and Treen. He had slept there a few times in the past and knew no one ever visited the spot but a gigantic deaf-mute named John, who came to tend his mother's grave.

When news of Edward's death and the reason for it came to Megaera, she had been frozen with surprise— and relief. Respectful of her seeming shocked grief, the sympathetic Justice of the Peace had encouraged her to retire to recover herself. Kind neighbors had arranged the funeral and kept her father from disgracing himself in public. If any of them had known what Megaera was thinking in those few days she kept to her room, people would have recommended she be confined to a straitjacket. However, the thoughts did not show in her remarkable violet eyes, bitter thoughts, at first only about the debts that would soon complete Edward's revenge even though he was dead.

If only she had known what he was doing, it occurred to Megaera later, she could have got the money away from him. She could have prevented him from betraying the gang so that the money, whatever it was, could be used to pay the debts. Megaera had wept long and bitterly, and everyone felt deep sympathy for her, believing she had loved her worthless husband in spite of, or in ignorance of, his faults. Sweet and innocent, most of them thought her, and marveled at how she had found the strength to manage the estates and her father without collapsing under the burden. This was the last straw, they surmised.

Robert Partridge, the family physician, had known better when he was summoned to attend Megaera. He was somewhat in her confidence because he treated her father and had treated Edward that time John had beaten him nearly to death. He knew Megaera with her big violet eyes, little tip-tilted nose, and sweet rosy lips was as tough as whipcord. He came in haste, but to congratulate her on her fortunate release, not to support her faltering spirit. In his hurry he nearly stumbled over big John's feet. The deaf-mute was leaning on the wall beside his mistress's door, trembling with fear. Partridge patted the giant's shoulder comfortingly, but it had little effect. Only Megaera could comfort him. She was the only person who could really communicate with John after his mother died.

As the doctor walked into the room and held out his hands to Megaera in a wordless gesture of understanding, John's history passed through his mind. The boy had been the last child of a shepherd and his wife, conceived by some freak of nature when both were too old to expect such a result from their intercourse. Partridge had not really been surprised when the woman had brought the three-year-old to his office because the child could not speak or hear. Children born so late in their parents' lives sometimes were defective. He had confirmed sadly that the condition was permanent. What had surprised him was that the boy was clean, well-fed, and responded well to signs his mother made to him.

Partridge had not seen John again for many years, had forgotten his existence, until he had been called urgently to Bolliet Manor to care for an accident victim. Thinking Lord Bolliet had injured himself in a drunken fit, Partridge had made haste. However, he had been directed to the stables, where he found thirteen-year-old Megaera kneeling beside a battered and torn giant, stroking him and making signs with her hands.

"Good God, who is this? What has happened?" Partridge had asked.

Megaera's eyes shot sparks of rage, but she answered collectedly. "This is John Shepherd. His father used to tend our sheep. When the old man died, I allowed his widow to stay on in the cottage. I visited from time to time to make sure she and John didn't starve. He can't speak or hear, you know. Some lunatics—I don't know where they could have come from—attacked him."

"He's grown to a fair size," Partridge murmured, kneeling down and looking at the cuts and bruises on John's enormous torso. "You'd think even deaf and mute he could defend himself."

"I'm sure he could," Megaera snapped, "but I think he didn't understand at first what was happening. When he realized, it was too late." Her eyes filled with tears. "They had put a rope around his neck and tied him up—I found him that way. He had been there two days. They left him to die!"

The doctor set his jaw with rage, but shook his head. "But how the devil did they get him tied up?"

"He must have let them. John never expected any harm. Old Goody Shepherd was always kind to him, and she never let him go to town or mix with people who would hurt him or make fun of him. He probably thought it was some kind of game."

"Too bad," Partridge said, keeping a wary eye on his patient while he probed around to determine the extent of the damage.

He was a little nervous, expecting that John might react violently to being hurt again after his bad experience, but the big man kept his eyes fixed on Megaera's face. Although John occasionally winced and gasped under the doctor's hands, he obviously understood from Megaera's expression that Partridge was trying to help him. It was clear that John was not an idiot, although his mind moved slowly. There were other peculiarities about him. He must be in his mid-twenties, Partridge thought, trying to remember what year he had seen him as a child, but he had no beard nor any more hair on his body than a young boy would have.

"Can you leave him for a while?" Partridge asked. "I want to examine the rest of him. Will he let me?"

"I'll tell him—I hope," Megaera replied. "I learned to talk to him a little." She made signs for *I have to go away* and then for *I'll come back soon*. Then she pointed to Partridge, stroked him, kissed his cheek, took John's hand and made it stroke the doctor, took the doctor's hand and stroked John's cheek. Last she made the sign for *Good*. "I hope that'll do," she said. "I'll be right outside. If he acts up, yell and I'll come. Better my sensibilities be offended by John naked than you get your neck broken."

In fact, Partridge had no trouble with John, who was as meek as possible, even though he was clearly distressed at having to take off his pants. His mother had taught him modesty. The doctor salved a bruise or two while confirming his suspicions that there was more lacking in John than voice and hearing. The scrotum was minute and empty, the penis no bigger than a child's. John was a natural eunuch. In a sense that was an enormous relief. There was no chance that the big brute would be driven by frustration to forcing himself on women.

It was more of a relief after John's hurts were dressed and he was bedded down temporarily in the barn, because Megaera said she was going to keep the deaf-mute at Bolliet. "It isn't possible to send him back to the cottage by himself. Goody died a couple of weeks ago. I didn't know what to do about John. It seemed cruel to take his home away as well as his mother, so I left him to see whether he could manage alone. Thank goodness I decided to go up there today to see how he was making out."

Partridge pursed his lips and frowned. "Do you

think it wise to keep him here?" he asked. For all Megaera spoke like an adult and did more about managing the estate than her father, she really was only a child herself.

"There isn't anything else I can do," she said, looking Partridge squarely in the eyes. "And if you are thinking I should have him locked up, I won't do it! It would be *murder*, plain murder. You know it would."

Of course, Partridge thought, as he presently held Megaera's hands and smiled down at her, as things worked out it was the best thing that could have happened. John was perfectly gentle—unless Megaera told him not to be gentle. God knew what would have happened to her if John had not been there to defend her after she married Devoran. It was after he had treated Edward for the beating John had given him that he told Megaera it was even safe to let John sleep in her room, if it was necessary, that he was not a man in the usual sense and would never have any interest in women.

"You'd better let John in," he said, releasing her hands. "He knows something bad has happened but he doesn't know what, and he's scared to death."

"Heavens," Megaera responded, "I forgot all about him. You know he follows me around like a shadow unless I send him away. He must have been there when Lord Moreton told me about Edward. I came right up here after sending the groom for Mrs. Levallis. Yes, let him in."

As soon as she made the sign for *All's well* and smiled at John, his trembling stopped and he sat down on a big chair reserved for him in the corner. Partridge shook his head. All the trouble had faded from John's face. He was as happy as—as happy as a clam, and just about as sensible. It was too bad that Megaera's emotional wounds could not be healed so easily. In one sense she was rid of Devoran, but in another she might never be rid of him.

"What will you do now, Meg?" the doctor asked.

She looked at him, much startled, wondering whether Edward could have told the doctor about the debts—Partridge was everyone's confidant. Then she realized he was again gently suggesting that she should go away as he had recommended many times recently. No one knew that she couldn't afford to leave Bolliet and might not even be able to continue to afford to live there. If her father had any idea of what he had signed all those years ago, he certainly had no recollection of it now. He would probably miss Edward. Megaera had never told him the truth. What good would it have done?

"I can't leave Papa," she said. There was nothing Dr. Partridge could do for her, so there was no sense in telling him her troubles.

"Don't be silly, Meg," Partridge said sharply. "There isn't anything you can do for him that the servants can't. And I'll look in twice a week, as I always do. If he should take a turn for the worse, I would let you know. It's no life for you here."

"He would miss me," Megaera protested.

"Whenever he happened to notice you weren't there," the doctor remarked dryly, "but since he probably wouldn't remember the last time he saw you . . . You aren't looking well, Meg. I've been worried about you for months."

"I'll think about it," she said with a tired smile.

Actually, Partridge might get what he wanted, if not the way he wanted it, she thought after the doctor left. She might have to leave Bolliet. There was not much left in the jewel box, and the interest was due at the end of the quarter. She went back to racking her brains for a new source of income, but she had been up and down that path many, many times. It was worn into ruts so deep that Megaera doubted she could see over them even if there were new fields to plow. She had hoped that Edward's death might open a road that had been blocked before, but if one existed, she could not find it.

In due course Edward was buried and Megaera was free to resume her normal occupations within the bounds of mourning. On the first day that it was proper for her to ride out, John made known to her that he would like to go up to the hut. He went there three or four times a year to air it, sweep out the dust, and make sure the place was watertight, as well as to tend Goody's grave. Megaera had tried to explain to him that he could bring the bits of furniture and crockery to Bolliet Manor and she would give him a room in which to keep his treasures, but John either could not or would not understand her. Perhaps the cottage was some kind of shrine to his mother.

That was a new thing to worry about. If she could not stay at Bolliet, what would happen to John? Usually Megaera sent him to the cottage alone, but this day, with the odor of the funeral wreaths still cloying the air in the house, she decided to ride up and see the condition of the place for herself. Perhaps if she were there she could explain to John about bringing his things home with him.

Her mind was busy with trying to formulate a set of signs that would get her point across, when John entered the cottage. An instant later there was the soft gobbling, which was the only sound John could make, and a shot rang out, followed by a shriek of pain. Megaera slid from her horse, but there was no place immediately available to tie the creature. She dragged it forward to the doorway of the cottage, just in time to see John lift a man off the bed and throw him heavily to the floor. He was half stunned but still struggling to reach a weapon in his boot top when John put a foot on him.

Fortunately John was near enough to the door for Megaera to reach him without dropping the reins. She signed *Stop* before both hand and leg were splintered. "You had better be perfectly still," she said to the man. "John can and will kill you without hesitation."

"He attacked me," the man groaned, "came into my house—"

"It's not your house," Megaera interrupted coldly. "I know it's John's."

Technically, of course, it was her father's house, but Megaera had no intention of identifying herself at the moment. As the man lay, it was impossible for him to see her. A quick glance around the cottage had told a clear tale. A bowl of dirty water and cloths with bloodstains on them bespoke an injury the man was afraid to have treated. The way he had struggled to reach his weapon and the fact that he had several in odd places about his person spoke of a criminal. Obviously he was a fugitive from justice.

There were, of course, many reasons for evading the law, but Edward's death and the raid on the smugglers' hideout were prominent in Megaera's mind. By now she knew that some of the smugglers had escaped. Naturally she associated this escaped criminal with the smugglers. She associated something else. Megaera had been through Edward's possessions since his death and had found several interesting things: first, a list of names and places matched with quantities of different types of liquor, but there was also money, jewelry, and clothing that had been purchased quite recently. Since Edward had not had a penny from the estate and no one would lend to him or allow him to buy on credit, he had found a substantial source of income—and that source of income must have been the customers listed.

John's eyes flicked back and forth between the man he had subdued and his mistress, so that Megaera did not need to touch him again before she signed *Tie*

him up. That caused some confusion. John knew
tie up, but such an order had never been applied to a
person. Megaera had to show him, hands crossed behind her back and then pointing to her ankles. She
stepped back as soon as she was sure John understood,
to find a place to hitch her horse. That did not take
long, but Megaera did not reenter the cottage. She
needed time to think.

Before John's slow mind came to grips with the
fact that his mistress had not come back and he came
stumbling out to seek her, several decisions had been
made. The first was that Megaera intended to transfer
Edward's source of income to the payment of the mortgages on Bolliet Manor if it was humanly possible.
The second was that to do that, one had to avoid getting caught, not only by the customs men but also by
the smugglers themselves who, if they discovered a
weakness anywhere, were bound to exploit it to their
own advantage. The third was that she would let the
man go whether or not he could help her make contact with the smuggling ring. The chief of the gang
had killed Edward, and Megaera was grateful.

However, decisions two and three required permanent concealment of who she was. Since Megaera did
not believe in honor among gentlemen—the only real
examples she had had were Edward and her father—
she certainly did not believe in honor among thieves.
She expected no gratitude. Who had ever shown her
any, except poor John, who was not a man and was
too stupid to think for himself. What she did expect
was that, if she let this man go and he guessed who she
was, he would try to extort money from her for not
turning him in to the law. Naturally the situation
would become even more acute if he could help her
embark on a career as a smuggler.

A shadow fell over Megaera and she jumped, but it
was only John. When he saw her look at him, he
signed *Done*. Megaera bit her lip. She wanted to talk

to the man but did not want him to see her. She was
certainly not the only woman with red hair in the
locality, but that characteristic would narrow the field
enough to make identification possible. She looked up
at John. *Cover his eyes. Then come here,* she signed,
but had to show him how to make a blindfold out of
a piece of cloth.

In a few minutes John was out again. Megaera took
a deep breath and stepped into the cottage. "You're
one of the escaped smugglers," she said. "I don't care,"
she added as he shook his head vehemently. "It's none
of my business. I've no love for the law, and nothing
against you."

As she spoke she looked the man over. His clothing,
although bloodstained and dirty, had been of reasonably good quality and had a crude, flashy style to it.
Megaera's eyes widened. Was this the head of the
gang? The man who had shot Edward?

"Then why the hell did your dummy tie me up?"
Black Bart whined. "I wasn't doin' nothin'."

"You shot at him. Call that nothing?" Megaera
countered. "You broke into his house."

"No one don't live here. I been by a hundred times
and it's been empty. What harm did I do to take a lay
down when I was hurt?"

"No harm in that, maybe, but John doesn't like
people picking his lock and using his house without
his say-so. When he came in, you shot at him too.
Lucky you missed. Take more than a bullet to stop
John—and you'd have been dead, the hard way. He'd
tear you apart piece by piece. Then you tried to get at
your other pistol. Why blame John for tying you up?
It was the only reasonable thing to do."

"What're you goin' to do wif me?" he asked fearfully.

"I told you—nothing. If you're one of the smugglers
and we can reach an agreement, you can stay here. If
not, John will carry you a few miles away, take away

those pistols of yours, and let you go. Either way we don't turn you in—that I swear."

"Then why the wipe over my face?" The voice was less whining, but not any more pleasant.

Megaera laughed. "Because I don't want you to turn us in either."

"You! You're a lady, ain't you?"

How could he have guessed that, Megaera wondered, and in the next moment realized it had to be her speech. She had tried to model her sentence structure on his, but her accent was different. Megaera's mind whirled. She had gotten herself into bad trouble. Then suddenly she saw a path to safety. One group of servants spoke nearly with the same accent as their masters—gentlemen's gentlemen and ladies' maids. She laughed again.

"Sure, I speak pretty so I'm a lady, am I? You remember *that*, that I'm a lady. John doesn't like it when I'm not treated with respect. Never you mind what I am. I came a long way to get in on the smuggling lay, and then I heard it was finished here. Is it true?"

Black Bart began to curse. Megaera listened calmly, although she found his language more original than Edward's. He kept going for a long time, saving his choicest epithets for her late husband, who he believed—quite correctly—had betrayed them. Megaera treasured up a few remarks about Edward that she wished she had learned earlier so that she could have said them to his face.

"You're beginning to repeat yourself," Megaera remarked after a while. "I understand that the cargo and the depot are gone. I don't care about that. What I want to know is whether the smuggler's ship was taken or whether he was scared away for good. If not, I'll find the money to pay for a new run, and I have a new and better place to hide the stuff."

There was a long silence. "This ain't a trap?" The whine was back in the voice.

"Ever hear of a lady customs officer? Don't be a fool. Anyway, you don't have to tell me anything now. I've business elsewhere. John and I will be back here tomorrow night after moonrise. If you want to do business, we can talk about it then. If you don't, just be gone and don't come back."

As she said it, she signed *Hold him* to John. When he was helpless in the giant's grip, she went over him carefully, extracting from various places two more pistols, two knives, and a lead weight in a piece of cloth. She then searched the cottage carefully but could find nothing besides the gun he had dropped when John had first seized him. Having removed all the weapons, she signed that John should come out and lift her to her saddle. When she was mounted, she indicated that the prisoner should be turned loose, and left. John was not very willing, and Megaera had to assure him that the man would go away soon.

After she was safely home, Megaera considered what she had done. She thought the remainder of her jewelry plus Edward's would bring in enough to pay for the smugglers' cargo, and that the cave that opened on the opposite side of the hill from the site of Bolliet Manor would serve perfectly to hide the smuggled goods until they could be delivered—not all in one night but a little at a time. The cave would serve her better than the smugglers because there were several interlocking passages behind it. One of the passages led right to Bolliet Manor and two others to smaller caves and, eventually, to other exits in the hill.

In fact, the cave had many advantages. She could reach it without ever apparently leaving her house. In addition, either the local people had forgotten the caves and passages existed or they were so terrified of them that they would neither speak of them nor go

near them. Megaera herself had only learned of their
existence because some antiquarian gentlemen had
come from London to investigate them, having found
references to them in letters written during the Civil
War. Apparently the Cavaliers had hidden from the
Roundheads there at some time. Perhaps that was
when the legend of their fearsomeness had begun, because there was nothing there—except the danger of
getting lost if one did not know one's way around. Megaera's father had uninterestedly given permission for
exploration, and Megaera had been curious enough to
follow the scholars around until the whole complex
was familiar to her.

That was the easy part. The hard part was going to
be to keep her identity secret. After all, there was no
way to blindfold a whole smuggling crew. First Megaera thought of disguises—a wig, a mask—but she soon
realized that such things would be worse than nothing.
They would draw attention to the fact that she had
some reason to hide her identity. She needed to be a
different person, recognizable as a definite individual.

Thus was born Red Meg—a stranger to the district,
a lady's maid on the run for stealing her mistress's
jewels. That explained the money and the speech.
John was no problem. Although his disability and his
size were distinctive, no one except the people immediately connected to Bolliet Manor—and Dr. Partridge,
of course, who was as good as mute—knew him. Like
John's mother, Megaera never let him leave the
grounds of the manor, except to go to the lonely cottage. Now he would have to go with her, of course,
but she was sure she could control him.

Megaera collected clothing here and there, a groom's
breeches, a boy's shirt, a jacket old and patched and
too large. She collected the appurtenances a person
would need to make life moderately comfortable in
the cave—an old bed and mattresses, blankets, braziers,
other old furniture from the attics. John spent the

whole day carrying the things into the cave. When it was all set up, Megaera dredged dirt through her hair, dirtied her face and hands thoroughly, smeared mud and soot on the old clothes. Finally she and John set out on the long tramp to the cottage.

It was not cold, but Megaera shivered all the way there. She recognized the chill as fear, but she was not sure whether she feared the smuggler would be gone and her last chance to save her home gone with him, or whether he would be there and she would be involved in an enterprise that could ruin her. That thought made her laugh in the midst of her fear. She could not be ruined any more thoroughly than she had been by her loving father and unloving husband. She could not even marry for money. Convention dictated a year of "mourning," and by then Bolliet would be in the hands of the moneylenders.

He was not gone, although Megaera had thought he was at first. She would not enter the cottage, fearing an attack even though she had taken his weapons. But he would not come out either, also fearing a trap. At last, knowing he could not remain forever in the cottage and believing that she would send the brute in after him, he emerged. It was the first contest of wills between them, and Megaera had won it. She was quick to follow up the advantage.

"Since you're here, you want to do business," she said briskly. "What do I call you?"

"Black Bart, but my name's Bertram Woods," he answered, scowling. "What's yours?"

"Margaret," Megaera replied readily. She had that all planned and was delighted it was going her way. She had even stopped shivering. "Some call me Red Meg," she went on.

"Margaret what?" Black Bart asked.

She laughed at him. "Love children don't have double names. Red Meg's good enough for you. Now where and when do we meet the smuggler?"

"Not so fast. Did you bring the money?"

Megaera laughed again, contempt clear in the sound. "Not a penny, nor will you see a halfpenny of it until I've collected from my customers. Then you'll get your cut—just like everyone else. You can get more if you get the men together and manage them, but I'll hold the clinkers and I'll deal with the Frenchy. No argument—take or leave."

Bart reasoned and pleaded, insisting that no smuggler would have anything to do with a woman. Megaera's heart sank because that was certainly possible, but she knew that if she did not control the money and the deliveries, she might as well give up the enterprise completely. She held out stubbornly, refusing to discuss the matter at all. Her way or not at all—and in the end it was her way, all her way.

Black Bart had given Megaera an ugly feeling from the moment she first laid eyes on him. Pierre Restoir, the smuggler, had an exactly opposite effect. He was a big man, his bald head and wrinkles betraying his age; however, his body was still strong and lithe and his bright dark eyes showed a spirit as young and lively as a boy's. Megaera liked and trusted him on sight, and, although he was obviously startled at having to deal with a woman, soon it was clear he was delighted with the arrangement. He was fair and reasonable in his demands; Megaera bargained hard because she had to wring every coin she could out of the deal, but they soon came to terms.

After their first transaction was complete, Pierre drew her aside and told her to meet him at The Mousehole to arrange future deliveries and payment. "For you, Mees Meg, eet will be better, and I do not like to come ashore when cargo ees deliver'," he said, speaking in his heavily accented English because he thought Meg did not understand French. "If eet become for me necessary to run, I should be on my ship. That other one, I would not trust 'im with the name

of a place friendly to me. 'E ees not 'onest, that one.
'E would betray a frien' and enjoy eet. But you, *petite
Megotta la rouge,* you would not. Also, eet ees not
wise that those others"—he glanced at the men who
had fetched the cargo and were loading it on the
ponies—"should 'ear too much."

"I must bring John," she said.

Pierre laughed. "But, of course. For me eet ees
safe—'e does not talk—and for you eet ees better 'e be
always near."

The boats were beginning to scrape onto the beach.
Red Meg came out of her vivid memories with a start
and began to direct the loading of the ponies. She and
Pierre were old friends now. Tomorrow night she
would meet him at The Mousehole, pay him, and
arrange for the next shipment in about two weeks. He
tried to come frequently from September through November or December. After that the weather got so
bad they could not count on a regular schedule.
Megaera stocked up over the autumn months—there
was plenty of storage space in the subsidiary caves—so
she could service her customers without interruption
over the winter.

Chapter 3

On the way back to London with Philip the next morning, Roger's qualms were eased. He was not less fearful or less guilt-ridden, but both emotions were made bearable by the glow of happiness that had transformed Philip. They were driving themselves without even a groom up behind because Roger had thought Philip would burst if he could not talk. He was so happy that even a hangover could not depress his spirits.

"I had better not take Blue Boy," Philip said, coming out of a few moments of frowning silence. "He's best for steady work, but a pale dapple like that is too noticeable. In fact, I wonder if all my horses are too good. Do you think I should buy some old hack?"

"Let's take it in stages, Philip," Roger suggested. "You have to get to Cornwall and meet Pierre at The Mousehole. Probably you're right that you should ride rather than arrive either by post or in your own curricle. The point is, I don't know how often Pierre comes over. With the watch being kept for French ships so intense, it might be difficult for him to get through."

"I do not believe it," Philip said, grinning happily.

"They are watching for ships of the line or a whole flotilla of little ones, not for one *chasse-marée·* And if Pierre were going to give it up or not come for a long time, he would have written to you. Someone at The Mousehole could have mailed the letter for him."

Roger suppressed a sigh. Philip was right. Pierre would have let him know if he did not intend to return to England for a long time. "All right," he agreed, "but I don't know his schedule. You might have to wait a few weeks or even a month, if you happen to arrive just after he made a delivery. You can't live at The Mousehole. I doubt it's a first-class posting inn."

Philip hooted with laughter. "It is probably worse than the Soft Berth was. I do not care for that, but they would not permit me to stay. They would tell a stranger there were no rooms. Where the devil did you say this Mousehole was?"

"Pierre said you must take the coast road out of Penzance. About a mile and a half along the road, there are a few houses. Just beyond the last one the road branches. You must take the left fork. Pierre said to look hard; it's only a rough track and pretty overgrown. Another mile and a half or so will take you to The Mousehole. It's on a tiny cove."

"Smuggler's rest, eh?" Philip suggested.

"Probably," Roger replied, "but if I know Pierre he doesn't land cargo there. I doubt he even brings in the *Bonne Lucie*. By the way, he also calls her *Pretty Lucy* when he's in England. For Pierre it would be too obvious to use a regular smugglers' place. I'm sure they know his business, but he doesn't do it there."

But Philip had not been listening. His brow was furrowed with his own thoughts and he was repeating "Penzance, Penzance," under his breath. Then he said louder, "Five miles from Penzance! That is what he said. Five miles from Penzance."

"No," Roger insisted, "I'm sure Pierre said a mile and a half—"

"Not Pierre," Philip interrupted, his eyes dancing. "Perce Moreton lives five miles from Penzance at a place called Sancreed. I think I might just arrive at Perce's—"

"Without an invitation?" Roger asked, horrified.

"I have had many invitations, but who wanted to go all the way to Cornwall at the time?"

"He may not be at home."

"Know he is at home," Philip said with a laugh. "On at me about the delights of Cornwall when he was trying to wean me from my 'wicked ways.' It will not matter if Perce is not there either. His mother and father know me pretty well. Always took me along with Perce for tucker when they came to visit him at Eton. Perce told them I was an orphan because you had run away to France— Oh, good God, that is perfect!"

Roger looked at his son warily. Joy and mischief mingled in explosive proportions in Philip's face. "I have a feeling that I am about to become the goat," he said faintly.

"Watch your horses," Philip recommended.

"I was driving before you were born," Roger pointed out, nonetheless checking on his team. His son was a notable whip.

"Naturally," Philip responded. "It must be that familiarity breeding contempt thing—unless, of course, you just do not have the knack . . ."

Roger could not help laughing. "It's you who are losing your knack, my boy. That red herring is far too smelly. Now just what does my being in France thirteen years ago have to do with Lord Kevern's parents?"

"Well, I do not think anyone ever bothered to explain to them what happened to you—I mean, the subject never came up. Likely Lord and Lady Moreton still think you are not much of a father, abandoning me like that right after my mother died—"

"I didn't expect to be gone for more than a few weeks," Roger said guiltily. "I'm sorry—"

"Do not be ridiculous," Philip interrupted. *"Grand-mère et Grand-père* were there. I worried about you, sir, but I did not feel abandoned. Anyway, it is going to be very useful now. I shall tell the Moretons that you have thrown me out."

"What!" Roger roared.

"Well, what other reason could I have for going to Cornwall, of all unlikely places? And for staying? And for coming back? You have paid my debts three times, given me a stake, and told me to get out and not come back. That is quite—"

"Quite outrageous!" Roger broke in. "Philip, you are enjoying this!"

"Certainly," Philip agreed promptly. "And you see it is reasonable that in such straits I would join the smugglers—to sustain my bad habits, I guess." He could see pressure building up in his father and added slyly, "Are you going to try to tell me you did not enjoy getting Leonie out of prison and helping all those people escape? Martyred, were you?"

"I was very worried about Leonie's safety," Roger said with dignity, but his lips twitched. Philip had punctured his sense of propriety, and he was proud of his son's quick wit.

It was really a believable reason for Philip to take up with Pierre, and what the boy was saying was, sadly, common enough. Irate or uncaring fathers had been known to disown sons for less than Philip had done. Many more simply stopped the funds that supported their wild offspring and let nature take its course. Debts and harassment, sometimes debtors' prison, usually tamed the cubs into more moderate behavior.

"What are we going to tell Leonie?" Philip asked next.

"The truth," Roger replied. "You know she can *smell* a lie on either of us, and she would be far more hurt and worried if she sensed that we were lying. Fortunately she has a great faith in Pierre. Knowing you are with him will be a great comfort to her."

Roger was right about that, but Leonie would not have made a fuss in any case. The light in Philip's eyes and the worry in Roger's demanded calm and support from her. She understood well the need to do one's duty; her father had done his regardless of consequences, and Leonie had been proud of him. Now she swallowed her fear for the young man who had seemed to be God's gift to fill the hole her brother's death had left in her heart. Philip's duty was to serve his country; hers was to make that service as easy as possible by allowing him to do it without being dragged at by her fears.

With Leonie only the positive factors of the adventure were discussed. Roger explained that Philip would be in no danger on the sea even if the *Bonne Lucie* should be sighted or even captured by a British ship. "First of all, Pierre has signboards with the English name, *Pretty Lucy,* which he places over the French name, and he has a Union Jack he can raise. And even if they're stopped, there will be papers identifying Philip and any vessel he uses for transport as under the protection of the Crown. The worst that could happen is that they would be brought to Dover or Portsmouth. There will be special clearance in sealed papers there."

"And in France?" Leonie asked. She managed to control her voice so that there was no tremor in it, only interest.

"Of that I am not certain," Philip replied. "I have no doubt that Lord Hawkesbury will have suggestions, but I think I will take Pierre's advice. From what

Papa says, the matter is urgent, but not urgent in the sense of days or weeks. If Pierre thinks I will need something special from the Foreign Office, I will simply come back to London. However, somehow I feel he will manage best from his end."

"Yes, he will know," Leonie agreed.

"And the Terror is over, my love. *Madame la Guillotine* is retired. Even if Philip is caught in France, he will be safe. Smugglers are encouraged by Bonaparte, you know. All he does is take away their gold for his war and send them out again."

Leonie smiled. "It seems a most sensible attitude."

Her eyes were on her embroidery, and the men did not see the shadow in them that turned their normal golden hue mud-colored. It was useless for her to say that she knew the same indulgence would scarcely be shown to spies. She could not imagine what excuse a smuggler would give for being in the government shipyards of Boulogne, but there was no sense in raising points like that either. They were as obvious to the men as to her. Some excuse would be found. Leonie just hoped it would be good enough.

In fact, it was this problem that held everyone's attention most closely in the private office Lord Hawkesbury maintained in his home. At the small desk near the window, Jacques d'Ursine was writing out the papers Philip would carry. No one, Lord Hawkesbury swore, beyond the four in that office would know of Philip's mission. That was why they were meeting in Lord Hawkesbury's home rather than at the Foreign Office. So why, Lord Hawkesbury asked, was Roger so reluctant to give any information on his French contact. Perhaps they could provide more help if they knew more.

Roger had already discussed this matter with Philip. Nothing was to be said about Pierre, absolutely nothing. Governments, Roger pointed out cynically, had no honor, even the best of them. What Lord Hawkesbury knew would get into some record somewhere. His intentions might be excellent; he might wish to be sure that Pierre was rewarded for his help, or protected. Nonetheless, when the emergency was over, other foreign secretaries might feel differently. Pierre would be known, a marked man and ship. Philip agreed with his father and merely made his face a blank as Roger replied to Lord Hawkesbury's urging.

"Impossible. He has my word that I would never name him or his ship. I have already violated my promise by giving this information to Philip. In the interests of the country I was willing to go that far. And, you know, my lord, that even with the best of intentions, absolute secrecy might not be possible."

"Are you accusing me—or Jacques—"

"Of nothing, my lord," Roger said hastily, although he was by no means as sure of Lord Hawkesbury's discretion as he would like. In company he felt to be secure, his lordship might say more than was healthy. The less he knew, the better off Philip would be. "However, you are an important personage. Your private residence is not a secret. It is not impossible that this house is discreetly watched."

"It may be, of course," Hawkesbury conceded, "but I hoped it would be thought that I would conduct only private affairs here. Perhaps it would have been better to meet at the Foreign Office after all."

"No, my lord. If I thought so, I would have said so. But we must work on the assumption that we *are* awakening suspicions somewhere. Philip must do his best to convince anyone who might be interested that his behavior is natural."

"Yes, of course. Do you have some plan for this?"

"Well, I—I have been—er—running into debt a bit, my lord, and I thought I might spread it around that my father had lost patience with me. It—er—is not completely untrue, except that it had nothing to do with the debts. So it would be reasonable, you know, that I should go into the country. Well, I would be going in any event. Hunting, you know."

"You aren't going to meet a ship in Leicestershire," Hawkesbury remarked.

"No, no, but—er—anyone who was watching me would rather stand out in such company. When I was sure there was no one, I could move on. Or if there were, my friends and I—I could say it was a joke or agents of my creditors or something—and we could—er—take care of them or him—whatever."

"I see. And then?"

"I cannot say for certain, my lord. I just do not know. However, I promise I will make all the haste I can. I understand that if there is a fleet, it must be quite ready, since no one in his right mind would think of invading during the winter storms."

"Bonaparte is not in his right mind," Jacques d'Ursine put in.

"I do not believe that," Philip said. "Those victories—"

"Luck! Dishonest grasping at other men's skill—" d'Ursine interrupted shrilly.

"Yes, yes, Jacques," Hawkesbury soothed. "Are you finished with those documents? And don't forget to include the identity papers that the Ministry sent over. We don't want to make this meeting too long, you know, in case someone *is* watching." He paused a moment to be sure d'Ursine had returned to his work and then looked back at Philip. "You know what information we need?"

"Yes. The number of ships and their condition of readiness first. Then, if I can, the condition of roads in the area, supplies, number of men employed, troops in readiness, anything that would help the War Office judge when an invasion might be launched and the number of troops that might be committed to it. And, of course, whatever I can pick up in addition."

"We *must* know about the ships. If we had had

more ships available in the Mediterranean, Bonaparte would be in our hands now. He would never have reached Egypt and never have come back either. And there was not even a threat of invasion then. Now, with the patrols we are forced to keep, the French have far too easy a time importing all kinds of supplies. Our blockade is much hampered."

"I understand," Philip assured him.

Before he could say more, d'Ursine rose and brought the documents to Lord Hawkesbury. He examined them and nodded. "This will cover most eventualities. You have an identity as Baptiste Sevalis, a Parisian merchant. It is the best that can be done if you will not be more specific about—No? Very well, then."

He drew a seal from a locked drawer; d'Ursine tipped wax onto the paper and Lord Hawkesbury applied the seal to the passes. The identity papers had been previously sealed with forged French seals. When all was dry, he passed the sheets to Roger, who read them and passed them on to Philip with a nod of approval. Philip did not bother looking at them. He would have plenty of time to examine everything later. He folded the sheets carefully and stowed them in a pocketbook, which he placed in an inner breast pocket.

A few more words were exchanged, but it was obvious that Philip was not attending and was all but visibly quivering with impatience. Hawkesbury smiled and asked if he was eager to be on his way.

Philip laughed and looked shocked. "Not today. If I am going first to my friends to divert suspicion, I must take clothing and my servants. All this must be arranged if I wish to go early tomorrow. If you will give me leave, my lord?"

"Of course." Hawkesbury stood and came around the desk to shake hands with him. "Good luck, my boy. You have those passes, your identity papers, and

that list of our men in that area of France. But be
wary. Not all of our agents are to be trusted completely."

"I will not go near any of them unless I am at my
last gasp, my lord—and I cannot think why I should
be."

Roger stood up also, but Hawkesbury had reminded himself of something else. The funding for
the venture had not gone through the complicated
channels yet, but the draft could be forwarded to
Philip anywhere if he wished to leave an address.
Roger said hastily that he would advance the funds
to be repaid when Philip returned and that Hawkesbury should hold the draft. Ungratefully, Philip was
almost audibly grinding his teeth with impatience,
and Hawkesbury's secretary obviously felt the same
way. Regardless of the fact that his employer was still
speaking, d'Ursine bowed silently and left the room
by a side door. Roger and Philip were not so fortunate.
Before Hawkesbury had finished his thanks, regrets,
warnings, and promises, d'Ursine had had time to
write and dispatch two brief notes.

One of these reached François Charon, an émigré
who dealt in foreign books and manuscripts. When
he had perused the note, he circumspectly burnt it
and rewrote the pertinent information—that a "Parisian merchant" named Baptiste Sevalis was in reality
an English spy—on a thin spill that eventually came
into the hands of Joseph Fouché. The other was delivered to the house of a young gentleman, also an
émigré, whose valet hesitated for some time before
deciding to wake him. Jean de Tréport was not the
easiest master to work for.

Outside of Lord Hawkesbury's house at last, Philip
flicked his whip and the boy who had been holding his
horses' heads sprang away. The animals surged forward, just a little too fast, as if sensing their master's
eagerness.

"Are you going first to Leicestershire?" Roger asked.

"No, of course not. I intend to do exactly what we planned. But listening to Hawkesbury gave me the pip. That man has flatulence of the mouth. Moreover, that secretary of his sounds a little mad. He is just the type to run all over town telling people how we are going to discover all Bonaparte's secrets."

Roger laughed. "I suppose d'Ursine *is* a bit unbalanced, but he's not a fool for all that. And as for Hawkesbury's talking, it's necessary in the Foreign Office. Look at the mess Cornwallis made of the peace because Talleyrand talked circles around him."

"You are not thinking that Hawkesbury would have done better, are you?" Philip asked, turning his eyes from the street in his astonishment and nearly running down an innocent, crossing sweeper.

"Watch where you're going!" Roger exclaimed, but he had to laugh at Philip's protest. "Unfortunately not. I don't think there's anyone in our government that can match Talleyrand for sly cleverness. But Hawkesbury might have exhausted him—or put him to sleep—so that a few reasonable provisions could be slipped in."

Philip shrugged. "All right for diplomatic conferences, but he still talks too much for my taste. I can just see him mentioning to a small, select group the latest effort to discover Bonaparte's intentions about invasion. Then one of them will mention it to a friend, a wife, a secretary. Pretty soon we might just as well have published what we are going to do in the Court Calendar."

That was just what Roger feared. He bit his lip. "If you've changed your mind, Philip—" he began eagerly.

"God, no!" Philip exclaimed, grinning. "I have not enjoyed myself so much since Perce and I took that boat out and nearly drowned. I would just like to escape the consequences this time."

The light remark sent a chill down Roger's spine.
He had caned both boys for their disobedience and
ill-judged daring, but the consequences this time
might be more permanent than a few welts. Then he
said, "That Perce! Oh, Lord!" because he suddenly
connected the boy with the friend of Philip's that had
hung around Sabrina for a while. He hadn't given
him much thought because he had realized that no
one had much chance once Lord Elvan entered the
field, but if he had then remembered the tall, fair
stripling with a cultivated expression of vacuity and
a devil of mischief in his pale eyes, he might have . . .
No, it was Sabrina's right to marry whom she chose.

Roger prayed he was wrong about Elvan for Sabrina's sake. She was so precious to Leonie, the last
of her father's family, the only one saved from the
shipwreck that had drowned her Uncle Joseph, his
wife, and his son. It had been thought that the two
little daughters were also lost, but a strong Irish maid
had been holding the little girls when Lady Alice and
her son had been swept off the lifeboat trying to save
Joseph. The small boat had been driven north by
wind and current and had come to ground at last on
a tiny island west of Scotland.

The people were poor and rather primitive; they
had done what they could for the survivors, but Sabrina's elder sister and the maid had died and Sabrina
herself had been sick for a long time. None of the
other survivors had known her, and she knew her
name, Sabrina Evelina Alice de Conyers—but that was
all. To the ignorant people of the island the name
was no clue to where or how to inform Sabrina's rela-
tives, if she had any. They knew she was "a lady,"
but that was all. No, Roger thought, life had to come
right for Sabrina. It was a miracle she was alive; it
was by a second miracle she had been found; surely
a third miracle would make her happy.

The ride was not long, and Roger brought his at-

tention back to Philip, offering a few practical suggestions about the kind of behavior that would attract
the least attention on the road. Once home, Philip
ran upstairs to his father's dressing room to change
into the riding clothes that had been laid ready
earlier. He exchanged his white nankeen pantaloons
for rather stained buckskins, his Hessian boots for a
pair with tan, turned-down tops and spurs. Philip did
not ordinarily use spurs, his horses being lively enough
without encouragement, but extra effort might be required from a tired animal on this journey. In any
case, he wanted to look more like a country squire's
son and less like a dandy.

His linen was rather too fine for his purpose, but
he could buy a shirt or two, or Pierre could supply
him with more appropriate wear when they met. He
put on the plainest shirt he had, tied a wipe around
his neck in place of an elaborate neckcloth, added a
buckskin waistcoat and a long-tailed black coat over
all. The worst problem was his greatcoat. It was a
delicate fawn color with too many shoulder capes.
Fortunately the weather was mild and he would not,
he hoped, have to wear it on the road. He looked
around the room, but the roll of extra shirts and
underlinen, a pair of knee breeches, striped stockings,
and slippers for evening wear was gone. Leonie must
have had it all attached to his saddle.

The last thing he did was to straighten the tops of
his boots and feel around the inner edge until he
found where Leonie had opened the stitching that
held the inner leather lining to the outer shell. He
slipped one of the documents d'Ursine had prepared
into one boot, the list of British agents in northern
France into the other, noticing that Leonie had re-
done the stitching so that there was no visible sign
that the boots had ever been opened. The identity
papers he left in his wallet. They might cause some
confusion if they were seen by local authorities in

England, but Philip wasn't worried about that. A touch with the glue pot and a moment or two to make sure that the openings of his boots were sealed, and the hiding place of the sensitive papers was secure.

The door opened just as Philip looked around the room one last time. Roger came in and silently handed over a two-shot, tap-action muff pistol, small enough not to make a suspicious bulge in a pocket. It was, of course, rather inaccurate and useful only at close quarters—five or six feet—or as a threat. The long-barreled Lorenzoni quick-loading pistols in their fine case were something else again. They were old but immaculately kept, as accurate as fine Manton dueling pistols, and had the advantage that a dozen balls and powder charges were carried inside each gun itself so that paper cartridges or a powder flask and balls were not necessary. Last, Roger handed Philip an arm sheath carrying an eight-inch-long, razor-honed dagger that could be strapped to a forearm or slid down a boot.

"I must say," Philip remarked, "that there are advantages to being the son of a gunsmith." That was a reference to his father's adventure in revolutionary France, but it did not produce the usual laugh, and Philip raised his brows. "Do you expect me to need to hold off an army?"

"Hopefully not, but it never hurts to be prepared," Roger said, keeping his voice steady with an effort. "There is another pair of pistols, good Parkers, in the saddle holsters, cartridges in the flaps, more cartridges in the saddlebags. Keep the Lorenzonis hidden. They're a good surprise to anyone who thinks you don't have time to load. You remember how to use them, don't you?"

"Of course," Philip replied, stowing away the muff gun and sliding the knife down his boot. "They were the greatest joy of my misbegotten youth. I thought I would *never* get old enough to be allowed to use them." He paused, then said awkwardly, "I wish you would not worry. I guess I have been behaving like a dreadful ass recently, but my brain is not yet pickled. I know this is important. I swear I will not act the fool and—and I will pay strict attention to what Pierre tells me."

Roger didn't answer that because he couldn't command his voice. He merely clapped Philip on the shoulder and they went down the corridor toward the back stairs. At the foot Leonie waited. She was dry-eyed and smiling, but her brunet skin was sallow with pallor. She embraced her stepson and kissed him on both cheeks, saying, "*Reviens bientôt, chéri.* We will be waiting."

To Philip's relief, neither followed him out the door. He understood that his father and stepmother were worried, but he was not. Thus he found their emotion irritating even while he was warmed by the knowledge of their love. In the alley beyond the servants' entrance was a rawboned bay called Spite. The name was a family joke; Spite had the sweetest disposition ever bestowed on a horse, but he had an odd habit that made him look vicious—of laying back his ears and showing his teeth. Philip never thought about that habit, he was so used to it, and in other ways the gelding was ideal. He had speed, stamina, took fences standing or flying, and would burst his heart going if it were asked of him. Last and best, he was not a handsome animal, and his description would fit about two thirds of the common hacks in the country.

Philip stowed what he was carrying in the saddle-bags, noting that there was just room for the pistol case. When he went up into the saddle, it was with a curious sense of release, as if the motion were a dividing line in his life. Technically he had been a man for years, living his own life in his own rooms in London or at Dymchurch House. His income was assured and his own to manage as he saw fit. Nonetheless, he had not felt like a man. Although his father did not intrude in his life, he was there—a firm bulwark ready to offer support or advice in any crisis.

That was over. Philip blushed briefly as he wheeled Spite out onto the street and headed toward Hyde Park. What a fool he had been for the past half year. But it was partly his father's fault. Philip had known he could go his length and come out scatheless. Mentally he shrugged. It was not worth thinking about now. He was really on his own. Pierre would help all he could, but Philip realized that once in France, Pierre probably could not do much. He was too obviously what he was—a Breton fisherman, and not young. Not a likely person to be wandering around military installations.

First things first. He had to get to Pierre. How real was the threat that someone would be warned that he was on his way? A possibility, but not a strong one, Philip thought. In any case, not a thing he needed to worry about while he was in London or the nearby towns. There was so much traffic on the roads near London that it would be impossible to determine whether anyone was following him or was just an innocent traveler going in the same direction. On a lonely stretch of road it might be worthwhile to look around, but not here. He rode contentedly, regardless of Spite's one real drawback, a bone-jarring gait that made long hours in the saddle painful and exhausting for the best of equestrians.

Just as Philip passed out of London proper, a young man was shown into the library of Roger's house. He bowed with a flourish but received only the curtest of nods in reply. Roger did not like Jean de Tréport. It seemed to him that this young scion of an émigré house had encouraged all of Philip's less endearing habits. The marks of dissipation on his face made him

look much older than Philip, although he was actually two years younger. His reputation, aside from the
drinking, whoring, and gambling—which were accepted as normal in the circles in which he traveled—
was good. He was honest in his play and paid his
debts and his share.

"I'm sorry to trouble you, Mr. St. Eyre," Jean said.

He had hardly any trace of accent, less than Philip,
because he made a conscious effort to eliminate it. His
parents had fled to England shortly after the Revolution began in France. Jean had been only a boy then,
and he said he had few pleasant memories of his
native land. Thus, when the old people died, he refused to go back even when the option was offered
by the amnesty. He was more Englishman than
Frenchman by now, he claimed, and besides, there
was nothing to go back for. His father had sold everything he had before leaving. There were no lands to
reclaim.

"No trouble," Roger replied civilly but without
enthusiasm. "What can I do for you?"

"Is Philip—is Philip in trouble?" Jean asked hesitantly. "We had an engagement for dinner last night,
and he did not come. His servant told me he had gone
off the day before in a violent rage, not saying where."

Roger set his jaw with distaste, but he knew this
was the opportunity for which he had been waiting.
"I have refused to pay his debts again," he said coldly.
"I do not know whether you consider that trouble.
And I have told him to stay out of Town." To Roger,
as to all Englishmen, "Town" without the article
meant London.

"He is gone then?" Jean asked anxiously.

"I have no idea," Roger replied, "but I think not.
If he is not back in his rooms, try Dymchurch House
or Leicestershire. I warned him to stay away from
those country houses where the play is high. Whether
he will take my advice or not, I cannot say."

"I see. Thank you." Jean bowed himself out on a wave of slightly incoherent apologies.

Outside, he walked swiftly around the corner. "He is gone," he said to another young man.

"Are you sure?" Henri d'Onival asked. "The note said he was supposed to leave for Leicestershire tomorrow."

"He is gone, I tell you. His father acted as if he had not seen him since Tuesday, but we know they were together this morning. St. Eyre told me to try Dymchurch if Philip was not in his rooms here. Thus Philip must be already gone and *not* toward Leicestershire, which his father also suggested to me—most innocently."

"You mean we are suspected?" Henri asked nervously.

"No, I am sure not. Old St. Eyre is a sly beast, even if the son is a fool. He will say no more to anyone. I think he wants the story of his refusal to pay spread about. It would explain Philip's absence from his usual haunts. Naturally, he does not want questions asked."

"But if he is not going to Leicestershire, where is he going? And how can we find him if he has left already? No, I do not like this. It is one thing to go with him as friends and find a way to search his things to remove these lists and passes, but to follow him elsewhere . . . No. Even if we could find him, he will be suspicious."

"Yes, getting the papers will be more difficult, but you know we were also supposed to discover who it is that he plans to meet. And we *do* know where he is going. St. Eyre let that slip before he thought his son would be involved. Hawkesbury told Jacques that whoever it is has a base in Cornwall. Now, I do not think Philip will skulk along back lanes. There is no reason for him to do so, and he would not wish to put up with the accommodation in country inns.

There are only two toll roads to the west; one runs to Bath and the other to Exeter."

"You mean we should each take one? I don't think that's wise. We had better report that the plans were changed—"

"No," Jean contradicted sharply. "Do you wish to return the money we were paid?" A significant silence answered him, and he went on. "I don't think we should separate. I'm almost certain he won't take the road to Bath. There's too much likelihood of meeting people he knows—his family and friends—returning from there. Let's at least try the Exeter road."

"Very well," Henri said.

He was beginning to regret having mixed himself into this business. It was one thing to spend his time in the company of young army and navy officers and pick up a piece of information here and there. The money was useful. Unfortunately, the costs of mixing were high and his parents' income was limited. Now there was almost nothing left. Insensibly, as his allowance dropped Henri continued to spend until it was more than he had—only a little at a time, he was no reckless debauchee—but now he was deep in debt.

Regret or no regret, he had to go through with it, Henri decided. He had not realized that tradesmen's debts were protected by law in England, and he had to have what had been promised when he came back with the papers and the name of Philip's contact. The alternatives were too horrible: debtors' prison or flight—and to where could he fly? No, he must steel himself to do whatever was necessary.

Jean did not have the small qualms that disturbed Henri. He had lived on his wits for years. His parents had left him enough to exist on a modest scale if he were careful. Had he felt inclined toward a profession or trade, he could have lived comfortably. Since he was inclined to nothing but drink, cards, and women, his income was not sufficient. Jean was no fool, however;

mostly he lived at little cost to himself, a welcome guest who enlivened dull country sojourns. In addition, he had been supplementing his income for years in ways he found pleasant and amusing. Discreetly he led "flats" to gaming dens. Later he received a percentage of what they had been fleeced. He was on the payroll of many a "madam" also. No one lost on that, for the houses to which he introduced his friends were delightful, if costly, and he had his entertainment free of charge.

This excursion into espionage was something new, but it paid well enough so that Jean welcomed the experiment. He had a vast contempt for those he lived on. It had delighted him to be able to refuse invitations he had previously accepted, knowing that his hosts would now need to scrabble about for an extra man. He was sure he would be welcomed back next season with relief after the fools they would need to invite in his place. Not that this adventure was his first. It seemed to be the most serious, however. What he and Henri had been given in advance to cover expenses was handsome. What was promised for the future, on successful completion of the mission, was munificent. Jean wondered where it came from. Perhaps when he returned from Cornwall he would squeeze d'Ursine a little and find out.

"I will meet you at the Sun, where we can rent a carriage and horses"—Jean pulled out his watch and snapped it open—"in an hour. That should be time enough to gather up what little we need. Remember, you will not need evening clothes, and do not bring a million neckcloths as if we were going visiting in a grand house."

Philip had done exactly as Jean predicted. He did not really expect to be followed, but despite his avowal of caution he would have been rather pleased if he were. At this point he was eager to taste the joys of being a hunted man, and it seemed highly unlikely that his adventure could really begin until he arrived in France. So he took the most open, obvious route and stopped for tea at a well-known posting inn. His promise to his father that he would do nothing wild restrained him from giving his name or doing anything special to draw attention to himself, but he could not resist riding on into the dark before he finally stopped.

This marked him as a man in a hurry, but to his disappointment no one seemed interested. Philip ate well and went up to bed early, wondering if Spite's even disposition and strength could make up for his uneven gait. He was not looking forward to the morrow. As he undressed, Philip eyed his boots uneasily. They were dusty and in excessive need of polishing. Moreover, it would be remarked if he did not put them out for cleaning—and that was not the kind of notice Philip wanted. He might be hungry for adventure, but he did not wish to endanger the success of his mission.

Having picked up each boot, examined and flexed the area that had been opened and found it sealed tight and capable of bending without giving away what was hidden, Philip put his boots out to be cleaned with all the others. It was, in his considered opinion, the safest thing to do, and he was right. Although concern—that the paper would crackle or the bootboy notice the slight bulge or the seal open owing to rough handling—stole into his dreams and made him restless, Philip found his boots and their contents intact in the morning. The fatigue of restless sleep only compounded the discomfort of Spite's rough gait. By teatime on Friday, Philip was very ready to linger on a comfortable chair in a private parlor of a large posting house. He was even tempted to ask for a chamber and go no farther, but conscience drove him on.

Outside of Salisbury, however, it began to rain, and Philip had had enough. He stopped at Wilton, quite unaware that the fast post-chaise, which had passed him outside of Stockbridge, was now behind him. It had stopped in a small lane until he rode by, and then traveled at a discreet distance along the relatively empty road, turning off into side roads to wait and leave the road behind Philip empty for a while each time it drew close. In Salisbury the chaise was much closer, close enough to see which hotel he stopped at—if he stopped, but he did not. On the road the distance was allowed to widen again.

The chaise went right through Wilton, but it was soon apparent that Philip was not on the road ahead. Back it came and stopped in the innyard. Jean hopped out and, to the ostler's amazement, walked into the stable. A quick glance told him what he wanted to know—that a still-damp, raw-boned gelding was munching contemplatively on a fine display of oats. Before the ostler could speak, Jean pointed out two stalls near the door and said that his horses should be settled in them because he intended to leave very early the next morning. He stayed to see the animals unhitched and bestowed in the spots suggested and to criticize the rubbing down.

It seemed unusual for a man to be so attentive to the comfort of rented horses, but they were a good team and the postillion did seem to be unusually stupid. The ostler accepted Jean's behavior without thinking much about it. Obviously the man intended to use the same team the next morning, and he wanted to be sure they were in peak condition.

That deduction was true, but it was not the reason for Jean's lingering in the stable. He knew Philip and Philip knew him well, and he was taking no chance on running by accident into his intended victim There could be no believable excuse for him to be on this road and stopping in the same inn. It was too much of a coincidence. However, Philip did not know Henri. It was therefore quite safe for him to enter the inn, make sure Philip was there, and rent a private parlor to which Jean could go directly and not leave until Henri had determined that Philip had gone up to bed.

The plan worked very well. Henri did not even need to ask where Philip was. The landlord, apologizing for providing only a small room for Henri and his companion, mentioned that his larger room had been rented less than a half hour earlier by a single gentleman. "A busy night," he remarked, rubbing his hands together and smiling. His inn, less than five miles from Salisbury, did not often have so much "gentle" custom, the upper-class travelers preferring to stop at the larger, better-appointed inns and hotels in Salisbury. This meant three expensive, special dinners as well as the rent for both parlors and extra bedchambers—and the gentry did not examine bills with the same care that merchants or other tradesmen gave to them.

The bad weather brought dark even earlier than usual in October. Philip was not in the least sorry. He was sick of his own company and doubly tired owing to his restless night and a full day of Spite's bone-crushing movement. As soon as he had eaten, Philip went up to bed. This time the fact that he had set his boots out did not cause him any qualms. In fact, even if he had been worried, it would not have kept him awake. He was so tired it was doubtful that a full-scale war outside his window could have disturbed him.

Certainly the quiet snick of his latch opening did not wake Philip. He did not even sigh or turn his head as Jean, his face hidden by a neckcloth raised over his nose and mouth, slipped into the room. Henri, similarly masked, hung back uncertainly until Jean stuck his head back out of the door. It was too dark in the inn corridor to see Jean's glare, but Henri knew what his face must look like, and entered. This was totally out of Henri's experience. He was frightened half to death. If they were caught, it would mean prison.

Jean closed the door softly behind his unwilling companion and moved silently toward the bed. Mentally he swore obscenely. He had had no idea how dark it would be. It was possible to see darker shadows that denoted the room's furnishings, but the bed was a heap of indistinguishable shapes. It was impossible to tell where Philip's limbs lay under the blankets or what was his head rather than a curve of the several pillows furnished by a thoughtful landlord in his best bedchamber.

Thus it was also impossible to fix his eyes on his target, rush to the bed, and strike Philip with the butt of the unloaded pistol he carried in his hand. He had to go right up to the bed, pause, lean closer. At that point the plan went a little awry. Jean bumped the bed lightly as he strained to see. Philip jerked. His sleep had been deep, but he had been sleeping for some hours and he was no longer exhausted. Although he had decided there was no foundation to his hopes that any adventure would overtake him before he left England, there was just enough suspicion left in him to bring him half awake before Jean brought his gun down.

Jean felt the gun hit something solid. Philip jerked again and then went limp. With a sigh of relief, Jean fumbled on the bedside table for the flint and tinder and lit the candle that stood ready. They did not dare light the branches of candles for fear the glow would be seen under the ill-fitting door or between the curtains. Besides, they knew there was not much to search. They had a good look at Philip when they passed him and saw he had virtually no baggage.

The roll of greatcoat and extra clothing was unstrapped first. It took longer than Jean had thought, and Henri was trembling with anxiety. Every garment had to be shaken and felt to be sure that the papers were not inside a sleeve or a leg. The saddlebags hanging over the back of a chair were next. Too nervous to feel through them, Henri dumped them on the floor. Jean growled at him and then growled again when he saw there was nothing in them of the least interest. He pawed through the evening slippers and the rolled stockings, fine silk, too thin to conceal anything.

"He has sent the papers ahead," Henri muttered. "There were knee breeches. He is going to visit someone."

"No," Jean snarled. "There was more in the saddlebags than this. Also he is such a fool that he is probably still carrying the papers openly in his wallet. That must be under the pillows."

The voices were low, but they were enough to cover the soft groan Philip had just uttered. The concentration on what they were doing and the light of the candle also concealed from them that Philip had raised a hand to his head. Jean's blow, although meant to stun for a considerable time, had been softened by a fold of the loose down pillows. Philip had been only briefly unconscious. By the time the saddlebags were dumped, he was aware but still too dazed to be certain what had happened. Now, just as the two turned toward the bed, Philip realized that his head hurt. He had been struck! He sat up, reaching under the pillow for his pistol and calling out.

Without waiting for anything, Henri dashed the candle to the floor and ran for the door. Jean might have stood his ground, but he was blinded by the sudden extinguishing of the light and startled by Henri's movement. He, too, ran for the door, just as Philip found his gun. Philip did not fire, partly because he knew he could not aim owing to his dizziness

and the dark but more because he realized his
assailants had left the room. For a few minutes Philip
struggled dizzily to rid himself of the bedclothes,
which were well tangled around his legs, so that he
could give chase. When he had finally pushed them
away, however, he did not bother to get out of bed.

Philip had no idea that other guests had arrived.
Tired as he was, he had discouraged the early attempts
at conversation the landlord had made. He assumed
that the attackers had found a way in or had bribed
the landlord or a servant. So, unless the men were
total idiots, they would have prepared a quick escape
route. He should have shouted or fired his pistol at
once, but he had been confused. Now it was too late.
There was no sense in rousing the whole place.
Whether the landlord was truly unaware or paid to be
unaware made little difference; in either case he would
be no help. Gingerly rubbing his head, Philip got up
and dragged a table across the door. It would not keep
anyone out, but it would make enough noise, scraping
across the floor, to wake him.

Chapter 4

In the morning when he saw the mess, Philip was furious. However, he knew the thieves had not got what they wanted. His boots had been in the possession of the servant whose duty it was to clean them, his purse had been under his pillow with the wallet and the muff gun, and the Lorenzoni pistols were under the bed behind the chamber pot. Philip had thought when he regained his senses that there had been no time for his assailants to search. Now he realized he had been wrong, but as he repacked his possessions he saw that nothing at all had been taken; even the packets of paper cartridges for the Parker pistols in his saddle holsters were there. Everything had been torn open and strewn around, but his watch and his snuffbox had not even been moved on the bedside table.

Initially, when he saw clothing and other articles strewn around, Philip thought of calling a servant to clean up. He reconsidered that notion in time. There would have been questions about what he had lost, on why he had not called for help. Possibly to keep a clean name the landlord would have demanded that he report to the authorities in the neighborhood. That would mean endless delays. Besides—Philip rubbed his

head, which was still tender and ached a little—he
would prefer to deal with his assailants himself. The
first round was a draw; the next he would win. These
had not been ordinary thieves—those would have taken
his watch and snuffbox.

When he came down to breakfast, the inn was quiet.
No one said anything to him about a window or door
found open. That might merely be caution, but it
might also imply that the landlord was party to the
deed. It was best, Philip thought, to take no chances.
He ate well but quickly, ordering that his horse be
saddled and ready as soon as he was finished. Since
Jean and Henri were long gone—they had left as soon
as it was light enough to see, well before the sun
rose—Philip never discovered that there had been
other guests at the inn.

As Philip directed Spite onto the road again, a stir-
ring of excitement filled him. They would try again,
but not, he thought, at an inn. They would expect
him to be on his guard there. *They,* Philip wondered,
why did he think *they*? He had not seen more than
one shadow in the room, and yet he was sure . . . Yes,
there had been at least two. He remembered now that
the door had opened before the shadow reached it.
Philip's brow wrinkled. Spite's gait was not soothing
his aching head. It did not seem possible to him that a
gang could be involved. That would be impractical.
Two or three men. What would they try next?

Philip looked around him, but this was a highly unlikely place for an attack. The grazed-over downs
rolled away on either side, ahead and behind. There
was no hiding place for anything larger than a partridge or a pheasant. It was simply not possible for
anyone to prepare a surprise attack on this section of
the road. Once again Philip searched the horizon on
every side, trying to be sure there was no fold of land
or patch of wood in which men and horses could be
hidden. If there was, it was too far away to make sur-

prise possible anyway. Philip dismissed the possibility
from mind—almost disappointed—and tried to think
ahead.

When Philip left the inn, the Lorenzoni pistols,
loaded and half-cocked, had been moved from their
box in his saddlebags to the tops of his boots. Simply
by dropping either hand down to his side, he could
draw a gun and fire. Moreover, the Lorenzonis could
be reloaded in about two seconds by the simple procedure of raising the muzzle and swinging a lever forward, then dropping the muzzle and swinging it back.
There was no need to fumble for a cartridge paper,
tear it open, pour powder and ball down the muzzle,
and ram it home before being ready to fire.

Added to Spite's surprising turn for speed and
ability to jump, Philip felt quite sure he could wound
or kill the men before they could hurt him. He had
one advantage over them, which he had deduced from
what they had done in the inn. Plainly they had some
reason for wanting to keep him alive. Nothing would
have been easier than to put a pillow over his face
while he was stunned and smother him. There were
two of them, and they could have overpowered him
even if he should have regained consciousness before he
strangled. Philip himself felt no such compunction. If
he could kill them, he would do so gladly. They were
French agents, enemies of his country, and enemies of
the most insidious kind. Either they could pass as
Englishmen or actually were English, and therefore
far more despicable, being traitors.

Had Jean or Henri guessed the pattern of Philip's
thoughts, they would have gotten rid of him when they
had the chance. Instead they imagined he would be
only frightened and wary. A long discussion resolved
into the decision to abandon all attempts to waylay
him until they were west of Exeter. There was no way
Philip could avoid passing through that city, the Exe

being too wide for a bridge below the town. Thus, all roads led into Exeter, and Jean was sure they could pick Philip up again when he entered or left. This plan had the further advantage that Philip might relax his guard if several days passed without any added alarm.

Their long hours in the carriage had produced one more idea—that it was stupid to expose themselves in any attempt to take Philip. Thus, Jean had found a person in the slews of Exeter who, for a few guineas and whatever Philip was carrying that was of value, would take on the task of holding him up. They told a tale of blackmail—Philip had obtained papers that could be used to ruin their business. They did not want him hurt if it could be avoided. All they wanted was the papers. The highwayman could have Philip's purse, his watch, his snuffbox—all his valuables. However, as the papers were almost certainly concealed on his person, he would have to be overpowered and stunned or bound and blindfolded so he could be thoroughly searched.

The highwayman made nothing of that. Sometimes men who traveled with valuables carried an extra purse to be flung to a thief. Often they went so far as to carry cheap watches or snuffboxes too. It was becoming a common practice of the more daring rank riders to search their victims. However, for that a really lonely stretch of road or a guarantee that no one would come along and interrupt was a necessity. If Jean wanted the job done near Exeter or the victim took the well-traveled coast road toward Plymouth, it would be necessary to block the road in both directions for at least a few minutes, until he could stun Philip and drag him off the road.

Jean and his hired man had argued over the price of such help and come to terms. Jean and Henri would block the road from Exeter by drawing their carriage across it. One of them could pretend to have fallen and been stunned. Anyone that came along could be stopped and asked for help. The highwayman would provide another of his ilk to stop anyone coming from Plymouth. The signal would be one pistol shot, which would serve the double purpose of frightening Philip into obedience. If Philip took the less-traveled road toward Launceston, the second man would not be required. It would be enough for Jean and Henri to block the Exeter side.

After all this planning, it was a sheer accident that Henri saw Philip enter Exeter. He was lounging in the breakfast room of the inn at which they were staying after a very late rising, idly watching the traffic that passed on the road. In fact, he did not know Philip by sight and would not have recognized him. It was the rawboned bay that drew his attention. Philip stopped to ask the ostler of the inn a question, and Spite laid back his ears and showed his teeth as if he were about to savage the man who had raised a hand to stroke him. When Henri had gone into the stable to order their horses put to after the abortive attack on Philip, Spite had turned his head and frightened Henri half to death with that gesture.

Henri leapt to his feet and ran upstairs where he burst in on Jean, shouting that their man was riding right through town. Jean wasted no time. He told Henri to follow Philip and, if he did not stop on his own, to accost him and hold him in talk. He would meet Henri with the carriage just inside the old town gate as soon as he could.

At the far end of the town Henri saw Philip turn into an innyard and dismount. As Philip handed his reins to an ostler he gestured to a postillion, to whom he talked for a while and then handed a coin. Discreetly, Henri idled about. It had occurred to him that the only thing Philip would want to talk to a postillion about was the condition of the roads. If he asked the same question of the same postillion, he would get the same answers, and perhaps even find out which road Philip planned to take.

In fact, matters worked out just that way. Philip had mentioned that he intended to take the upper, less traveled road to Bodmin. Since the ostler had led Philip's horse into the stable, Henri assumed that he had stopped for a meal rather than a cup of coffee or mug of ale. He would have time to pass the information to Jean and his hireling rank rider.

The highwayman was waiting a little distance from Jean's carriage and was not ill-pleased at the news. It meant that he would not need to share with any associate. He grunted acceptance and rode off, making for a convenient spot he knew well from previous robberies. Henri climbed into the carriage with a deep sigh of relief. When Philip rode past them without a glance some time later, he sighed again. He just knew that they would be able to follow him without difficulty and that no one would come along the road behind them to interfere with their plans. From the lucky chance of spotting Philip, everything had gone just right. He felt much better now, sure that good luck would follow good luck.

Philip was of an exactly opposite opinion. He believed that when anything has been running very smoothly, there are bound to be little unseen bumps to throw it off the track. His wariness was increased rather than decreased by the untroubled ride and quiet nights he had had. He knew that all roads south of Bath led to Exeter. Thus, before he mounted to leave the town, he made sure his Lorenzoni pistols had fresh powder in their priming pans and were at half cock.

At first he rode slowly, giving Spite a chance to digest what he had eaten. It was a very lonely road. If ever there was an appropriate place for his pursuers to fall on him, this was it, Philip thought. Even the weather threatened; it was a dull, gray day. After a moment's thought Philip unrolled his greatcoat and put it on. It would fall low enough to hide the pistol butts sticking out of his boots. Preparations made, Philip touched Spite with his spur and cantered on for about a quarter of a mile. There was a sharp curve in the road ahead. Instinctively he tightened his rein and Spite slowed.

It was fortunate he had done so. Just around the turn a masked rider waited with his horse athwart the road. As Philip appeared he brandished a pistol in each hand and shouted for Philip to "stand and deliver." If Spite had been going faster, Philip might have had his hands too full with his horse to plan his moves. As it was, he uttered a startled gasp as he pulled Spite to a halt. The highwayman laughed.

"Get you down," he ordered, and fired the pistol in his left hand. "A warning," he said. "The next one will hit."

The highwayman's horse, accustomed to shots, stood like a rock, but Spite danced and bucked to Philip's intense delight. Since the stupid clot had already fired one gun, he had only one shot left and probably would not dare fire again. Even if he did, there was little chance of his hitting Philip while Spite was cavorting all over the road. The man shouted threats, but Philip allowed Spite to whirl right around while he shoved his left arm through his reins so that both hands were essentially free. As his right side was hidden by the movement, he dropped his hand and pulled one of the Lorenzonis from his boot. A single pull brought the gun to full cock and, as Spite came around the full turn, Philip raised his arm and fired.

Simultaneously he dug his spurs into Spite's ribs and bent low. The horse sprang forward frantically. Surprised out of his wits, by the shot and by Spite charging down at him, the highwayman forgot all about his instructions not to harm Philip and fired his second pistol. However, his horse, which was proof against pistol shots, was not indifferent to collisions. Seeing Spite thundering toward her, the mare began to move aside, and the variety of motions made the highwayman's shot as wide as Philip's. As he bent, Philip reloaded his gun.

Spite had just passed the highwayman's mare, but Philip now grabbed the reins in his left hand and wheeled the horse around. He had no intention of galloping off down the road. For one thing, that was an open invitation for a bullet in the back; for another, Philip had no idea the man was only hired help. He thought he was facing one of the French agents and was quite determined that the world would be better off without him. He could not understand why the "agent's" companion had not burst out of hiding or fired at him from concealment. Perhaps there had been only one man.

Even so, had the highwayman fled, Philip could not have brought himself to shoot him in the back. Instead, shouting curses, the man was fumbling in his pocket, either for a cartridge with which to reload his gun or possibly for a third pistol. Philip did not wait to find out. From nearly point-blank range, he shot him in the head.

The body went over sideways, limp hands dropping the reins. This, together with being twice charged by Spite, was too much for the mare. With a whinny of fear the animal took off down the road. Philip started to follow, thinking it would be best to examine what the man was carrying. However, when the bumping tipped the corpse over so that one foot tangled in the stirrup and it was dragged, Philip drew Spite in sharply. His gorge rose and tears filled his eyes.

In the excitement of the fight he had acted as circumstances dictated, but the sight of that limp, helpless thing that had once been a man bumping along on the road brought home to him what he had done. He sat trembling, wishing it undone, blaming himself for aiming for the head rather than the shoulder. It was no good now telling himself that the man had been a spy, perhaps had been planning to kill him. When he was in France, he would be the spy. How was he different from the man he had killed? All he could see was that pathetic body being dragged along by a terrified horse as it rounded the curve in the road.

Philip fought back the lunch that was rising in his throat, wondering whether he should try to pursue the horse so that the body could be . . . Could be what? Philip knew he dared not permit himself to be embroiled with the authorities over this shooting. He was not afraid of being accused of murder. The mask on the corpse's face and the fired pistols, one of which was lying on the road and the other probably in the man's pocket, would tell their own story; however, Philip would have to identify himself and explain what he was doing in the area.

That was impossible. Probably he would need to remain in Exeter until proof of his identity could be obtained—and that would be vastly complicated by the false French identity papers he was carrying. That he had killed a French agent would be no compensation for the lost time. What England needed to know was whether or not an invasion was imminent. Surely that was the important thing. Philip bitterly regretted what he had done, but it could not be undone by involving himself in endless delays and explanations.

Just as he reached that conclusion he heard shouts and the jingle of carriage harness that an abrupt change of pace causes. Philip wheeled Spite and spurred him into a headlong gallop. Whatever was left of the man he had killed would be taken care of by whomever was coming down the road. He could do nothing more than they would; he knew nothing about the man, except that he was a French agent, and now that he was dead perhaps that was better left unsaid. He had sounded English when he called to

Philip to halt; perhaps he had a wife and children. Even if the wife knew her husband's profession, it was unlikely she was involved, and the children certainly should not be branded as traitors.

It was only later, after Philip had stopped for the night in a miserable inn in Okehampton, that it occurred to him that any agent's confederates should be ferreted out. It was too late to go back now, and the other arguments for staying clear of the business were still good. The best move under the circumstances would be to write to his father and report the whole affair. Roger could inform the Foreign Office, and they could work through the local authorities without giving away his own part in the matter.

Philip slept uneasily, disturbed by dreams of flying horses dragging bodies with only half a head. The only comfort he had when he wakened, shuddering, was that he no longer needed to listen for an invasion of his room in the night. Although his basic premise was wrong, his conclusion happened to be correct. Temporarily he had rid himself of his pursuers. In swerving to avoid the highwayman's frantic mare, Jean had lost control of his own horses; the traces had become entangled, one horse had stumbled, pushing against the other, which swerved still farther, so that the carriage had ended in the ditch with a broken wheel.

Neither Jean nor Henri was much hurt, but both were bruised and shaken, and when they had finally disentangled the frightened horses and ridden them, most uncomfortably bareback, back to Exeter, they encountered a small crowd gaping interestedly while the town constables made ready to carry their accomplice's body away. Here they learned that the highwayman had been killed by a shot in the head. Henri almost fainted, and for the first time Jean became seriously worried about the spirit and abilities of their opponent. It had never occurred to Jean that Philip would resist the highwayman. One look at Henri underlined the fact that he would be little help. Jean would simply have abandoned his companion in Exeter, except that Philip knew him and did not know Henri. He could still be useful in watching the quarry.

It was easier for Jean to make that decision than to convince Henri to go along with it. When Jean threatened to abandon him, Henri received the information with enthusiasm, promising to return immediately to London or find a convenient house party to attend and swearing that he would say nothing, absolutely nothing, about this venture. This innocent remark opened a whole new vista of horrors to Jean, since he was quite certain by now that Henri was totally incapable of keeping any secret for long, particularly one that he could use to make himself seem mysterious and heroic.

Jean's next idea was to kill his companion, but he realized he would be suspect at once. He would have to wait before silencing Henri for good. He set himself to convince his unwilling companion that graver and more horrible results than anything Philip could do would follow failure to accomplish their mission. Furthermore, he said, he did not wish to be shot either. They would not themselves come in contact with Philip. They would be more careful, hire a group rather than one man. In fact, they would wait until he had made his contact with the shipmaster whose name they were to discover and accomplish both purposes at one time.

Eventually Henri agreed; but between his resistance and the dilatory ways of those who went to bring the carriage back to Exeter and the wheelwright who repaired it, they were many days behind Philip. Jean was furious. The only point that they were certain Philip would touch was Bodmin. After that he could go either north or south on any of hundreds of cart tracks that led to the numerous if tiny fishing villages and smugglers' ports of call. In any of those villages

Philip would stick out like a sore thumb, but it would take weeks or months, possibly even years, to investigate them all. Long before they found the village, Philip would have made his contact and departed for France.

It was not a cheerful prospect, and Jean did think briefly of abandoning the quest. However, there was still a substantial sum remaining of what d'Ursine had given him, and he was not yet ready to give up the even more liberal payment promised if he brought back the papers and the name of captain and ship. There would be no harm in inquiring along the road running west from Bodmin. If Philip's goal was near Land's End, the number of villages he could aim for would be drastically reduced. They might even find him before he left for France.

Chapter 5

On the night Philip wrote to his father to describe his encounter with the highwayman, Megaera set out to meet Pierre at The Mousehole to pay for the cargo he had delivered. She put on the coarse clothing of the Red Meg persona, but she did not bother to dirty her face and hair. There was no chance, in her opinion, that Pierre would ever meet Mrs. Edward Devoran and recognize her as Red Meg. It was thus silly to have to wash her hair, which hung nearly to her knees and was no light task.

She passed down the chimney stairs, John preceding her with the lamp, and through the passage. When she had first threaded her way through the branching tunnels, she had had to lead John. Now he knew the way from the house to the main cave by heart. He still got confused when the kegs needed to be moved to the subsidiary outlets, but he was learning and soon would be able to do all the transferring alone. That would be very convenient, since John could sleep all day if necessary. Megaera could not do that without causing anxiety among her servants.

That anxiety, unfortunately, would not be confined to her own staff. Many servants in the local "big houses" were related, and even more of them were acquainted with each other. Since gossip about their masters and mistresses was the main staple of conversation among them, and since that gossip moved up the social ladder as well as down, any peculiar behavior on Megaera's part would all too soon be known all over the neighborhood. Thus Megaera found herself very short on sleep for about two weeks out of every month over the normal delivery period, and just now, when Pierre was showing up more frequently than usual, she was nearly staggering with weariness.

At least, she thought as she mechanically followed John, there would be no deliveries to make this time. The kegs Pierre had delivered would merely be stored. They would come to no harm in the cool, dark caves waiting until the bad weather made crossing the Channel and unloading the *Bonne Lucie* too dangerous. Then she would still have stock to deliver. Meg was proud of her forethought; her customers would be pleased with her service. Often, now, when payment was left in the agreed-on place or when the money was handed over in person at the time the kegs (or bottles) were delivered, there would be a note or word-of-mouth request that she deliver to a new customer.

Business was expanding both because her deliveries were regular and dependable and also because there were none of the petty depredations that sometimes accompanied deliveries by other smuggling bands. Since Megaera made all the deliveries herself with John's help, she could be sure that nothing would be damaged or stolen. She had the advantage of a completely safe hiding place, so that she was in no hurry to rid herself of the cargo. Deliveries could be made a few at a time instead of all in one night.

The men who brought the cargo from the ship to the main cave had no idea that there were subsidiary caves in the hillside. All they knew was that Megaera paid them as they unloaded the cargo into the cave and sent them away. This, as well as the strict rules about not annoying the villagers, was a cause of dissatisfaction to some of the men. But most did not mind, knowing that their job was the least dangerous part and glad to be free of making the deliveries. By and large these men were decent fishermen and farmers who merely wanted to increase their pathetically small livelihoods.

There was, however, a more lawless group. These men had been accustomed, under Black Bart's management, to taking a woman here and there, a chicken or piglet or two, sometimes even things of greater value. They had also been accustomed to holding back a few kegs of brandy to be broached and drunk. Red Meg paid a little more than Bart had, it was true, but she had taken most of the fun out of the work and they resented it.

Megaera had never noticed the resentment. She had the prejudices of her class in full measure and assumed that all the lower orders would have the same attitude toward her as her own servants and the tenant farmers that lived on her land. Because she paid them fairly, she assumed they were satisfied and dismissed them from her mind. She was not surprised, of course, when she found evidence several times that some men had returned to search the main cave. It was natural, she had thought, that such creatures should want to steal a few kegs for their own pleasure or to sell privately to increase their profit.

The evidence had merely proved to Megaera that she had been very wise to remove the temptation from their path. Obviously if they had to pay for their drink, they were much less likely to overindulge to their own, their wives', and their children's detriment. Besides, the extra keg or two were that many more coins toward the redeeming of the mortgages on Bolliet Manor. Megaera would not spare a penny from that purpose for anything.

If it had been possible for John and herself to unload the *Bonne Lucie* alone, she would have dismissed
the gang entirely to save what she paid them, but that
really was beyond her ability. She was not strong
enough to handle kegs, and John could not manage a
boat. The men were necessary. The only expenditure
Megaera really resented was the extra share she paid
Black Bart. He did nothing except complain, and she
suspected that the two men who had tried to become
familiar with her had done so on his instigation.

After the first had approached her and been felled
by John, Megaera had found her father's pistols and
taught herself how to use them. By the time the next
cargo came, she was wearing them ostentatiously. She
had drawn on the man who had grabbed and tried to
kiss her. John had broken his arm before she nerved
herself to fire, but she had pretended that was an act
of mercy—and the men had believed it.

There had been no further trouble, and Megaera's
sense of fairness had prohibited any attempt on her
part to get rid of Black Bart, even though he was
totally unnecessary to her now. After all, he had introduced her to Pierre and originally assembled the band
of men she employed. That she did not like him and
would prefer to deal with Thomas Helston, a stolid,
solid farmer from Treen—who could be trusted to get
the men together as well or better than Bart and
whose large, industrious family would benefit from
the extra share—was not reason enough to cut Bart out.

Nonetheless the idea occurred to her continually.
Black Bart made her nervous. He never did or said
anything obvious enough to merit John's attentions,
but there was a look in his eyes, a shade in his speech
and manner that disturbed Megaera very much. Recently she had even begun to consider paying only
the interest on the mortgages and collecting a large
enough sum to offer Bart as a final payoff. If she

could clear her conscience that way, it would be worthwhile to remain in debt a few months longer.

The trouble was, she did not really believe she could rid herself of the man that way. Either he would lay an information with the revenuers or, far more likely, would try to raid her group and steal their cargo. It would be possible, Megaera supposed, to fight him off, but she knew the tales about the smuggling gang wars in the seventies and eighties of the last century, and she shrank from the bloodshed and violence. To her mind she was doing no one any harm by her current enterprise. She would rather endure Black Bart and the uneasiness he aroused in her than begin the bad old days again.

For the hundredth or thousandth time Megaera was searching through her mind to find a method she could use without violating her notion of what was just and would still keep Bart from troubling her after she paid him off. She knew one way, of course. She could identify him as the man who had murdered her husband. That would be terribly unfair. For one thing, Megaera was not really sure it had been Bart, although she did not think, now that she knew them, that any of the other men customarily carried pistols. Stout cudgels, which could also be used in helping them climb the steep path from the cove to the cave, were the men's customary weapons. For another thing, Megaera was grateful to the person who had removed Edward from her life. She did not want anyone punished for that.

Down the ladder from the high opening, John and Megaera came out into the small area she had screened off from the wide expanse of the cave as her "living place." John lit a candle from the lantern and then moved toward the front of the cave where he had tethered a sturdy pony earlier in the day. By the light of the candle Megaera emptied the dried scraps of food from a plate on the table into a bucket and put some fresh "remains," which she had brought from the house, onto the greasy, unwashed plate. She shuddered slightly at the thought of living in such squalor—not the damp dark of the cave but the idea that she would not wash the dishes if she should be reduced to such a condition. However, the point of her disguise was that Red Meg was a sloven. If the men searched the cave, it must seem that she did live there, and in conditions that matched her filthy person.

While she was arranging evidence that the cave was lived in, John saddled the pony, then set down the lantern and went outside. When he was sure that no one was riding in the immediate area—a most unlikely accident, but Megaera insisted on caution—he led the pony outside. He did not remain near the opening of the cave but moved east about a hundred feet and stood holding the lantern. It was not likely that any-one would see the light, but Megaera did not want to take the chance that a shepherd or late home-goer would notice and thus become aware of the cave en-trance.

A few minutes later Megaera came to the mouth of the cave. The moon had not yet risen, and after she had blown out the candle and stuck it in a convenient niche to be relit on her return, she could barely see enough in the faint luminous skyglow not to trip. Cau-tiously she made her way out, feeling for stable footing on the rough ground as she turned right, to where John waited. All her attention was directed to her goal and her footing. She never saw a shadow rise from where a man had lain concealed by the dark and the low growth of brush.

There was a single snap of a dry branch, a brief rustle—enough to warn Megaera. She ducked and darted forward, avoiding the blow that had been in-tended to stun her. However, she had no time to turn or draw a pistol before she was seized. Black Bart cursed viciously, furious at missing his chance to subdue Meg without fuss or trouble. Rage and terror had flooded Megaera, giving her more strength than would be expected from her slender fragility. She twisted and writhed like a wildcat, clawing and kicking while Bart tried to swing his pistol so that the butt would stun her.

He missed her head again, striking her shoulder so that she screamed—but the pain apparently only gave her more impetus. A violent kick from her boot heel caught Bart right on the shin, and it was his turn to howl with pain. Now Bart regretted that he had not tried to shoot her, but he had been afraid he would miss in the dark. Then she could have darted back into the cave. He could just about enter one without falling apart, but he knew he could not follow her far inside.

Even as he had attacked her, Bart had not been sure what he would do after he stunned Meg. He would rob her and rape her—of that he was certain—but whether he would have killed her at once or kept her prisoner until he had tamed her he could not decide. Now he knew he would kill her. A wildcat like this would never tame. She was not whimpering in pain but screaming with rage, fighting him harder even as he tightened his grip and struck at her again.

Megaera hardly felt the blows that hit her. In fact, although Bart was bringing the gun down as hard as he could, the barrel of a pistol was not weighted properly for striking. In addition she was moving so violently that many of the blows missed and the others only glanced off her arm and back, except for the first which had bruised her shoulder. She struggled like a madwoman, knowing her only hope was to break free and run to John.

It did not occur to either Bart or Megaera that John could notice what was going on. Since he was deaf, no sound could reach him; since he carried the lantern so that Megaera could find him and the pony, he would be blinded by the dark. Thus, as frantically as Megaera struggled to free herself, Bart struggled to hold her. If she got loose, he would be finished in this area in the smuggling business or any other. Most of the men would stand up for her, and the dummy would kill him on sight.

What neither Megaera nor Bart realized was that John was not totally unaware that something was wrong. He had noticed Megaera come to the cave entrance because he saw the brief glow of the candle before she blew it out. Instinctively he knew how long it should take his mistress to reach him, and she had not come. At first he thought she had paused for some reason—often he did not understand the things she did—and he waited.

However, Megaera was the focus of John's whole existence. She was the one who had saved him when he was bound and left to die; she was the only person with whom he could communicate; most important of all, she made him feel useful and important. Without any sexual overtones, of which he was incapable, John loved Megaera with his whole heart and soul. He adored her as a goddess. He had no other deity—even his mother could not communicate abstract ideas to him in dumbshow. Megaera was John's everything, and the few seconds' delay stretched to minutes and hours in his anxious mind.

He stared toward the cave, seeking her shadowy form advancing toward him. He knew the ground was rough and began to fear that she had tripped and fallen. As soon as that thought occurred to him, he would have run back, but he was constrained by what he was supposed to do. Never, never had he ever disobeyed or deviated from what he knew Megaera expected of him. Still, the notion that she had hurt herself grew with each passing second. Surely if she were hurt, he must disobey the order to hold the pony and wait. John's mind moved slowly and, although he was no physical coward, he was utterly and completely terrified of Megaera's disapproval.

She had not come. She had to, but she did not. Sobbing with anxiety, John set the lantern down and wound the reins of the pony into the bush beside which he stood. It was too long a time. She should have come by now. He stared back into the dark—and something flickered against the sky, a double darkness that moved. A sigh of relief moved John's giant chest. She was coming. But another moment passed and she did not arrive. John saw the fleeting movement of shadows again, but it seemed to be in the same place. A furious gobbling came from his throat and he began to run back, slipping and stumbling in his haste.

Megaera was nearly done for. No matter how furiously fear pushed blood through her body to provide energy to her muscles, she was a small girl and her strength was nothing in comparison to her opponent's. Despite her flailing and kicking, Bart had got one arm firmly around her and was trying to cock his pistol so that he could press it against her head and fire. She had frustrated his attempts to do so twice—once by wrenching one arm free and drawing her own gun. But there was no chance she could cock it, and Bart had laughed as he knocked it out of her hand. The second time he did not laugh; in fact he nearly lost his hold on her when she turned halfway round toward him and kneed him in the groin. Unfortunately the angle was wrong and Megaera's strength was already failing, so that the blow was more startling than disabling.

It was infuriating, too—so infuriating that Bart stopped trying to cock his pistol and raised it to strike at Megaera again. It was a mistake. Before he could hit her the sound of John's blundering advance, as heavy and inexorable as a charging bull's, changed the situation. Bart knew his opportunity was gone. Even if he

let Meg go and cocked his gun, there would be no time
to get them both. If he shot John, Meg would shoot
him—if the bullet stopped John at all, which Bart
doubted. And if he shot Meg, John would tear him
limb from limb. Certainly it would be impossible to
steal the money she must be carrying to pay Restoir.

He did the only thing remaining for him to do in
the circumstances, shoving Meg forcibly away from
him so that she staggered backward. She would have
fallen painfully, but John was closer than Bart
thought. The big mute caught his mistress before she
hit the ground, gobbling his distress while Bart ran
off into the darkness. He paused once, cocked his gun,
and turned, but Meg and her servant were still locked
together and were so dim that he knew he would miss.
Bart dared not fire on a chance. That red-haired bitch
would know he couldn't reload quickly in the dark
and would send the dummy after him. He turned to
run again, but before he moved, Meg's voice came.

"Get out of the country," she screamed. "It's your
only hope. I know you killed Devoran, and I'm going
to lay an information with Mrs. Devoran. Maybe the
beaks won't listen to me, but they will to her. You
show your face again near Bolliet or Treen and you're
a dead man."

It was the best she could do. Had Megaera been less
breathless and exhausted, she would have pursued
Bart. Now that he had attacked her, her conscience
was clear. She would have shot him or had John break
his neck without a qualm. But there was no way to
send John after him alone, because he could hardly
see her gestures. It would be impossible to explain to
him that he must chase, catch, and kill a man. Besides, there was another consideration. Bart had a gun
and Megaera would not for a moment think of risking
John's life to assure her own future safety.

After her first shock had passed, Megaera was a
little surprised that John had not pursued Bart on

his own. She had had to order him to hit the man who had made lewd suggestions to her—but of course he had not heard them. He had attacked the man who had grabbed her, without instructions, as soon as he had seen her draw her gun, indicating the man's act was offensive to her. By now John had helped her back to the cave and run to the pony to get the lantern. It was then that she realized that John had never known someone had attacked her. He had never seen Black Bart in the dark, and she had been catapulted into his arms well away from her attacker. With all his attention on her and unable to hear the crashing brush as Bart ran, John would never have noticed Black Bart's escape.

That was unfortunate, since Megaera had no way to tell John that a man he knew as part of the gang—and therefore as trustworthy—was no longer a "friend." Tears of fear and pain and loneliness rose in her eyes. Now that she no longer needed to defend herself, she ached all over from the beating she had taken. She was shaking with fear and fatigue, but she could not even lie down and rest. She *had* to ride to The Mousehole and pay Pierre.

God knew what Pierre would think if she did not come, and there was no one she could send. Even if John knew the way—and that was most doubtful—she had no way to explain to him that he must give Pierre the money and a note. No, she must go herself. As she made the decision, her tears spilling over because she hurt so and the thought of riding the four miles to The Mousehole was so frightening and depressing, John came back with the light. He began to tremble when he saw her tears, fearing he had done something wrong, and Megaera had to wipe her face and force a smile and assure him all was well—which made her feel even more hopeless and lonely.

In her attention to detail, Megaera had furnished the cave with a broken comb, a small mirror, and the

other articles of a female toilette. Aside from the fact
that her hair had come down, she was surprised to see
how little her violent struggle showed. Probably she
would be black and blue all over the next day, but for
now, once her hair was done again, she thought she
looked much as usual.

To John's dull perceptions or to a person who did
not care about her, that might have been true; but
Pierre Restoir liked and admired his partner and his
mind was not in the least dull. Even in the dim light
of the old inn where smoking oil lamps, hung from
age-old rafters, provided all the illumination, Pierre
could see Meg's unusual pallor and the fear in her
large, violet eyes. He jumped to his feet and led her
to the corner table near the back door that was his
customary place.

"What 'as happen', Mees Meg?" he asked anxiously,
speaking to her, as he always did, in English.

Because she did not need to control her emotions
for fear of frightening John, having left him in the
stable with the pony, Pierre's question brought tears
to Megaera's eyes again. "Bart jumped me as I came
out of the cave," she confessed, her voice trembling.
"John was ahead and didn't notice anything was
wrong for quite a while. I had a devil of a time fighting Bart off."

Pierre growled deep in his throat. "I warn' you," he
said severely. "Did I not say to you to be rid of 'im,
that 'e was dishonest?"

"Yes." Meg sniffed back tears. "But how could I? I
made a bargain with him, and he hadn't done anything until tonight."

"That ees true," Pierre admitted, frowning. Then
he shook his head. "The poor John, 'e ees not clever.
Also, because of 'is deafness, 'e cannot protect you
when 'e cannot see you. Eet ees not safe, Mees Meg."

Megaera shuddered. "I will be more careful," she
sighed.

"That ees not enough," Pierre protested. "You need someone to assist you. I see you shake, Mees. You should not 'ave come."

"But if I hadn't, you would have thought I—"

"That you intend' to cheat me? No! I am not so much the fool. But I would 'ave worry much what had 'appen'. Ees there no one you can trust, Mees Meg? You are young—beautiful—ees there no man . . ."

"No!" Megaera exclaimed forcibly.

"You do not trust any of us except poor John, eh?" Pierre said, restraining a smile out of sympathy for Megaera's shaken condition and her youth. "One man 'as betray' you, I suppose, so all are under suspicion. But . . ."

"Now you are saying *I* am a fool," Megaera interrupted. "You are right that I have reason not to trust men, but I'm not so silly as to think all are the same." She smiled. "I trust you, Pierre."

"Much good that ees," he grumbled. "When you need me, I cannot be 'ere. Eet ees not safe for you that my French and Breton crew come ashore. I wish . . . Perhaps I will think of something. In the meantime, you will be careful, yes?"

"Yes. Don't worry about Black Bart. I happen to know that he killed a—a gentleman in a nearby town. I have a way to tell that man's wife. She's clever. She'll think of a way to set the law on him if he shows his face in this district again. I don't think he'll trouble me anymore."

"Perhaps not," Pierre said, but somewhat doubtfully. "That idea ees a good one, but 'e ees sly, treacherous, that creature. Do not trust too much to the law. For money they can be blind, and they are not too clever also."

"I know. I'll be careful."

Megaera reached inside her long jacket and undid the money belt she had strapped around her slender waist. She touched Pierre's foot in warning and then handed over the belt cautiously under the table while she went on talking about the precautions she would take. There were one or two soft clinks as Pierre transferred the golden guineas to some small sacks, but Megaera knew the sound of their voices would cover them. After he had cleared the belt, it came back by the same route. Without looking at what she was doing, Megaera folded the cloth into a soft roll and stuffed it into the pocket of her jacket that was hidden by the wall near which she sat. Only when that was done did Pierre return to real business.

"I will come again two weeks from Tuesday," he said, "unless the weather ees too bad. What code this time?"

"Three short, one long, one short for the house on the cliff to warn me to come down. I'll give you two long. You give me one long, one short, a blank long, and one more short to confirm at the cove."

Pierre grunted as he wrote the signals down, using a tiny piece of charcoal on a dirty scrap of paper which he stuffed back into his tobacco pouch when he was finished. Some smugglers might have objected to the involved code, which changed for each delivery, but Pierre liked the idea. It was a sign of Red Meg's caution, and daring though he might be, Pierre also believed in taking every precaution possible in business matters. No one except himself and Meg knew the code; no one could learn it by watching. Thus no one could lure either of them into a trap. Pierre liked the idea so much that he had begun to use it for his pickups in France, when those were made secretly.

Now, of course, Pierre mostly took on his cargo publicly. Since Bonaparte had taken over the government of France, things had changed a great deal. In a sense they were better. Bonaparte had no objection at all to smuggling wine and brandy and tobacco into England. He needed money to continue his wars; he needed good English woolen cloth for overcoats and uniforms and blankets for his army and good English leather boots to put on his soldiers' feet.

Pierre was delighted with the new system—but that did not mean he approved of Bonaparte. Other things were not as satisfactory. All controls on everything had been tightened. There was not a port a ship could sail into, not even a simple *chasse-marée*, that it was not boarded and examined. This annoyed Pierre on principle, although it did him no harm. He had far more tricks for hiding his ill-gotten profits than all the customs men in France could uncover. Sometimes a layer of fish was stuffed with gold pieces; sometimes the guineas were nailed to the hull of the *Bonne Lucie* well below the waterline.

Often Pierre did not sail into a port directly. There were as many lonely coves on the rocky Breton coast as in Cornwall. A brief trip in the ship's tiny boat and the loot was hidden safely to be picked up when convenient. Of course, the gold Pierre carried home was only a small part of his total profit. Most of it went in purchase of those British manufactures Bonaparte desired.

These Pierre brought openly into port, showing bills for about one-third higher than he had actually paid. Since the value of his outgoing cargo was often known, at least approximately, and Pierre willingly opened his strongbox to show what remained between what he had been paid and the cost of his cargo (there were never more than five or ten English guineas there), the bills looked legitimate enough. He got his money plus the legal profit allowed, which gave him a most respectable earning ratio and, equally important, the pleasure of cheating the government that was trying to control him.

The only real problem Pierre had was the purchase of the English goods he needed. During the spring and summer immediately after the declaration of war, the English factors who had been dealing with him had been willing to continue selling to him direct. As feeling against Bonaparte rose with the threat of invasion and news of French victories, however, the merchants in Falmouth had become afraid someone would report them for dealing with the French and accuse them of treason.

Pierre had been wondering whether he could ask Meg to do the buying for him. She was English and might be able to purchase the relatively small quantities of material Pierre carried without question. This was no time to add any problems to those she already had, Pierre decided. Perhaps she would have thought over his advice and found a more normal assistant than John to help her by the time he returned. If she had, he would see what could be worked out. If not . . . Wait and see, Pierre told himself as he escorted Megaera to the stable and offered to ride home with her if she felt she needed more protection than John could afford.

Impulsively Meg raised herself on tiptoe and kissed Pierre's cheek. "You're a dear. No, I'll be all right. No one followed us—I'm sure of that. I was nervous as a cat and watching carefully. So I'm sure I'll be all right."

"If 'e knows where you live—" Pierre began.

"No—and I have more than one hidey-hole," Meg said, most untruthfully. "I'm not going back to the place he knows. I'll warn the men in the gang, too. One of them can take over everything Bart did. He's a decent man, has a wife and children and every reason to avoid trouble. Don't worry about me. I can take care of myself."

Megaera hoped the assurance carried more conviction to Pierre than it did to her. The truth was that she was miserable and frightened. She desperately wanted someone to talk to, someone who would help and protect her, but she knew that Pierre had his own affairs. Besides that, it was very dangerous for him to be in England. Nor did she dare confide in any of the local men. Sooner or later a close association of that type would expose the connection of Red Meg with Mrs. Edward Devoran, the daughter of Lord Bolliet.

Chapter 6

Philip rode to The Mousehole three days after Pierre left. He had no trouble finding the inn, which was the only building larger than a miserable hut. Not that the inn was much better. It was very old and sagged crookedly, as if the spirits served in it for centuries had permeated the beams and made it drunk. The plaster between the beams was cracked and peeling, the beams themselves ashen gray with lack of treatment. The thatch looked near as old as the house itself, flattened, ragged, covered with some gray-green lichens or moss that could withstand the salt air and salt spray that came in from the sea.

Inside, the place looked less ready to collapse but no less aged. The ceilings were low, black with accumulated soot from the fires and smoking oil lamps, which, Philip suspected, made darkness barely visible at night. Even on this fresh October morning one could hardly see enough to avoid the large, rough-hewn tables and benches. The windows were few and grimed with years of dirt. Although accommodation had been far more Spartan than Philip was accustomed to since he had passed Exeter, the inns on the main road had been decent and clean.

"Yes?"

The landlord, who had come out from behind the scarred, greasy counter, was no more inviting than his inn. He was big and the dark eyes in his craggy, gray-stubbled face were hard. His voice, though raised in question, rejected an answer, implying the visitor had made a mistake by entering and should leave at once. At first Philip was affronted. He was accustomed to an eager welcome from landlords, and the poorer the inn the more eager the welcome, usually. Before he made the mistake of showing his resentment, however, logic and his sense of humor came to his rescue. In a smugglers' den strangers could scarcely be a pleasant surprise.

"I want Restoir," Philip said without preamble. Ignoring the fact that the landlord was already shaking his head in denial, he went on. "Six feet or thereabout, maybe fourteen stone, black eyes, gray hair—what's left of it. He's the captain of a *chasse-marée*—a fishing boat, I mean, the *Pretty Lucy* or *Bonne Lucie*. Never mind saying you do not know him. I do not care whether you do or not. All I want is to leave a letter for him."

Philip reached into his pocket and drew out the folded sheet together with a golden guinea. He flipped the coin toward the landlord, whose hand flicked out to snatch it from the air with a speed that warned he would be a bad opponent. The coin disappeared and the hand went out again to take the letter.

"You can leave it," he growled. "I never saw the man nor heard of his boat, but if he ever comes in, he'll get the letter. What do you want him to do?"

"Nothing," Philip lied blandly. "He wants me. I will be around for a month or so. I have business here anyway. If he still wants me, he will know where to find me—and if he does want to find me, it will be well worth your while that you passed the word."

The landlord shrugged. "Like I said, I never heard

of him or his boat—but all kinds of people walk into
The Mousehole. I'll spread the word you're around,
if you want. What business?"

"Restoir knows, and that is all that counts. My name
is Philip St. Eyre."

He left without another word, hoping he sounded
like an illicit customer for Pierre's goods rather than
a customs agent or any other officer of the law. He was
almost certain the landlord would pass on the letter.
Pierre had told his father he could be reached through
the inn called The Mousehole, so Pierre must have
warned the innkeeper that there might be messages for
him.

The denials meant nothing. It was not likely that
the landlord would admit knowing a French smuggler in these times even if the man was hiding behind
the counter or sleeping off a drunk in a room upstairs.
Besides, Philip was sure he had seen a flash of recognition in the man's eyes, even as he was shaking his
head in negation. Now there was nothing to do except
wait and pray that the weather would not suddenly
turn nasty and prevent Pierre from coming across.
Usually he made about one trip a month, so the time
limit Philip had set should be adequate.

If the weather played him false, Philip thought as
he rode up the miserable track that was all the road
there was to The Mousehole, he would have to visit
the inn again and reinforce his payment. He hoped
sincerely that it would not be necessary, as a repeat
visit, too much interest on his part, or the appearance
of being willing to wait beyond the time he had
already stated might make the landlord suspicious.
No, it would not matter, he decided. Suspicious or
not, he would pass the letter. There could be no danger to him in that—or to Pierre.

Filled with pleasurable anticipation, Philip kicked
Spite into a canter as he headed back toward Penzance.
According to the instructions he had been given, it

was necessary to go back to the second fork in the road and take the right-hand turn this time. About a mile on, that would bring him to another road where he must go left. At Drift someone would be able to direct him to Moreton Place near Sancreed.

This information was quite correct, and just as the family were sitting down to tea, Philip pulled the bell. At this point his carefully constructed plan almost went awry. A week on the road had done his outer garments little good, and the Moretons' well-trained butler was not accustomed to young men traveling without baggage or a valet. He therefore looked most coldly on Philip when he asked to be announced.

"If you will give me your card, sir," he said disdainfully, "I will carry it to his lordship."

"I do not have a card," Philip said impatiently. One does not, after all, carry English visiting cards when one is about to embark on a career as a spy in France. Philip was rather annoyed with himself. He could have brought *one* card along, but he had carefully divested himself of anything that could be used to identify him. "I am a friend of Lord Kevern's," he added. "My name is St. Eyre, Philip St. Eyre. Lord and Lady Moreton know me quite well."

"If you say so, sir," the butler responded with patent disbelief, beginning to close the door in Philip's face.

It was infuriating, and Philip barely restrained himself from pushing in by force. That would scarcely be polite behavior, however, or calculated to please Lord and Lady Moreton. Philip was just resigning himself to a ride all the way back to Drift, when the rattle of wheels drew his attention to a fine sporting curricle bowling up the drive. He hoped it would be a member of the family rather than a visitor, and he grinned with relief when the butler said, "Here is Lord Kevern now," obviously expecting Philip to cut and run.

When he stood his ground, the butler began to look

worried. He did not open the door any wider, but he stepped out himself. "I am very sorry, sir, if—"

"Perfectly all right," Philip replied, smiling. "I am a little travel-stained, I know. And it was foolish of me to forget my cards."

Before he could say any more, Perce Moreton rounded the corner of the house nearly at a run, then drew up short to gape. "You didn't ride that ugly bonesetter all the way out here, did you?" he asked in amazement.

"Ah—yes, I did," Philip replied, "but I think we had better go in before we discuss it any further."

"Butler closed the door in your face, eh?" Perce said next, mounting the flight of wide, shallow steps. "Don't blame him. Wouldn't let you in m'self, only that I've known you so long."

"What do you mean, butler?" Philip asked, diverted from a defense of his appearance that he had intended to make by blaming the roads and inns of Cornwall for his soiled and wrinkled clothing. "Do you not know the name of your own butler?"

"'Course I know his name, you fool," Perce exclaimed, but without heat. "That's it." He paused to consider this statement, then wrinkled his forehead and laughed. "Been with us so long, never thought about it, but it's a bit confusin', I guess, to have a butler named Butler."

"You mean Butler is his name?" Philip asked, his voice rising a little.

"Er—yes."

Philip shook his head sadly. "It is just like you, Perce. I cannot think of anyone else who would be silly enough to have a butler named Butler."

As soon as Lord Kevern had addressed the disreputable-looking visitor in terms of familiarity, Butler had stepped back and opened the door wide. He listened to the lunatic conversation about his name with a perfectly unmoved countenance, although once when the young men's eyes were locked together he had raised his own to heaven. Two of them! No one at the Rich Lode ever believed him when he said Lord Kevern was the worst devil of all m'lord's sons. And it was true enough that the capers he cut were usually very clever. Looking at his blond, bland face with its vacuous expression and listening to the nonsense he talked, Butler could see the reason why people discounted him. That was a mistake.

Meanwhile, Perce had propelled Philip through the now wide and welcoming door, protesting, "He ain't *my* butler. M'mother hired him, you know, or maybe he was in the family—" He stopped and turned to the butler. "Who hired you, Butler?"

"I came as pantry boy in your grandfather's time, my lord," Butler replied, his face properly wooden but a smile in his eyes. "Master Ives employed me by recommendation, and I worked my way up through footman."

"There!" Perce exclaimed, steering Philip through the entrance hall and thrusting him through a doorway on the left into the library. "Can't keep a good man down just because of his name. Must reward merit and ambition, you know." His face changed as he shut the library door, and he said, "Trouble, Phil?"

"Ah—yes and no," Philip answered. "As you know I was jigging a little too fast. I—ah—tripped a couple of times and my father lost patience and suggested a— a long trip into the country."

Philip swallowed. It had sounded amusing to him when he told Roger he would blame him for his excursion into Cornwall. Now, however, he was suddenly, achingly aware of how good and loving his father had always been, how uncomplainingly he had paid for his son's stupid excesses. The words stuck in Philip's throat. It was one thing to tease his father, another entirely really to blacken his name.

"You mean your father pushed you out?" Perce asked, his face blanker than usual.

Unable to speak, Philip nodded.

"For good?"

"No, of course not. Just until—until my debts are paid."

"Cut you off with a shilling, eh?" Perce's blue eyes might well have been marbles, they were so glassy and emotionless.

"Yes," Philip grated.

"Come off it," Perce said sharply. "I know your father. Know your stepmother, too. She'd kill him if he ever thought of such a thing—which he wouldn't."

"Damn you!" Philip exclaimed, grinning. "Why the devil did you make me say all that when you knew. . . I cannot tell you anything else, though. I know your tongue will not wag, Perce, but it is not my secret."

"That's all right," Perce agreed instantly. "Pretty sure I know anyway. Nothing else could've hiked you out of the 'slough of despond' you were in. Never mind that. What're we going to tell m'parents is more to the point. How long will you be staying here?"

"I do not know, perhaps a month—six weeks, even, if the weather turns very bad. Perhaps only a few days. But there is something else. I may have to return, possibly several times."

Perce thought that over, looking more and more like an idiot the faster his mind moved. "Then we have to use that story. M'father won't believe it—he sits in the Lords and knows your fa—but I can tip him the wink and he'll be mum. M'mother will swallow it whole, which is all right. You'll suffer for it, though. She'll sigh all over you and 'poor boy' you to death. Serves you right, m'lad. It's all to the good, anyway. At least she won't shove m'sisters down your throat. Dreadful muffin-faced things they are."

Since Philip knew that Perce was quite fond of his

sisters—he was forever buying trinkets and lace and
ribbons and dispatching these items to them—Philip
did not take his description too seriously. He appre-
ciated the gentle warning in what his friend said,
however. This was no time for him to become interested in a woman or to permit one to become
interested in him. Obviously Perce had guessed immediately that Philip would be engaged in some kind
of venture in France. Philip could only hope it would
not be as obvious to anyone else.

He was delighted with the way things had worked
out, since Perce took charge of explaining his unannounced arrival and the possibly erratic nature of
his visit, thus freeing him from the necessity of ma-
ligning his father. Perce also supplied horses, extra
smallclothes, stockings, and shirts. Unfortunately
Philip could not cram his broad shoulders into the
willowy Perce's coats, but that troubled neither of
them since it was an excellent excuse to avoid the
round of visits to the neighboring gentry that Lady
Moreton might otherwise have enforced. One could
not present one's son's friend when he had only one
tatty coat and a soiled greatcoat and no money to
buy another.

Instead, Perce took Philip all over the countryside,
from Land's End to Saint Michael's Mount both by
road and over field and barren upland ridges. Philip
did not ride Spite, and he wore one of Perce's hats,
which altered his appearance surprisingly. These
peregrinations were remarkably useful. Philip learned
that The Mousehole was less than four miles away,
if one climbed a stony headland instead of going
another five miles around by the roads.

They did some hunting with a pack owned by Mr.
Levallis of Treewoof, but it had not much in common with the long, smooth runs of Leicestershire,
where only hedges, ditches, and stone walls were
obstacles. The countryside was wild and rough, and

the sport was more exciting from the immediate danger of precipitous rises and unseen cliffs than from wild gallops and soaring jumps. It was devilishly frustrating, in one way: there were so many earths for the foxes that it was rare to get one to run more than half a mile. On the other hand, there were a devilish lot of foxes, and when one was lost another turned up almost immediately. As far as Philip was concerned, that was perfectly satisfactory. He didn't care if they never killed a fox. He was only interested in the thrill of the chase.

He was enjoying himself and said so, apologizing to Perce for having resisted visiting his home previously. Two weeks passed most pleasantly, and before the simple pleasures had a chance to pall, a most disreputable individual delivered a note to the servant's door of Moreton Place. He did not wait for a reply or, more surprising, for a tip, but merely thrust the folded paper into the hand of the servant who came to the door and left as hastily as he had arrived.

It was a grubby piece of paper, and the boy who received it was obviously distressed. It was not the sort of thing that could be placed on the table where the mail went. Had not Butler had rigid control over the servants' hall and been, in addition, aware that Lord Kevern's guest was up to something, such a note might have been disdainfully dropped in the fire. Fortunately the boy who accepted it was far too much in awe of Butler to do anything without his sanction, and he presented the unappetizing missive to his superior.

Butler took it, bent his eye on the lad, and said, "Keep your mummer shut. You never got this. You don't know nothing about it. If I hears a word of it, I'll know where that word came from, m'boy, and you won't like it."

He then ascended the back stairs, more quickly and a good deal less majestically than he ascended the front ones, and tapped quietly on Philip's door. He was well paid for his effort—in general butlers were far too lofty personages to carry notes; that was what footmen were employed to do—by the expression on Philip's face (and the golden guinea Philip passed to him) when he handed the note over. The expression satisfied his curiosity—this note was the thing Mr. St. Eyre had come to Cornwall for—and the golden boy handed over mutely testified the need for secrecy and Philip's appreciation of Butler's sagacity. It also gave the lie to the gossip related by her ladyship's maid—that Mr. St. Eyre had been turned out by his father and was desperately strapped for cash.

Completely unaware of how much Butler knew and of how little harm the knowledge would ever do him, Philip choked down his excitement and tore open the note. It was only two sentences: "Any time after moonrise. I hope that Roger and Leonie are well." At first startled by the non sequitur mention of his father and stepmother, Philip recognized the cleverness in a moment. Perce knew his parents' names; possibly Lord and Lady Moreton did also, although Philip was not certain of that, as they did not happen to move in the same social circles. Everyone had sedulously avoided mentioning Roger and Leonie at all, lest it make Philip self-conscious or unhappy. In any case, there was probably no one else in Cornwall who knew. Thus Pierre had fully identified himself without writing one single word that could connect him with Philip or vice versa.

It was hard to make ordinary conversation at dinner and through the afternoon and evening, but Perce and Lord Moreton understood what must have happened and they helped cover Philip's occasional lapses into absentmindedness. These woke sympathy rather than suspicion in the female sector of the family, and the kindhearted attempts of Perce's mother and sisters to divert Philip's mind from what they thought were

his troubles and regrets served admirably to pass the
hours until he could reasonably excuse himself.

He spent a little time getting his armament in perfect order and then, when all was quiet, went to the
stable and saddled Spite himself. The horse had had
a long rest after the heavy work of carrying Philip
from London to Sancreed. He was almost too eager,
taking the road from Moreton Place to Drift at a fast
canter that was dangerous in the deceptive moonlight.
Philip, being just as eager, had not the heart to check
him, but when he directed the animal across the road
into the trackless countryside, he had to pull him in.
There were few places flat or smooth enough to make
even a trot safe, but the steep climb and the equally
precipitous descent were sufficiently taxing that by the
time Philip rode Spite into the stableyard of The
Mousehole, the horse had worked the fidgets off and
was happy to lip over some hay quietly.

Philip entered the inn with his heart beating so
hard he thought everyone would hear it. He had not
noticed what the outside of the place looked like in
the moonlight, but as he glanced around for Pierre
he could not help but see that the worst deficiencies
of the interior had disappeared. The lamps that hung
from the rafters were dim and smoky, but that was
all to the good. In the soft light, the shadowy corners
looked cozy, and the bright fire, crackling and spitting
over its salt-impregnated fuel, lent an air of bon-
homie and cheerfulness to what, in daylight, was a
miserable room.

The landlord had started to come around his
counter when he saw Philip enter, but as the young
man passed under a lamp and his face became clear,
the big innkeeper turned back to pouring drinks without a word. There must be very few strangers who
came to this place, or the landlord had a remarkable
memory for faces. Philip realized he was known and
approved. In the same moment and for the same rea-

son, Pierre recognized him. He stood and gestured. Philip hurried toward him.

"There is nothing wrong?" the older man asked anxiously.

Philip's letter had said only that he was in Cornwall and it was urgent that he see and speak to Pierre. "Nothing," Philip assured him hastily. "Papa and Leonie are quite well, and everyone else also. It is business I need to talk to you about."

Pierre's eyes widened a little, but he nodded. "Talk. It is safe here, especially as we speak French. There is no other ship in, and my boys"—he nodded at men seated at other, less private, tables—"are safe enough."

"For this?" Philip asked, so low Pierre had to lean until his head almost touched Philip's to hear. "I am supposed to obtain information that will be used against France."

Pierre lifted his brows as far as they would go. Then he shook his head to stop Philip saying any more. Without another word he rose, Philip getting up at the same time. Together they walked out of the inn and down the uneven street. Although the weather was clear, it was sharp with a wicked little wind that nipped at ears and noses. The street was empty.

"One can never tell," Pierre said softly. "I would say my men did not care for their mothers and fathers, much less for France or for anything—except their own pockets and pleasures—but you can never tell. I have heard one or two speaking with pride of Bonaparte's victories. It is possible that a madness of patriotism could fall on one of them. Safety is best. What is this about?"

As they climbed down the side of the pier and walked along the rocky shore, which was utterly deserted, Philip described the problem. He explained about the conflicting information and the necessity of discovering whether Bonaparte really would be capable of invading England and, if so, when the invasion might come.

"They were working like devils on it in July—that I know," Pierre replied. "That is the last time I was in Boulogne. I brought a load of cloth and shoes. . . Of course! You are the answer to two problems that *I* have, my son. But I will tell you about that later. Let us think of your matter first."

"It is simply this. I must get into the port and ship-yards of Boulogne and see for myself how far the fleet is advanced, how many ships, what kind, whether men and supplies are available to use the ships—all that and anything else I can learn also." He hesitated and then said quickly, "Pierre, Papa said you would not care, but—but if this will make you feel a traitor to your country . . ."

"How many times must I tell you that France is *not* my country," Pierre said firmly. "I am a Breton, and I have no cause to love the French. And even if I were French, I would do what I could against this Bonaparte. No, I do not long for the old king. He was a fool, and this heir who is in exile in Germany, this so-called Louis XVIII, is even worse. Louis XVI was only stupid; this one is venal and bitter as well."

Philip grinned, much relieved. He had been troubled that Pierre would help him because of the long ties of friendship but would be unhappy about it. "Well, but you must have *some* government," he remarked. "Do you want to be like those crazy Americans who cannot have the same leader for more than four years at a time and even change those who represent them every two years so that no one can know what to do about anything before he must go on the hustings again?"

Pierre snorted. "I am not so sure they are crazy. If a man must give all his attention to being elected, he will have less time to persecute his countrymen by writing silly laws. However, I am afraid that even the precautions the Americans have taken will not save them."

"I do not think that the purpose of the American Constitution was to prevent the lawmakers from making laws." Philip sounded a little choked as he restrained himself from laughing. Pierre's ideas on government always gave him the giggles.

"Then they *are* crazy," Pierre stated, sounding so disappointed that Philip could no longer help laughing aloud. Pierre cast him a jaundiced look. "You have been corrupted by your father's notions. For a barrister it is reasonable to desire more and more silly laws. It is his life's work and much to his profit to protect his clients against such laws. Naturally! If there were no laws, there would be no lawyers. But you . . . Pah! The English are more crazy than the Americans. Everything has either a custom or a law."

"We are a—a conservative people," Philip offered merrily. "We like to have rules and live within them."

"You, my son?" Pierre laughed. "You never heard a rule but you must break it within the minute. How many years did I listen to your father moan that he was more often in your school than any other parent in its history. Did they say, Philippe, speak English—then you spoke French. Did they say, do not do this—then you, who had never desired to do such a thing in your life, did it at once. Did they say, do this thing—then you, who had done it every day for years, dug in your heels and would not do it again for begging or for whipping."

"Oh, come now, Pierre, I was not so bad as that," Philip protested, blushing.

"You were! But since your father was not much better, I do not know what he was moaning about. You both think just as I do, but all you English are mealy-mouthed. Take your father talking about Leonie as Mademoiselle de Conyers to me, as if he hardly knew her, when—"

Pierre stopped abruptly and swallowed hard. Philip let out a single whoop of laughter and then clapped his hand across his mouth. There was no doubt that his father did tend to wrap things up in white linen when he could. However, Philip was not shocked by Pierre's revelation. French-born Leonie was far franker than her husband, and Philip had known for some years that his father and stepmother had lived as man and wife in France without benefit of blessing by the clergy. Leonie could see nothing wrong with what she had done, and said so.

"Do not be vulgar," Pierre said repressively. "The young should not criticize their elders and betters."

That made Philip laugh again. "I have not said a word," he pointed out innocently. "How can I be critical or vulgar?"

Pierre snorted again. "It is not hard for an Englishman to be both without trying," he teased. "But I should not let you divert me in this way. What I started to say was that this Bonaparte is worse than the kings. They were born to power and could let things alone. He cannot stop prying and adjusting and arranging. If the French are not rid of him, they soon will not be allowed even to breathe except by his order. No, I will feel no shame, no guilt for helping you. The French are, most of them, too stupid to understand, but I am doing them as well as myself a great service by helping you."

"And the English also," Philip said seriously.

"No," Pierre said, also seriously. "An invasion would cost some lives, but it could not succeed in the end, and I think the English could break Bonaparte more quickly that way. However, that is not for us to decide. Your government has asked you to do a thing, and you think that thing is right and desire to do it. For me, who does not care who governs anywhere, that is sufficient. Now, what is your plan?"

"Truthfully, Pierre, I have none. I have papers as a

merchant, but I am a little worried about using them.
I thought it would be best to ask your advice, since you
must have a better notion of what is happening in
France than we can have."

Pierre smote himself in the forehead. "It is time for
me to die!" he exclaimed theatrically. "I have heard
you say something so eminently sensible that I have
nothing to argue about. I cannot believe it! I retract
my words. You do *not* take after your father. Never
did he not have a plan and uphold it in the face of
every argument of good sense and practicality."

"And his plans always worked," Philip remarked
rebelliously.

"That is true," Pierre conceded with amused sour-
ness, "but my plans would have worked just as well
and would not have been so hard on the nerves."

"I have no objection to quiet nerves," Philip
claimed, not too truthfully. "I had some excitement on
the way here."

"What do you mean?" Pierre prompted when Philip
hesitated.

Philip then described what had happened at the inn
and his shooting of the highwayman. His voice faltered
over the latter, and Pierre put an arm over his shoulders and squeezed briefly.

"Better he than you, my son, and likely you did
him a kindness. He was killed clean. He felt nothing,
not even fear. Do not give the matter another thought.
Remember, if you engage in this adventure, he may
not be the last. However, we will try to avoid that. I
do have a plan."

"Let me hear it," Philip said cautiously.

He had heard Roger's arguments about Pierre's
plans. Too often the reason Roger would not listen
was because the plan entailed Pierre taking all the risk
while Roger sat safely in a hideaway. Being eager for
action himself, Philip could understand how that
would be easier on Pierre's nerves. It was always easier

to face danger oneself than to permit a loved one to do so.

"I can obtain for you papers that will identify you —as of the *Douane*, you understand, the customs. That is better than a merchant. An officer of the *Douane* is free to travel and also it is a good reason to be curious and poke your nose into many matters. Unfortunately, this will not make you free of military installations. Bonaparte's grip on the army and navy is much stronger than on any other part of the government. Of course, there is much corruption on the procurement end. Even God, I think, could not enforce honesty in the purchase of military and naval goods. However, there are spies watching everywhere, and informers watching the spies. Moreover, the number of military inspectors is smaller and too many are known to each other."

"Do not bother apologizing," Philip laughed. "I am completely enchanted with what you offer. By God, if I cannot find a good excuse to get into Boulogne's port and naval yards as a customs officer, I am an idiot. There are so many—"

"Wait," Pierre interrupted. "I am not finished. Last July when I went to sell cloth and shoes at Boulogne— that was when I discovered the spies who spied on the spies and found an honest man could not make a decent profit—"

Philip snickered, and Pierre scowled at him, but neither was interested in reviving the familiar, serio-comic argument about the distinction between illegal and dishonest.

"It is not decent," Pierre went on with real anger, "for a price to be agreed upon and then a new official to come forward, all of a sudden, and announce a tax on all sales. Always the tax is paid by the final purchaser. That is custom."

"You see," Philip teased, "there are uses for custom and law."

Pierre hit Philip gently on the head. "Quiet, whelp. Do not be impertinent."

Philip laughed. "But, Pierre, you are not reasonable. If the government is the final purchaser—as it must be at Boulogne—it cannot pay tax to itself. That is silly. But, still, money is needed to pay for the material. So the seller pays the tax, which makes it possible for the government to buy again."

"I may or may not be reasonable," Pierre remarked dryly, "but I am not a fool. All such a procedure results in is raising the price of the goods—and by far more than the value of the tax. I was willing to sell direct to the government in Boulogne. Now I take my goods elsewhere, sell to a private procurer. Sometimes he sells to the government, more often he sells to still another private party. Each time the price goes up, and the final seller, knowing he will be taxed, merely increases *his* price by the amount of the tax or, perhaps, a little more."

Philip made a moue of distaste and shrugged. He knew what Pierre said was true, but he was not interested in trade. Although the attitude was changing slowly, the heritage of the land-based aristocracy was strong in Philip. He accepted that involvement in trade to make a living was degrading—but not, naturally, in the course of an adventure. He felt his father's stint as a gunsmith in revolutionary France was a brilliant act, and was himself quite prepared to be anything, including a cowman or a street sweeper.

"That is not to the point," Pierre went on. "What is important is that I dealt with the master of the port in Boulogne, and he has a daughter of whom he is dotingly fond."

"Daughter," Philip echoed, instantly alert. "Do you think—"

"Very likely," Pierre assured him. "She is young, not very attractive—less from bad features than from bad manners. She is awkward and spoiled. She interrupted her father and myself several times with nonsense, which a well-regulated daughter would never do, and her father did not reprimand her. Now, it is possible she is affianced or married since then, but I think her father is the stupid kind of man who wishes to hold his daughter for himself."

"But then he would scarcely welcome my attentions to her."

"But no," Pierre said, smiling, "on the contrary. If it is clear that you will only stay for a short time, that you have come only to investigate some particular problem, for example, and your permanent base is far away, then the gentleman will be glad for you to escort his daughter. You will not be a suitor for her, you see, only an amusement."

"That will be an interesting experience," Philip remarked, laughing. "Every Papa I have ever met seemed positively panting to unload his dear daughter—or daughters."

"I may be wrong. Be careful what you say in the beginning," Pierre warned. "If he *is* looking for a husband, do not undeceive him. Murmur hints that you have influential friends—"

"So I have!" Philip put in, grinning.

"—and that you could obtain a transfer," Pierre continued, ignoring Philip's mischievous interjection.

"Yes, all right, but I hate . . . I mean, it seems unkind to raise such hopes in a young woman," Philip said.

"Omelets cannot be made without breaking eggs," Pierre replied indifferently. His opinion of women, except for Philip's stepmother and Red Meg, both of whom he had come to admire and appreciate, was very low. "Soon enough she will find someone else—or do you believe your charms are fatal?"

"Not that," Philip said, still a bit disturbed, "but one does not like to imply a promise to a woman. . . . However, you are right, of course. One cannot consider such things when the welfare of one's country is at stake. I shall do my best not to wound the poor creature, but I will not allow that to stand in my way."

"Bravo! Spoken like a true patriot," Pierre laughed. "You are very like your Papa, but I think a *little* less silly about women. Now, let us go back to the inn. I will have to return to France to obtain the papers. It will be safer if my crew thinks you are a refugee who will do some purchasing for me and then come back with the goods to France. I have had trouble buying in England these last few months because the fools think I am French and either believe refusing to sell to me is patriotic or believe they will be called traitors if they sell. I will explain to you what is necessary for you to do. It would be good for the crew to hear us talk about that. Also, there is a problem with the—the lady who is my contact here in Cornwall."

"Lady?" Philip repeated, grinning. "A female smuggler is scarcely a lady."

"Not by birth, perhaps," Pierre admitted, but there was a note of doubt in his voice that Philip did not pick up. Pierre had certain suspicions about the girl known to him as Red Meg that he did not choose to examine because he felt it was none of his business. "Nonetheless," he went on, "Mademoiselle Meg is a lady in her dealing with me and in her behavior."

They had walked back much more quickly than the slow pace they had kept to while moving away. Still, Pierre had enough time before they reentered the inn to explain what had happened between Black Bart and Meg and describe his uneasiness about her safety.

"I was going to ask her if she would be my purchasing agent," Pierre finished as they entered and resumed their seats at the table in the corner. Pierre signaled for drinks to be brought and went right on talking, ignoring the landlord who brought the tumblers of brandy to the table. "She is most certainly English and could buy without question. However, it would be better if someone I know went with her."

Philip understood that. It was for the benefit of the landlord, to demonstrate his trust in Philip. Actually Pierre had made it clear that his purpose was not to check on Meg's honesty but to protect her. John's devotion was no match for his limitations. Once they were sure Bart was out of the area or caught by the law, the need for protection would probably be over, but if Philip could be with Meg for the next two weeks, Pierre said, it would be a big load off his mind.

"I will do it gladly," Philip answered, smiling.

"Good, then you had better drink up and get back to where you are staying. Mademoiselle Meg will be here tomorrow night, about the same time you came. We will all speak together then and settle one way or another."

Chapter 7

Although there had been no sign of Black Bart in the two past weeks, even when she and John had made several large deliveries, Megaera was shaking with nervousness as she prepared to meet Pierre. She knew it was ridiculous. Certainly Bart would make no attempt on her tonight of all nights. He must know that she would be doubly on guard after what had happened. Knowing it was ridiculous, Megaera still took every precaution, having John drive the pony out first and emerging herself in the shelter of the animal with pistols drawn.

Nothing happened, but Megaera was exhausted by the time she and John reached The Mousehole. She had been obliged to be doubly alert, for she could not count on another pair of ears—or even eyes, because there was no way Megaera could think of to explain to John that he must watch for an ambush.

Megaera's face was so blanched, her eyes so wide when she entered The Mousehole, that her fear was apparent even in the dim light. Pierre jumped to his feet and went over to her, asking anxiously whether she had been attacked again. As she laughed shakily and disclaimed, honestly blaming her nerves for her appearance, Philip had also risen and turned. He barely restrained a whistle and a grin of appreciation when he saw the woman to whom Pierre was speaking. No wonder he called her "a lady" and worried about her. His father had always said Pierre was completely impervious to feminine charms, but, of course, he was growing older and the girl—what a beauty!

No, Philip thought, bowing with grace when Pierre brought her to the table, it would be no hardship at all to guard her. He murmured something polite in French, noting her surprise that Pierre was not alone. She smiled at him, however, and interest seemed to drive much of the fear out of her. Philip, who had never seen Megaera before, had thought her beautiful even while she was pale and her expression rigid and distorted by fear. As the fear dissipated, animation filled the large eyes, the corners of the pretty mouth curled up, and the lips resumed their normal rosy color. Philip was enchanted. He had probably seen more beautiful women, but never in an overlarge and unclean man's jacket and well-fitting but stained and worn buckskin breeches.

Megaera was not as impressed with Philip's appearance, but that was because she did not pay it particular attention, not because she thought him unhandsome. She had first glanced at him only briefly when Pierre asked permission to introduce her to someone "very close" to him. He had a proposition to make, he said, that might increase Meg's profit, but this young man, Philippe Saintaire (Pierre simply used the name Roger had adopted when he was in France) would have to be involved.

It was a mark of Megaera's trust in Pierre that she felt no more than a deep interest in who "Philippe" was as she agreed to meet him and listen to Pierre's proposition. What in the world could "very close" mean? Surely Pierre would have simply said so if the young man were his nephew. And he could not be

Pierre's son because the names were different . . . or
could he? As they approached the table Megaera studied Philip's fine-featured, dark-eyed, dark-skinned face.
There was certainly a Gallic look to him, not particularly like Pierre but not unlike either.

There was no rule that a son needed to resemble his
father, and why should Pierre conceal the relationship?
Then Megaera had to be careful not to giggle aloud
or smile too broadly. Dear Pierre, he must be afraid
of shocking her. She remembered that he had said once
when they were talking that he was not married. Very
likely this Philippe was his natural son. As a country-
woman who managed her father's estate, Megaera
could scarcely be shocked by an illegitimate birth, but
it was sweet of Pierre to think she needed sparing.

They all sat down together. Pierre, speaking in English for Meg's benefit, began to describe his problem
and his need for a purchaser who was plainly and
clearly English—which Philip was not. Megaera was
definitely interested, especially when Pierre mentioned
the commission to which she would be entitled. Pierre
was intrigued by her interest. He knew what kind of
profit she must be making on the smuggled goods. He
knew she drove the hardest bargain she could. It was
obvious she was not spending the money on herself.
Even though simple caution would prevent a clever
woman like Meg from coming to a place like The
Mousehole in silks and jewels, she could have bought
a new coat or some trinkets to show him privately.
Pierre knew Meg trusted him.

The natural assumption was that Meg dressed as she
did deliberately and that she needed money desperately for some important purpose. Once or twice
Pierre, who was a rich man, had hinted that he might
be able to help if she would tell him what the problem
was, but she had frozen up instantly, becoming distant
and "different." That "difference," a hauteur of manner, plus the clothing that did not fit and almost dis-

figured her person, added to her rigid and painstaking
honesty, made Pierre reasonably sure that Meg was no
common farmer's wife or dishonest lady's maid driven
from her place.

Although his curiosity was aroused, Pierre knew it
was none of his business. It was Meg's secret, and he
had neither the right nor any reason to pry. He
glanced at Philip, wondering whether the young Englishman would note the incongruity between Meg's
dress and manner and be able to guess the cause. Then
he had to struggle against laughter as, previously, Meg
had to struggle against suppressed giggles. The attention Philip was bestowing on Meg was scarcely owing
to his recognition of a problem. However, Pierre
thought mischievously, it might certainly lead to the
disclosure of Meg's secret—any secret.

None of these thoughts had prevented Pierre from
detailing what he needed and the easiest way to go
about getting it. Megaera listened, frowning. The deal-
ers were mostly in and around Falmouth, which was
about thirty miles away. That meant two days away
from home, and it would not be possible to take John.
Even if he were not frightened to death by the many
carriages and crush of people, he would be in danger
through his deafness and his ignorance of what dangers to watch for. Megaera shrank from the thought of
riding thirty miles alone, seeking a hotel without her
maid and footmen.

One half of her brain was calculating how much the
commission would reduce the principal on the mortgages. The other half was telling her she was an idiot.
How could she worry about going to a hotel alone
when she was not afraid to direct a smuggling operation? But it was not physical things Megaera feared,
really. Anticipation of an attack by Black Bart set
her nerves on edge and set her trembling, but the
haughty contempt of a landlord made her soul shiver.
What if she should be turned away from the decent

hotels? Her eyes roamed over The Mousehole, and she shuddered a little. Would she have to stay in a place like this? Only by coming here to deal with Pierre had she grown accustomed to the place. The first times, John had been with her and no one had dared insult her. Now, of course, she was known. No one would think of interfering with Pierre's business partner, even if she was a woman.

"I am afraid," Pierre said, hesitantly, "that you would 'ave to—er—pretend to be—er—ah—a woman of substance. Otherwise, English as you are, the factors might not wish to deal with you. There ees great demand now for the goods I usually buy, but I gladly take luxury goods—only I do not know the men 'oo deal een them. Een the past an old Breton smuggler was not the kind they wished to sell to. And I prefer to deal weeth 'onest men. Also," his eyes twinkled, "eet ees less expensive that way, even weeth your commission."

Megaera bit her lip. That meant hiring a carriage, some kind of servant. No, she did not dare do such a thing locally, and where she was not known it might not be possible. She made a rapid mental review of her own staff. They were loyal, but it would be impossible to hope they would not slip and call her by her real name. Regretfully, she began to shake her head.

"Philippe 'ere would do all the necessary, except actually bargaining with the factors," Pierre urged. "I promise you 'e ees 'onest and trustworthy. All you would 'ave to do in addition ees arrange for storage of the goods until I return."

For a long moment Megaera stared across the table at Pierre. It seemed that he had guessed she had some reason for not wanting to be seen locally. His face was impassive, but behind his eyes some expression lurked. Distrust? No, not that. It did not matter. He had solved her problem.

"Very well," Megaera agreed, "but do you intend to wait? Is that safe for you, Pierre?"

"No, no. I said you would 'ave to store the goods. I will sail again—tonight, in fact, with the tide."

"But—"

"Philippe does not go. 'E will stay 'ere to assist you in any way you desire."

"Here?" Megaera looked around The Mousehole with an expression of horror.

"No," Philip said in English, grinning. "I will find a place; or perhaps you could recommend one?"

"You speak English!" Megaera exclaimed with relief. She had just started to wonder how Philippe could do what Pierre promised when the only words he had said were a polite greeting in French.

Pierre laughed. "Mees Meg, you think me a fool? Of course 'e speaks English, as well as you do," he added mischievously. "Now let us arrange the signals and then I must go. Philippe shall see you safe wherever you weesh to go. No, do not shake your 'ead. I tell you, 'e weell not betray you. Eet ees no longer enough, the poor John. I see 'ow you look when you come een. For a little while, until thees black devil ees taken or we are sure 'e 'as fled, you must 'ave weeth you a man who can 'ear and theenk quickly as well as see."

Before the attack Megaera would have fought such a suggestion tooth and nail. Now she bit her lip and looked uncertain, but the memory of that horrible ride, expecting every minute that someone would spring out at her, tipped the scales. She watched while Pierre passed Philip most of the little sacks of gold.

"He can come to the place the kegs are brought," she said slowly. "All the men know that, but I . . . It isn't that I don't trust you, Pierre. It's just . . . I have a reason. . . ."

"No reason you should trust *me* anyway," Philip put in cheerfully. "After all, Pierre might be prejudiced in my favor. In fact, he is—anyone could see that.

I might have concealed my evil nature from him all these years. S'truth, he does not know *everything* about me."

Pierre snorted and hit Philip in the head. Philip laughed up at him. Megaera's eyes widened in surprise. If her father had had a sense of humor, it had been drowned in the bottle long before she was old enough to recognize it. Edward certainly had none. Thus it took her a few seconds to realize that Philip was teasing, rather than actually warning her against himself and confessing something bad to Pierre.

"I'm sure he doesn't," she said tartly as soon as the notion became clear. "However, it's useless to think you can jolly me. If you have gone to all the trouble of concealing your worst side from Pierre for many years, you will not expose it to me. I have no sense of honor at all, I warn you. I would immediately lay an information and betray you to your—er—friend."

Pierre smiled at them indulgently and recalled Megaera to the matter of the light signals. She named the blinks and he wrote them down, thinking with satisfaction that she and Philip would get along well. He rose and said good-bye. Both nodded absently and returned to their wary yet interested contemplation of each other. Pierre shrugged and strode away.

"Well," Philip began, "can I not convince you to take me as a guest—a *paying* guest?"

"Not as a guest, a tenant, or anything else," Megaera said, but her eyes twinkled. "You may or may not have an evil nature, but you certainly have a *curious* one, and I am not going to satisfy it. I will tell you that I am not hiding anything *shameful*—"

"That is not clever," Philip interrupted, shaking his head sadly. "Really, you do not appear to be at all experienced at concealment. Perhaps you hope to convince me you are a murderess or something equally awful by such a statement, but your effort at a sly leer is not at all the thing. Now—"

"Don't be so ridiculous," Megaera laughed. "Why in the world would I want you to think I was a murderess?"

"To inspire awe in me, of course. Also, to keep me from contemplating cheating you or—er—importuning you."

"I have the best guarantee against 'importuning' in the world," Megaera said dryly. "John may not be able to hear any distant threat, but he can see one close by."

"No, no," Philip protested. "Never would I do anything so crude as to importune you by force. Have you not already warned me that you would split to Pierre? And has not Pierre warned me about your giant—and not too clever—protector?"

"Then what did you mean, Philippe?"

"You had better call me Philip," he remarked, avoiding her question.

The truth was that he hadn't meant anything. He had merely been waltzing around his notion that she wanted him to fix on some reason, even a discreditable one, for her secretiveness so that he would not seek out the truth. However, the jesting remark about importuning her had brought to his mind the actual possibility of doing so—not by force, naturally. Philip would not have dreamed of doing that, not even with a girl he picked up in the street. However, there were much pleasanter ways of "importuning."

"Will you not have something to warm you before we leave?" he went on hastily, before Megaera could repeat her question. "It is really quite chilly out."

Megaera looked around at the inn again, wrinkling her nose. It occurred to Philip suddenly that her speech was very fine, not a false gentility spread over a common accent, and also that she was not accustomed to the crude surroundings of The Mousehole. This increased his curiosity about her, but he knew it would be a grave mistake to allow that to show.

"I assure you the wine and brandy here are far

above the quality of the place itself," he said with a gentle laugh. "At least, the brandy is. I have not tasted the wine, but—"

"Do you think they even carry any?" Megaera asked, looking sidelong at the few men who remained now that Pierre's crew had left.

They were not prepossessing specimens, certainly, and quite unlikely to have a taste for fine wine. Philip shrugged. "I can ask. If there is no wine, perhaps brandy-and-water? Or hot rum with lemon? No, perhaps there would not be lemons here—but perhaps there would. Sailors are very partial to lemon or lime, you know."

"No," Megaera admitted, "I don't know. I admit my acquaintance with sailors is small, but that is true of a great many people. Do you think my tongue will wag if you make me drunk?"

Philip assumed an expression of injured innocence. "Not at all," he disclaimed. "Simply I do not wish you to be chilled and delay Pierre's business."

"Oh, what a clanker," Megaera groaned, but she could not help smiling, and she did not at all wish to refuse the drink and have to leave. She had not had such an enjoyable time in years. "Very well, order what you think I will like. If I don't drink it, you may."

"But that will make me drunk," Philip protested.

"And how will that make you different from any other man?" Megaera remarked with such bitterness that Philip leaned forward and took her hand.

"What have I done to offend you?" he asked earnestly. "I was joking, I swear—"

Her expression softened and she patted the hand that held hers before she withdrew it. "Sorry. It has nothing to do with you. I'm a little too familiar with the effects of overindulgence in brandy. Forgive me."

"If it distresses you," Philip assured her, "I will not drink at all. It is of no consequence to me. I only thought you would be cold on the ride home—truly."

His response astounded Megaera, who had expected
him to laugh or to say something stupid about his own
ability to hold his liquor or, if he wanted to be cruel,
ask why she was encouraging the habit by bringing
duty-free liquor into the country. The odd thing was
that the response astounded Philip, too. He had been
walking around better than half soaked for almost six
months—brandy on the table with his breakfast to dull
not only the aching head and heaving stomach engendered by the previous night but also the boredom and
frustration of his life. Of course, as soon as he had
taken on this piece of work he had cut down his drinking. It would not do to be fuddled with French agents
after him. However, it was a surprise to him that what
he had said was true. He had no desire at all for another drink.

Even more surprising was his resentment for Meg's
sake. After all, it was more usual than not that any
lower-class woman would be well acquainted with
fathers and brothers and husbands the worse for drink.
That was far less frequent in his own class, not because
the men drank less but because they did not do so in
the presence of their women, and there were servants
to care for them (or take the punishment) when they
became helpless or obstreperous. But Philip could not
associate this delicate, violet-eyed girl with the lower
classes, and he felt a sudden strong desire to protect
her from needing to deal with such degradation.

Megaera was smiling a little mistily. She knew Philip
had not meant he would forswear liquor entirely, but
no man had ever offered so much as not drinking in
her presence. The suggestion raised this man, whom
she believed to be an illegitimate son of a common
smuggler, to a level of thoughtfulness and generosity
never achieved by any "gentleman" of her acquaintance.

"Don't be silly," she said softly, patting his hand
again. "I would prefer that you don't get awash, but I

have no objection to a sip to keep out the cold. I'll even join you—if I can stomach what they serve me."

Philip looked at her anxiously for a moment to be sure she meant it, which pleased Megaera even more by proving what he said had not been an idle gesture, then turned and motioned to the landlord. After some negotiation—The Mousehole was not equipped to cater to refined tastes—a drink was settled upon. It was at that moment that Philip realized he did not know what to call Meg. To the landlord he said, "For the lady," and that covered it, but sooner or later he would need to address her by name. Pierre called her "Miss Meg," but it was obvious that she was fond of the old man. She might not wish to extend the liberty of such familiarity to so new an acquaintance.

"Miss—what?" Philip asked.

"What do you mean, 'miss what?' I didn't say I was missing anything."

"No," Philip laughed, "I meant, what am I to call you?"

"The men call me Red Meg," she said, smiling. "Pierre, a polite Frenchman—no, Breton, I'm sorry. He becomes quite incensed when I mix them up. Anyway, Pierre adds an honorific—Miss Meg. Either will do."

Philip was silent while the landlord put the drinks on the table and he paid. Then he said slowly, "Would you not . . . When we go to Falmouth, I will need to show a proper respect. Will you not tell me your surname?"

"Well!" Meg exclaimed. "If you are not the most persistent, curious . . ." She paused then and thought about it. It did not matter why Philip had made the point—he was right. She would have to give a name to the factors with whom she did business. "Very well," she said, "you may call me Margaret Redd when we go to Falmouth. Here you'd better say 'Meg' like everyone else, or I probably won't answer you."

"Just as you like," Philip answered. It was obvious

to him that Redd was not Meg's name, really. "I did
not wish to offend you by assuming the same familiarity that Pierre might have won by long acquaintance."

Megaera did not answer that. She lifted her drink
and sipped it because she was afraid her voice would
be unsteady. She was deeply moved by the delicacy
Philip showed toward her. He could not have been
more thoughtful of her feelings if he had met her in a
fine drawing room rather than this dirty, smoky, common alehouse. Strangely it did not occur to Megaera to
be worried by this. Having blocked Philip's attempt to
discover her name—only she no longer thought it was
that as he had looked honestly surprised when she
accused him of curiosity—she never feared that he
might have recognized her breeding. She put his
thoughtfulness down to the natural politeness of Philip's French breeding—but she liked it, and him, more
than any man she had ever met, except Pierre, who
was too old in Megaera's opinion to be considered a
"man."

Since Megaera did not want her silence to become
noticeable, she cast about in her mind for a safe subject and found one immediately. "Did I understand
your fath—oh, I'm sorry, I meant Pierre. Did I understand correctly that he doesn't care which of several
types of merchandise we buy for him so long as these
are ready in stock?"

Philip had opened his mouth in surprise when Megaera almost called Pierre his father, but before she was
finished speaking he decided that it would be very
wise to permit her to keep this particular delusion. It
would solve many problems, giving him a background,
explaining Pierre's faith in him, and, best of all, preventing Meg from asking questions he would find difficult to answer. Obviously, from her swift apology and
her blush, she believed he was a bastard and might be

sensitive about it—or she herself felt it improper to mention. Either way she would avoid the subject of Philip's antecedents, and that was all to the good.

Thus he ignored that part of her remark and answered the question about business. "Yes. Since the war all English goods are scarce and valuable in France."

Megaera was again silent for a moment, sipping her drink while a new problem came into her mind. "I have just thought of something quite dreadful," she said hesitantly. "I suppose you are the wrong person to talk to, but—but—isn't it wrong for me to help buy things that will aid the French war effort? Oh dear! I've given Pierre my promise, and I must—"

"But there is no reason to worry," Philip hastened to assure her. "Pierre and I do not love the French, and particularly not Bonaparte, any better than you. I know Pierre does not sell to government procurers. I swear that is the truth," he added when he saw the doubt in Megaera's eyes, and explained about the taxes and Pierre's determination to avoid them. "So, you see, we are doing Bonaparte more harm than good. Besides, if Bonaparte cannot get English cloth and leather, he might be forced to start making such things himself—and that would be bad for our trade."

"*Our* trade?" Megaera echoed.

"I have lived in England a very long time," Philip said hastily, cursing his slip. "To speak the truth, I am more English than French in my sympathy—if not in my speech."

Megaera frowned suspiciously, then her face cleared. Of course, Philip's mother must have been English. Perhaps he had only gone to live with his father after she died, or perhaps she had come back to England when Philip was a boy. There were many explanations, and each would account for Philip's fluency in English as well as his attachment to the country. Megaera could not doubt the honesty of that slip. It was, she

was sure, quite unintentional and betrayed the truth—
that after his loyalty to his father, Philip preferred
England to France.

It was such a pleasant conviction and made Megaera
so happy that it did not occur to her it was just the
kind of "slip" an agent would make to induce the conclusion she had reached. She was fortunate, for suspicion would have made her miserable to no purpose at
all. As it was, she smiled brilliantly at Philip, feeling
even more comfortable and attracted to him.

The sensation was mutual. Philip had not previously
given any thought to the subject, but he suddenly
realized that it *was* unpatriotic to deal with French
smugglers. The gold and silver paid for brandy and
wine—utterly useless products, although delightful—
were supporting the war Bonaparte was waging.
Philip was surprised by this revelation. He had bought
plenty of duty-free liquor himself. The Soft Berth at
Kingsdown still was a smugglers' den. There were
plenty of Frenchmen and Dutchmen who made the
short run from the northeast coast of France or Holland to the Kentish shore, even though Pierre no
longer did so.

And more than guineas crossed in the smugglers'
vessels, Philip guessed. French agents must cross and
come ashore, perhaps as crew, just as he intended to do
in the other direction. Perhaps they concealed their
purpose sometimes, but often enough, Philip was sure,
the English contacts of the smugglers either did not
think about it or did not care that they were helping
seed their country with spies. It was a pleasant thing
to know that Meg was certainly not one of those who
did not care. Now, Philip decided, he could make sure
she would think about it in the future. She might even
be a help in catching an agent.

"I am glad you spoke of that," he said. "Pierre and
I, as I said, do not love the French and do not wish to
assist them. Neither do you, I am sure, yet both of us

may do so without intention. I know Pierre does not give passage to French agents, but other smugglers may do so—"

Megaera gasped with surprise. It was obvious she had never thought of it. Philip nodded in recognition.

"Yes, and even Pierre might be tricked by a crewman who might desert or meet someone secretly to pass information. Again, Miss Meg, we can be helpful."

"Tell me how—and call me Meg. Never mind the 'Miss.'" She leaned forward eagerly and took an unguarded swallow of the drink she had been sipping with careful reserve.

"Two ways. Make sure no one who comes ashore to help unload cargo slips away—"

"Pierre's men don't unload my cargo."

"Good. That is one less chance, but I do not believe that to be true in all cases. Perhaps the men who work for you also work for some other group. Probably they would not tell you, but it does not matter. Most of them are loyal Englishmen. They are only trying to make a little extra money, which they need—"

"As I do," Megaera interrupted again. In the next moment she was appalled at what she had said, and she hastened to add, "Please don't ask why. I won't tell you. I—I just couldn't. . . . I didn't want you to think . . . Go on, tell me what you want me to say to the men."

Philip was most interested in Meg's spontaneous remark, but he judged it wise to pass it for the moment and continued blandly, "What I have just been saying to you. That they should watch for anyone coming ashore and staying, or coming and accepting papers, a wallet, anything, from a stranger. Even more important, they should watch for a stranger who seems to be joining the smugglers and who is not a known member of the crew. That is how agents most commonly cross to France. After all, the packet boats no longer run. They do not have much choice. A French naval vessel would have to sneak in to pick them up. That would not be easy, and there would be the complication of getting word to France that a pickup is required. Whereas a smuggling ship may come in quite often and be safer— you know how frequently Pierre crosses. Also a naval vessel will often ignore such a ship, even if it is recognized as French. The navy is as fond of brandy as anyone else."

"I'll tell my men," Megaera agreed earnestly. "You're quite right that they are mostly decent men who need money. Certainly even the ones who make a living in evil ways by choice would not, most of them, wish to help French agents. But you said there was something else we could do."

Philip grinned and his eyes danced. This idea was the best he had had in a donkey's age. It would increase Pierre's profit, give him far more time with Meg, and do as much damage to the French war effort as one small, virtually unarmed vessel could do while improving England's balance of trade. Megaera, watching him, smiled in sympathy, and Philip laughed aloud.

"What is it?" she asked.

"I have thought of a way to serve all our purposes," Philip replied. "When Pierre buys, he always takes whatever the factors who will deal with him will give him. This is often heavy goods, sometimes, I suspect, stolen or diverted from the port at Falmouth and, indeed, these goods might be useful to the army and navy Bonaparte is forming. But we have two weeks. You heard Pierre say he would prefer luxury goods. We can afford the time to look in many different warehouses and to buy small amounts here and there."

"Well, yes. . . ." Megaera had her doubts about the time, but she didn't want to discuss that now. "But buy what?"

"Indian goods," Philip answered, his eyes glowing. "Rugs and shawls, Indian muslin, fans and feathers. France must be starved for Indian goods. Her trade has been blocked off since May. I do not suggest silks, because silk is being made at Lyons again and the ladies of the court are forbidden to wear anything else. However, my fa—someone I know told me that Bonaparte's own wife ignores the rule and appears in public in Indian muslins. There are many new rich among the French, and they are all hungry for display."

"But what if the factors Pierre dealt with do not handle such goods?"

"Pierre dealt with men who would overlook the fact that they were selling to a smuggler, and French at that. No one would suspect *you* of such a thing." Philip laughed aloud.

"N-no."

Megaera sounded uncertain, and Philip began to assure her that no woman so young and lovely could ever be suspected, that if he had not been assured by Pierre most seriously of her profession he would have believed it a joke. Megaera smiled at the compliments, but, of course, Philip's assurances were of little value. She was not in the least worried about being taken for a smuggler; she was worried about just the opposite. What she was thinking about was the possibility of being recognized as Mrs. Edward Devoran in Falmouth.

Naturally she had never dealt with wholesalers, but what about other tradesmen? After careful thought Megaera decided she had done no business in Falmouth for years and had not even been in the town for a very long time. Also, the chance of meeting anyone she knew socially there was minimal. "Very well," she said, tossing off the remainder of her drink with a casual abandon that set her coughing. Philip leapt up and patted her solicitously on the back and the paroxysm soon stopped. Meg stood up. "I suppose you want to start tomorrow," she said. "That will be all right, but I must be back here before Wednesday night. I have deliveries promised that night, and I like to be on time."

Philip was considerably surprised by the early date she set, but he did not allow it to show. In fact, he was well pleased. He could always insist on returning sometime later during the two weeks if he couldn't think of another way to spend time with her. He agreed easily and walked with her to the stable. His eyes opened a little when the mountain of man that was John rose from the bale of hay on which he had been sitting. Pierre had said "giant," but Philip allowed for exaggeration. Actually the word was fairly close to the truth. Philip was not surprised to see that only Meg had a mount. It would have needed a draught horse to hold John, and it would be pointless since he could surely keep up with Meg's pony afoot, unless Meg chose to gallop.

His eyes opened even wider when Meg seized his wrist and laid his hand to her cheek and then to John's. In the next instant he understood that she was introducing him as a friend to be trusted, which permitted him to react properly when she kissed his cheek and said, "Kiss me." He therefore returned the salute as chastely as she had given it, but his internal reaction was so much the opposite that, considering the circumstances, it surprised him.

Megaera was equally surprised at her reaction. When she had first been married, she had responded quite naturally to her husband. She had never loved Edward, and she had disapproved of his method of winning her, but he professed love for her and she had been very willing to learn to love him if she could. Since Edward was normal sexually and Megaera was a beautiful girl, he had made a modest effort during the first few weeks of marriage. Megaera had just about begun to enjoy his sexual attentions, although she still did not like Edward himself, when he had grown bored by her simplicity and begun to look for variety.

Because Megaera had never loved Edward at all, in fact she had not even liked him, she had not associated the pleasure of her body with sentimental emotion. It was quite clear to her that any man with whom she was willing to couple could wake similar sensations in her. Two things had kept her chaste: pride and the failure of a sufficiently attractive man to appear.

The pride had not only prohibited Megaera from looking among the lower orders for a lover but had prevented her from giving the slightest evidence of dissatisfaction with her husband. Of course, every man and most of the women in the neighborhood knew how unworthy was the recipient of this seeming trust and affection. However, a decent man would not consider causing Megaera the misery of exposing her husband just on the expectation that she might then be induced to start an illicit love affair.

Those few who were unscrupulous enough to try it got short shrift. Megaera by now had enough experience of weak and deceitful men to recognize them within moments of their opening their mouths. Nonetheless, the method she chose to drive them off, those who chose to undeceive her about Edward's character—an icy assurance that she knew her husband quite well enough without outside instruction—only confirmed the neighborhood's impression that she was so bewitched by Edward that no other man had a chance.

After his death Megaera had unwittingly reinforced this idea still further. At first she had been besieged by suitors. She was her father's heiress; the Bolliet lands were in good heart. What could be more appealing than a beautiful, rich widow who was known to be willingly blind to her husband's faults? In the beginning Megaera was both too sour from her first marriage and too positive that the moment she confessed she was really penniless, about to lose Bolliet, her current swains would melt away like spring snow. She should have had more faith in her own appeal. Among the men were a number who would have taken her gladly, paid off the mortgages, and made excellent husbands. But Megaera was in no mood then for experimenting with any man and turned all away, saying that she did not intend to marry again.

Once she had begun smuggling, she never gave the matter of marriage—or of men—another thought. Occasionally she was aware of a vague physical need, but usually she was too tired from her double life to feel desire when there was no man to stimulate it. Now, suddenly, as she took Philip's hand and kissed his cheek, she was painfully aware of him as a male creature and a desirable one. Mrs. Edward Devoran would have thrust that feeling away and buried it. A lady could not desire the illegitimate son of a Breton smuggler, no matter how handsome his face or elegant his manners.

Before Megaera could withdraw into herself, she became aware of her surroundings as well as of Philip. At once a weight of oppression rolled off her. Mrs. Edward Devoran could not consider a smuggler's bastard, but for Red Meg he was a perfect match. So she did not drop Philip's wrist immediately, merely signed to John that he should get her pony. As the big man turned away Megaera opened her fingers and allowed her hand to slide down the back of Philip's.

Philip was far from innocent where women were concerned, but his experience with ladies was limited. He avoided young marriageable girls like the plague, having never seen one with whom he would consider spending his life. Since he did not desire marriage, he feared to wake expectations that could cause pain, being genuinely kindhearted. He had had one affair with a married woman of his own class but had found it most unsatisfactory. She was lovely to look at, and her husband was such that Philip could understand and approve the lady's desire for a lover. However, he had not enjoyed the sneaking, hiding, and lying and had been repelled by the totally unnecessary revelations the "lady" had made. The last straw was when he discovered he was not her only stud.

Thereafter Philip had confined his attentions to the professionals who worked in bawdy houses. These came in a wide variety, from filthy, crude sluts who would do anything, to gracious "ladies" whom a man needed to woo as delicately—and much more expensively—than any duke's daughter. Philip opted for the middle range—good-looking girls with enough veneer or refinement to be clean and refrain from any disgusting behavior but who were frank about their desires, both physical and financial. He had several favorites, who greeted him with crows of delight—for he was a strong, patient lover and a generous one who nonetheless had proved that he was no chick for plucking. He would pay well for good service but could be neither gulled nor overawed.

The girls seemed to appreciate it, although Philip was too wise to question deeply what they thought. It was enough that several had said outright that, if he wanted sole possession, they would be willing. Philip had considered it with one or two of those who made the offer. It would be a little more expensive but a little more convenient in that he could be sure the girl would always be free when he wanted her. He had discovered, however, that he had no such inclination and did not mind at all that the girl he used on Monday would be performing for someone else on Tuesday. Nor did he care that a girl he asked for specifically might be busy; there was always another ready, and he preferred variety.

Accustomed to the straightforward advances of such young women, Philip might well have missed the significance of the delicate, suggestive touch of Meg's fingers on the back of his hand. He did not, because he was already thinking along the same lines himself.

Ever since he had made that teasing remark about importuning her, he had been thinking about her as a woman rather than as Pierre's smuggling partner. And everything she had said and done had made her more desirable.

Long used to Leonie's intelligence and practicality, Philip was enchanted by Meg's business sense and quick understanding. One reason he had never considered marriage was his horror at the thought of being tied permanently to one of the giggling, simpering misses presented as marriageable. When Meg had taken hold of his wrist, made him touch her, kissed him, and asked to be kissed, he understood there was no sexual significance to her actions. Nonetheless, a surge of desire had gripped him, stronger by far than any induced by the most blatant overtures of any light-skirts.

Thus, when the tips of Meg's fingers slid over his hand, Philip shivered. The gentle touch affected him much as the "electric" fluid with which some of his friends at Oxford had been experimenting. His skin tingled and he felt the hair on his body rise. There was, too, a wash of heat in his genitals, but that, although more violent and demanding, he could deal with more readily than that subtle tingling. It was the latter which rendered him breathless and mute so that he could only stare down into Meg's face and swallow hard, like a cursed fool.

Chapter 8

The momentary awkwardness did Philip no harm with Megaera, who, as aware of him as he was of her, recognized his response. In fact she was much flattered because she knew—had even expected—she might be seized and mauled about as soon as she offered the invitation. Instead Philip seemed doubtful—not that he lacked eagerness, but he seemed to be uncertain she had intended an invitation. That was very pleasant. Megaera's knowledge of casual relationships between men and women was virtually nonexistent, but from the maidservants' complaints against Edward she assumed they were brief and violent. Her protest to Edward had brought the defense that the girls had "asked for it." But when Megaera tried to discover how they did so, it appeared that a glance or a slight hesitation in leaving a room was sufficient.

Only when John brought her pony did Megaera begin to wonder whether Philip's hesitation might have been owing to his fear of John rather than his respect for her. The discussion they had had about "importuning" came to her mind, and she bit her lip with vexation. By then Philip had fetched Spite, and they set out northwest over the sharply rising land to

pick up the road that led to Bolliet. Both were silent.
Megaera was wondering how she could test Philip's
reaction to her, and Philip was wondering whether it
was fair to embark on a love affair with her when he
would be gone in two weeks and might never return.

"This is where we leave the road," Megaera said
after about fifteen minutes. "Look carefully at that
lightning-struck tree. Beyond it is a tall peak that
shows between the two remaining living branches. You
cannot see that now, of course, but it is clear in day-
time. We go by west of the tree. There is the crest of
a hill, but we go around, keeping on the low side. If
you climb too high, you will find yourself lost."

"I am lost already." Philip laughed awkwardly. "I
will never find it. This is not my kind of country at
all, and a lot of my time has been spent in Town—I
mean towns."

Megaera peered at him through the dark when he
said "Town," recognizing it as an unintended reference to London. She put the odd remark aside. There
were, as usual, many explanations, and she did not
really care much about Philip's background. He was
the son of a friend and had proved himself, despite
his origin and his trade, no enemy of her nation. The
slight mystery merely lent additional charm to his
elegant French-accented speech and manners and to
his handsome countenance.

"Tomorrow you won't need to come farther than
the tree," Megaera said. "That's where I'll meet you.
If you need to come to the cave, I'll send John to meet
you. In daylight you won't have any trouble."

Philip frowned. "If it is so easily found, is it safe
for you?"

"How do you mean, safe? The men all know it, of
course. They have to bring the goods here. It just isn't
possible for John and me to unload fast enough by
ourselves. It's safe enough from the local people. Many
don't know about it, but most are just scared to death

of the cave. There are all kinds of stories about 'creatures' that live 'under the hill.' But I've never seen or heard a thing. For all I know those rumors were started on purpose before I came here. If you mean safe from the revenuers—no place is safe if an information is laid. I move the stock as soon as I can. Most of the time the cave is empty. It's just a place I can be reached—if you want to reach me."

"Good!" Philip said emphatically. "But should I not see you safe to where you live? I mean—what good is my bringing you to the cave, if—"

"I'll stay here tonight," Meg said abruptly. "I have a bed and blankets and such. With John sleeping across the opening and a noise trap that will wake me, I'll be safe enough."

Her tone did not invite argument, and Philip rode on in silence. It seemed odd to him that the girl should be so secretive. Her looks were so distinctive, and her servant more so, that it didn't seem possible she could hide her identity, but if that was the way she wanted it . . .

"I did not mean to pry," he said softly. "Believe me, your safety is of great importance to me, and I agree that what I do not know I cannot tell. That is wise. I only wish to be sure this Bart person does not—"

"There's no danger of that now," Megaera remarked. "He wouldn't try to get me at any time except when I go to *meet* Pierre. Silly, that's the only time I carry any large sum of money."

"Then why—" Philip began, and shut his mouth abruptly, flushing at his own stupidity.

Although he could not see it, Megaera had blushed hotly also. She had not meant to sound so blatantly inviting. Actually she had not intended any invitation; she had only answered with the direct truth, not thinking how it must sound. They rode on in awkward stillness, but fortunately the level area narrowed and Megaera kicked her pony into a trot for a few steps so that she could precede Philip. That made speech difficult and was an adequate excuse for the silence.

After her first appalled reaction, Megaera told herself it was all to the good. She was *supposed* to be coarse and common. She had thus done just what she believed such a woman would do. It was ridiculous to care what the bastard of a common fisherman-smuggler thought of her. She was not Mrs. Edward Devoran, with a family name and honor to protect and noble standards to live up to. Now she was Red Meg, who wore an old, dirty, man's jacket and breeches that would have caused Mrs. Edward Devoran to faint with embarrassment and horror. So what if Philip thought her a common whore! The defiant thought was accompanied by a rush of tears and a stuffed nose, which made Megaera sniff.

First mute with embarrassment at his gaucherie, Philip had remained silent because of confusion. There was so great a dichotomy between that delicate, thrilling touch on his hand and the crude suggestion of Meg's remark. The two simply did not go together. The open invitation was the sort of thing one of the girls in a whorehouse might have said. The touch on his hand was something a shy girl might do to encourage a hesitant suitor.

Had that gentle touch been an accident? Philip could not believe it—partly because he didn't want to believe it. There was something exciting, exciting in a clean, fine way, about the delicate invitation that he could not bear to discard in exchange for a crude pleasure he could find anywhere. But if the shy desire to encourage him was the truth, what could Meg's purpose be in permitting him to accompany her, saying she intended to sleep in the cave, had a bed there, and nail the whole thing together by admitting she knew Bart would not attack her on the homeward journey?

At that moment Philip heard the sad little sniffle. Perhaps if he had not heard, he would not have noticed the surreptitious gesture with which Megaera wiped tears from her cheeks. He did see, however, and the quick motion plus the sniff was so eloquent and so satisfactory an explanation that Philip nearly laughed with joy. He would have spurred Spite forward to comfort her at once, except that John was between them and Philip did not know the ground. He dared not go around in the dark where, if Spite put a foot wrong, they might tumble over a drop. It might not mean much but a few bruises to Philip, but the horse could break a leg.

It did not matter. When they came to the cave, he could show that he understood. Philip was now sure that the three things had nothing to do with each other at all. Meg had allowed him to accompany her for several reasons: because Pierre had suggested it, because (he hoped) she enjoyed his company, because she had to show him where to meet her, and also because, however sure she was Bart would not try to attack her when she had no money, she was woman enough to be nervous. In this light the remark she had made was no more than the simple truth—a confession rather than an invitation.

Fool that he was to have hurt her. Obviously in her innocence she had not realized the implications of her simple statement until his crude half question had made them plain. He hoped the aftermath of her tears of shame would not be so much anger that she would not listen to his apology. Philip opened his mouth to call out, but at that instant John trotted around from behind Meg's pony. Philip pulled up Spite as he saw Meg slide down from her mount. However, as he rose in the saddle to dismount also, Meg said coldly, "Don't bother to get down. John is just going to look over the cave. Then I'll tell him to take you back to the road."

"Please do not be angry at my stupidity," Philip said. "I will not dismount if you do not wish it, but allow me to say how sorry I am for offending you. I understand why you are angry, indeed I do. It was most ungracious to sound as if it were too much trouble for me to accompany you. I—"

"Oh, come down," Megaera interrupted. "It's stupid to talk at each other with you atop that horse."

Philip swung his right leg over and came off the saddle. "Thank you. You are kind. Pierre would be furious if he knew how I had insulted you. He thinks the world of you, and you are so—so practical I forgot that knowledge that a thing is so in the head does not always quiet the heart."

"What in the world does that mean?"

"Only that I should have understood that you were nervous, even if you did not believe Bart would try to attack when you had no money. I am such a fool. . . ."

"I wasn't angry about that," Megaera said, laughing softly. "I *was* frightened half to death on the way here and very glad of your company on the way back. I—I misunderstood your—well, not your question but—but why you didn't finish asking it."

Philip cleared his throat. "Meg, you are entirely too truthful and innocent," he said with jocular disapproval. "I presented you with a perfect excuse for being angry with me. It cost me considerable pains to think it up. You are supposed to use it, not uncover the vulgar truth."

To his surprise Meg did not laugh but took a step closer and said, "I prefer the truth, and I thought the same as you, but—but I didn't intend it that way."

"I know that. I have just told you so, both roundabout and directly." Philip took her hand as it came up to make a gesture.

"Yes, but—but I'm afraid that what put it into my mind . . ."

Her voice drifted away as Philip drew her closer by the hand he held. She did not resist, but he could feel her trembling and her eyes were as wide as they had been when she had come into The Mousehole.

"You need not fear me," Philip murmured. "You must know I think you very beautiful, very desirable, but I would not . . . You have only to say, 'Stop. Go away.' I will obey you."

"I have only just met you," Megaera whispered.

It was too dark to see that she was blushing, yet Philip knew that. "Sometimes it is that way," he said gently. "For me also—"

"Oh, a man—" Megaera's voice was suddenly hard and she uttered a slight, bitter laugh. "A man looks and wants."

"That is not what I meant," Philip protested sharply. "I am no innocent. I am not likely to confuse you with a woman who can be bought for a few shillings."

Megaera did not reply. She knew any man who was not an idiot would have said the same. Nonetheless the words were a sweet balm, and she told herself that there was a ring of sincerity in Philip's voice. And, indeed, she did not hope or desire to make any profit out of their relationship. The trouble was that she could not think how to advance from the current position. Just then John emerged from the cave with the lantern, which he extended toward Megaera. She withdrew her hand gently from Philip's grasp.

"What time shall I meet you tomorrow?" she asked.

"Oh, Lord! I have to get a carriage, and I think the nearest inn that has post horses will be in Penzance. Not before ten, Meg—which means, I am afraid, that we will not have much time for business when we reach Falmouth—not enough, anyway."

"There must be at least one respectable hotel in which we could stay," she said, and then her breath drew in sharply.

Philip began to laugh. "Meg, you *must* learn to

think before you speak—or else not give way to second thoughts. I assure you I will not mistake your meaning another time. Yes, I am sure there will be decent hotels. After all, naval wives doubtless require respectable accommodation. I am glad you are willing to stay in my care. We can talk about the arrangements on the way. You look very tired."

"Yes, thank you," she said, like a child, then turned to John and signed that he should lead Philip back to the road and that she was going directly back into the house.

It was convenient that Philip could not understand the gestures, but Megaera was aware that he was watching keenly. All too soon, if they spent much time together, she would not be able to count on her instructions to John being secret. She must remember that this was an entirely different man from the slow country clods with whom she was accustomed to dealing. She must also remember that, no matter how attractive, he was only Pierre's bastard. Her secret must not be exposed. Probably Philip was honest, as Pierre was honest. Nonetheless the relationship between Red Meg and Mrs. Edward Devoran must never be known.

Megaera sighed as she passed through the cave and went around a rough outcrop of rock. Behind it she stuck her arm into a deep fissure and felt around until her hand found a large knot of rope. Pulling on this dragged a ladder out of a dark hole well above Megaera's head. She climbed the ladder, crawled into and beyond the small opening, and stood up. She pulled the ladder up behind her with considerable effort. As she laid it down so that the legs were on the higher area that made the opening so small, the rope slid back into the narrow crack that extended down to the floor of the main cave and disappeared from sight.

The ladder was new; John had built it to be sure it would hold his weight, but it was not the first to lie in that position. Its ancestor, which had been found by the scholarly gentlemen investigating the cave, was the best proof that the long-dead owners of Bolliet Manor were probably no better than they should be. Megaera was horrified to learn that they had probably been wreckers, who had kept goods and perhaps prisoners in the caves.

She was not thinking now, as she had so often before, that the family had come full circle. Her mind was a muddled mass of doubts, fears, and desires made more confusing by her fatigue. By the time she had stretched her aching limbs in her comfortable bed, she was almost ready to back out of the whole enterprise. The few extra pounds' commission would not be worth the agony of spirit, she told herself. The decision quieted her enough so that she slept, but not for long. For the first time in more than a year she dreamed of making love and woke up weeping.

The few hours of rest had revived her somewhat, and the dream, leaving her unfulfilled, had sharpened her appetite. First she realized that she could no longer back out; she had promised Pierre she would buy the goods for him. *And don't be a fool,* she told herself. *This is a golden opportunity. Philip is handsome, gentle, and, best of all, has no acquaintance in the neighborhood. There is no chance that he will ever meet Mrs. Edward Devoran. Besides, he won't stay in Cornwall after his business is finished. He'll go back to France with Pierre.* That produced a sinking feeling of disappointment rather than relief, but Megaera's spirits rose again when she remembered that, if the buying trip were successful, Philip would surely come back to repeat it—especially if he wanted to see her again.

The second time it was even easier to go to sleep. This time she slept peacefully, although dreams continued to flit through her brain. They were sweet dreams—of soft whispers, gentle touching, kind looks. Megaera was a child, then suddenly a woman, but the

man, whose face was a dark blur, was always the same
—father, lover, protector, he was uniformly loving. He
comforted the child, who had scraped a knee, then
suddenly was kissing the woman with passion. His
breath was sweet, untainted with liquor—and Megaera
knew she was safe forever.

Before Megaera had even got into bed, Philip waved
good-bye to John and set off at as fast a pace as he
dared to where a secondary track, which went eventually to Buryan, met the road that ran past Bolliet.
Here he turned due north, steering by the stars and
by his memories of rides with Perce. He went a little
astray, but it was a fortunate mistake and brought him
out right at Drift rather than at Catchall, which was
half a mile farther west along the main road. He was
not really surprised to find it was Perce who opened
the door for him.

"You're late" was all he said.

"Yes, and I must leave very early. I do not think I
will be back—not for some time." Philip's eyes twinkled. "I think I have found a way to restore my
fortunes."

"Yaas," Perce drawled. "Pay those debts that have
been on your mind so much. You wouldn't like some
company?"

"With your French accent?" Philip shuddered and
laughed.

His friend shrugged. Actually he was good at lan-
guages. He spoke French, German, and Italian fluently
and could manage a little Russian as well—but he
spoke every one like an Englishman. Worse, he knew
"English" was stamped on his face, so that it was true
he would be more a danger than a help.

"Damn!" he said softly as he closed the door. "Is
there anything you need? Money?"

"No. I told you. I am about to make my fortune.
You need not worry. I will be quite safe." The dis-

belief on Perce's face led him to say a little more. "I have met an old friend of my father's. Believe me, I am more likely to be stifled by protection than exposed to any excitement."

Actually Philip was not much interested in his adventure in France at the moment. That excitement had been temporarily superseded by another. He was no less determined to do what he could to help his nation and foil Bonaparte's plans, but he could not do anything about that until Pierre's return—and he was meeting Meg tomorrow.

Perce had not answered Philip's nonsensical assurances as to his own safety immediately, merely staring at him in frustrated silence. Then he sighed. What could Philip say? "Do you want a nightcap?" he asked.

"No. Lord, I must reek of brandy already—but it was good brandy, I must say. That is what comes of drinking at a— Never mind. I had better go to bed before I say what I should not. But Perce, do you know where your unstamped brandy comes from?"

"The same place yours does, you idiot—France. Where else? And there is *no* stamped brandy in Cornwall," Perce answered sardonically.

"No, you fool. I mean, who brings it?"

"How should I know? Do you think m'father or I accept the kegs? For God's sake! He's a justice of the peace!"

"Who does accept them?"

"Butler, I suppose." Then Perce cocked his head. "Is it important? Do you want me to wake him?"

"No, of course not. Just curiosity."

"Oh? I thought maybe you were drumming up trade or looking for information about your future business rivals."

Philip laughed as he set his foot on the stairs. "No, you have the wrong end of the stick. I am not selling. I am buying—and not brandy. My interest was personal. I have heard . . ." Then he paused, feeling ashamed of himself. He had no right to pry into Meg's life, really. She had a right to her own secrets.

"What?" Perce urged.

"That there was some trouble," Philip finished lamely, needing to say something.

Perce wrinkled his forehead. "You know, I heard that too, but it was some time ago. Nothing serious— a petty theft or two, a servant girl complaining she was mauled about. Wait," he added as they reached the top of the stair. "I *have* heard something else. Now, who was it that told me? . . . Well, never mind. It seems the trouble has stopped and there's a big brute delivering now, really big—and—yes, he's a deaf-mute. Damn! I do remember. It was Levallis told me. Seems a maid went out to the jakes or something and ran into the brute. Screamed the place down. Everyone ran out, even Levallis himself, but the creature just put the kegs down. It was a sure thing he never heard the girl. Didn't touch her or tell her to be quiet or anything. Didn't say a word to the others either. Just set down the kegs and walked away."

"Oh, thanks."

Philip didn't know whether he was more disappointed or relieved that Perce knew nothing about Meg. Apparently she was as secretive with her customers as with Pierre, or perhaps John made the deliveries alone.

"As long as the trouble is over," he said to Perce. "My—my new employer is, according to his lights, an honest man."

"I see." Perce's lips quirked. "Wants to be sure his clients are satisfied. Yes. Very reasonable." They had reached the door to Philip's bedchamber. Perce put his hand on his friend's shoulder. "Be a little sensible, will you, Phil? If you weren't around to give me a start now and then, I might freeze over solid."

"We will be wicked old men together, I am sure,"

Philip replied. "Will you say everything proper to your parents and sisters for me? Beg pardon for my sudden departure. I will write, of course, to thank them and to beg permission to return. I will be back, you know."

An enormous urge to tell Perce about Meg, to confess that he had finally met a woman who could arouse more than carnal interest in him, filled Philip. He shut his teeth hard. Perce would think he was insane! Imagine a St. Eyre feeling that kind of interest in a girl of common birth who headed a gang of smugglers. When he thought of it in those terms, Philip himself wondered whether he was insane. He struck his friend lightly in the solar plexus, forced a grin, and went into his room.

Of course he was mad, he told himself as he slipped off his clothes. Meg was beautiful, and she might even be a decent woman, but she was out of the question for him. Doubtless he was reading all sorts of things into her that did not exist. He smiled wryly, trying to ignore the weight of disappointment that settled on him. It was all Pierre's fault—calling her a "lady" and telling Philip to protect her. No doubt she was about as helpless as a fully armed dragoon. He remembered the pistols strapped around her waist. Almost certainly in the hard light of day he would see her as she was. Philip set his teeth and imagined Meg in the kind of clothing his bawdy-house girls decked themselves in. He fell asleep with that picture in his mind and a big empty hole in his chest. By morning the notion was fixed, and he could laugh at himself without feeling his throat tighten.

Philip left Moreton Place before anyone but a few servants was awake. In fact he saddled Spite himself, rode to Penzance as quickly as possible, and breakfasted while the hired horses were put to the carriage he had chosen. Megaera had been up even earlier than Philip. She had packed a small old portmanteau of her father's with her soberest gowns—and most frivolous nightdresses and underlinen. The second dream had hardened her final decision, although she was well aware of its falsity. Even if Philip wished to be her lover and protector, she could not accept. There could be no permanent relationship between them. All the more reason why Red Meg should taste what would be forever denied to Mrs. Edward Devoran.

Before the maid came in with her morning chocolate and to make up her fire, Megaera had carried the portmanteau to the cave and returned to her bed. When the girl came in, Megaera told her to send in Rose to pack a bag. She told her personal maid that she was going to pay a visit and would be away for a night or two. She discussed with Rose some slight changes in her evening dresses to make them appear fresher. It was difficult to have much interest in gowns she knew she would not wear, and she was rather impatient with the way Rose dwelled on details.

"And the carriage, ma'am?" Rose asked. "Which will you take?"

"None," Megaera replied. "I will ride over to the vicar's house where I am to be taken up. Do not be so prying, Rose, but go fix my gowns."

The maid did as she was told, but she was puzzled by her mistress's manner. Her lady hadn't been interested in the dresses, not really, but she was excited and eager to go. Also it was very odd for her lady to say she was prying by asking about the carriage. After all, someone had to tell the footman what to tell the coachman. And if her lady was to be taken up, why at the vicar's house? Why not at Bolliet?

Then Rose's face softened. Could it be a man? That could explain why her lady was meeting him at the vicar's. Rose knew that Megaera couldn't bear to lock her father up, but it was plain as a pikestaff that any decent man would be scared off by such a father-in-law. But then surely her lady would have wanted to look her best. So why did she hardly look at her gowns? And besides, what man in the district didn't know about Lord Bolliet?

Fortunately Rose was very romantic and very fond of her mistress. She shook off all practical objections, telling herself that the look in her lady's eyes could only mean a man. She even found reasons for Megaera's lack of interest in her gowns. Her lady was incurably honest, much to her own detriment, Rose thought with irritation. Probably the gentleman was *not* local. He would not know that there were money troubles—all the servants knew that much because of the cutbacks in spending, but they had no idea how acute the problem was—because of that monster her lady married and because of his lordship's little weaknesses. Her lady would wear the old gowns to show she was not rich. That was it.

That was the story that went around in servants' hall, and even Mr. Crystal, the butler, could not really deny it. His glimpse of Mrs. Devoran when he served breakfast tended to confirm Rose's contention. Mr. Crystal could only hope that his poor, poor lady would not suffer anymore. He had not seen such a light in her eyes for many years. All he could do for her, however, was to suppress gossip as much as he could in the servants' hall and promise to pin back the ears of anyone who dared to let a word slip to his lordship. Fuddled as he was, he might take it into his head to interfere in some way.

Not in the least aware of the conspiracy of helpfulness surrounding her, Megaera wore away the hours until nine o'clock. Then she had her mare brought around, had her elaborate portmanteau strapped behind the saddle, and set out. Mr. Crystal, seeing her off, frowned. She should have taken a groom. Of course, it was only about two miles to the vicar's house, and Mrs. Devoran's horse knew the way by heart, even if Mrs. Devoran herself should be somewhat distracted.

Still, a groom would have lent propriety. He sighed. There was no use talking about propriety to Mrs. Devoran. In fact she was a stickler usually, but when she got an idea into her head she just did things her own way.

Having held her mare to a staid trot as long as she could be seen from the house, Meg quickened her pace once she was clear. It was odd that the passage from the house to the cave could be traversed in a few minutes on foot, but it took almost ten minutes to ride around the hill. And no one would ever guess that Bolliet Manor was on the other side. It looked completely wild country as soon as the formal park was hidden. All to the good, Megaera thought. That increased the likelihood that no one would ever associate Bolliet with the cave.

John was waiting to take the mare in and transfer the sidesaddle to the pony. Meanwhile, Megaera removed her fashionable riding habit and replaced it with a sober walking dress from her period of half-mourning. It was pale gray with black ribbons and, in spite of its sobriety, highlighted her red hair and creamy complexion. The high waist did her no disservice either, emphasizing her slenderness and her firm, high bosom, although the dress covered rather more of her breasts than was fashionable. A darker gray pelisse covered her, and a bonnet with a long poke shaded her face. At this hour of the day there was some chance of passing someone she knew on the road. Meg hoped Philip—she shivered inside a little as she said his name to herself—would have obtained a closed carriage, but if he had not, the hat would conceal her face and hair.

She dressed in front of John without the slightest embarrassment. Dr. Partridge had been right about John. He was not the least bit interested in such things. He did look at her from time to time, but only at her face and hands to see if she wanted him to do

anything. It was impossible to feel anything more
about John's occasional glances than about those of
her pony or mare.

When she was ready, John led the pony out. Megaera glanced around to make sure no one was walking
the hills. Shepherds sometimes came by or boys from
the village to snare rabbits or birds. Today, fortunately, the hillside was empty. John lifted her to her
pony and picked up the old portmanteau. The elegant
one had been placed out of sight in one of the passages. It was difficult to ride in the tight skirt. Megaera
could not fit her knee over the rest. She could only
perch on the saddle with one foot in the stirrup. However, John walked beside her and she rested a hand
on his shoulder. He would catch her if she slipped.

They arrived by the blasted tree without any un-
toward incident. Megaera was lifted down and the
portmanteau set beside her. She signed to John that
she was going away for three days (he would not worry
if she came home sooner but would be frantic if she
were late) and that he must take the pony back to the
cave and keep the mare there until she returned. There
was no way she could tell him to meet her because
she was not sure exactly when she would return, but
Philip would surely see her to the cave, so that would
be all right. Now she glanced anxiously down the road
and pulled her watch from a small pocket in her skirt.
She was early, and it would be very bad if someone
saw her standing by the side of the road.

Megaera waved John away. As usual he was reluctant to leave her alone anywhere except in the house.
She had to push him on his way, but having him around
was the worst thing. He was just too noticeable. Megaera herself could probably hide behind the tree if
necessary. If anyone noticed her at all, she would be
thought to be a servant girl waiting to be picked up.
However, John was hardly out of sight when Megaera
heard a carriage. She retreated cautiously to the tree,

but it was Philip and she came toward the road, lugging the portmanteau.

As soon as he saw her Philip pulled up his horses, wound the reins around the whip holder, and jumped down. He took the portmanteau from her hand, looking somewhat stunned. He had convinced himself that she would be swathed in purple satin, tawdry tinsel, and unsuitable, moth-eaten ostrich plumes. A thin little hope, peeping through those images, showed a sweet little maiden in pale sprig muslin and white lace mittens. What he saw was a beautiful and dignified woman, most tastefully attired; Leonie could not have looked lovelier nor more appropriate. Philip swallowed hard.

"What's wrong?" Meg asked anxiously. "Is something the matter? Pierre? Don't tell me—"

"No, no. I have heard nothing, but I am sure he is safe away. It is you—forgive me, but you are so exquisitely beautiful and so—so right!"

She laughed, her creamy skin flushing deliciously. "That isn't very polite. You aren't supposed to apologize for compliments."

"Not for the compliment, but I did not wish that you think I would—would take advantage because you are alone."

Megaera did not answer. What could she say? She was delighted by the proof that the respectful attitude was not generated by fear of John, but she hoped he was not going to carry it too far. Not to scratch dirt over a dead thing—Megaera *wanted* Philip to take advantage of her. She contented herself for the moment by smiling brilliantly at him as he helped her into the carriage. Philip asked her to take the reins while he went to the horses' heads to back them around. Normally he would have done it from his driving seat, as he was a top sawyer, but he did not trust the hired horses to respond just as they should. He told himself that he preferred Meg to think he was less

experienced in handling the ribbons than he actually
was; really, however, she had become so precious that
he could hardly bear that she should be bumped on
the rough road, not to think of tipping her into a
ditch.

When they were facing in the right direction, he
took the reins from her. She had been about to ask if
he would prefer her to drive, seeing how cautious he
had been about turning the carriage, but two minutes
of watching his hands betrayed his skill. Since it had
not occurred to Megaera that Philip had any secret to
keep, she leapt to the correct conclusion—that his excessive care had been to spare *her* the smallest uncertainty. She blushed again with pleasure. Never in her
life had she been treated with such tender consideration.

"I have been wondering what we should say at the
hotel," she began, after a glance at Philip showed her
he was looking at her with a bemused expression whenever he could spare a moment from the road. "Do you
think they would believe my maid broke a leg?"

"I am sure they will believe anything you choose to
tell them," Philip responded, "but I do not think we
should pretend you are accustomed to a personal abi-
gail. We are supposed to be in trade."

Since Megaera had not the faintest notion of the
great state in which rich tradesmen lived, she made no
objection, merely looking respectful of Philip's wider
experience. "Is it proper for a woman in trade to go to
a hotel alone?" she asked.

Philip passed his tongue over suddenly dry lips. "But
you will not be alone. Accompanied by your husband—
or your brother," he added hastily, swallowing, "no
questions would be asked."

Megaera was silent, staring straight ahead. Her heart
was beating so fast and hard she was surprised that her
pelisse did not flutter with its violence. Philip had certainly wasted no time. Was he so sure of her, Meg

wondered, that he did not feel it necessary to woo her?
A flicker of hurt and anger stirred. She turned her
head, prepared for a confident smile and planning to
wipe it off his face with a whiplash repudiation. Instead she saw a flush almost as deep as her own, and
lips tight with anxiety. The hurt and anger dissolved
into tenderness. It was not overconfidence but under-
confidence that had driven him.

"I don't think," Megaera said, her voice trembling
between nervousness and laughter, "that anyone would
believe I could be your sister."

A huge sigh whooshed out of Philip, and he turned
his head for a glance at her. He was smiling now, but
with relief, not contempt. "I thought you would hit
me," he said, looking back at the road, which was
rutted and bumpy. "I would have well deserved it,
but I did not mean to say that right off. The words just
came out. Thank God, you are an honest woman,
Meg, not a simpering idiot. Now I can talk sense. You
do forgive me for being so—so—"

"Importunate?"

Philip laughed. "I did not mean it that way." Then
he took the chance to turn his head again, his face
serious. "You are free to say 'no' at any time, my dear.
I took an unfair advantage, I know, but I honestly
believe we will draw less notice as husband and wife.
It is a common thing for a man to have a shop where
articles of dress are sold while his wife is a dress-
maker in the same establishment. In such a case they
might well share the duties of purchasing."

"You're quite right." Megaera nodded agreement.
"There was just such a shop in Penzance."

In the past, before her father's gambling and Edward's chicanery had stripped them bare, Megaera
had bought trifles for herself there, although serious
shopping had been done at Exeter. After the "fall,"
Mrs. Beeble had made for her the few dresses she

absolutely needed. In fact Mrs. Beeble had made her mourning clothes, the very dress she was wearing. There had been neither time nor money to send to London for "blacks," and even if she had had both in sufficiency, Megaera would not have dignified Edward's death by spending more than necessary.

The knowledge that reason as well as desire had prompted Philip's suggestion removed the last of Megaera's feeling of awkwardness. Indeed, she began to feel wonderful. The worst was over—the embarrassment of agreeing—the best was yet to come. Her spirits soared. She began to chatter as she had not done since the knowledge of the debts Edward had saddled Bolliet with had fallen on her. She asked Philip about Falmouth, and when she learned that he had never been there and knew less than she, she speculated about the town with such abandon that Philip begged her to stop. She was making him laugh so much, he claimed, that he would drive them off the road.

"Besides," he went on, "we must be sensible. We must think up a story to explain why we, who have never bought there before, are now buying in Falmouth."

"To set up a new business," Megaera responded promptly. "That would be a good reason to buy in small quantities from a number of different factors. Until we were established, we would not know exactly what would sell best."

They had time enough to polish their tale to perfection so that all the details were firmly fixed in both their minds. Either could be questioned or just talk idly without fear that any story would contradict the other's. A great deal of amusement was extracted from this practical purpose also. They invented an entire family tree for both between gales of laughter. There were sober parents, silly sisters, industrious brothers, eccentric aunts and uncles, and wastrel cousins. Meg-

aera was so happy that her breath kept catching on
tears. She had not laughed so much or felt so free since
she had married Edward. The long nightmare was
over at last. This must be the dawn of a new life.

Chapter 9

With some effort Philip and Megaera presented a sober appearance when they entered Falmouth. It would not have done at all to laugh uproariously as they drove through the streets. The sobriety soon became real enough because they had a little difficulty in deciding where to seek accommodation. Philip had naturally gravitated to the most elegant establishment, which was on the main street of the town and easy to find. Megaera, wrenched from her happy delusion of freedom and a new life, realized she could not stay there. Of all places, that was the most likely one for her to meet a member of the social set in which she lived. Nervously she protested that it would not be suitable for persons in a small way of trade.

Philip slipped an arm around her waist. "Perhaps not, but we do not need to tell anyone here what we do. I want you to be happy."

She hesitated. It was so strange to hear a man say he wished her to be happy that she could hardly bear to frustrate his desire, no matter how silly. But it would be too dangerous.

"I would not be happy," she murmured. "I would

feel that people were staring at me, wondering what I was doing there. Please, Philip."

"Of course, Meg. Whatever you like," he replied at once, making her completely happy again.

Megaera could hardly believe the good humor in his voice. On the rare occasions when Edward had offered her a choice and she had chosen differently than he would have done, he was scarcely civil, not to mention good-humored. But Philip's pleasant mood held even after the next two places they examined were obviously hopeless. Megaera shuddered at the looks of the loungers in the yard and at the appearance of the yard and hotel. Philip took her away at once, one arm protectively around her. Back on the main street he sat frowning for a moment.

"I'm sorry, Philip," Megaera whispered, trying to forestall an outburst of rage. "Perhaps—"

"What a fool I am!" he exclaimed, smiling at her. "I must ask one of the factors Pierre recommended."

It was the solution, of course. In another half hour they were ensconced in a clean, quiet establishment on a peaceful side street conveniently near the port and commercial area but screened from them. When they were shown to their room, a large chamber with the bed screened off so that it could also serve as a sitting room, Philip asked solicitously whether Meg wanted to rest awhile. She burst out laughing. It was so ridiculous to think she might be fatigued by a three-hour drive in a carriage after her exertions over the past year. The expression on Philip's face when she laughed was not so funny. It made her breath catch, and she stepped back a pace. Instantly Philip turned away and walked to the window.

"Do you wish to go out at once," he asked, "or can I order tea or some wine for you? It is too early for dinner."

"Let's go out." Megaera's voice quivered slightly. She had made him angry now, she was sure, and it was so stupid. What difference did it make whether she yielded at once or a few hours later?

"It is not kind to laugh at me," Philip protested, but he was laughing himself as he turned back toward her. Since he had mistaken the frightened shake in her voice for repressed mirth, he also misunderstood her expression of astonished delight. "What did you expect," he went on wryly, "when you are so beautiful and we were sitting so close. Do you think I am made of stone?"

Megaera recovered quickly. She thought again she had been a fool to refuse Philip, but now it was because her own desire had been awakened. He was so handsome, so different from the fair men to whom she was accustomed. Nonetheless she knew her instinct had been right. Another time a quick union with half one's mind on something else might be enough; for their first time, it would be all wrong.

"I'm not laughing at you," she said. "What makes you think I'm any better than you are? But you know it wouldn't be right."

"Such devotion to duty!" Philip exclaimed, his eyes gleaming. "I assure you Pierre would not expect it."

"So long as Pierre gets goods to sell at a reasonable price, he wouldn't care if we took no longer than five minutes over it," Megaera replied tartly, realizing that Philip was teasing her again. "It was you who wished to do Bonaparte a bad turn by buying only luxury articles."

"I know," Philip admitted sadly, "but my love of country has been completely subverted."

That was irresistible. Now Megaera had to laugh. Nonetheless, she moved firmly to the door and opened it. Philip followed, sighing dramatically, but he was really very pleased. It had occurred to him also that he wished to linger over his pleasure. They set out on foot, visiting the recommended warehouses first and asking for referrals to other factors who would be likely to carry the goods they wanted. In a very short time Philip decided he knew why Pierre had insisted that Meg do the buying. She had an eye for real quality and drove a bitter bargain.

Philip was really amazed at what could be purchased for a small sum. He had been thinking in terms of the prices ladies paid for single items or a few yards of dress fabric in fashionable shops in London, since he had no experience with wholesale purchases. But even when he corrected his line of thinking, it seemed that Meg was obtaining a great deal for very little. Soon he began to wonder whether Pierre would have sufficient cargo space for what the gold he had been given would buy. Between warehouses he mentioned this to her.

"I'm surprised myself," she replied. "The prices are reasonable to begin with, and they let me beat them down in the most extraordinary way. With that first man, I thought perhaps the goods might have been stolen, but they are all behaving alike."

"Perhaps it is not so unreasonable," Philip remarked slowly. "I have just thought that much of what we are buying may have been lying in the warehouses for a long time. Do you think that perhaps these goods were *meant* for transshipment to France and the war stopped the sales?"

"You're probably right," Megaera agreed, looking with admiration at Philip. "Now I'm really delighted. Think of all the good we're doing."

"Yes, but could we not stop doing it now?" Philip pleaded. "I cannot see how Pierre will manage to stuff all that we have already bought into his ship. What will we do with the extra?"

"I have plenty of storage space," Megaera replied heartlessly. "The ponies can bring the goods down when we pick up the kegs, and the boats can run out with a load just as easily as running out empty."

Her eyes gleamed with enthusiasm. Philip groaned, but Megaera's blood was up. She had not had a good shopping binge for years, and it did not matter a bit to her that none of the articles would belong to her. It was the shopping and choosing that she loved rather than the having. However, Philip did not need to suffer much longer. It was growing late, and she was wise enough not to wish to give an impression of hurry or urgent need. Moreover, Philip found a source of private diversion.

While Megaera was examining a case of bird plumage and haggling over broken feathers and other imperfections, Philip discovered a display of Indian jewelry. The items were inexpensive. They were not of gold or precious stones, but they were very lovely. Bracelets and necklets of polished wood were inlaid with traceries of mother-of-pearl in delicate, exquisite designs. Philip summoned a clerk and hushed him.

"For my wife," he mouthed, "a surprise. She works so hard."

A conspiratorial smile acknowledged the tribute, and the pieces were laid out. Philip was enchanted. A marvelous fragrance wafted from the wood. He felt like buying them all, but that would have been ridiculous, and he finally chose three bracelets, a necklace, a pair of earrings, and two combs that had a matching pattern of a greeny-blue mother-of-pearl that would go magnificently with Meg's red hair. He paid the full price the clerk asked, which occasioned a look of surprise until he said, "Put the rest away. I do not want my wife to see them. You will not make much more than I have given for these after she is finished chaffering, I assure you."

The clerk looked across the warehouse at his master, who was wringing his hands at that moment and swearing he would be driven to the workhouse if he acceded to Megaera's demands. He heard her unshaken and completely unsympathetic voice replying that she preferred it to be his master than herself, and that since neither was in the least likely, his master should stop complaining and apply himself to considering her offer realistically. The clerk shrugged, smiled, and slid the trinkets into a box, which he closed. The gentleman he served obviously knew his wife.

With his purchases wrapped and in his pocket, Philip strolled back to Megaera who, flushed and triumphant, had concluded another purchase. "Enough, my love," he said firmly. "It is time for dinner. You must not wear yourself out." He turned to the factor, in whose eye he thought he detected a gleam of satisfaction mingled with exasperation; however, the respect with which he bowed to Meg as Philip paid the agreed-upon advance showed he had not got the best of the deal. "We will arrange about transport tomorrow," he said to the man, cocking a cynical eyebrow. "You have quite worn out my poor, frail Meg."

A rich color suffused the factor's face, and Megaera opened her violet eyes as wide as they would go. Before an explosion could erupt from either, Philip hastily shepherded Meg out of the building. She began to laugh.

"How could you?" she gasped. "Why did you? I thought the poor man would burst."

"I am sorry," Philip said, but with a quite unrepentant face. "You *look* fragile and delicate. You *should* be worn to a wraith by all that arguing."

Megaera laughed again. "No woman is worn out by chaffering. I have known some die-away creatures, who did nothing but lie on a sofa and whine all day, to leap to their feet and shout like fishwives for a bargain."

"Very strange," Philip mused. "It is considered very bad *ton* for a man to argue about the price of anything. Oh, he might say 'too much' on a horse, but for clothing, or a gun . . ."

It did not occur to Megaera that it was odd that Philip should talk about the *ton* any more than it struck Philip odd that Megaera should be acquainted with ladies who could afford to spend all day lying on a sofa. To Pierre, who was not of their class, it had been immediately apparent that Megaera was a "lady," just as he would have recognized Philip as a member of the gentry even if he had not known him. The factors, too, knew they were dealing with gentry, but they were not surprised.

Although they did not believe the tale of the new shop and dressmaking establishment, they pretended to do so. Many impoverished families did some backdoor trade, which they concealed from their equals. It was none of the factors' business; all they were interested in was selling their goods. Only Philip and Megaera, who were, so to speak, born to the speech and manners of their class, found them so ordinary as to be unnoticeable.

"Well," Philip continued, abandoning discussion of the inexplicable differences between men and women to further a far more pleasant result of that difference, "you *must* be tired even though you do not feel it now. I think we should dine quietly in our chamber."

Megaera dropped her eyes. She had been so absorbed in what she was doing that she had lost awareness of Philip as a desiring and desirable male. His voice, however, was only friendly, still carrying a hint of laughter. There was nothing at all suggestive about his tone. Megaera remembered the times she had used words with double meanings without recognizing that fact until it was too late. So she nodded her head, not daring to answer for fear her voice would betray her.

Betray what? Alone in the bedchamber, where a maid had already lit candles to supplement the dying light of the short autumn day, Megaera was thrust back into the indecisions of the previous night. Philip had seen her to the door, murmured that she should make herself comfortable while he went down to order dinner. "Comfortable." What did he mean by that? But again there had been nothing in his face or voice, no offensive leer or suggestive glance. He had looked happy, his dark eyes alight, his fine mouth gently curved, not quite smiling but hinting at it.

But there was no excuse for indecision. Philip had said she could back out at any time, but Megaera knew she could not—not now. When they had first arrived, she could have done so. Philip had offered her the opportunity. Possibly she could even have said she had changed her mind any time during the afternoon. Her last chance had been when he suggested they dine in their bedchamber. If she had refused, she could have told him while they ate that she was not willing.

Suddenly she laughed aloud. It would have been a lie. In fact she was not at all unwilling, and the only reason she was shilly-shallying was her old-fashioned notion of propriety. There was always a great outcry against the reading of novels and the harm they did to the delicate minds of young females. In fact the damage they did was to promote overdelicate feelings and overscrupulousness. The heroines were either so lachrymose over their tiny indiscretions or so horribly punished for them that any normal woman was filled with guilt for normal feelings.

As she removed her hat and gloves and hung her pelisse in the press standing against the wall, Megaera became indecisive again. She now admitted to herself that she wanted Philip and intended to yield to him, but she was embarrassed at the thought of needing to say so. The solution presented itself as she turned from the press and hit her foot against her portmanteau, which the servant had left beside the bureau when she had unpacked it. There was no reason in the world why a "wife" should not relax in dishabille after a hard day's work.

Trembling with nervousness lest Philip come back too soon, Megaera began to remove her clothes. She could have rung for a maid to help her, but a year of dressing and undressing herself in her smuggling clothing had made her swift and skilled at buttons and ties

in a way most unusual for a girl of her class. Most of
them had never dressed or undressed themselves in
their lives, and Megaera had found it awkward at first,
but she was used to it now.

Actually there was little enough to do. The black
velvet spencer could be drawn off easily. The low-bos-
omed gray twill gown was a little more difficult because
of the myriad tiny buttons that closed the sleeves. However, it was a well-worn dress and the button loops
slipped over the buttons without trouble. Automatically Meg hung up her spencer and gown. That was
another thing ladies did not do, but obviously one
could not leave unusual garments lying about for a
maid to pick up. Megaera was so accustomed to hanging her smuggling garments in a locked press in Edward's room that she sometimes hung up her own
dresses—which horrified Rose.

Underneath the dress was virtually nothing, although not so little as some really fashionable ladies
wore. Megaera was not one who drew on a pair of
knitted silk, flesh-colored tights, pulled a diaphanous,
short-sleeved gown over them, and considered herself
fully clothed despite freezing weather. She wore a delicate tucked and ribboned chemise and a straight petticoat with a flounced hem over knee-length, lace-edged
drawers, which hid the garters that tied her silk
stockings just above her knees.

Young and slender and with a body hardened by
much walking and riding, Megaera did not bother with
a body band to flatten her stomach or a breast band
to lift her breasts; the one was as flat, the other as high
and firm as any woman could desire. As she stripped
off her undergarments she cast a single look down at
her body and smiled. No one could disapprove of that
milky skin, delicately veined with blue, or the small
dark-rose nipples that crowned her breasts.

In the next moment, however, she frowned. A nightdress was going too far. Besides—the frown smoothed

out—her pantalets and chemise were really much prettier than any of her nightdresses. She pulled those delicate garments back on and found a soft blue crepe peignoir frothed with ecru lace. It had been part of her trousseau, but she had only worn it three or four times. Her lips grew hard for a moment. The time during which she had wished to please and attract Edward had been very brief, and it was seldom that she needed a peignoir even during those few weeks. Usually Edward was out in the evening, returning only long after Megaera was abed.

She pushed that memory away forcibly, but she had little time to brood in any case. She had barely taken off her shoes and stockings and replaced them with a pair of velvet slippers when there was a scratch at the door.

"Who is it?" Megaera called, suddenly afflicted with a horrible sinking feeling.

Had Philip found a group of male cronies to occupy his time? It was just the sort of thing Edward had done, even on their wedding trip. He would tell her to go to their rooms, saying he would be coming to join her—and then send a message by a waiter to inform her he would be delayed because he had found a partner for piquet or a group that wished to play basset. And Edward had never given her warning of his coming by scratching at the door.

The answer to her question brought a flush of pleasure to Megaera's face. She should have known better, she told herself as she called, "Come in." Philip might be only a smuggler's bastard, but he was a greater gentleman than Edward had ever been. He would not walk in unannounced, not even into the room of a woman who had agreed to act as his wife on only a few hours' acquaintance.

He proved himself a "gentleman" even more thoroughly when he entered. Although his eyes widened and he swallowed hard, he said nothing. Instead he came forward, lifted Megaera's hand, and kissed it formally. Philip was a sensitive young man and he had seen not bold invitation but extreme nervousness on Megaera's face. He was grateful to her for her delicate reply to a question he had no idea how to ask.

"Each time I see you," he said, "you are more beautiful than the previous time."

"Don't say that," Megaera replied, pretending crossness, but she did not pull her hand from Philip's grasp. "It is impossible to maintain such a record."

"Not for you."

Gently he drew her closer. She did not resist, but he could sense tension in her. Nonetheless he kissed her, lightly in the beginning and then, when she did not try to escape him, more demandingly. At first she seemed totally passive; then, slowly, her free hand crept up his arm toward his neck. At this interesting moment there was a new scratch at the door.

Reluctantly Philip lifted his head and stepped back, calling, "Just a moment." He did not move away immediately, but looked down at Megaera, who met his eyes. She appeared a trifle dazed, but more at ease. Philip smiled at her. "I told you," he murmured. "You are more beautiful than ever."

Then he kissed her forehead and led her to a chair near the window. "Come in," he called when she was seated.

The waiter entered carrying a salver that held two bottles and two glasses, which he set on the table. Philip nodded to him and said he would pour himself. Megaera noticed that the man did not linger, and she guessed that he had been given his pourboire earlier or that Philip had promised he would take care of the staff later. Probably both, she thought amusedly when she saw the alacrity and depth of the servant's bow as he let himself out.

"I was not sure just what you would like to drink, my dear," Philip said, "or whether you would prefer that I did not drink at all."

"No, don't be silly." She shook her head. "You are the most considerate person I have ever met. You cannot forgo your pleasure to pander to my prejudices."

"My pleasure is pleasing you, not in a glass of wine, Meg," Philip said. "I am drunk enough, having tasted your lips. Believe me, it will be no sacrifice to drink ale or cider instead of wine, and I have ratafia for you."

"That's the prettiest speech I ever heard," Megaera exclaimed. She tried to laugh, but her eyes were full of tears, and she had to get up and go over to look at the bottles to conceal it. "You have some very tolerable sherry here," she remarked, striving for calm. "I know. I brought it into the country myself. I wonder which of my customers sells to this inn. I don't distribute so far. I'll have some of this, if you please."

The reminder that she was a smuggler was very deliberate. Philip's consideration, the nearly formal tone of what could only be considered a courtship, was touching her more deeply than she desired. It was very necessary to remind herself that he could never be anything more than a casual lover. Red Meg could want him, but Mrs. Edward Devoran must not fall in love with the illegitimate offspring of a Breton fisherman. There was also the possibility that recalling Philip's attention to her profession would change his manner. That would hurt, Megaera knew, but it would be most salutary.

In fact, if her statement had any effect, it was the opposite of what she feared—or hoped. Philip followed her to the table and uncorked and poured the wine, smelling and tasting it before he offered a second glass to her. Then, instead of renewing the embrace, he gestured her back to her chair and took the one opposite.

"There is one thing we have not considered," he remarked, sipping the wine slowly. "I think it will not be possible to have the goods we have bought delivered either to The Mousehole or to the cave."

Megaera blinked, then her lips twitched. "Are you making polite predinner conversation?" she asked.

Philip's eyes twinkled. "Well, yes. Obviously this is not a subject particularly dear to my heart just now, but I dare not kiss you again because I do not believe I would be able to stop."

"Would that be so terrible?" Megaera asked, her eyes fixed on her glass.

"Yes it would, my beautiful darling," Philip murmured. "I want very much to love you, but not in haste or with an ear cocked for the coming waiter. You would not like to know there was a man waiting outside the door guessing all too accurately what we were doing."

Megaera shuddered. "How ugly."

"Yes, and besides, the lovely dinner I ordered, picking and choosing with such care what I thought would please you, would be all spoiled. That would be an appalling finale to an appalling performance, do you not think?"

"I certainly do!" Megaera agreed, laughing delightedly. "What a clever devil you are. First you turn me down and then you make me glad of it. And you're right about the goods, too. I must think of a place where they can be left without arousing suspicion."

"I am afraid I can be of no help in that, except . . . If we only had one wagonload, I could hire a wagon and drive it myself, but I am afraid we will need more than one."

"You *are* clever, Philip. I could drive the second wagon if we need one."

"Could you? It is not the same as handling a string of ponies. I am not sure you are strong enough, my love. Those cart horses are very powerful, and the

hired beasts have often been abused, so that their
mouths are shod in steel.''

"Yes, probably, but they're also worn down. You
could pick a placid team for me. Surely they would be
less trouble than a pair of whisky-frisky, high-bred,
overfed carriage horses.''

"And when have you driven a high-bred pair?"
Philip asked.

Megaera bit her treacherous lips and turned her
head away. She knew she should tell Philip that the
coachman in the house where she had been employed
had been cozened into teaching her to drive, but she
could not. She preferred simply not to answer. Let him
think what he liked. As long as she could she would
not tell a direct lie. Philip saw her distress and remembered immediately that she was very secretive about
her background. He reached across the table to touch
her hand.

"Sorry, Meg, that was not really a question. I know
you do not like prying, and I had no intention of doing
so. Forgive me?"

"With all my heart. I wish . . ."

But that was a lie. Megaera did not wish she could
tell Philip the truth because she did not believe things
could be the same between them if he knew she was
the daughter of a baron and the heiress of a considerable estate—if she could ever free it from debt. Surely
that would make him either self-conscious or con-
ceited. It is not every smuggler's bastard who had the
daughter of an old and honorable family as a mistress.

The thought was so ugly that tears filled Megaera's
eyes, but she was saved from needing to explain by
the arrival of dinner. It took two waiters and a maid
to carry all the trays of dishes and arrange them, and
by the time they had done so, Megaera had forgotten
all about the degradation of her fine old family name
and was laughing helplessly.

"Philip, you are mad," she protested. "Is this your

tastefully selected dinner? Do you think I am a wolf
or a lion? Or are you expecting an army to join us?"

He looked around at the multitude of dishes with a
faintly bemused expression. "I do seem to have over-
done it a bit," he admitted, then glanced at her with
a glinting smile. "I am afraid my mind was not *completely* on the dinner. The landlord kept suggesting
things and—and I am hungry. They all sounded
good. . . ."

"I'm hungry too," Megaera confessed, still laughing,
"but . . . Well, we shall do our best."

They did, making up for a very scanty luncheon, but
without visibly diminishing the quantity of food. However, Philip had the brilliant idea of keeping back
those dishes which did not need to be hot to be tasty.
They talked easily about food, about wine, about the
business they were doing for Pierre. When they could
eat no more, Philip rang to have the dishes, except for
two or three, removed. He refilled the glasses with wine
and, as he bent over her, Megaera sniffed.

"Have you taken to wearing scent?" she asked.

"Scent?" Philip repeated blankly. "Do you think I
am a man-milliner? No. What can you mean?"

"I don't know, but you do smell delightful. I noticed
it before, but I thought I was imagining things. You
must have touched something in the warehouses I suppose." Her eyes danced. "Very nice. I would encourage
you to continue to use it, but it's a little too delicate
for your coloring."

"Good Lord," Philip said, reaching into his pocket.
"I forgot. I meant to give you these when we first came
in. Look, Meg, they are only trumpery, but are they
not pretty?"

He laid the things he had bought for her on the
table with so innocent an expression of pleased surprise that no woman in the world, no matter how
hardened to selling her favors, could have mistaken
his delight in giving a pretty toy for an attempt to

pay for what he hoped to receive. Since such a transaction had never entered Megaera's mind, there was no shadow on her face to spoil her cry of pleasure.

"I shall treasure them always," she promised, tracing the glowing mother-of-pearl inlay.

"Well, no, they are not worth 'treasuring,' but they are pretty, and the scent—"

"They are treasures to me, Philip," Megaera said. "I think I will never own anything as precious."

"Meg, darling . . ." Philip's voice sounded frightened, and he drew her up to him and held her tight against him.

She clung fiercely, fighting tears and despair. She could not love him. She *could* not! A night's pleasure now and again, that was reasonable, but she could not *love* him nor allow him to love her.

Until that moment Philip had been thinking—as his stepmother would have said with crude French cynicism—with what was in his breeches. He was a considerate, well-bred young man. Kind even to the girls he paid, he had responded unconsciously to Megaera's delicate behavior with gallantry. He knew he preferred being with her to being with any other woman in his entire experience, but he had not considered what that meant until Megaera's simple avowal had pierced his heart.

As he thought them Philip was aware that the words were a silly, conventional cliché of women's romantic novels. But they were also horribly descriptive. Quite literally he had felt as if someone had thrust something sharp through his chest. As beautiful as she was, had no one ever given poor Meg even such worthless trinkets before? Only Philip knew that was not what she meant. It was how they were given, why, and by whom that had invested carved wooden beads with a value far above emeralds and diamonds. In fact, had the things had any intrinsic value, Meg might have been bitterly hurt.

Having got so far in his thoughts, Philip dared go no further to wonder why he was so filled with joy by Meg's confession of love—for that was what her words had meant. It was easier to shut his mind. Instead of facing the terrifying notion that a St. Eyre had fallen in love with a woman who ran a crew of smugglers, he pushed her face up to his and fastened his mouth to hers. Desire, that was what he felt—not love, desire.

There could be no doubt that he felt desire and that Meg was responding to him. Their embrace was so violent that after a moment the buttons on Philip's coat began to cause her acute pain. She struggled to continue kissing Philip and still ease the pressure, but he let her go as soon as he felt her movement.

"Your buttons," Meg gasped before Philip could ask what was wrong.

It was a most fortunate interruption. The too-intense mood was broken. Both were able to laugh while Philip tore off the offending garment, and it provided the perfect excuse for removing Megaera's clothes. Murmuring sympathetic nonsense, Philip opened her peignoir and began to kiss her "bruises." His lips found her breasts, but the tucked and ribboned chemise, enchanting as it was, impeded progress. Philip slid the peignoir over Megaera's shoulders, and the costly garment fell to the floor unheeded in a crumpled heap. The chemise straps followed, but Megaera's fine upstanding breasts, nipples now erect with excitement, supported the chemise and it would not slip off by itself.

Not at all discouraged by this impediment, Philip went to work on it—but not by any crude expedient such as pushing the chemise down with his hands. He did allow his fingers to pluck gently at the back, but lips and chin worked at the front—kiss, push, kiss. Megaera's hands fluttered uncertainly to Philip's shoulders, to his hair, to his cravat. Here they steadied. The process that directed her actions could not be

called thought. The excitement that was sweeping over
her had suspended rational decision, but Megaera
knew what she wanted anyway. She had an intense
desire to see and touch Philip's skin.

She drew the pin from his cravat and dropped it
to the floor. The folds loosened at once. Her attempts
to pull it off were somewhat uncertain, distracted as
she was by the waves of pleasure Philip's mouth was
creating, but she got it loose and dropped it just about
the time that one rosy nipple was bared. Philip seized
on it at once, nibbling gently with lip-sheathed teeth.
Megaera sighed shudderingly and she caught at
Philip's shoulders because she felt her knees were
about to buckle.

Although Philip was by no means calm, he was not
as lost in a sea of sensation as Megaera. The sensations
were, after all, quite familiar to him. He was thus
still capable of keeping a fixed purpose in mind, and
that fixed purpose was to make this experience as
perfect as possible for his partner. Oddly enough, the
need to think and plan, to restrain the satisfaction of
his desire, heightened his enjoyment enormously. He
was aware that he had no hold on Meg, that he must
make her willing to participate again by his own skill
as a lover.

He was also aware that her reactions to him were
completely real, totally honest. This time he was not
a paying client who must be flattered and cajoled into
coming again and into paying a little extra. Although
he did not think of it consciously, the realization came
to him that what he had assumed was pleasure in his
company and performance might well have been no
more than acting. Even if it were not, it could have
no meaning. Clients were not chosen for their youth
and good looks. As a relief from the old, the ugly, the
cruel ones, Philip might be pleasant.

Meg, he was sure, had never been a whore. He
guessed she was not a virgin because of her readiness

to yield to him, but it was obvious from her actions that her sexual experience must have been very limited and that she had been a passive rather than an active partner. Everything she had done showed that it was he, as a particular person, rather than the act itself, she desired. And that, untainted by any commercial transaction, was both so flattering and so stimulating that Philip, who was normally a considerate lover, was pushed to an even keener sense of his partner's needs.

Having interpreted Meg's quick clutch at him with perfect accuracy, Philip released her nipple and caught her up in his arms. She was light enough and co-operative enough—flinging her arms around his neck to hold herself close—that he could free one hand to push the screen away and pull back the counterpane and blankets. As he set her on the bed he slid his hands up and pulled the chemise off over her head. The cessation of active stimulation permitted Megaera to catch her breath. It did nothing, however, to diminish her desire to see Philip's bare body.

"Take your clothes off," she said, far too deep in her physical need to be shy.

Philip licked his lips and took a deep breath. Meg's demand had driven him dangerously near a crude grab at quick satisfaction by exciting him far beyond his normal level of passion. The naked desire for him was very different from the prostitutes' practiced—and, now he realized, indifferent—attempts to stimulate him. He yanked off his shirt, pulled off his boots, and shoved breeches and underpants off his narrow hips in one motion.

Meg's sigh, her half-parted lips, the wide-opened eyes that ran up and down his body in eager examination, made him tremble with desire. He was at the bed in an instant, touching, kissing, fondling. Meg sighed and quivered, stroking the smooth, dark skin—so different, so exciting—winding her fingers in the black curling hair that grew in a wide triangle on Philip's chest. She returned his kisses, pressing her lips to his neck when his mouth was busy elsewhere. Abandoning his chest, Meg began tracing the thin line of hair that was different, flat and sleek, and descended from the down-pointing apex of the triangle and grew over Philip's belly to widen into the pubic bush.

Softly, under his breath, without releasing the breast he was alternately kissing and sucking, Philip began to groan. He could not hold off much longer. One hand found the button of her pantelets. He fumbled but found the minor hindrance exciting rather than frustrating. The girls in the bawdy houses never wore such inconvenient garments. Under their wrappers they were usually nude. Fortunately the button came undone before Philip lost patience and wrenched it off. One hand slipped under, seeking Meg's Mount of Venus and what lay beyond. Meg began to whimper and twitch, thrusting uncertainly toward the touch that was driving her wild.

Her response made it impossible, and clearly unnecessary, for Philip to wait. He lifted his head momentarily to see what he was doing and stripped off Meg's pantelets, mounted her, positioned himself, and thrust. Meg cried out, partly in relief but also a little in pain. She was not a virgin, but it had been a very long time since she had had congress with a man. For all her desire and her eagerness, she was stretched by Philip's considerable endowment. He paused at once, breathing painfully hard, obviously very surprised.

"Sorry," he gasped. "I am sorry. I did not guess—"

"Never mind," Meg whispered, winding her legs around him to help him along. "I love you. I want you. Love me."

Chapter 10

Philip took full advantage of Megaera's urging. His surprise had cooled his initial heat, and he moved cautiously until he was sure he was no longer hurting her. It took longer than he had expected from her eagerness to satisfy her, but she came to climax at last, crying out and clutching convulsively at her lover. Philip then abandoned himself to his own pleasure. This seemed to give Meg as much delight as her own orgasm, which was another pleasant surprise to Philip. Oddly, Meg went even further. When Philip had caught his breath and began to lift himself off her, she held him tight. "Did I not content you, darling?" he asked, somewhat startled and worried, knowing there was nothing more he could do for a while.

"Oh, yes," Megaera sighed. "Nothing so wonderful ever happened to me before."

"How you flatter me," Philip said. His voice was light, but he was quite sincere. "But, love, I will crush you if I lie atop you now."

"I don't care. I can't bear it to be over."

Her naïveté was adorable—and totally convincing. Philip knew that either he was her first lover or, if she had been used before, it was just that—she had been used, not loved. He kissed her lips gently, then her forehead, cheeks, and chin, little light kisses of affection rather than passion.

"Do not talk so silly, my darling. Love is never over. It only rests to renew itself. Let me turn so I will not hurt you. I assure you that you cannot wish to lie closer to me than I wish to lie to you."

He rolled sideways, pulling her with him, surprised to feel himself growing harder instead of slipping out of her. There was no drive to the sensation yet, only a lazy urge not to withdraw. Philip was perfectly content to remain coupled, and Megaera could hardly believe her own joy. Edward had succeeded in arousing her several times, but he had never brought her to climax because he never cared enough to notice. Even if he had, he would not have bothered to hold back his own pleasure to satisfy her. And when he was finished, he was finished. There were no sweet words, no soft kisses, no postlove fondling. Edward simply withdrew, left her, and went to sleep in his own room.

At first Megaera continued to cling as if she expected Philip to push her away (that had happened to her too), but it very soon became apparent that he had spoken the truth. She could see that he was enjoying her, admiring her, truly as eager to listen to her soft murmurs of love as to reply to them with kisses and caresses. It was all so full of joy. Philip laughed at her fascination with his dark skin, with the way the hair grew on his body, but he laughed kindly, inviting rather than rejecting her attentions.

Slowly the gentle touches of investigation grew more directed. The kisses lasted longer, lips parting to invite the tongue's invasion. They made love a second time, more slowly but with even greater intensity because they were more sure of each other and did not need to hold back anything for fear of offending.

When they were finished this time, Megaera did

not cling. Her contentment was thus even greater because, although Philip lifted himself off her at once, he drew her back into his arms and held her most tenderly. After their exertions they slept very soundly; nonetheless each was dimly aware of the other's presence, neither having ever before slept a night through in the company of another person. It was strange to wake in the morning touching one another, and a joy so incomparable that it was near to pain for each to see the delight in the other's face.

They made love once more with the dim light of early morning stealing around the edges of the curtains, and slept again, to be awakened by the maid's voice reminding them that they had asked to be called by eight of the clock. Philip groaned, answered the girl, then turned and looked at Meg pathetically.

"Are you really going to make me go out and hire a wagon?" he asked. And then he put back a tendril of hair that had fallen over her face and sighed. "You are *so* beautiful, Meg. I cannot believe it, but what I said—oh, half jesting—it is true. Each time I look at you, you are more beautiful than before."

Megaera's eyes filled with tears, but she did not dare answer in kind. She was treading very dangerous ground. Everything Philip said, everything he did, raised him higher in any comparison with the men of her own class—at least those with whom she had an intimate acquaintance. And Philip was sounding more and more as if he really loved her. No, she could not encourage that; it would be cruel to allow him to believe she could be his. Only she could not—not if her life had hung on it—hurt him at that moment. All she could do was avoid the problem.

"I hope," she said as tartly as she could, "that your eye trouble does not interfere with your selection of the cart horses."

"What eye trouble?" Philip asked, so puzzled that he let her go and leaned back.

"The eye trouble that makes you see me so peculiarly." Megaera forced herself to laugh, but it came out as a shy, gentle sound rather than the hard, cynical chuckle she had hoped to achieve.

Philip laughed too, but he sighed resignedly and got out of bed when she held off his attempt to kiss her again. "Slave driver," he groaned. "I never met such a woman. What does Pierre have which I do not have that inspires you to such devotion?"

"An unlimited supply of brandy and wine," Megaera replied, but her voice was happy.

She had escaped any declaration of love on Philip's part. He was only teasing her now. She lay a moment longer to let Philip finish using the chamber pot, then got out of bed too. The disorder in the room made her blush faintly. Her peignoir lay where Philip had dropped it in the middle of the floor; her slippers came next, one at a time, as she had pushed them off while Philip carried her to the bed; her pantelets and chemise were on the floor also, but beside the bed. Megaera giggled as she suddenly thought one could follow the "rake's" progress by the position of the discarded garments.

Philip's clothing was even more widely scattered because he had flung each article away in haste when he undressed. He had pulled on his drawers and breeches and then opened the door to take in the morning tea tray. Now he was wandering around, picking up and putting on a stocking here, a boot there, mumbling to himself about how things had gotten into such peculiar places. Megaera paused in her own dressing to watch him, almost sick with the intensity of her tenderness. She had not realized her feelings could be so fierce nor so strongly aroused by such simple, silly, everyday actions. Then she turned away sharply, knowing she must not permit herself to think or feel that way.

She had both petticoat and dress on when a more obscene epithet, quite loud, drew her attention. "What's the matter?" she asked.

"Sorry." Philip looked abashed at the language he had used. "I have pulled two buttons off my shirt. It does not matter. My waistcoat will hide it."

"If you can find the buttons, I will sew them back on," Megaera offered.

Philip looked around vaguely, clearly without much hope, but one button showed up nearly at the toe of his boot, white against the dark carpet. Megaera found the other almost as easily. It was only then that Philip asked how she would sew them on.

"With needle and thread," she replied, laughing at him. "No rational woman goes abroad without a paper of pins and needle and thread in her reticule. If she has them, there is hardly ever a need, but does she dare step one foot out of the house without them, then some great clumsy brute puts a foot on the flounce of her skirt instantly."

"But you do not have a flounced skirt," Philip remarked.

Some of the things women did and said puzzled him. Usually he paid no attention, having little interest in matters that seemed of enormous importance to them and of monumental insignificance to him. Now it was different. He found himself passionately interested in everything Meg did and said. He wanted to know her thoughts and why she thought them— even about needles and thread. He wanted to know everything about her. Meg looked blank when he spoke and then raised her eyes to heaven as she took the shirt from his hands.

"Philip, you are still asleep," she said. "All I meant was that a sensible woman is prepared for tears or seams coming undone. A woman's clothing is made of more fragile materials and also has more of a

tendency to get caught in things than a man's. And
some gowns are flounced. One always carries needle
and thread."

"Oh."

She glanced up briefly from her threading of the
needle and looked hastily back at her work. The expression on Philip's face was dangerous, terribly dangerous. "No," she gasped. "It is impossible. You must
return to France when Pierre comes."

There was a minute of silence so deep that it was
apparent Philip was holding his breath. Then air
sighed out of his lungs. "Yes." The word was spoken
so softly that Megaera hardly could hear. Her hands
trembled and she pricked herself. She could sense that
Philip was no longer looking at her. She sewed, half
blinded by tears that she would not permit to fall,
bit the thread, started on the second button, then
dared a glance at him. Philip had walked to the window and was looking out.

"It is not in my power to refuse to go," he said. "It
is not a question of money, Meg. I have an obligation.
I cannot explain it, but you must believe that if it
were a matter of choice I would never leave you. Give
me these two weeks, Meg—or however long until
Pierre comes back."

The sick terror that had gripped Megaera after she
spoke receded. She had thought that either Philip
would be furious or that he would laugh cruelly at
her for thinking he wanted more than a night's
pleasure. The answer she had was a terrible double-
edged sword, Megaera knew, but just now she did not
care. All that mattered was that one edge had killed
her fear and given her happiness. Later she would pay
and pay bitterly for this present joy, when the other
edge came to bear and loneliness cut her. For this
moment the relief was so great that she closed her
mind to the future. All she permitted herself to think
about was the tender pleading which confirmed that

Philip felt as deeply about her as she did about him.

"Yes," she whispered.

Philip was beside her immediately, pulling the shirt out of her suddenly idle hands, seizing them, kissing them. "I will come back," he promised. Then he realized he might not be able to come back. He might be caught, imprisoned, even killed. "If it is possible," he amended. "I . . . God, I want to tell you, but it is not my secret, Meg. You understand, do you not?"

"Yes. Yes, I do understand."

Megaera thought she did, assuming Philip was speaking of some obligation to his "father." She assumed, also, that Pierre might be involved in more activities than simple smuggling, and that Philip might be indispensable to those other activities. It did not occur to her that Philip might be in danger, only that Pierre might send him far away—to India, or the West Indies, or to Louisiana.

And Megaera understood obligation to one's parent, even when that parent had done little besides engendering her and causing trouble. Surely if she could endure her father, refrain from making him a prisoner in his own home, struggle to keep him from drinking himself to death even though that death would be a release for her, then surely Philip owed a "father" such as Pierre a devoted duty. It was wrong for Pierre not to have married Philip's mother, perhaps, but Megaera knew there must have been a good reason for it. Pierre was an honest man; he would not slough off a responsibility to a pregnant woman or his child. In fact Megaera knew he had not done so by the warmth and affection openly displayed between Pierre and Philip.

"Oh, Meg," Philip exclaimed, "you are the most wonderful woman alive, I swear it! Anyone else would have pouted and wept and fallen into a fit of the vapors because I did not set her above my duty. I do not know how I . . . Never mind. We have two weeks.

That can be a very long time. Let us not think about anything else."

"But we must," Megaera reminded him with a smile in her voice. She pulled her hands gently out of his grasp and picked up the shirt. "I must think of how to spend the rest of Pierre's money, and you must think of how to transport the goods, at least as far as the blasted tree."

"Yes, but first we must think of breakfast. I hope this tea is not stone cold. No, it is not, but there is nothing here but toast fingers. Give me that shirt, Meg, and I will go down and order breakfast."

"There is all that food from last night," Megaera protested. "We never touched it after—" She stopped abruptly and blushed.

Philip laughed. "No. Not that I was not hungry," he said wickedly. "It was just that I knew I would fall flat on my face if I tried to get out of bed. You wrung me out finely, my love."

"Liar," Megaera retorted. "It was only that your mind had fallen into a hole, and . . . Oh, dear! Stop laughing like that, you monster. You know I didn't mean *that*." She paused while Philip choked on his own mirth, then said with dignity, "In any case, there is plenty of food."

He looked under the dish covers while Megaera fastened the thread on the second button, then took his shirt and put it on. "The cold meat is fine for me," he agreed, "but do you not want eggs and streaky rashers, or—"

"No! Goodness, Philip, if I remain in your company long I will be too fat to walk. You will need to wheel me about in a barrow. Consider my poor pony. Tea and toast is quite enough for me. I must go down to the jakes. Will you fasten my sleeves, please? I find they are much easier to undo than to do up."

"How convenient," Philip murmured, kissing her on the ear as he began to button her sleeves.

After a moment he started to wonder who did up all the tiny buttons if Meg found them difficult. In fact, those on the right sleeve must be almost impossible to do with the left hand alone. Surely it was necessary to hold the sleeve together with one hand and button with the other? Could Meg have a maid? Nonsense, Philip told himself. It was ridiculous. The buttons were only difficult for him because he was unused to such tiny things so close together. Women knew how to manage from long practice, and the only reason Meg had asked him to help was, no doubt, that she was in a hurry to use the jakes.

When Megaera returned they breakfasted, Philip substantially and Megaera lightly, then went out to complete their round of the warehouses. Neither had ever been so comfortable or content. The underlying tension of the preceding day—the desire and uncertainty—was gone. Passion remained, but both knew it would be satisfied at a proper time and place, and it gave a warm, heady spice to the day's doings rather than making them nervous. Deep back there was a shadow, of course, but it did not come forward to cloud the mind and heart while one was busy and happy.

At last they came to the end of Pierre's gold. Philip was relieved that two carts would not be needed. A really large one with four horses plus loading the carriage with as much as it would hold should be sufficient. Philip spent the afternoon picking up from one warehouse after another, then arranged to have the loaded wagon stored in a strong locked shed so that the goods would not be stolen overnight. He said he was exhausted, for he had helped load and was not accustomed to that kind of work.

Megaera received that statement with more sympathy than Philip expected and promptly urged that they should have dinner in their room again rather than dining out. She did not ask whether Philip was

revived by the rest or by her presence or had perhaps
pretended to be more tired than he was to encourage
just the decision she had made. Megaera did not
know and did not care. Any of the suppositions were
flattering to her, and she had intended to find an
excuse of her own to stay in if Philip had not provided one. She told herself she was trying to avoid
the danger of meeting someone she knew in the town,
but she certainly made no effort to avoid Philip's
advances. In any case his fatigue—if he was fatigued—
did not affect his sexual performance. It was Megaera
who had to remind him, reluctantly, that they were
to be called at first light. It would take much longer
to draw the heavy wagon mostly uphill toward Bolliet
than it had taken to drive the light carriage down to
Falmouth.

For Jean and Henri the weeks since they had lost
Philip had not been nearly as pleasant as they had
been for their intended victim. It had taken far longer
to fix the carriage than could have been expected. Jean
believed that the wheelwright put off working on their
job whenever any other work was offered to him, because he was prejudiced against the French. This
added to the fury Jean felt over Philip's escape. His
first impulse to abandon the project disappeared, and
as his rage increased, it made him more determined
to catch and kill St. Eyre.

When at long last the carriage was repaired and
Jean had grudgingly paid the charges, they resumed
their journey. Because Jean did not wish to leave a
trail of inquiries about a man who soon would be
found dead, they took the chance of driving directly
to Bodmin. There Jean sent Henri to ask the questions. Perhaps he would be able to be rid of two
problems at once by having Henri associated with
Philip.

Once St. Eyre had been killed, Henri could be killed also. The weapons could be left, one in each dead hand. A duel in which both had died would explain both deaths without any need for further investigation, which might be embarrassing. It would clear up the problem of how to be rid of Henri without suspicion falling on himself. All he had to do was appear as little as possible. This was not difficult. Jean allowed Henri to question ostlers, stableboys, and innkeepers while he did the heavier task of unstrapping the luggage and following the servants up to inspect their room.

After Bodmin their progress was slow because it was necessary to stop at every inn where Philip might possibly have spent the night. Henri became rather over-full of tea and coffee, but he did pick up Philip's trail. He had made no effort to conceal it, of course, but it would have made no difference if he had. Henri remembered how he had identified Spite in Exeter. Although more than a week had passed and many innkeepers and servants had forgotten Philip, the ostlers and stableboys remembered Spite's frightening if harmless habit.

At Penzance the trail ended. They tried St. Just first, then St. Ives, then all the towns that were well-known havens for smugglers. Henri had a reasonably logical story now. They were on the trail of a French agent, a man who pretended to be either born of a noble English family or an émigré loyal to the country that had provided a haven for him. This man was trying to escape via a smuggling ship, with stolen papers that would protect either himself or another spy and was also carrying out important information.

To support this tale Jean had prepared some papers with large seals stamped on red sealing wax. Since most of the people to whom Henri spoke were illiterate, these seals were sufficiently impressive. A few could read, but even they were ignorant people. Jean took good care to direct Henri to avoid anyone who might have authority or knowledge enough to realize the documents were only a crude sham.

They were not ill received. Cornishmen might be sympathetic to smugglers, but they were as opposed to "Boney" as any other Briton. Along the roads questions about the "French" stranger were answered with alacrity and honesty—no one had seen him in any inn past Penzance where he had asked the road to Drift. But at Drift no one had seen a "Frenchman" riding a horse that laid back its ears and showed its teeth.

If Henri had asked for Mr. St. Eyre in Drift, he would have been directed to Moreton Place. Everyone in the town knew Philip, but they knew him as Lord Kevern's school friend. What was more, he had never stabled Spite in Drift nor, after the first time when he asked directions to Moreton Place, had he ever ridden Spite into town. He had been resting his hard-worked mount and taken a rest from Spite's cruel gait himself by riding Perce's horses. Thus, whatever Philip's accent and however close his features to Henri's description, no one connected the two. Lord Kevern's friend, who escorted the Misses Moreton and was so elegant and polite, could not possibly be in any way connected with this French spy that was being sought.

Two days later—in fact Philip and Megaera were about halfway to Falmouth at the time—Perce stopped at the Rich Lode in Drift. Naturally enough the landlord told him of their one bit of excitement.

"What did they say this man looked like?" Perce asked. It was a likely story, and Perce wanted to spread the word among his own friends.

The landlord obliged with a description of Philip and Spite. Perce himself did not recognize the description of Philip particularly—there were a large number of dark-eyed, black-haired, dark-skinned, tall, athletic men in the world—but the moment the landlord mentioned the rawboned bay that put back his ears and showed his teeth, Perce had all he could do to keep his mouth from dropping open.

"Why didn't you send the man along to m'father, Felton? Surely the one to help catch a spy is the JP. What did he look like? What did he say his name was?"

"I didn't see him myself, my lord," the landlord replied. "He talked to Jemmy the ostler. To tell the truth, I didn't think about it till now, but it's a bit odd he didn't come in and speak to me. As to Lord Moreton, I just supposed he *had* been at the Place and his lordship told him to come down here and ask."

"I'll check that, but I don't think he was. I don't like this either, Felton. That horse they mentioned is Mr. St. Eyre's mount."

"Mr. St. Eyre?" Felton echoed. "But surely that must be a mistake. Mr. St. Eyre isn't a French spy."

"Of course he isn't! Went to school with him! I've known him since we were boys and he hates Bonaparte worse than we do. What I don't like is this man sneaking around asking about him. If you want information for an honest purpose, you go to the authorities. Now, it may be a coincidence, but if it's Philip he wants—well, I want him first. Do you mind if I have a talk with Jemmy?"

"No, of course not, my lord. Do you want me to have him in?"

"No. He'll think he's done something wrong and forget half of what he knows out of fright. I'll go out to the stable. But if that man shows up again or if anyone asks for Mr. St. Eyre by name or by description, send him up to the house. Mr. St. Eyre isn't there anymore—but don't you say that. I want to know why someone is looking for Philip and who it is."

Having received the landlord's assurances, Perce went out to the stable. Jemmy was by no means an idiot; indeed, he was very clever about horses, but there his mind stopped. All Perce could ascertain was that Jemmy had been shown a paper with a big red seal on it. This had so fixed his mind that he had no idea what his questioner looked like. He could describe the carriage and the horses minutely; however, this was not much help since both were the commonest kind of rented article. Jemmy would even be able to recognize them again, but it was unlikely from his lack of articulateness that anyone else could.

There was nothing more to be discovered, Perce decided at last, tossing Jemmy a coin and telling him that he must tell Mr. Felton at once, *at once,* if anyone came around showing papers like that again. Also, Jemmy was to tell anyone who showed him big red seals to go up to Moreton Place, where his questions would be answered better. Perce was just turning away, much disturbed, when Jemmy dredged one more fact from his memory.

"They wus two," he announced.

"Two?" Perce repeated, puzzled.

"Niver give me t'orses t'old. Summon in t'chaise 'eld 'em. Niver come out, though."

That did not make Perce any happier, but he thanked Jemmy, took his own horse, and rode slowly home. Never in his life had he been at such a loss. He had no idea what to do. It was clear enough to him that the men who were hunting Philip had simply reversed the situation to some extent. They must be French agents. Whether the talk of the papers and information Philip was carrying was true or not was irrelevant. Someone was trying to stop him from getting to France. Perce cursed so long and so viciously that his horse picked up his pace, sensing his master's rage.

He could not warn Philip because he had not the faintest idea where Philip had gone. There was a chance that he was already in France, which would solve part of the problem, but Perce did not think so. Philip had said that he would send or bring Spite back to Moreton Place before he left. It would be safe enough to leave him there where there were so many other horses that Spite would be lost in the crowd.

However, even if Philip was safely across, these men should be apprehended. They were a danger in themselves, being spies. In addition, they might lie in wait to catch Philip on his return. Perce had no idea when this would be. Philip had implied a few weeks but admitted this was only a wild guess and it might be considerably longer. In fact Philip had said that he might not be returning to Cornwall at all. In that case, Perce was to bring Spite back to London when he came to Town for the Season.

What impeded Perce was the fear that any action on his part might endanger his friend or expose him. What was necessary was to spread the word that the spy hunter was really the spy. Perce gave this matter considerable thought and decided that French agents, although not welcome, would scarcely raise the same passion in Cornwall as customs inspectors. Yes, that was it! That would work!

Perce decided he would pass the word that the man or men claiming to be seeking a French spy were really customs inspectors attempting to obtain information on the smuggling gangs through this device, that the person they said they were seeking did not exist. The only trouble was whether the tale would spread fast enough. Unfortunately Lord Moreton was of a sufficiently ethical nature that he would have no dealings with smugglers. He did not carry these principles to any ridiculous lengths, of course. He bought his wine and brandy from the "gentlemen"—although at present it seemed to be a "lady" who was delivering the goods—just like everyone else. Nor did Lord Moreton go *looking* for evidence of smuggling. However, he would not out of hand acquit a man against whom evidence was brought, and he would not ignore evidence concerning smuggling if a complaint was made.

Thus, the "gentlemen" did their best not to provide evidence around Moreton Place. Aside from actual deliveries, the gangs avoided Drift, Catchall, and Sancreed. If any of the tenants on Moreton lands were employed by smugglers, they kept it secret. Ordinarily this was an agreeable arrangement all around. The smugglers were safe as long as no one complained, and Lord Moreton was not forced to choose between offending his neighbors or his conscience.

In this case, however, Perce was at a marked disadvantage. He did not have the direct leads to any gang that many members of the gentry had. He would have to pass the word through his friends, who could pass it along to their tenants who were involved with smugglers. On the other hand, word that came out of Moreton Place would carry considerable weight. Lord Moreton would not *support* the smugglers, but no doubt people would believe that he would resent "foreigners"—that is, customs inspectors from London or any area outside of west Cornwall—who invaded his territory.

As a first step Perce rode home and warned the head groom and Butler about anyone who came inquiring about Spite or Philip. Such a person should be held, without violence, if possible, but any way if strong measures were needed, until Perce or Lord Moreton had seen and spoken to him or them. Then he told his father, who was not in the least surprised, having guessed (as Perce had known he would) the truth. Lord Moreton approved his son's plans, although in fact he had not expected Perce to bother making any. After he had absorbed the full impact of the working of Perce's mind, he had something to add.

"Perhaps we can take it from both ends, Perce. You pass the word among the young bloods, and I'll pass it among the local customs men."

Perce burst out laughing. "By God, Fa, that's clever. I never stopped to think the thing all the way through. But wouldn't they think it's odd that the inspectors didn't go to them first?"

"Of course not! They're all so corrupt that they expect both periodic investigations and undercover attempts to catch them and the smugglers they protect. What I will suggest is the truth—that the men are not investigators but French agents. The locals may not believe that, but they'll jump at the chance to use that excuse to seize them and bring them to me, which will expose what they really are."

"Yes . . ." Perce drew the word out, frowning. "But I think you'd better make it damn clear that whoever catches them must hand them over. After all, Fa, we don't want these men knocked on the head and dropped off the nearest cliff. Not that they'd be any loss, but I think they should be questioned."

"Yes, indeed. Good gracious, Perce, I never knew you had even a thread of social conscience. I'll have to revise my view of you. Would you like a seat in Parliament?"

"I might some day, but not yet, Fa. The trouble is, I don't know what I want. If I thought I'd be a shade of use, I'd have asked for a pair of colors, but I can't believe that another inexperienced subaltern would be any real advantage to our army. I'd do as a staff officer, but—"

"For all his fat and bluster, York is a good man, Perce. He loves the service—"

"No! I know, Fa, with Fred on the *Royal Sovereign* and Robert in India you aren't too eager to have me in the mess too. That's why I haven't plagued out your life, but I—I don't know how much longer I can bear to do nothing. Aide-de-camp to York won't do. I know his good points, but his ADC's aren't among them. He does the work with the men at the Horse Guards and keeps the ADC's around to play cards with him."

"I didn't know, Perce. I'm ashamed to admit it, but you had me completely fooled. I kept thanking God that you were content to . . . Dammit, boy, that face of yours is like a wax mask. You could—" Lord Moreton's voice broke off abruptly. "That face must be worth a fortune at a gambling table—*and* it would be at a diplomatic conference, too. Possess your soul in patience for a little longer, Perce. We'll see what turns up."

With that Perce was reasonably content. His father was a sensible man, what could be called a real downy bird, and would neither forget nor suggest another palliative like the Duke of York's staff. Perce knew his responsibilities as his father's heir. He could also see that the struggle against Bonaparte was likely to be a long business. He could wait to deliver a telling blow against his country's enemy in a way that would not be too likely to leave Moreton Place without a master. For a moment he fixed his attention on doing what he could to help Philip along with his bit.

Unfortunately, as far as laying hands on Jean and Henri, Perce was too late. Although the people in inland towns answered questions willingly enough, those in smuggling centers were deaf, dumb, and blind. Having made inquiries at those coastal villages they could reach and drawn a blank—no one had *ever* seen or heard of a smuggler, or a stranger either, on the entire coast of west Cornwall, as far as they could tell—Jean and Henri had returned to Penzance. Henri again proposed abandoning their quest. By now, however, they had spent a good part of the money d'Ursine had given them on the task he had assigned. Jean pointed out that they had expended a great deal of time and energy, too, and they were no better off than when they first took the job. If they did not bring back the papers and the name of the ship and captain who was willing to transport English spies into France, they would get nothing for their pains.

They had been going about it the wrong way, Jean

said. He should have realized no one in a smuggler's haven would talk to an official of any kind. What they needed was someone involved in the smuggling. He could question, find Philip, and hire a gang to kill him and to discover what they wanted to know.

Naturally enough Henri was delighted with this idea, particularly since Jean took it upon himself to make these arrangements. Henri had been greatly irritated by having to do all the questioning and then being blamed when there were no results. Jean's purpose was far from beneficent. He intended to be the one to hire the gang so that they would obey him. It would be much easier that way to arrange Henri's death at the same time as Philip's.

At first it seemed that Penzance would be no more fertile a field than the smaller coastal villages. No one knew of any smuggling; no one had ever heard of any man employed in such an enterprise; there were no ships plying between Cornwall and France. Had not he heard there was a war? Being cleverer than Henri, Jean drank the excellent French wines served and changed his tack. He was not interested in ships or smugglers. He knew nothing of whether transport to France was possible. There was a man who had stolen papers from him and he wanted the papers back. He wanted a native Cornishman to find the man for him. He was not interested in anything else.

He left his name in many places together with the name of the inn in which he was staying. The next day there was a message. If Jean would come to The Pirate on Water Street after dark, he would learn something to his advantage.

Much encouraged by this sign of interest, Jean hurried to the assignation. The alehouse—for that was all it was—was not prepossessing, but Jean was not in the least put off by the blistered sign that creaked over the door, the desperate need for paint of the weathered boards, or the smell, smoke, and filth of the common room. Nor was he in the least surprised when the room fell silent on his entrance. He was quite accustomed to that hostile silence by now. This time, however, it did not last long.

A heavy, brutal-looking man rose from one of the side tables and asked if he was John Treeport. Concealing a shudder at the mangling, he agreed that was his name.

"And you're looking for a Frenchy what's took summat of yourn?"

"Yes," Jean agreed.

"Tall cove, wery dark o' t'skin?"

Jean took a breath. It seemed as if after all his trouble he was finally approaching the pot of gold. "Yes. Have you seen him?"

"Yair." It was a lie. He had never seen Philip, but that did not matter in the least. All he had to do was to repeat Jean's description back to him. "Black eyes, black hair, riding a big bay what bites."

"Yes! Yes, that is he. Where—"

"Wait up now. What's in it fer me?"

"Let's sit down," Jean said. "This man has done me and this country a grave injury. I will pay, of course, for information alone, but he is a very dangerous person, and my own companion is in his power, I believe, although I discovered this only recently. I will pay much better for . . ."

Jean hesitated, not wishing to say in plain words what was obvious—that he wanted Philip dead. Probably it would make no difference. No one would take this dirty brute's word above his, even if he did intend betrayal. However, Jean did not need to search for a euphemism.

"Want 'im 'ushed then?"

"Hushed?" Jean repeated.

"Put t'bed wiv a shovel! Deaded!"

"Yes—that is, he is very dangerous—"

"Carries bulldogs, does 'e?"

"Bulldogs? No. I don't believe the man has a dog with him. Why—"

"Don't be a fool, will 'e? Has 'e barkers? Pistols?"

"I'm very sorry that I am unacquainted with thieves' cant," Jean said coldly. "Yes, he does carry pistols, and a knife, too. In fact he has already shot one man dead— right through the head."

If Jean had not been so intent on his own indignation, he might have noticed a most unnatural gleam of satisfaction in the eyes of his companion, who now introduced himself as Black Bart and said firmly that, in this case, he didn't think he and Jean alone would be able to do the job. Since Bart had never heard of Philip before, Jean's questions about him started a plan in his head, and although he had no idea where Philip was, he was not in the least afraid of Philip's ability with pistols. What had come to him after he heard of Jean's search for a man who would hunt down someone for him was a marvelous plan to fool everyone all around and accomplish his own purpose, which was to kill Red Meg. When Jean agreed to what he said with alacrity, Bart was halfway home.

Jean, of course, had no intention of assisting personally at all, although he intended to go along. He made no protest when Bart suggested six men. He bargained a little over the price, but it was not, to Jean's mind, exorbitant for a murder, and he yielded on that, too. His pliability did him no good in Bart's eyes. He was now, in that "gentleman's" opinion, a mark to be gulled on all points. In any other situation Bart would have taken Jean's money, knocked him on the head, and dropped him off the pier. However, he had his own row to hoe. He would hire the men Jean wanted, but not to look for or kill Philip—in whom he had not the slightest interest.

Through the men in Megaera's group who preferred "the good old days," Bart was aware of the days when Pierre brought a cargo. From his own investigations and guesses he had discovered that Meg paid Pierre on the night following the delivery at The Mousehole. What he planned was to use the men for whom Jean was paying to ambush Meg before she got to the inn. This would have to be done quite near the place, since Bart had no way of finding out just how Meg came to The Mousehole. Knowing her, he even suspected that she used a different route every time.

The reasons Bart had not made any attempt to kill Meg and John previously were two: He had no money with which to hire men—every penny he had ever made he spent as soon as it came into his hands—and he did not want to admit that he wanted to "get" Red Meg. Since he had been in Penzance, Bart had found there was an exaggerated opinion afloat about her. John had been invested with an aura of invincibility, and Meg herself was reputed to be a witch.

Although Bart knew better and said so, he also knew it was useless to argue. Had he had enough money he could have compensated fear by payment. But this would be much better. The men would think they were going after some stupid French spy. He would bring them to a confrontation, shoot Meg himself, and the others would take care of the dummy out of self-defense. Then he could shoot Jean, too. Probably he would even have some more money and a watch on him. It would be a nice profit all around.

Jean's questions roused Bart from this pleasant reverie. "No, I don't know where 'e be now," he admitted, "but I knows where 'e *will* be, and I've friends what'll warn me when 'e comes. There's a place what we can 'ide. We'll need 'orses. It's, oh, four miles—thereabout."

"When will this be?"

Bart shrugged. " 'Nother week, maybe. Can't be sure. Gi' us t'clinkers so I can pay t'men."

But Jean was not such a fool as that. He had not carried more than a few guineas with him. These he gave Bart, ostentatiously showing that his purse was empty. "That's enough to hire the horses and give the men a taste. I'll pay half the remaining sum when we start and half when we return here—if the French agent is dead and I have recovered the papers."

Bart scowled horribly, but he realized that this man had dealt with his kind before and was not really a silly mark. It didn't matter, since his purpose was to kill Red Meg, not to make money. Nonetheless, it really sealed Jean's death warrant as far as Bart was concerned, and he made a mental note not to underestimate Jean again.

Chapter 11

As Philip remarked, two weeks can be a long time, especially if one is sad or in pain. Unfortunately, when days are peacefully slept away and nights are full of work and joy, two weeks can fly swiftly away.

While Philip and Megaera waited for John to bring the ponies to carry Pierre's goods to safe concealment in the main cave, they had decided on what to do. Philip would return the wagon to Falmouth, picking up Spite from the stable in Penzance so that he would have a mount for the ride back. Meanwhile Megaera would arrange the return of the chaise. She did not say how and Philip, growing wise, did not ask. During the day and a half it would take Philip to return the wagon, Megaera made more habitable the one remaining room in the house on the cliff.

That house had almost certainly been inhabited by wreckers—Megaera feared they were members of her own family, although she made no effort to find out—in the seventeenth century. As the Bolliets grew more respectable they began to frown on so brutal and inhumane an activity. The small house, so convenient for setting fires to lead ships astray so that they would founder on the rocks instead of making a safe harbor,

had been abandoned and allowed to fall into ruin.
One room, where the chimney provided a strong base,
remained reasonably sound.

When she began smuggling, Megaera had had John
tighten this room until it was weatherproof, and she
had furnished it partially with a table and a comfortable chair. Whenever Pierre was due, she had to spend
several hours, as a minimum, and sometimes nearly
all of two or three nights, waiting for his signal there.
Now she completed the furnishings with a bed, another
chair, a small hob for the fireplace, and such pots,
plates, and utensils as would be necessary to reheat
food brought in. Wine, naturally enough, was plenti-
ful, and Megaera had John bring up a small cask of
ale from the house.

Her next task was to cover her absences, for she
would be away far longer each night than usual. In the
past Megaera had used the small hours of the night to
deliver, which was why she kept to a limited geograph-
ical range and sold in bulk to subsidiary suppliers.
Having thought the matter over, she fixed on the romantic nature of her maid and decided to take Rose
partly into her confidence. After she returned to the
house and was changing from riding dress to evening
clothes to dine with her father, she confessed to Rose
that she intended to be away nearly all night every
night.

There was no need for Megaera to say she had taken
a lover. Rose would leap to that conclusion without
being told. Trouble and compassion filled Rose's face;
she was terribly, terribly worried. She knew this was
wrong. Her lady was not the kind to play with a man
who would not or could not marry her. Yet it all fitted
together now. Rose was sure Megaera had not been
"taken up" from the vicar's house. She had ridden
somewhere to join this lover. And now he had come
closer so her lady could spend some time at home and
not arouse suspicion.

"Oh, madam—" she began.

"Let me be, Rose," Megaera said fiercely. "I know what I'm doing and it will only be for two weeks. Only two weeks. . . ."

"I'll help you, my lady. You know I'll do anything. I only . . ."

"Thank you, Rose, but you mustn't worry about me." Megaera's violet eyes stared out into space. "I understand what I'm doing. I'm not a fool. This is the way I want it to be. All you have to do is make sure no one else knows I'm gone."

But it really didn't matter whether any of the other servants found out. The upper servants, Megaera knew, were all devoted to her, and any lower servant would be bullied and terrified into silence. For a woman in her position, taking a lover was an "acceptable" secret, and the entire household would rally round to protect their mistress from her friends and neighbors. Megaera was in such a glow when she went down to dinner that it penetrated Lord Bolliet's alcoholic haze, and he complimented her on her looks and regretted that he had arranged to meet some friends after dinner.

Megaera accepted this statement with good grace. Her father's "gentleman's gentleman" and "groom" always accompanied him now when he went out. They knew who were acceptable companions. If Lord Bolliet attempted to join any company with whom they were not familiar, they would gently steer him along better-known paths—men who knew he could not pay gaming debts and would sometimes let him play with them out of pity. Actually it was far more likely these days that Lord Bolliet had no intention of going out and "meeting friends"; it was a euphemism for drinking himself insensible in his own chambers. He often said he would go out, then took another couple of drinks to "steady his judgment"—and then decided he was too "comfortable" to go out. Megaera did not even sigh. In a sense her father had been dead for many years.

This night she hardly heard, although she replied suitably. Every part of her except her body was already in the cave waiting for Philip. Since it had been clearly stated that Philip would be leaving with Pierre, Megaera had not felt it necessary to keep any check on her feelings. She knew she would suffer after he left, but she would not think about that except in a positive sense. After he was gone, there would be practical sense in weeding him out of her heart. She would recognize how ridiculous it was to mourn the departure of a smuggler's bastard; his image would pale —after all, she could hardly remember what Edward looked like; she had only a vague idea that he was fair and flabby.

At present Megaera felt fully justified in enjoying her brief fling to the uttermost. And enjoy it she did. Each evening, as soon as dinner was over, she fled the house to meet Philip at the cave. There she changed her clothes and they waited until it grew dark enough to load the ponies for deliveries. Megaera had had to decide whether to include Philip in these expeditions. If she did so, it would be necessary for her to expose to him the network of tunnels and the subsidiary caves. The decision did not take long. She excused her precipitate capitulation to the desire for every second of his company she could glean by telling herself that he *could* not betray her. He would be gone, probably forever, in two weeks. The only tunnel she did not show him was the one that led to Bolliet Manor.

Philip was even happier than Megaera. He did not need to fear the pain of any permanent separation—at least not if he survived his mission to France. Although he did not define to himself exactly how he would maintain the relationship between himself and Meg, he did not spend much time worrying about it either. He would "arrange something." Many men he knew kept a mistress in high style. Why should he not do so also? In any case the problem was at a distance. He reveled in Meg's company in the present and looked forward with anticipation to the future. When he had done his duty to England, he would come back and make some settlement that would make Megaera his forever.

The only shadow on Philip's picture of a perfect future was his fear concerning Meg's activities. More and more often as he laughed with her or loved her he would remember there had been an attack on her. And there was the ever-present danger that local customs officers might be forced into making an arrest, or that London would initiate another cleanup of smugglers like that of 1802. He tried to convince her to give up the trade or at least suspend operations until he returned, but he met a blank wall. Although she was deeply moved by Philip's concern for her safety, Megaera had her own duty, which was saving Bolliet.

Most of the time these shadows and the awkward places where conversation touched on the secret spots in each life did not in the least mar the joy Philip and Megaera felt. They discovered similarities in outlook and interests that should have raised the strongest doubts in each mind about the genuineness of the other's role. Instead both marveled at the wonder of meeting a person whose finer nature had triumphed over an unsavory background.

They worked during the early hours of the dark, making a quicker job of it with two men moving the kegs and cases of bottles. Philip was at first puzzled by the fact that Meg stayed out of sight so carefully, even sending John to collect payments. Then he called himself a fool. John was awe-inspiring; Meg was not. Just one look at the big deaf-mute gave customers a marked disinclination to hesitate, argue, or cheat about payment. John could not be questioned or threatened. For those who knew a woman ran the gang, seeing John

gave the impression that any woman who could manage him must be a fierce Amazon. Those who did not
know would assume a powerful and brutal male leader.
Altogether it was a logical move, and it never crossed
Philip's mind that Meg concealed herself because her
customers might recognize her as a social equal.

When business was finished, pleasure reigned su-
preme. John was left at the cave to disperse the ponies
to their fields or stabling, and Megaera and Philip rode
cross country and climbed the back slope to the ruined
house on the cliff. Generally Megaera brought food
from the cave (which had come earlier from the
kitchens of Bolliet Manor). Sometimes Philip purchased some from an inn. They ate and talked and
made love. At first light, Megaera would leave. She
never permitted Philip to accompany her, because she
did not wish to explain why she went into the cave
and never came out.

After her first refusal Philip did not ask again. Their
two weeks were too precious to spoil with arguments
about anything. It would be soon enough, when he
returned, to invade Meg's privacy to discover what he
would need to offer her in cash and security to wean
her from her unsavory profession. He had not forgotten
that she said a desperate need for money had driven
her into smuggling, but he expected that his task
would be made much easier by being able to reveal
the truth about himself.

Usually Philip was too grateful to be allowed to
sleep off his hard work and hard lovemaking in the
warm bed, which was still faintly scented with Meg's
sweet body, to resent being excluded from part of
Meg's life. He felt a little guilty, because he was aware
that she must be as limp with sexual satiety as he was,
but it was her decision to go alone.

Insensibly the days flew by until the last. Megaera
had thought of canceling her deliveries for that night,
but she did not dare because she felt that any break

in the routine would make the pain of parting more excruciating. Everything was as much the same as they could make it—except for an occasional silence and the fact that neither wished to eat the customary supper. It was after they got into bed that their mutual awareness of parting became apparent. There was a ferocity about the way they claimed each other, and both seemed insatiable.

Since that first night in Falmouth there had been no exigency about their lovemaking. Sometimes they coupled when they first got into bed, but as often that was only a time for sleepy fondling and soft, loving words. Sex came later, after a few hours of sleep or sometimes not until morning, when both were rested. This last night was different. They united explosively as soon as they had torn off their clothing, but Megaera did not release Philip after climax. As she had that first time, she clung to him and, as he had that first time, Philip did not fail her.

Exhaustion claimed them both after that, but not for long. Again, as on that first night, each was constantly aware of the other's presence, but there the similarity ended. In Falmouth there had been peace in the awareness; now it was like the effect of strong drink on a high fever. As soon as his body would rouse, Philip was all over Megaera again—and she received him as if she had not touched a man in years. Both knew they were behaving foolishly, that flogging their bodies into orgasm after orgasm could not keep the hunger and loneliness of the future at bay, but neither could stop. Even when it was no longer possible to distinguish whether climax was pain or pleasure, they touched and caressed and coupled.

Light brought sanity. In the dawn their last caresses were tender rather than passionate, Philip whispering assurances to Meg that he would return as soon as he could, Megaera replying that she would wait forever. In the stress of the moment she had forgotten Mrs.

Edward Devoran completely. She was all Red Meg, all simple, direct woman. Philip was her man and she was his woman and there was no consciousness of class or birth.

"When I come," Philip said, "I will leave a message for you in the cave, if you are not there."

"Leave a message for me?" Megaera repeated blankly. "But won't you come ashore with the kegs? I will be on the beach."

"I—" Philip started to say that he might not return by sea, and swallowed the words. "I might not be able to do that," he said. Then, hurriedly, "Do not lose hope, Meg, if it takes long. I *will* come. If I am alive, I will come."

"Alive?" she breathed. "Why should you say—"

He stopped her mouth with a kiss. "Only because my duty may take a long time to discharge. And I know you will begin to wonder whether I have forgotten you. Never think it, Meg. It may be many months, but I will come. I will never forget you. Will you wait for me?"

"Yes."

She stared at him in the pale light of dawn. He appeared more tired than when they had gone to bed —which was not surprising. His large, dark eyes looked anxiously at her from under lids heavy with lack of sleep. They were ringed with mauve, and his cheeks appeared hollow under the heavy black stubble of beard. Usually Philip shaved when they returned to the house after delivering the orders. Megaera enjoyed watching him and liked the faint odor of shaving soap that clung to him. Last night he had not bothered because of their eagerness to make love.

Suddenly she wondered why she was killing herself to hold on to Bolliet. Why not let the gull-gropers have it? Mrs. Edward Devoran could simply disappear. Red Meg could marry a smuggler's bastard. She sat up abruptly. That was insane! She could not abandon her father. He would be thrown out to die like an old bag of bones. And the people on the estate? What would become of them? But she could not take back her "yes" either. She bent to kiss Philip one last time. When he came back, she would tell him—something.

Gently she disengaged herself from his clinging arms. "I will meet you at the cave at the usual time," she said. "What do you want done with Spite?"

"I have a place to leave him," Philip replied, his voice harsh.

Megaera nearly went back to the bed, but she knew that would only make it more painful. She dressed quickly and then, quite suddenly, fled the house without saying another word. Philip had started to get up too, which was unusual, but he only called her name as she went out the door and he did not follow. He could scarcely pursue her stark naked as he was, but it would be wrong anyway, he told himself as he permitted his eyes to close. A faint, reminiscent smile curved his lips as he slid deep, deep into an exhausted sleep.

The smile was still on his lips when he woke some hours later, the sun shining full in his face. He stretched slowly. The night he had put in had almost made the parting worthwhile, and he had nothing to fear. Meg was honest as the day. She had said she would wait, and she would. It would not be so long. He would make all the haste he could.

Philip whistled happily as he pumped water, stirred up the fire, and set a small pot to heat shaving water. He washed sketchily, shivering in the chilly room at the touch of the cold water. Would there be time, he wondered, to take a bath at Moreton Place? No, that was ridiculous. Even Perce would find it hard to explain a friend who came in to take a bath and left again, and there would be no way to keep that information from Lady Moreton. Anyway, he would suit his role better as he was. Philip looked at his watch and whistled again. He had slept longer than he thought. It wouldn't take long to ride Spite over to Moreton Place and leave him in the stable yard, but it would take considerably longer to walk back from there to the cave.

Then he realized he would have to make a detour to the cave first to leave his saddlebags and clothes roll. It was enough to carry himself all those miles from Moreton Place without having to carry baggage too. He reminded himself to ask Pierre whether it would be safe to carry the Parker pistols and the muff gun into France. They were English-made and might betray him. The Lorenzonis were safe—not that he would part with them even if they were not. But it was as likely that a Frenchman would have a pair of Italian-made guns as an Englishman. His clothing too—but Pierre would know.

Even with detours and the long walk, Philip reached the cave before Megaera came through the passage from Bolliet Manor. She had guessed he would be early and had come early herself, but she could not come before dining with her father, and on this night when she would be returning alone to the cave with the men, she needed the pistols and other things she kept hidden in the passage, so she could not ride around the hill, as she had been doing to deceive Philip.

Megaera peered cautiously out of the passage before allowing John to lower the ladder. Fortunately, although she could hear Philip moving around, he was on the other side of the screen that hid the "living" area. John dropped the ladder very slowly so it would not make a noise when it touched the floor, and Megaera clambered down as fast as she could and ran quickly out into the main body of the cave, calling, "Philip, is it you?"

As he turned she clasped him in her arms and kissed him hungrily. It was a device to give John time to come down, push the ladder back into concealment, and come out—but Megaera enjoyed it very much. So did Philip, although he guessed the purpose.

"And where did you come from, bunny dear?" he asked mischievously when she heard John coming and broke the embrace.

The question was more for the pleasure of seeing Meg drop her eyes and blush furiously as she told a lie than with any real desire to know. Philip was curious about her secret, but he was certain after the two weeks of intimate living that there could be nothing shameful in it. The dreadful difficulty she had in lying, as well as Pierre's assurance that she was honest, precluded a criminal background. Philip was curious but not in any hurry to have his curiosity satisfied. When he told Meg his secrets, he was sure he could winkle out hers.

"From one of the other caves," Megaera said, hanging her head.

It was harder and harder to lie to Philip, particularly since she trusted him implicitly now. The only reason she had not confessed and lived with him in the greater comfort of Bolliet Manor was her fear that the knowledge that she was "a lady" would make him feel awkward or embarrassed. She could not speak now, either. It would make him unhappy, and that word "alive" had haunted her all day. She believed now that Philip was going to do something dangerous. If that were true, he must have nothing to distract him. He must be secure and confident so he could think only of his own safety.

"Little liar," Philip said, kissing her lightly on the nose. "There is another passage you have hidden from me. Never mind, love, I will not pry now, but when I return we will have a reckoning."

"Oh, Philip—"

"Never mind, I said. You are such a terrible liar, you

could not convince me. Meg, for the last time, will you not just leave this cargo in the cave or sell it all to someone else to distribute? I am afraid for you."

"Afraid for me? Don't be silly, Philip. Don't you worry about me! Only come back safe. I'll be fine. I'll wait however long. Just come back safe."

"Love, love, of course I will be safe. Whatever put the idea that I would not be safe into your beautiful head?"

Clearly he didn't remember what he had said that morning, half asleep as he had been. He must not worry about that either. Megaera looked up and smiled. "Oh, Philip, everything is dangerous. Every trip Pierre makes he might be caught. I'm sure disposing of the goods we have for him will be dangerous. Such things must surely be forbidden—well, you told me yourself that Bonaparte had forbidden them."

Philip laughed and kissed her nose again. "Adorable idiot. Pierre has never been caught in nearly forty years. Do you think he will suddenly forget everything he knows, just because I am with him? I may distract you, my love, but he is quite indifferent to my charms."

But then it was dark and John came with the ponies. They made their way to the cove. Pierre was not delayed either by a cruising ship or by contrary wind; his signal flashed right on time, and after Megaera had answered with hers they were all too busy to be sad or frightened. Pierre's goods, which had been brought down by the ponies, were loaded into the outgoing boats. Philip had no chance after that to think of anything but what he was doing. Unloading from and reloading the small dinghies was a ticklish job. It was only in the early hours of the morning, when he had finally maneuvered himself into a spare hammock and stretched his aching limbs, that he realized he had overlooked one essential thing that might be of enormous value to Meg.

He sat up so suddenly that he banged his head on a beam and almost fell out of the hammock. Ignoring the muffled laughter of a couple of newer crewmen who did not know him, he went to find Pierre and tell him he had changed his mind about going ashore to meet Meg when she paid for the cargo she had received. It had been agreed between them that Philip would not come. Both felt it would be too painful to part again under the restraint necessary in The Mousehole.

How much Philip's regret over this decision inspired his idea, he did not investigate. However, when he told Pierre that he wanted to leave two letters with Meg—one explaining that if she should by any mischance be caught, she should send the second letter to his father and appeal to Roger for help—Pierre agreed that the notion was most excellent. He grinned a little, but he was kind enough not to mention that it would be easiest simply to entrust the letters to him. Pierre did not think much of women, but he was by no means immune to their charms. It might be long in the past, but Pierre could remember finding excuses to see this or that pretty creature one last time. He simply furnished Philip with writing materials and told him he was going to bed.

Philip did not find either letter easy to write. He did not wish to give his father and stepmother any reason to think he was acting like an idiot and contemplating a permanent association with an obviously unsuitable woman. This would cause them considerable anguish and could not help Meg. Not that his father would not exert himself in her behalf—he would, of course, but he might also insult her by offering to buy her off.

In this Philip wronged and underestimated his father, who would have recognized Megaera's quality instantly. Roger might have been stunned to find a lady of quality engaged in such an enterprise—although that was doubtful too. After twenty years as a barrister there was very little that could surprise him. Nonetheless, since it was not likely Roger would be too dazzled by Megaera's beauty to notice anything else, he would have known her for a lady. Furthermore, having a reasonably clear understanding of his son's character, he would have welcomed his peculiarly employed but gently born prospective daughter-in-law with open arms—after extricating her from the grip of the law.

Like most sons, however, Philip did not guess his father was so perspicacious. Therefore, he controlled his transports about Meg's character and person as well as he could and tried to place emphasis on how well Pierre thought of her, how eager she had been to make sure the smuggling did not give aid to Bonaparte either through helping his agents or providing goods useful for war, and how helpful she had been to him. This was a waste of effort. When Leonie saw the letter, she would read between the lines immediately. Philip, though, was well satisfied with his effort when it was completed.

The letter to Meg was even harder to write. Philip hoped, of course, that she would never have to open it. However, if she did, there was no way to guess when it would be. He did not dare confess his mission lest the letter fall into other hands. In the end he decided to tell her nothing, only that if she should be taken by the law she should demand that Roger St. Eyre, M.P., of Stour Castle, Kent, be informed and the second enclosed letter be delivered to him. Using the name of a gentleman and member of Parliament would obtain consideration for her immediately. No local official would take the chance of offending a man who might be of importance, and if the arresting officers were from the Customs Service in London, they might know his father. Now if he could obtain Meg's promise to do as he asked, Philip felt he would not need to worry about her.

He was completely happy when he and Pierre were
set ashore at a quiet beach not far from The Mousehole. There was a rough pier near the inn itself, but
Pierre preferred not to use it. He believed it was unwise to appear at the same time and place in a vulnerable position—and there was nothing more vulnerable
than a man caught on a ladder between a pier and a
moving boat—too frequently. Thus he came ashore
sometimes east, sometimes west of the place and
walked, which also gave him a chance to look over the
ground and the inn with some care.

The beach on which they landed did not run all the
way to The Mousehole. A rocky headland protruded
right down into the water. This was not at all unusual,
and Philip and Pierre scrambled up the flank of the
hill by the light of the dark lantern Pierre carried, for
it was a nasty night, cold and misty with light rain.
When they reached the top of the rise, Pierre stopped
to look around and orient himself. He knew the area
well, but in the absence of moon and stars he had to
use the lantern to identify a landmark he knew to be
nearby.

It was not where he expected, but they could not be
lost as long as they kept the sound of the surf to their
left. They walked a few minutes, Pierre occasionally
turning the light inland, hoping to pick out a cairn of
stones. Apparently in the dark they had missed the
beach he wanted and landed at one even farther east
than he had intended. They walked for nearly ten
minutes before he spotted the pile of rock; it was a
good deal farther south than he expected. He uttered
a short exclamation, and they turned toward the
marker. They would come out on the road at the very
northern edge of the straggle of huts that surrounded
The Mousehole rather than on the shore near the inn.

This was scarcely important, as they had plenty of
time, and Pierre and Philip walked along talking
softly in French of Pierre's success in obtaining an ex-

cellent set of papers for Philip and Philip's success in obtaining a cargo of great value for Pierre.

"Yes, well, I hope it is not too dangerous to handle," Philip said.

Pierre laughed. "You mean now that you are of the *Douane* you will report me?" Then, before Philip could react to this teasing, Pierre said, "My God, a thought of the most excellent. So you shall, Philippe!"

Aware that Pierre could not mean this literally, Philip did not cry out in protest but only remarked calmly, "Here is the road, do not fall into the ditch."

Pierre started to swing the lantern to delineate better the edge of the rain runoff ditch, when a voice cried out, "It is he!" and almost before the last word a pistol barked. Another voice, deeper, hoarser, shouted, "No!" but Philip and Pierre were already in the ditch, and Pierre's pistol had returned the shot in the direction of the sound. It seemed as if he had been more successful than he intended, for a scream rang out and a shadow darted across the road.

Actually Pierre had only intended to warn off whoever had been lying in wait. He assumed it was a case of mistaken identity, since no one could possibly have known where he and Philip would come from. An ambush laid on the road could not have been intended for them. It had been blind chance that brought them there. Pierre's mind went no farther than that, but Philip's leapt to the next conclusion. An ambush on the road might have been meant for Meg. She would come that way and she would be carrying a large sum of money.

The Lorenzoni in his right hand spat fire, and the shot was returned with better aim—or better luck than could be expected in the dark. The ball whistled by fairly close. Pierre uttered a wordless protest, but before he could reach out and catch Philip, the younger man was up and running along the ditch. Pierre's mind formed some choice expletives, but he did not utter them aloud. He was using his mouth for the more sensible purpose of tearing open a cartridge to reload. There were two more shots fired, and another scream before he was ready. Now he had time to curse, and he did.

Three brief points of light close together coupled with a roar of sound betrayed the position of more of the attackers. Pierre fired in their direction, and the corner of his eye caught two more flashes too close together to be separate men. That was Philip, firing both guns. There was no vocal response to any of the shots. All had seemingly missed. Pierre cursed again, but with relief at the knowledge that the second cry he had heard had not been Philip's. Without stopping to reload this time, he continued along the ditch in the hope of catching his too-adventurous companion. It was clear to Pierre that there were too many attackers for simple robbery to be the motive. He thought they had got mixed into a war between two smuggling groups or between a smuggling gang and customs.

It occurred to him that the one French word nearly every smuggler knew was Customs—and that he might have been talking too loudly. It was just after he had said something about Philip being of the *Douane* that the voice had cried, "It is he!" and the shooting had started.

"Philippe!" he shouted, reaching for him but missing. He had underestimated the distance in the dark.

Pierre was not as young as he had been, and dashing around in ditches after a scrambling climb was telling on him. If Philip heard, he gave no sign. Pierre was close enough to see him dimly. He was working the lever of one of the Lorenzonis—presumably the other was already loaded. Hastily Pierre leapt and grabbed, but Philip had already moved. Pierre's foot came down on a stone that shifted, and he fell headlong, just as a gun went off nearly in his ear.

He did not see what happened next but knew from

the results. Before he could get to his feet, another gun
went off, very close, and a heavy weight smashed him
flat. Apparently some fool, seeing both Philip's pistols
go off, had run down to the edge of the ditch to shoot
him at point-blank range, assuming he couldn't reload
in time. That was his last mistake. The Lorenzoni re-
peaters could fire twelve shots each at only two- to five-
second intervals. Nonetheless this was a near disaster.
Pierre heaved frantically at the dead weight pressing
him down into the glutinous mud. With no one to
protect his back, it would not be long before Philip
was shot down despite his superior guns.

It was a devil of a job to get out from under the
body. The ditch was narrow and the weight could not
be thrust off by rolling over. Gasping for breath, Pierre
tried to crawl out from under by going forward. He
had just freed his head and shoulders when he heard
a woman shriek briefly in surprise, two more shots, a
hoarse gobbling, an agonized male scream that went
on too long and broke too abruptly, some alarmed
shouts—and then silence.

Chapter 12

The confusion immediately after the precipitous departure of the remaining ambushers was little less than the confusion of the gun battle itself. Philip shouted both Meg's name and Pierre's, not knowing which one to succor first. Pierre's hoarse bellow that he was all right sent Philip in the direction he wanted to go— and almost got him killed because John grabbed him, not recognizing him in the dark. Megaera had to fling herself right on top of John, and even at that she only saved Philip a broken neck because her weight knocked John's hands loose.

When that little fracas was over, it took a few minutes to calm John, who was weeping with fright at nearly having killed his only friend and displeased his "goddess." Then they were able to look for Pierre, who had sensibly stopped struggling as soon as he realized the attack was over. John heaved the body off him at once and helped him to his feet and out of the ditch. There were a few more incoherent sounds while everyone made sure everyone else was unhurt.

"Lunatic!" Pierre exclaimed, as soon as he was sure *son fils* was intact. "Why did you return their fire after

my warning shot? Why did you not give me a chance
to say we were not customs agents?"

"Customs? Good God, I never thought about it. I
assumed it was Black Bart after Meg again."

There was a moment of silence. Meg shuddered and
Philip held her close. Pierre emitted a low whistle.

"Of that I had not thought," he admitted. "I do not
think 'e know this place, but we 'ad better see if we
'ave the good fortune to 'it 'im, or if anyone is alive
'oo tell us what was this about. Our lantern is in the
ditch somewhere. Do you 'ave one, Mees Meg?"

"John dropped it, I think. It must be somewhere,
but I suppose the oil is all spilled."

After they wiped the lantern so the whole thing
would not catch fire, there was still enough oil to burn
for a little while. The body John had heaved out of
the ditch obviously had no life in it and was not
recognizable. One whole side of the head had been
blown away. Megaera choked and hid her face in
Philip's breast. He swallowed hard himself and looked
away. Pierre shrugged and moved on to where a
shadow lay, darker than the road surface. When Pierre
shone the light on it, his breath drew in sharply. He
had seen many, many dead men in his life, but there
was something terribly wrong with this body. It was
crushed and twisted in a most peculiar fashion, all out
of shape like a bug that had been stepped on.

Just as he was about to move away, the eyes opened.
Stifling his pity and revulsion, Pierre knelt down.
"'Oo were you trying to get?" he asked urgently, quite
loud. Sometimes the dying will respond to something
far outside their own concerns when there is enough
force in the question.

"Agent," the broken body sighed.

Pierre grimaced angrily. It *had* been a mistake, and
three men were dead because of it. He hesitated a moment, fumbling for his knife. This poor creature could
not survive long and it was senseless to let him suffer.

"French agent . . . said papers for Boney . . . not . . ."
The thread of a whisper finally stopped.

Knife in hand, Pierre waited, bending still lower.
Then he sat back on his heels and slid his knife back
into its sheath. There was no need to use it. The open
eyes still stared at him, but they were empty with death
now. So it had *not* been a mistake after all, and it was
fortunate indeed that Philip had reacted as he did. The
attempt had been meant to take Philip. Pierre did not
need elaborate explanations to understand that the real
agent had reversed his and Philip's roles and had hired
men to kill Philip. Both men he had examined were
local hired help. He moved on to the last body and
his breath drew in again, but not because of the
wounds—one in the shoulder and the second in the
throat. It was pleasure that made him breathe deeply
this time. For once luck seemed to be with them. This
was no local hired man; he was dressed like a gentleman.

"Philippe, come 'ere," Pierre called. "We were both
wrong. Eet was not a gang after customs men nor Black
Bart after Mees Meg."

Philip tried to make Meg stay with John, but she
clung to him and perforce he brought her with him.
She began to shake when she saw the body; this was
the man who had run right into her pony, waving a
gun. She had shot him in frightened reaction, her
pistols being drawn and cocked because she had heard
gunfire and also heard Pierre shout Philip's name. It
was only after she had fired that she realized the man
had not been attacking her but had been running
away from the battle behind him. Then, before she
could do anything, John had grabbed another man
and broken him.

It was horrible! She felt sick and weak, and then
she heard Philip exclaim, "Jean! Good God, Jean de
Tréport. But what—"

"The dying man said they 'ad been hired to kill a French spy—'e can only 'ave meant you, Philippe."

"God in Heaven! I felt there were two of them that first time in my room, but when I killed the one on the road and no one tried to help him, I thought I was mistaken. I can hardly believe . . . But he knew I was no spy. Yet you must be right. It was my name, not the fact that you mentioned customs. Do not cry, Meg, my love. You have saved my life."

"You mean that man—those men were trying to kill *you*, Philip?"

"It looks that way," he said grimly. "Jean knew me. I thought, in fact, that we were friends. Now I suppose it was because—" He hesitated, unwilling to say too much but realizing he must give Meg some explanation, "because I knew too much about him and would not give him information."

"Oh!" Meg exclaimed, having absorbed what Philip had said. "Oh, the monster!" She pulled herself more erect, no longer trembling. "I am sorry I only shot him twice!" she said ferociously.

Philip and Pierre both burst out laughing. "Twice ees enough, Mees Meg," Pierre chortled. " 'E could not be more dead if you 'ad shot 'im a 'undred times."

"No, and it is a shame to waste powder and ball," Philip remonstrated with mock seriousness.

Indignation had completely eliminated any shred of sickness or remorse. Megaera looked at the corpse with the cold, indifferent glance she would have bestowed upon a rat in a barn. "Do you want John to get rid of the bodies by dumping them off the pier, or should we just leave them here?" Then something odd struck her, and she looked toward the huddle of huts. "But where is everyone? It sounded like a war was going on when I was riding down the road."

"That is just why it is so quiet," Pierre pointed out, grinning. "People 'ere do not intrude on other people's wars. And yes, Mees Meg, eef the poor John can take away the bodies, eet would be better for all. Those 'ere, as I said, do not wish to draw the attention. They would be angry with us for causing so much inconvenience."

"No, we cannot drop them off the pier," Philip said, "at least not de Tréport. He must be found. I will go with John while you and Pierre finish your business, Meg. I will take them across to the main road. That will be a nice neutral place, not too close to any village."

John had followed them, and Meg signed swiftly that he was to go with Philip and obey him. She gave Philip one long look, but he was not standing on ceremony because of Pierre, and took her in his arms and kissed her. He could not see her face clearly, but he felt the warmth of her blush and he kissed her nose and murmured that she should not be such a goose. It was an enormous relief to him to know that the attack had not been directed against her. Doubtless the Black Bart man had left the area when she threatened him.

Pierre took Megaera away, and Philip set about his cleanup job briskly. He and John loaded two of the bodies on the pony which, being of placid disposition, had not run far. John slung the third corpse over his shoulder, as indifferently as if it were a sack of wheat. When they reached the road, Philip went through Jean's pockets, but he found nothing of significance. He had hoped there would be some clue as to whether Jean was working on his own or for someone else. He accepted the lack of evidence philosophically, however. On an adventure one cannot have everything handed out on a platter. The fact that he had been able to recognize Jean was very good luck. He could pass the information along to his father, and all of Jean's associates would be most carefully watched and scrutinized.

It was only a mile as the crow flies to the main road

north of The Mousehole, but finding a path passable
to the laden pony took them almost a full mile out
of their way. By the time he got back to the inn, a
little more than an hour later, Megaera had become
very nervous, although Pierre kept telling her it was
impossible for Philip to cover the distance in less time.
Between what had happened and the exertions and
lack of sleep the previous night, she looked wan and
exhausted.

Philip took her hand and held it tightly while he
assured her that all had gone well. Then he explained
about "a man he knew" who had considerable influence in the government and gave her the letters to
his father and the one that explained how to use it,
both wrapped in blank covers. Next he told her what
to do with the letter to Roger and that it was explained more clearly under the cover. Last he got a
dirty but usable sheet of paper and some gritty ink
from the landlord. With these he wrote a brief, sput-
tery note to Roger, not describing what had happened
—that would have taken too long—but telling him he
had discovered Jean de Tréport was an agent for
Bonaparte, that the man was now dead (he would
explain when he saw his father), and his friends and
associates should be watched.

This he gave to Megaera when they were outside
the inn, pressing a gold piece into her hand and telling her to arrange for the letter to go express. "Find
a way to get it on the earliest mail, love," he begged.
"It is very important."

"Yes, I will," she assured him. "Don't worry about
the letter. And you mustn't worry about me either,
Philip. I will be very careful, I promise. I wish you
could promise the same."

"But I can, sweet, really I can. It is not dangerous,
what I am about to do, only, perhaps, time-consum-
ing. Wait for me, Meg. I will come."

"Yes, but now you will go," Pierre said. "Philippe, we will miss the tide. Come."

There was no arguing with tides. Philip did not dare pause even to kiss Meg. That, he was afraid, could not be done briefly. With one last look over his shoulder, he walked down to the pier where Pierre's boat was waiting to take them back to the *Bonne Lucie*. He was glad the parting had been so abrupt. It was easier that way. He was also much easier in his mind. Probably Meg was right and there was virtually no chance of the law catching up with her, but should that odd chance happen, his father would get her out of trouble. There were a lot of strings in Roger's capable hands, and he had a powerful pull.

Neither Philip nor Megaera gave Black Bart a second thought, and if Pierre did, he was far too wise to mention that just as the lovers parted. The same could not be said the other way around. There was nothing Bart *could* think of besides Meg and Philip. He could not believe his bad luck. Who could imagine that the man Treeport wanted should appear. He had been furious when Treeport precipitated the attack. It had been Bart who shouted, "No!" after Jean fired the first shot. The last thing in the world that Bart wanted was for Pierre to be hurt. He was aware that Pierre did not like or trust him, but he believed the smuggler would do business with him when there was no one else.

Once Pierre had returned the fire, however, the men, who were scarcely a disciplined group, simply did what was natural to them. They were beyond Black Bart's control, and he knew it. The best he could do was hold his fire and hope he would be able to kill the one Jean had said was a French agent. Bart was indifferent to Philip's reputed treasonable activities, but he wanted to finish the shooting before Red

Meg heard it and was warned off. However, he could not even accomplish that purpose. The "French" devil never seemed to have to stop to reload, and killed the man who seemed to have a perfect shot at him.

Then he had missed his chance to kill Red Meg too. Because he was so sure she would be warned off by the gunfire, he had not been watching for her. When she appeared with blazing pistols and had killed one man and, a moment later, John had killed still another, Bart decided that the ambush had somehow been betrayed to her and a counter-trap had been set for him. He had all the money Jean had given him in his pocket, having found very good reasons not to pay the men in advance.

Crouching low, gasping curses and curses and curses, Bart ran to where the horses had been hidden. This time he would have to get out of west Cornwall, at least for a while. Red Meg would not be content with a warning this time. She would start a hunt for him, put pressure on the law—after all, she already paid them to turn a blind eye to her deliveries; she could pay them a little more to catch him on some charge. Sure, they would take him for smuggling. The men in Meg's gang would give evidence. The customs men and the JP would be able to show the officials higher up that they were *not* corrupt. Hadn't they caught and convicted a smuggler?

Weeping with fury and frustration, Bart whipped his horse viciously. It was a miracle that the beast did not stumble in the dark and throw him, but it carried him over the headland and back to the road a safe distance away. Horse and saddle had been rented; remembering that gave Bart his single spark of satisfaction. Jean had rented the horses; he had told Bart to do it, but he was too smart for that. It would serve the idiot right to have to pay for the animal. Long before he reached Penzance, Bart turned off the road and headed north. Sooner or later he would strike a track that would take him east. He had heard there was a lively smuggling trade in Polperro and Looe. That should be far enough that Red Meg's dogs couldn't sniff him out.

Henri d'Onival was also on the road—or, rather, beside it. When the first shot had been fired, he had screamed with terror. That was the cry that made Pierre think his random, warning shot had hit someone. However, Henri's only pain had been an agony of fear. Without thought he had run across the road, away from the terrifying sounds of gunfire. Blind with panic he had stumbled and fallen into the ditch on the other side and had lain there throughout the whole fight, shivering. He had heard Megaera's pony coming down the road but had not recognized it for what it was. To his fearful mind the sound was magnified into a whole army coming to attack them from behind.

The two shots Meg fired and the two screams—hers and that of the man John crushed—convinced Henri that his position was little safer than those of the men who were still fighting. He crawled forward in the ditch as fast as he could, ignoring bruised knees and torn hands, and then, when silence had fallen, he got to his feet and ran. He ran until he fell from exhaustion. By the time his driven body had recovered, his absolute panic had receded. Now Henri remembered the horses hidden not far from the road. But to get a horse he would have to return to the scene of the battle. He shuddered convulsively and began to walk. Nothing would make him go back. Nothing would make him remain another day. Nothing would make him continue this horrible enterprise. Whatever Jean said or did, Henri determined he would not listen. He would return to London. He might be penniless, but he would still be alive. He would find some other way to pay his debts.

It was nearly morning by the time Henri made his way back to the inn in Penzance. On the way he had had another terrible fright. The sound of horses had sent him cowering into the brush by the side of the road. He feared it was the "law," or whoever else had come down the road and attacked them from behind, searching for survivors. In fact it was the survivors themselves. Henri was lucky in his fear, however; the hired men were angry enough to kill him. They thought they had been tricked into an attack on Red Meg's gang, and they would not have waited to listen to any explanations. Had they seen him, Henri would have been killed and delivered to Red Meg as a burnt offering—a token of good faith that they had been tricked and had not intended to start an intergang war.

Although he was a little afraid of Jean, Henri was so much more afraid of being involved in another situation like the one he had just escaped, that he knew he could outface his partner. And during the long walk home he had conceived a brilliant idea. He did not need to complete the job to be paid. All he had to do was to threaten to expose d'Ursine—a nice show of indignation at being asked to spy against the country that had sheltered him and his parents. Yes, d'Ursine would pay—and pay.

Henri was very much surprised to find that Jean had not yet returned when a grumbling servant had finally been aroused to let him in. Trembling with joy, seeing a way to free himself from the threats and importunities of his partner, Henri ordered the servant to wake an ostler and tell him to ready the carriage. He ran up to the room, pulled the remaining money out from where Jean had hidden it, threw his things all anyhow into his portmanteau, and ran down again to wake the landlord and pay the bill.

The innkeeper was surly at first but when he saw Henri's battered and muddy condition, he added up the account and took the money. It was all too apparent that the two men, who had been heard to quarrel, had come to a violent parting. The landlord was somewhat surprised at which one of the two had come out the victor, but he wanted neither a murderer apprehended on his premises nor a violent confrontation—if the other of the pair were still alive—so he took his money and helped Henri leave as quickly as possible. If the other did not show up, the innkeeper knew he could sell his clothes and other belongings. If he did show up, he could throw him out if he didn't have money to pay the bill again, or he could sympathize with him if he did.

Unaware of the clearing of the area, Megaera stood watching Philip go down to the pier. She stood there long after he was made invisible by the misty rain and darkness, telling herself that she could still see him. Finally, however, the wet began to penetrate her heavy jacket and she knew she was only pretending. The boat must be halfway to Pierre's ship already. Megaera heaved a deep sigh and blinked back tears. Sweet. It had been heavenly sweet, but now the bitter aftertaste would begin.

Still, when she reached home and got into bed, she found that there was no time for bitterness or tears. She was so tired between fear and excitement and the fact that she had slept hardly at all the previous night, that she fell asleep as soon as her head was down. Compensating, she slept very late the next morning. Rose did not wake her. She had become accustomed to her mistress sleeping late this past year, although not so late as these last two weeks.

Thus Megaera came slowly awake when she was fully rested. She woke up happy, as she had ever since she had given herself to Philip in Falmouth. In the next moment she remembered that this morning was different from those other mornings. She was not going to spend the day in a rosy haze, just killing time

until she could go back to Philip. Philip was gone.
Then, before her heart could sink, before the bitterness of loneliness could overwhelm her, she remembered the letter she had promised to send out in the
mail.

With a gasp of alarm Megaera jumped out of bed
and looked at the little gold clock on the nearby
table. It was too late to catch the morning mail at
Penzance, but a groom could catch a second coach
that started after one o'clock. She flung on a peignoir
and rang furiously for Rose. Between dressing, telling
the maid to send a footman to the stables to warn
a groom he would have to ride to Penzance to catch
the afternoon mail, and finally going out to the stables
herself to give the groom the letter and the money
to pay the express charges, Megaera did not have time
to become depressed.

Even after the groom had ridden away, spurring his
mount to its best speed, life conspired to hold off
sorrow. Looking around, Megaera noticed subtle signs
of neglect. The horses were not suffering; the grooms
of Bolliet were chosen equally for their love of their
charges and for their skill in handling them and their
trappings. However, cleaning and repair, particularly
of the stable and yard, were not favorite duties. Lord
Bolliet seldom came down to the stable. Even when
he did, he saw little. In the last month Megaera had
been distracted, first by her worry over what Black
Bart might do next and then because of her total concentration on her affair with Philip. She had not, she
realized, visited the stables herself for some time—and
it showed.

The head groom was summoned, and his ears were
well reddened by the time Megaera let him go. But
his neglect was only a symptom of a more basic dis-
ease. Megaera realized she had been concentrating so
much on her smuggling activities that she had been
neglecting her other duties. She returned thought-

fully to the house to examine the private books she
kept. The outlook was brighter than she had expected.
She had two quarters worth of interest in reserve, and
it was time for rents to be paid by the tenant farmers.

With a sense of horror Megaera realized that she
had no idea what kind of harvest it had been. She
knew that she must have discussed such matters with
her tenants, but her mind had been so far away that
she could not remember what had been said. It was
time, and long past time, that she should pay some
attention to the estate. If she did not, she would soon
be ruined in a way other than unpaid debts. Land in
which an owner had no interest was soon mistreated
and exhausted. Megaera knew that not all Bolliet's
troubles were owing to what Edward had done. In
the years between her mother's death and her own
development to an age where she could control her
father, the land had been mismanaged. It was only
now really recovering, and she had nearly let it fall
into bad heart again.

In many places such close attention was not necessary. The rich heartlands of England produced well
even with indifferent care, but in Cornwall land could
not be neglected. There was great contrast in the
arable land. There were rich valley folds, but these
were narrow and steep-sided. Most of the land was
thin soil over rock, some of it so poor that it provided
grazing only for a few sheep. The remainder would
bear crops if carefully tended, but neglect of any kind,
particularly in manuring the land or not permitting
the fields to lie fallow, brought about swift disaster.

During the years Lord Bolliet drank and gambled
and Megaera was too young to have either understanding or authority, several farms had been completely ruined. Two still lay derelict; one, that to
which the cliff house belonged, was probably spoiled
for all time. The other, Megaera had been thinking
of renting again. The hay taken from the fields had

been good that last August. It was time to consider that and also to talk to the farmers about what should be planted. Megaera had developed a painless technique for this and for preventing the tenants from appealing to her father, who had a tendency to agree to anything to get rid of the men. She went round late in the autumn, asking what needed repair before the winter storms. At the same time crops and fields to be left fallow were discussed.

By experience the tenants had learned that, if they did not abide by these informal "agreements" or have very good reasons for any changes they made, Mrs. Edward Devoran would make their lives a living hell. The smallest aspect of what they did would suddenly come under scrutiny from the mash fed the chickens and the shoes on the horses (if one had any) to their wives' housekeeping. It was not worth it—and it did not pay either, the longtime tenants told the new ones. Mrs. Devoran read all the books on new methods of farming but she wasn't one for fads. She took advice from the best farmers in the neighborhood to be sure the books were "right for Cornwall." What was more, she was not above taking advice from her tenants—if she thought it was for the good of the land.

It was time, Megaera told herself firmly as she came away from the stables, for Mrs. Edward Devoran to take over from Red Meg. There were a few deliveries still to make, but not many. Nearly all Red Meg's customers were well stocked, knowing the coming of the winter gales would cut down the smuggling traffic. The decision was no wrench for Megaera. She was glad to avoid the "smuggling lay" right now. Deliveries would bring Philip too much into her mind, whereas Mrs. Edward Devoran's activities could have no association with him. What could a smuggler's bastard know about the management of land?

Megaera almost wished that Pierre's regular run would be interrupted too. Philip had told her it would

be "a long time" that she must be prepared to wait,
yet she knew she would expect to see him when
Pierre came again, that she would be miserable when
he was not there—even though she knew he could not
be. No, she would not think about that. There was
work for Mrs. Edward Devoran. Philip had nothing
to do with Mrs. Edward Devoran—nothing at all.

It was fortunate that Philip knew nothing of Red
Meg's alter ego. It was the security he felt in her love,
the certainty that she would be waiting and they
could come to some permanent arrangement, that
made it possible for him to put her—not out of his
mind; he could never do that—in the back of his consciousness. The knowledge that Meg was his was a
warm, comforting glow that helped rather than hin-
dered his concentration on other things.

The *Bonne Lucie* had made the crossing without
difficulty. There had been sail on the horizon to the
west in the morning, possibly an English vessel patrolling, but the *chasse-marée* was in no danger. She was
of small draft and rigged for speed; she could easily find
protection in the shallow waters of some cove on the
coast long before the ship could come up to her—if
it should be in the least interested in doing so. Since
the sail disappeared it was apparent that whatever
ship it was had not thought the *Bonne Lucie* worth
investigating.

By noon they were lying-to under a steep headland.
With a glass Philip could see that there was a village
where the land fell away into a valley to the north.
The ship's boat went ashore, and a little while later
a horse and rider set out from an area hidden by a
fold of the land. The rest of the day was spent idling,
Pierre complaining that the delicate cargo Philip and
Meg had chosen precluded fishing, an activity in which
an honest Breton fisherman *should* be engaged. It was
impossible, he said, to contaminate such fine fabrics
and feathers with the unromantic aroma of fish.

The tone was light, but the lookouts kept sharp watch. Bonaparte had no objection to smugglers who brought in woolen cloth and leather. Boots, jackets, and guns were welcome also, but frills and feathers, which would drain the purses of the people without providing material benefit or assistance to the war effort, were forbidden fruit. Because they were forbidden, they were so much the more valuable. Pierre might complain as a jest, but he would be well pleased —so long as they could avoid the unwelcome attention of French revenue officers.

They had a plan even for that, but it was only a delaying tactic. Philip, who had his forged papers ready, would say the cargo was already confiscated and under his control. Unfortunately, as soon as the customs men had time to think, they would know he was lying. His "guardsmen" would have been members of Pierre's crew, and they did not have the proper uniforms. Pierre growled with irritation when he mentioned that. Bonaparte was uniform mad. *Everyone* wore uniforms, even the least, last, jumped-up civil guard. The worst of it, Pierre confessed, was that it worked—at least a little. The uniforms seemed to rouse the pride of the men. It cost much more to bribe them when they were in uniform.

First Philip laughed, but he stopped abruptly to remark that if what Pierre said was true, the identification papers he had were useless until he discovered what uniform he would need and could obtain one.

"Yes, yes," Pierre said. "It will be waiting for you in the village. One of the women is a good seamstress and has prepared one, but it could not be finished until you could be fitted."

"She knows this?" Philip asked. "Is she to be trusted?"

"Do not teach your grandfather to suck eggs," Pierre snapped. "She knows only that I have need of a uniform for a false officer of the Customs. And trusted?" He laughed. "Do you think anyone in this village loves the customs service? Besides, she was one of my women. Yes, she is to be trusted."

Chapter 13

The overland journey to Boulogne was easy and pleasant. Philip felt that Bonaparte's penchant for uniforms, however much it might annoy Pierre, was a most excellent thing. It enabled him to place nearly every official he met, and it gained him courtesy from innkeepers and other civilians. Of course, it made the common people chary of talking to him. But, since he was not really a revenue officer, that did not trouble him at all. He was not in France to collect hearsay information about smugglers but to see with his own eyes what was taking place in the shipbuilding facilities and, if possible, the armed camps around Boulogne.

After Pierre's goods had been safely landed the night they arrived, by much the same method as the casks of liquor had been landed on the Cornish coast, Philip had spent almost two weeks preparing for his role. First he had pretended to be a civilian who had come to visit a relative for a holiday on the Breton coast. This "relative" was a friend of Pierre's, a wealthy local farmer of unimpeachable honesty, who happened to have an ineradicable grudge against Bonaparte. His son had died in the holocaust created by

General Brune in response to the First Consul's suggestion that "it would serve as a salutary example to burn down two or three large communes chosen among those whose conduct was worst." Bonaparte meant that there had been uprisings against his taking power in those places. Monsieur Luroec's son had had nothing to do with the anti-Bonaparte uprising, being solely interested in farming his land. It was merely his misfortune to be in the local market town selling produce when General Brune created the "spectacularly severe act" that Bonaparte felt would be "the most humane method" of handling the situation.

Needless to say, this accident did not endear the First Consul to Monsieur Luroec. He was too careful, too conservative, to burst into violent opposition—and he had other children to protect—but whatever he could do to undermine Bonaparte or his government was done with enthusiasm. He welcomed Philip into his home, provided him with a horse and saddle (for which Philip paid), introduced him to all the other men of substance in the neighborhood and town as his "cousin," and wrote to his wife's family in Normandy asking that they offer hospitality to his young cousin who would be passing through their area soon.

Philip told everyone that his mother was from the Côte d'Or, which was quite true, and his father had migrated when young to Paris—which was also true, in a way. He claimed that owing to the disruptions of the Revolution, he had never traveled out of Paris before. He asked a million questions about how things were done in the provinces, concentrating on the Customs. This, too, seemed very reasonable to every one. After all, Philip claimed he had been newly appointed to a clerkship in the *bureau de service* in Paris. What could be more natural than that he should wish to know what was done and how it was done by local officials. Obligingly his various hosts invited men from the customs service to meet their Parisian fellow worker.

The local officials were delighted to know someone who would soon be working in the central seat of power. Philip had sensibly protested that he had not yet been in the offices, that he had chosen to take a brief vacation before beginning his new work, and that he did not yet know a single person in the service. Nonetheless they told him all their problems, for future reference. By the time he was finished listening, Philip knew a great deal about Customs and, incidentally, about the officials in Paris who were responsible for the orders that went out to the local officers.

Philip learned something else of great interest. Monsieur Luroec might hate Bonaparte because he associated him with his son's death, but by and large the French did not. The First Consul had given them back stability, reasonable laws, reasonable taxation, sound money. The émigrés in England were sadly mistaken in thinking that the people feared and hated the "Corsican." The truth was that they loved him—and had good reason to do so. He was politically as incorruptible as Robespierre (as long as no one threatened his power) but completely human, warm in his dealings with everyone, and, if given to occasional bursts of temper, not above apologizing for them. Most of all, of course, it was the economic security and growing prosperity that the French loved. Philip might know that this was based on a false foundation—the huge sum extorted from the conquered nations—but the French neither knew nor cared. Bonaparte had put food in their stomachs, coins in their hands, and they loved him.

Philip made only one mistake and that, fortunately, was after he had obtained most of the information he needed. Quite casually one of the men asked how he had obtained his appointment, since he seemed to have no connection with or knowledge of the service. Philip had thought that out in advance, but he did not realize the effect his answer would have.

"My father knows Joseph Fouché," he said.

Instantly there was a deathly silence. Those men who had complained of inefficiency or corruption went pale. Philip had known, of course, that Fouché had been Minister of Police; he also knew that Fouché had been very powerful. It had not occurred to him that the name would *still* inspire such terror. Philip had been thinking of men in England who had been influential and were now out of office. Often they still had friends and could do favors. It was fortunate that Philip was a quick-witted young man. He realized at once that a disclaimer would get him nowhere, that he was already branded as dangerous to talk to. Thus, when one of the men asked stiffly whether the nation "would have the infinite happiness of seeing Monsieur Fouché back in office," Philip replied, "We hope so."

The guests stayed another uncomfortable half hour to prove they had nothing about which to be guilty or fearful. Later some sought private interviews with Philip, to assure him that they adored their superiors in Paris and considered every official of Bonaparte's government perfect. Philip did his best to calm their unspoken fears. He was sorry to have caused them, but he was too sensible to deny he was a spy in Fouché's service. First of all, no one would believe him anyway; second, no one would talk about him or "wonder" about his appointment to any other person as long as he was thought to be Fouché's man.

Sooner or later it would occur to everyone that, if he had been Fouché's spy, he would never have permitted his master's name to come into the conversation. However, the fear Philip saw was so powerful that he hoped he would be finished with his task and back in England before anyone had the nerve to mention him again. As he thought over his "gaffe,"

he became better and better pleased with it even
though it had cut off the flow of information. He
moved on to Normandy two days later, hoping that
his rather sudden departure would fix the idea that
he was an agent of the police and had obtained all
the information he wanted.

In Normandy, Philip learned some very disquieting
news. Bonaparte himself was said to be in Boulogne.
He had established himself in a small chateau, Pont
de Briques, right at the gate of Boulogne and was
personally overseeing the preparation of an army and
a fleet of invasion. In this situation the First Consul
had shed the imperial splendor of the court he held
at the Tuileries and with which he had toured
Flanders and Holland. He was visiting in person the
workshops and camps to raise enthusiasm for the invasion of England to the highest pitch.

This was not good news, and at first Philip was
gravely disturbed and considered making his way back
to Brittany at once to bring a warning of imminent
invasion. When he rethought the matter, however, he
realized there could be a second reason for Bonaparte's presence. If, in fact, the preparations had been
lagging behind schedule, the First Consul might have
felt it necessary to prod them forward in person.

Philip's next impulse was to rush to Boulogne at
once. This idea he also dismissed on second thought.
It would do England no good at all if he were caught
and killed. Thus he followed his original plan, except
that he did not claim total ignorance of the central
office of the Customs this time. He said instead that
he had always been chained to a desk and wanted to
know the realities behind the reports he read. He
asked more intelligent questions and received further
enlightenment. When asked how he had come into the
service, this time he was evasive until he felt he
had drained the wells dry. Then he let slip the "connection" with Fouché. It worked just as well the

second time, and Philip left for his final goal with confidence that he would not fail out of ignorance of the role he was playing.

Before he introduced himself to the *Chef du port maritime*, Philip made a number of quiet visits in the surrounding area. He avoided the various army camps and concentrated on the coastline, particularly the little bays and inlets so useful for small vessels that wished to land cargo without "benefit" of government supervision. He made these little trips in civilian clothing and escaped challenge, although he would not have minded being asked to identify himself.

It did not take long to find what he wanted, an abandoned rough shed mostly overgrown with brush and weeds now sere and dead. He was careful not to disturb the herbiage at that time, but when he returned, far more secretively, late that night, he boldly broke away a path. Having deposited in the shed the contents of one large portmanteau, carefully wrapped in an English woolen blanket, he cautiously retraced his steps to the local road. Once on this he no longer took any precaution against being seen, but rode back to his lodging and wakened a servant to let him in. He knew such behavior might rouse suspicion, but he did not deign to explain himself, and the next morning he came down to breakfast in his uniform.

After that there was no need for explanations. Philip rode directly into town and inquired for the *Chef du port maritime*. When he gained admittance, identified himself, and the usual amenities had been exchanged, he asked the obviously puzzled harbor master whether, to his knowledge, the customs officers in the area were honest.

Monsieur Fresnoy immediately became more cautious than puzzled. He did not wish to say he did not know. The harbor master was not responsible for the behavior of the customs officers; his duties were with the ships, assigning mooring and regulation of the building and repair—but no senior officer likes to admit ignorance. Least of all did any official wish to fail, even in peripheral duties, when Bonaparte was virtually breathing down his neck.

Moreover, Monsieur Fresnoy's nose was just a shade out of joint. Since it had been decided that the main portion of the invasion fleet would be built at Boulogne, he had been pushed very much into the background. The work was being supervised directly by the First Consul. Fresnoy did not resent that, of course, but when Bonaparte's other duties drew him elsewhere, matters were not passed back into his hands. Monsieur Decrès, Minister of Marine, had special deputies to direct the work. Monsieur Fresnoy thought that was a mistake because he knew the people and the area; however, he understood the Minister's action.

Before the First Consul had decided to invade England, Boulogne had been essentially a commercial port (except for the brief interval in 1797 when the Directory had also envisioned an invasion). In addition the Revolution had taken an enormous toll of naval officers; a great many had been executed for royalist sympathy. Thus there were too few experienced officers available for manning port facilities. Men of proper rank and experience were found for the great naval ports of Cherbourg, Brest, and Toulon, but for Boulogne it was thought sufficient to have a man who knew the sea. Monsieur Fresnoy, retired from his career as captain of a merchantman because of an injury, honest and knowledgeable, seemed ideal.

When the plans for invasion of England had been revived, Monsieur Fresnoy had expected to be dismissed to make way for someone better fitted to oversee such an enterprise. This was not, however, the way Bonaparte worked. Honest men who had given good service were not cast aside—at least not unless they appeared to embody some kind of challenge to Bonaparte himself. Since the latter did not apply to the totally apolitical Monsieur Fresnoy, he was not deprived of his position; merely, the necessary work was separated from his duties and given into hands Bonaparte thought more expert. Monsieur Fresnoy was grateful that he had not been dismissed, but, having watched the work for five months, he had begun to feel that he could have done it just as well, and that would have brought him into intimate association with the First Consul and perhaps led to greater things.

Thus, Monsieur Fresnoy was undecided as to how to react to Philip's inquiry. His first instinct was to temporize, and he asked, "Why do you ask such a question?"

Although Philip could have grinned with delight because the answer was exactly what he wanted, he maintained a slight, worried frown. "I am of the the Customs," he replied, "and I have been on vacation in Brittany and here. Last night I was—ah—er—out rather late."

The harbor master smiled very slightly and nodded. Philip was a very handsome young man. It was perfectly reasonable for him to "be out late" on vacation. Monsieur Fresnoy loved and admired the First Consul, but his preachments and efforts to establish "morality" left the former sea captain totally indifferent. Philip smiled back tentatively and then looked worried again.

"Well, I was passing a little cove—I do not know its name; I am a stranger here—and I saw a boat. I was a little—er—ah—a little drunk, I am afraid, so it seemed very strange to me that a boat should be out late at night. I never thought about it being a fishing boat, you see."

"Well, was it?" Monsieur Fresnoy was slightly annoyed. Did this officious young man think he was going to get a medal for reporting that a boat anchored for the night in a cove outside of Boulogne?

"Er—no, it was not. I am sorry to make such a long

story. I was only afraid that to someone accustomed
to fishermen and other such harmless activities my
suspicion would seem ridiculous. Sober, I would not
have thought of it myself, but drunk as I was I became sure it was smugglers."

"One boat? Or do you mean a ship?" Landsmen,
Fresnoy thought, seemed to believe the two words
were synonymous.

Philip smiled shamefacedly. "One very little boat.
Silly, was it not?" Then he frowned. "But what I found
was not silly. I know the First Consul banned all im-
ports of English goods and, more especially, those luxurious items that are of no benefit to the country.
Why should a silly woman wear Indian muslin when
she could wear French silk? The First Consul is perfectly right. The silk is even more handsome."

"Yes, but what has this to do—oh, I see. You *found*
Indian muslin?"

"Yes, and other things. What worried me this morning, when I was no longer drunk, was the—the small-
ness of the 'shipment' and the—the openness of the
man's behavior. That was why I came here instead of
going to the Customs director, whom I know to
be in Boulogne. My cousin in Brittany has a friend
who not long ago used to trade in Boulogne, and he
spoke of you as a very honest man. I do not wish to
make trouble for anyone, which is what would happen
if I went back to Paris and reported what I have seen.
So I came to you."

"But why? I have nothing to do with customs. In
fact, I think our customs men are honest. I do not say
there may not be one who has stepped off the straight
path, but in general—and I am sure the director . . ."

"It would be a very foolish thing for the director of
the district to endanger his position and reputation for
a few bolts of cloth and a few boxes of feathers. However, to speak plainly, such a man does not like to be
told his business by—by a nobody like me. Moreover, it

will not be pleasant for him to need to begin an investigation of his personnel."

"And if I accompany you he will be forced to do so, eh?" Monsieur Fresnoy said wryly. "Does it occur to you that he will not love me for this either?"

"Oh, no, sir," Philip hastened to assure him. "He will blame that on me. I will tell him just what I have done. Moreover, he will know you could not refuse me."

Monsieur Fresnoy's eyes narrowed. "I do not see how this can benefit you, then, since you will still gain Monsieur le Directeur's animosity."

"No, I will not," Philip assured him earnestly, "at least not if he is an honest man. Oh, he may be angry at first, but as soon as he begins to think the matter over he will think differently. After all, I am sure he does not want a corrupt officer in his brigade. Second, since you know of this problem and I am *sure* he will investigate, there will be no need for me to report anything to my office. As I said, I do not wish to report this. You know and I know that this may have nothing to do with any customs officer. There are so many coves and little empty beaches. The whole Grand Army could not patrol every one. But the office of the Director General will assume inefficiency. . . ."

There was a brief pause after Philip's voice died away. Monsieur Fresnoy looked at his earnest, anxious expression and smiled. "You are a very clever young man, and thoughtful and patriotic too. Yes, indeed, I will go with you."

Philip dropped his eyes and looked modest while he murmured his thanks. He did not smile, for he was still only at the beginning of his path, and he certainly did not want the harbor master to guess how comical it was that they should be in perfect agreement. He, too, thought he had been clever and patriotic.

It happened that the director of the customs office was in and was willing to see the harbor master imme-

diately. Philip was grateful. This was the only part of
the operation that was really risky, and he was glad he
would have no time to get nervous and do or say
something silly. He had no idea whether this bureau
chief happened recently to have been in Paris or
whether there was some department rule a high official
would know that precluded the role Philip was playing. In addition, if the man was suspicious and wanted
identification, Philip had no idea whether his forged
papers would pass the inspection of someone who knew
what the papers should be. Until now everyone had
accepted him on the wealthy Brittany farmer's word.
The harbor master's clerk had looked at Philip's
papers, but only cursorily, and there was no reason
why he should be able to tell forged papers from genuine ones.

Monsieur Fresnoy was a clever man and, for his own
sake as well as Philip's, started the conversation with
a large dollop of butter. Instead of repeating Philip's
suspicions of complicity in smuggling, he explained
that this young clerk of the Customs, Philippe Saintaire,
was most sensibly in awe of his own superior and
sought the intervention of someone with authority
outside of his own service to introduce him. Then he
went on to describe what Philip had seen in the cove.
The reaction was more violent than Philip or Monsieur Fresnoy expected. The director turned brick red
and snarled.

"Can you find the place again? Do you have proof?"

Monsieur Fresnoy stiffened imperceptibly. How
could he have forgotten to ask those questions himself? A single glance at Philip reassured him that he
had not been wrong in his judgment of Philip's character.

"Yes, sir, to both," Philip replied promptly. "As to
proof, of course, I could not be sure that the goods
would remain where I found them until I could get to
see you. Frankly, sir, I was afraid to seek out anyone in

authority last night. Monsieur Fresnoy has been most
kind, but I confessed to him I had—er—been making a
little merry and was not completely myself."

"Then you are *not* sure, really."

"Oh, yes, I am sure. I was not—ah—so merry as that.
In fact, what I found shocked me so much . . . Well,
I could not carry it all, but I brought what I could
back to my room at the inn. I was afraid to carry such
stuffs around with me, but if you would send an officer
with me—"

"Yes, very wise."

The director jangled a bell and a clerk came in to
receive the order. Monsieur Fresnoy rose, saying he
imagined he was no longer needed. Philip hastily got
up also and took his hand.

"I cannot thank you enough, sir," he said. "If you
would permit me to call at your house to express my
gratitude—if I am not too bold. . . ."

"Not at all," the harbor master replied, thinking to
himself that this was a most polite and proper young
man. "You have no engagement this evening?"

"No, sir, unless—" Philip turned to look at the director, who waved a negation at him. Philip then smiled
at the harbor master and bowed. "Then this evening—
at what time?"

Monsieur Fresnoy looked at the dark, handsome
face, remembered Philip's implication with regard to
what he had been doing the previous night. Clearly
this was a correctly brought up young man, who understood the amenities. One worked off one's lust on the
class of women who did such things; one did not seduce
one's equal's (or superior's) daughters. He named a
time, said a polite farewell to the director, and went
away thinking that Philip might be an amusing companion for Désirée.

The rest of the morning and the early part of the
afternoon were too busy to permit Philip time for
thought. It took all his concentration to remain in

character, not to seem to know too much or too little, to seem interested enough in the problem of who was doing the smuggling. This last, naturally enough, was scarcely a subject on which Philip desired that the truth be uncovered. However, he soon realized he was not the first to bring information that English goods were being smuggled into this area.

At first Philip could hardly believe his good luck, but when he was finally dismissed with a commendation he realized that it was the most natural thing in the world. Boulogne was full of men becoming wealthy from the huge shipbuilding contracts, plus naval and army officers who were training the men who would sail the invading fleet and take part in the proposed invasion. These contractors and officers had been here for months and could expect to remain for months longer. Doubtless their wives had come to stay with them. There would surely be social affairs to mark the economic rejuvenation and to relieve the tedium of camp life. The women would need constant additions to and refurbishments of their wardrobes, since each group moved in a closed social circle in which one saw the same people over and over. There would also be the subtle striving among the women that always existed in closed social circles, the desire to lead the pack in fashion and elegance. This was the perfect situation for a market in forbidden trifles.

What a fool he had been, Philip thought. He should have known that Pierre would not have suggested his taking along some of the goods unless smuggling was likely. On the other hand, to Pierre, smuggling was likely anywhere. He seemed to think it was the natural condition of man. Well, perhaps he was right. Philip lay back on his bed and finally allowed himself to laugh heartily. What a tale he would have for his father and Leonie—and for Meg. It had worked so well!

The harbor master had been too interested in his story to check his credentials, and, after all, it was not his business. But the way he had introduced him to the Director of Customs had certainly given the impression that Monsieur Fresnoy knew the man he was introducing. He had even managed to surmount a last, unexpected danger when the director had offered to write to his superior to commend him for his alertness and devotion to duty even on vacation.

Philip had gasped with shock—and had barely managed to change that to an indrawn breath of amazement at the director's generosity. Surely it would be too much trouble, he had said politely, envisioning the hunt for him that would begin as soon as the director was informed that no such man was employed in the *service de bureau*.

"Not at all," the director insisted, a little surprised, for it seemed a bit odd that so clever a young man should not wish to capitalize on his achievement.

Fortunately, by that time Philip had caught his breath and had a moment to think. He lowered his eyes and bowed. "Since you are so kind," he murmured, "could you do me the infinite favor of—of giving the letter into my own hand. I—I am new in the office, you see, and my name might be meaningless. Letters can get lost . . ." Philip allowed his voice to drift away.

The implications were plain. This clever young man had been too clever, perhaps, and annoyed his fellow workers or offended his superior. Or, simply, he was clever enough to wish to carry a commendation personally to someone higher up than his own superior. Well, why not? Ambition and cleverness should be rewarded. The director nodded and smiled.

"Very well, come tomorrow afternoon. My clerk will have the letter for you."

Philip confounded himself in thanks and bowed himself out, remembering not to sigh with relief or wipe his brow until he was well away from the director's office. That had been a narrow squeak and, really, it was not yet over. In well-meaning innocence the director might still write to someone in Paris to commend him, thinking that such an action would serve to confirm the letter he would carry.

It would behoove him, Philip thought, sitting upright, to move as quickly as possible to get his information. There was no time to spend courting the harbor master's daughter. He would have to use more direct methods. However, he found that he was not to have any choice about meeting Mademoiselle Fresnoy. He had hoped to be shown into the harbor master's study, where they could talk in privacy and he could be politely indifferent if the daughter invaded her father's sanctum, as Pierre said was her custom. Instead he found himself shown into the parlor and introduced to Mademoiselle Désirée.

Philip did what he could. He first thanked the harbor master most sincerely—he was quite genuinely grateful to the man and hoped Monsieur Fresnoy would not get into trouble if the truth were later discovered. Then he mentioned the letter of commendation and, using that as a wedge, inserted the information that he did not expect to be in Boulogne longer than a week. All the time he had been speaking, he had been aware of occasional, but very intense, glances from Mademoiselle Désirée. It was an odd sensation, like little flickers of heat that touched him. Yet he could not catch her looking at him even once. Each time he turned politely toward her to include her in the general, impersonal remarks he was making, her eyes were demurely lowered, fixed on some small piece of needlework she held in her lap.

It was when he began the next stage of his attack, which was to regret that he probably could not obtain permission to get into the port facilities and dockyards, that her eyes first met his. The brief flashing glance gave him a shock. It was avid and at the same time calculating, but so swiftly veiled that Philip could hardly believe the demure face he saw held those eyes.

"But why not, m'sieu?" Désirée asked.

"Alas, I have no official reason to be there, and I must assume they are closed to the merely curious, since the work is for the war—"

"Naturally we cannot have a stream of visitors who would impede the work," Monsieur Fresnoy said.

"Oh, I would keep out of the way and, truly, I am so ignorant about ships that I would not know what questions to ask nor would answers do me much good. I suppose the desire is foolish, but . . . All day I work with reports of ships and tonnage and the names of far places." Philip sighed. "It is all words on paper. I had hoped to see how ships are built and to see how they are launched. It would make it all real to me. Ah well, I suppose I should have got permission in Paris. . . ."

"I do not see what harm it could do for Monsieur Saintaire to see the yards and docks, Father," Désirée urged softly, "particularly when his patriotic act can leave you in no doubt as to his loyalty."

"No, no, of course it would do no harm, but I do not have time to escort him, and—"

"Oh, I would not expect that!" Philip exclaimed, horrified. "But is it too much to ask—or is such a thing impossible—for a pass?"

"That would not do," Désirée said. "The yards and docks are very dangerous places. You say you are ignorant of ships and shipbuilding. You might be hurt yourself or cause an accident wandering about. Father, if it were agreeable to you, I might serve as guide to Monsieur Saintaire. I could ask Jeannine to go with us so that all would be proper."

To Monsieur Fresnoy it seemed perfectly natural that every man in the world should find ships and everything about ships the most interesting subject that existed. It also was pleasing to him that so well-bred a young man, who did not ogle his daughter, should entertain her for a few days. Monsieur Fresnoy was aware that Désirée lived too quiet a life, but he could not bear to think of her associating with the young officers of the army and navy who were here today. They might well be here long enough to win his daughter's affections, but they might also be killed in the invasion. And there was no one else. No shipbuilder in Boulogne could spare time or timber for merchant vessels, so those were all dropping anchor in other ports. Thus there were no young men but those Monsieur Fresnoy considered unsuitable for one reason or another.

Philip would be a safe escort, Monsieur Fresnoy thought. No girl as sensible as Désirée could fall in love in a few days. Even if that were possible, the young man had the accent and manner of a gentleman. He was in a reserved occupation; he was clever and ambitious. They could write letters to each other, if they wished. Perhaps if interest grew between them, Monsieur Fresnoy would permit Philip to visit again— in a year or two. Then, perhaps in a few years more . . . Yes, if Désirée fixed her attention on a most suitable young man who was employed in Paris, she would be less likely to be interested in someone closer, more dangerous to her father's peace.

In no time at all Monsieur Fresnoy permitted himself to be talked around. It was safer for Philip to go with Désirée and her friend. Désirée was well known in the shipyards. In the past he had spent much time there, and she had often brought him something to eat if he was too busy to come home. Even now he was in the shipyards quite often to smooth things over between Parisian officials and the north-coast shipbuilders or to settle disputes between the workmen of disparate origins who had different ways of doing things. The former sea captain was accustomed to many accents, many ports, many different ways of living.

The very last thing Philip wanted was a guide, par-

ticularly a feminine one who would doubtless be bored
and want to leave almost as soon as they arrived. He
had been hoping to "get lost" in places his pass did
not entitle him to go to, counting on his uniform,
which might not be familiar to workmen who had no
reason to examine uniforms closely, to protect him
from questions. He murmured that Mademoiselle
Désirée was "too good," she must not trouble to go
into a noisy, dirty place most unsuitable to her delicate
gender, that he would be very careful and neither cause
nor fall into an accident.

The faint, polite protests that were all Philip dared
allow himself did him not the slightest good. Désirée
would be delighted; her father was "very happy to
accommodate him." Philip could only thank both
with as much enthusiasm as he could summon up and
hope he would be able to keep the pass and get in another time. Perhaps, he told himself as he walked back
to his lodging that night, it would be all for the best.
At least he would be recognized as a guest of the
harbor master. But while the surface of his mind remained occupied with the question of his mission, a
vague puzzlement stirred below. Every outward aspect
of voice and manner marked Mademoiselle Désirée a
proper and modest girl. Still . . .

The pleasant surprises started as soon as Philip
arrived at the harbor master's home at the appointed
time the next morning. Désirée and her friend were all
ready to go, a pleasant change from the few times
Philip had escorted English girls, who seemed to think
that an hour's wait would endear them to their escorts.
Then, there did not seem to be any secrets to be kept
about the yards or docks at all. Désirée was obviously
well known and was greeted with respect. No place was
forbidden. Philip's questions were all answered with
the greatest good humor and apparent frankness.

At first Philip was very careful, despite his fear that
Désirée would wish to leave too soon. He asked every

question with respect to merchant vessels, where and how cargo would be carried, where and how cargo could be hidden. His "ignorance" was instructed. These were not cargo vessels. They were meant to carry guns, men, and horses—for the invasion. Philip waxed ecstatic with patriotism.

"I am very happy to hear such sentiments," a pleasant tenor voice behind him remarked.

Philip turned, smiling, to repeat his enthusiasms in new words, but the smile froze on his face when he saw the two girls curtsying deeply. It was Bonaparte himself, at the head of a modest group of master craftsmen and naval officers. Philip bowed also, holding his breath. From the back many uniforms were indistinguishable from one another, but the First Consul could not fail to recognize the service to which Philip "belonged" as soon as he saw the front. And, indeed, the next words out of his mouth were, "You are of the *Douane*. What are you doing here?"

"I am in the office of clerks," Philip got out, "and all day I read and write of ships of which I know nothing. I was curious, my lord."

Was there a flicker of satisfaction in Bonaparte's eyes at the use of the honorific reserved for the very highest nobility? Philip could not swear to it because the penetrating blue-gray eyes did not linger on him but passed to the girls, who promptly curtsied again. Bonaparte opened his mouth to say something, then recognition came.

"Ah, Mademoiselle Désirée!" A swift glance around. "Is your good father here?"

"No, sir. He could not take time from his work to escort Monsieur Saintaire, yet he felt Monsieur Saintaire deserved to see what he wished because of his service to the state, so he asked me to show him what I could."

"Yes?" Bonaparte encouraged. "Service to the state? How has Monsieur Saintaire served the state?"

Given tacit permission, Désirée launched into a description of Philip's discovery of the "smuggled" goods. She glossed lightly over the time of his discovery, saying he had been returning from a visit, which Philip assumed was what her father had told her. Decent girls were supposed to be ignorant of the existence of whorehouses. Also, she somehow implied that it was the Director of Customs who had introduced Philip to her father and recommended that the young man's curiosity be satisfied. Philip was puzzled by this, since Désirée knew the true facts, but he guessed it was because she did not wish her father should bear the blame of permitting an unauthorized person into the facility. Whatever her reason, Philip was delighted, since it would have been embarrassing to have to explain why he had gone to the harbor master rather than the director to report. Moreover, the way the story was coming out, it sounded as if he had been recognized and accredited by the director of his own service.

While Désirée spoke, Philip had ample opportunity to examine the bogeyman all England feared. He did not look much like a bogeyman. Bonaparte was about average height, or a little below, for a Frenchman—which made him a good six inches shorter than Philip's own six feet—and he was rather handsome. The blue-gray eyes were large and of a very intent expression under a lofty forehead with fine, down-slanting eyebrows. His skin was very clear and very pale, particularly white on his hands, which Philip felt were too small and too graceful for a man. There was, however, nothing unmasculine about nose and chin, the former long but straight and handsome, the latter strong and determined. His smile, directed now at Désirée, was peculiarly charming, the lips very mobile and expressive.

"So," Bonaparte said, turning his eyes on Philip again, "a most honest and patriotic young man."

"It is difficult to be otherwise when you are an example to us all, my lord," Philip replied, taking a chance and laying flattery on with a trowel.

He was rewarded with a brilliant smile, which confirmed what that first flicker of satisfaction at being called my lord had implied—that Bonaparte was a man who enjoyed flattery. Further confirmation came in a kind but condescending dismissal of the ladies to a "more appropriate occupation," coupled with a gracious invitation to Philip to accompany him on his tour of the shipyards. Philip choked, nearly strangling on laughter. Surely this must be the first time in history that the leader of a nation invited an enemy spy to accompany him on a tour of an installation preparing for invasion of the spy's country. The mild strangulation did Philip no harm; Bonaparte took it to be an expression of unbelieving awe, and Philip encouraged this useful delusion for all he was worth as soon as he caught his breath by stammering thanks and gratitude.

Several times more that morning Philip was forced to cover hidden emotions with gasps of spurious admiration—but the emotions were no longer mirth. Nor was the admiration all assumed, for it was impossible to be in Bonaparte's company without admiring the man. His manner to the workmen was perfect. There could be no doubt that his presence and comments—he had a surprising grasp of anything that was told him—did inspire them to the greatest effort of which they were capable. It was remarkable, too, that a man of such vanity should be able to listen to and accept statements from the experts who accompanied him that obviously went against his desires.

Naturally, Philip had made himself inconspicuous among the First Consul's entourage. The invitation did not imply that Bonaparte intended to act as a personal guide—for which Philip was truly grateful. He preferred that the penetrating gaze of the First Consul be turned on men and things other than himself. His speech, he knew, was perfect—and Bonaparte, whose mother tongue was Italian rather than French, probably would not have noticed any irregularity in that anyway. His manner was good enough in general—in England he had always been accused of being "French" in his ways. Still, there was something in those blue-gray eyes that made Philip too aware that he was *not* French. Such a feeling was dangerous; it could cause awkwardnesses that would not appear if it did not exist.

However, as an anonymous member of the group that trailed Bonaparte, Philip had the enormous advantage of having his questions answered without needing to ask them. Bonaparte was as interested as Philip himself in how long it took to build a ship, in whether it would be possible to speed the process by adding men to the labor force or by any other expedient. Nor could any spy have been more interested in how many ships had already been completed and of what types they were.

All this was the most wonderful good fortune, and the answers Philip had to his unasked questions were in some measure consoling. It was immediately clear that no invasion would be launched that year. Not nearly enough ships were ready to carry an adequate force across the Channel. Privately, Philip did not think the fleet could be ready during the early part of the next year either. That was not his responsibility, however. If he brought home the information he had, those more expert than he could calculate a probable date far better than he could. In fact Decrès's deputy was assuring the First Consul that the ships could be ready by the summer of 1804, and the master ship-builder, although he did not dare contradict the deputy of the Minister of Marine, was biting his lips and looking very nervous. Philip assumed from this that the deputy's prediction was oversanguine and that it might not be until 1805 that the fleet would be ready.

Nonetheless Philip felt cold with fear. It seemed to him that however long the event was postponed, it *would* come. There was iron-hard determination in Bonaparte's face, and when he spoke of the need to conquer and for all time control "perfidious Albion," his voice rose and thinned into a cry of fanaticism. It must be war to the death. Either England or France must go down to utter defeat. Philip realized it would not be enough to prevent or defeat an invasion, to win some battles, and to make a peace. Bonaparte would only begin all over again. To achieve a lasting peace Bonaparte would have to be destroyed—killed or removed from power in such a way as to be sure he could never grasp it again.

Chapter 14

Philip went back to his inn, after Bonaparte had finished his tour of the Boulogne docks and shipyards, in
no mood for polite conversation. His mission was complete. He had the information for which he had come—
straight from the horse's mouth as it was said—and it
was not very pleasant. In the privacy of his room he
wrote down in brief and cryptic form everything pertinent that he had heard and seen. He did not think
the letters, which were abbreviations of English names
of ship types, and numbers would be meaningful to
anyone who found them, and to be sure he interspersed
totally irrelevant symbols and numbers between the
real information, marking the irrelevant materials with
checks, dashes, and little stars.

He put the paper into his pocketbook quite openly,
hoping that no one would ask what it meant or think
it important. A little thought produced an explanation
if anyone did ask; the symbols could be initials and
the numerals prospective contributions to a worthy
cause. Deciding exactly what the worthy cause should
be was the next step, but Philip never got that far. A
scratch at the door heralded a servant with a delicate
missive. Philip restrained his groan and his expletives

until the servant was gone, and then expressed himself freely for a minute as he perused the invitation to dinner penned by Mademoiselle Désirée.

His first impulse was to refuse, but he did not dare. He had said he would be in Boulogne for a week. If he disappeared suddenly, that would be suspicious. In general, perhaps not, but to leave abruptly on the very day he had toured the docks and shipyard was stupid. Nor could he say he had been recalled to his office. Such an order would naturally come through the director's office. Perhaps a sick relative? No, Philip told himself. He was merely indulging himself because he didn't wish to sing praises of Bonaparte, as he knew he must to remain in character.

There was nothing he could do but accept. He would have had to make some kind of farewell visit anyway, so the note he wrote and sent with a servant from the inn was graceful. The combined efforts of his father, grandfather, and grandmother-by-marriage had finally drilled into him the need for graceful forms to avoid hurting and offending those who did not know him well. It was fortunate, however, that his host and hostess could not see his sullen expression as he wrote. By the time he set out for Monsieur Fresnoy's house, the expression was gone. Philip knew that the invitation was tendered out of pure kindness for a young man alone in a strange place. He could not be ungrateful, no matter how inconvenient the kindness was in reality.

Philip spent the first few minutes of his walk to Monsieur Fresnoy's house thinking up praises for Bonaparte that would not stick in his throat, but his mind was soon distracted. He had the strangest impression that someone was watching him, and the sensation did not pass as he completed the length of the street—which it would have done had someone been peering out of a window. Philip stopped abruptly and turned, at the same time clapping a hand to the pocket in which men carried their purses. Pickpockets were rife and clever, and such a gesture would imply no personal uneasiness, only that Philip thought someone had tried to rob him.

The street was quite full at this time, of course. All sorts of people were there, well-dressed ladies and gentlemen either going out or home to dinner, officers and men of the army and navy on and off duty, laborers and sailors going about their business or seeking amusement, and the usual number of ill-clad loiterers. As swift as Philip's movement had been, he did not surprise anyone with what might be considered an unhealthy interest in him. Several people had noticed his action and also glanced around, but there was no one close enough to him and no one who started to run on whom to pin suspicion. Philip shrugged and continued on his way, his hand ostentatiously on his pocket.

As he walked Philip wondered whether he had somehow given himself away and was being watched by the spy-catchers of the Ministry of Police. In the next moment he told himself that was ridiculous. Why should such men bother watching him? Surely it would be safer to arrest him and try to beat the truth out of him. Perhaps no one was watching him and following him at all. It could be his own awareness of his mission that gave him the feeling he was suspected. He could think of only one reason for not being taken into custody at once. It was possible that they wished to discover whether he had any confederates.

If so, of course they would be sadly disappointed—or would they? Would they accuse Monsieur Fresnoy and Désirée because they had helped him quite innocently? That was an ugly thought. Philip remembered his father's tales of Paris in the Terror. Innocence was no armor then, for there was no justice to protect the innocent. But Philip's memories of Roger's and Leonie's vivid descriptions of the haunted, fearful people checked his flight of fancy in that direction. Bonaparte might be an enemy of England, might even be a fanatic who wished to rule the world, but he was no madman like Robespierre, who thought he could build a pure and secure nation on a foundation of death and terror surrounded by a sea of blood.

The morning Philip had spent in the First Consul's company was proof enough that he did not inspire, nor wish to inspire, a generalized and unreasoning terror. Philip did not doubt that the man could be terrible enough when he wished, but that would be to a particular person or group for a particular reason—and the reason would be made clear to all. No, what Bonaparte had offered France was exactly the opposite of what Robespierre had inflicted on the country. Frenchmen did not walk in fear. Possibly personal enemies of the First Consul would not receive justice, but the ordinary man, the lower levels of officials, felt secure and worked hard out of patriotism and enthusiasm.

Once again Philip wondered whether he was imagining the sensation of being followed. When he came to the quieter street on which the harbor master lived, he quickened his pace, like a man who was eager to arrive at his destination. He had hoped that he would be able to identify who was following him, but when he stopped suddenly again and looked back, this time without pretense, there was no one among the few passersby that he could associate with his uneasy feeling.

Naturally enough Philip said nothing about being watched or followed to Monsieur Fresnoy or his daughter, and the experience benefitted him in that it filled his mind to the exclusion of any animosity he might feel toward Bonaparte on his country's behalf. The things he had planned to say flowed easily enough from his tongue, and after that he found to his relief that his host was very willing to move to other subjects. Before long the beauties of the Pas de Calais country-

side had been introduced into the conversation by
Désirée. It was an unexceptional subject, one where
total ignorance on Philip's part was perfectly reasonable.

There was no need for Philip to do any more than
listen and agree that "it must be lovely." He could
safely voice a formal and rather insincere regret that
the brief time remaining to him before he must return
to his duties would not permit him to see more.

"But why not?" Désirée asked. "Did you not tell
Papa that you would remain in Boulogne a week? The
town itself is not so pleasant now that it is overrun
with soldiers and sailors. You would do better to go
out into the countryside."

Because he was preoccupied with hiding his irritation at Désirée's too-accurate memory—Philip had
hoped to be able sometime that evening to say his
farewells and announce he was leaving—he fell right
into the neat little trap she had laid, although at the
time he did not know it was a trap.

"It is not very interesting to go sight-seeing by
oneself," he remarked with pretended regret. "And it
is rather cold to ride about on horseback for pleasure."

"That is true," Monsieur Fresnoy replied. "It is
necessary to share such pleasures and, of course, November is not the time of year in which the country
looks its best."

"No, Papa, but for some things it really is better
when the leaves are gone from the trees. The views
from the hills are seen much more clearly. Indeed, in
summer it is often impossible to see anything because
of the trees."

"That, too, is true, my love," Monsieur Fresnoy said
indulgently, smiling at his daughter. "Why do you not
take Monsieur Saintaire for a drive in the carriage to
your favorite spot in the hills?"

"What a good idea, Father," Désirée said with
innocent enthusiasm. "May I take Jeannine along

also? We could then go to her aunt's house near Amble-teuse. And the moon will be full. You would not object if we drove back after dinner, would you? You will not be lonely dining by yourself?"

"Not at all, my love. In fact, I will not *be* dining by myself. Monsieur Champagny has asked me several times to join him, but I put him off because it is not a proper house for you to go to—his sons so coarse and wild and no other woman. I am sure I can arrange something. By all means, go to Madame Miallis if you will not cause her any inconvenience."

At the beginning of this conversation Philip had opened his mouth several times to protest, but there was really no opportunity and, on second thought, he was very glad neither father nor daughter had noticed. After all, what could he say to excuse his refusal? And, in fact, it was far better for him to go. What could be more innocent than an excursion into the countryside with two young girls? No one in his right mind could consider them conspirators, and it was ridiculous that a spy or saboteur or whatever else he was suspected of should waste his time in such a frivolous manner. Certainly it was a more sensible thing to do than to leave Boulogne abruptly.

Thus Philip accepted with becoming gratitude. Actually his pleasure was not all assumed. He had found Désirée and Jeannine good, if somewhat silly, company on the way to the shipyards. The rest of the evening passed pleasantly. Philip spoke of his work in Paris and Monsieur Fresnoy of his. Désirée played and sang to them. At ten Philip rose and said his adieux. Monsieur Fresnoy, however, said he would send a servant with him to the main thoroughfare. With all the soldiers and sailors in town there had been robberies, especially in the quiet, richer residential sections. Philip accepted with alacrity. The last thing he wanted was to kill or injure someone in self-defense and come under the close scrutiny of the police.

The servant left him at the corner of the boulevard, where there was little chance of any attack so early. Although not so full of people as when he had gone to the harbor master's house, there were a sufficient number to warn off thieves, and the moon was bright. As he walked along Philip wondered whether a full day and evening of Désirée and Jeannine would be endurable. They were rather silly, but one could never tell. Of course, Meg had never been silly—at least, not silly in a boring sense, although she could act silly enough when she wanted to make him laugh.

The thought of his Cornish beauty wakened a desire to see her and was so compelling that Philip forgot completely about whether or not he was being followed. Thoughts of Meg also aroused other desires. Philip had been celibate far longer than was usual for him, not so much out of fidelity to Meg—naturally he would not consider a brief connection with a prostitute as being unfaithful—as from lack of opportunity. He had been too busy, too intent on his purpose. Now he thought about seeking out a whore, but he did not know Boulogne well enough to find a house that kept women of the better sort, and he had no intention of exposing himself to the danger of trying the dirty and disease-ridden trulls that roamed the streets.

As he entered the inn Philip wondered whether he could ask the landlord about where to find a suitable companion. Often innkeepers had girls on call for their guests. However, Philip had deliberately chosen a very respectable establishment, and he was aware that Bonaparte, although not exactly perfect himself, frowned on the immorality of others. It would not be wise to take the chance of bringing himself to the notice of the landlord for such a thing. Since he had hesitated a trifle, he ordered a bottle of wine, and when it had been carried to his room, he filled a glass and sank into a chair by the fireplace.

Deliberately fixing his mind on trifles, Philip pulled

off his boots and sighed. To someone accustomed to
having his boots cut and fit exactly to his feet with the
care and passion Cellini must have put into his pure
gold salters and cups, the items he now wore were a
sore trial. They were not too small or tight, but they
caught his toes and heels in unaccustomed places. To
Philip's mind they had the even greater disadvantage
that they fitted his calves far too tightly to hold either
the long barrel of a pistol or a knife. He could wear
the knife in an arm sheath, but the pistols had to go
into his pockets, which made for a slow draw.

Philip sipped his wine and looked into the fire, trying to think of a logical excuse for leaving Boulogne
before the week was out without raising suspicions in
anyone. But the dark red glow of the embers where the
fire was cooling put him in mind of Meg's hair, and
the ache in his loins when he thought of her made it
hard to think of anything at all, much less specious
excuses that would convince the cordial Monsieur
Fresnoy. Cordial. Philip fixed on the word. Was Monsieur Fresnoy too cordial? Was it his men who were
following . . . Nonsense! Philip had been going to
Fresnoy's house. Only a lunatic has a man followed to
his own home. And Pierre said that Monsieur Fresnoy
was honest.

Then suddenly Philip remembered what else Pierre
had said—that Monsieur Fresnoy might want a tem-
porary amusement for Désirée. That fitted the harbor
master's cordiality, and Philip remembered something
else—the flickering hot glances cast at him by the
"modest" maiden herself the first evening he had been
at Fresnoy's house. He had not caught her at it, and
he could not remember anything like that tonight—or
did he? Had some of Désirée's glances while she was
playing and singing been a little more—more interested than they should have been on so brief an acquaintance? It had been she who suggested guiding him

on the tour of the shipyard. But it had been Monsieur Fresnoy who suggested the sight-seeing in the country.

Irritated, Philip tossed down his wine, undressed, and went to bed. It took him a long time to fall asleep, and he had some peculiar dreams when he did. One in particular was so frightening that it woke him, but when he recalled what he had been dreaming he laughed aloud. Désirée had been following him, invisibly stalking him through the streets. He knew it was she, although he could never catch even a glimpse of her, and a sense of horror had grown in him. It was particularly weird because he had no feeling that harm was intended—at least not the kind of harm that comes from knives or guns. It had been—it had been as if she intended to—to *eat* him. Philip shook with mirth.

The laughter lightened his mood and he slept more soundly, but by then there was little left of the night and he woke late and needed to hurry over his washing and shaving. He cut himself, too, cursing the French razors that Pierre had given him to replace his own fine English pair. He had some trouble stopping the bleeding and could only be thankful that the cut was under his chin and would not show. Still, he grumbled to himself that if Bonaparte could use English razors, as it was rumored he did, there must be a supply of them in the country. By the time Philip had cleaned himself up and changed his shirt he was dreadfully late. He did not stop for breakfast, rushing along the streets as fast as he could walk. He never gave a thought to whether or not he was followed, and could concentrate on nothing but how late he was.

His breathless and apologetic arrival dispersed the gloom on the faces of the two young ladies as soon as he assured them the delay was only owing to having overslept. "I am so sorry," he repeated. "It was foolish of me not to tell the landlord to have me called, but I went to bed so early it did not occur to me that I

would not be awake at dawn. I—I did not sleep well."
At that point Philip stopped abruptly, realizing he
could not explain why he had not slept.

"It does not matter at all," Désirée said, "as long as
you are here now."

She smiled at him, and Philip swallowed. It was obvious that there was no need at all for him to explain
why he had not slept. Monsieur Fresnoy's "innocent"
daughter had leapt to the right conclusion, and in
her father's absence did not try to hide her knowledge.
The only thing she had not understood was who had
generated Philip's discomfort. But thoughts of Meg
had not caused all his discomfort; the look that accompanied Désirée's innocuous words reminded Philip
very acutely of the predatory follower in his dreams.
Of course, separated from the association with the un-
feminine and doubtless unsexual follower in the street
the previous evening, the impression Philip received
this time was far from horrifying.

The drive was rather long, but it was enlivened in
several ways. Désirée insisted on sitting forward, although Philip protested vehemently if briefly before
accepting the arrangement. He might have been impatient about verbal polite prevarication when he was
younger, but he had always been protective of women.
The forward seat of a carriage was far less comfortable;
the movement of the horses and the bumping over
rutted roads tended to jolt anyone seated there toward
the rear seat. Depending on the condition of the road,
it might take considerable strength to maintain one's
position.

At first Philip did not understand why Désirée
would hear no argument against her taking that uncomfortable position. Politeness would not permit her
to allow her friends to sit there, but it was common for
any male, even a guest, to sit forward when the other
occupants of the carriage were female. However, Désirée was adamant and Philip yielded, thinking it was

more reasonable to change position with her when she
became uncomfortable than to argue. Before that,
having seen a servant carry a picnic basket into the
carriage, Philip confessed he had had no breakfast. It
would be easier to eat, he thought, when he did not
need to hold on with one hand or brace himself against
being flung into the arms of the girls opposite.

That idea passed through his mind without his
realization that Désirée intended to fall into his lap—
which would have proved a sad lack of deviousness in
Philip's thinking processes if Désirée had known of it.
She, however, accepted his protest as polite rather than
meaningful and smiled on him while he ate, thinking
that it was delightful to have met a young man who
understood her without explanation. This lack of
comprehension of each other's intentions might have
led to an awkwardness had not the terrible condition
of the road leading to Ambleteuse provided a clarifi-
cation.

The first bumps precipitated Désirée into Philip's
lap. He clutched her instinctively; she clutched him
back. Philip was aware of soft, plump breasts and
well-padded hips. Without letting go he inquired
anxiously whether she was hurt—but he was not such
a fool as to offer to exchange seats. After a moment
he restored Désirée to her position. Jeannine, gazing
fixedly out of the window, recommended that he look
to the left where a few hundred yards from the road
the cliff fell away into the sea. It *was* a magnificent
view. Philip had just enough time to remark upon it
before Désirée was bounced into his arms again.

As Jeannine had not turned her head and was com-
menting quite loudly about how she could never tear
her eyes from this breathtaking prospect, Philip took
advantage of his own "breathtaking" opportunity and
kissed Désirée before replacing her on the forward
seat. Far from protesting at the "outrage" done her,
Désirée looked rather hurt at the briefness of Philip's

"insult." Therefore, the next time opportunity knocked, Philip no longer hesitated about flinging wide the door. He swung his legs aside, took the lady into his lap, and kissed her at leisure. She responded with an enthusiasm but with a lack of finesse that left Philip still unsure of how far he would be able to go.

Under the circumstances Philip was stunned for a few minutes after they got down from the carriage. There was nothing immediately wrong. The house and grounds were typical of the haute bourgeoisie, well cared for, spacious, and dignified. However, the "aunt" who met them in the parlor after they had been admitted by a servant was the kind of aunt Philip knew very well indeed. In fact she was no more nor less than a high-class procuress. French or English, the speech and manner were unmistakable.

Involuntarily Philip stiffened. However naughty Désirée and Jeannine might be, this was no place for them. Girls of decent family simply did not . . . But before the thought could finish, a young man, also in uniform, had rushed past Jeannine's "aunt" and caught Désirée's friend in his arms. It was immediately apparent why Jeannine had been so obliging in the carriage, but Philip still suspected that neither girl understood to what kind of a house they had come.

The question that flicked through Philip's mind was whether it would be worse to tell them or to leave them in ignorance. In the next moment that answered itself. This was not the first time the girls had been here. Jeannine, at least, was very much at home. Her relationship with the young man who had greeted her so passionately seemed well established, and soon Philip realized she *did* know where she was. That reduced his responsibility to explaining to Désirée as soon as they were alone. This was not long delayed. Jeannine and her Georges disappeared even more promptly than a hired whore and her client. Philip was shocked.

He was about to protest, when the "aunt" returned

and invited them to accompany her, but Désirée rose so eagerly that he had no chance. On second thought, it was a better idea. Closed into privacy he could explain without fear of interruption or denial.

The first check to Philip's noble intentions was his surprise at the size and elegance of the suite of rooms. The second was the avidity with which Désirée flung herself into his arms. It would have taken cruel force to thrust her away. Philip had to kiss her, and he was distracted by his own unsatisfied appetite. She was a very pleasant armful. Eventually realizing that he must explain at once or it would be too late, Philip detached himself.

"Désirée," he said, after clearing his throat, "your friend has misled you, I fear. The woman who lives here cannot be her aunt—at least . . ."

"No, of course not," Désirée replied. "I know this is not her aunt's house. It is Georges's doing, and it is not really wrong. They are married, Georges and Jeannine. It is—their parents would not hear of the match, so they had a civil marriage. It was some stupid quarrel from many years ago. Of course, if Jeannine gets with child, the old people will have to give in. But to get with child, she must find a time and place to be with Georges."

"I see. But Désirée—"

"Do not tell me it is wrong for me to come here. I thought you understood. I desire the same pleasure Jeannine has."

"Your husband will give you that, Désirée," Philip said, choking down both disappointment and a desire to laugh.

"I have no intention of having a husband," Désirée said coldly. "Do you think I am such a fool I do not know when I am well off? With Papa I can do as I like—always. Why should I give myself to a man who will think he has the right to tell me what to do, use

my property as his own, tell me what I can spend of my
own money—and everything else, including how often
to breathe."

For a moment Philip stared at her openmouthed.
"You have a point," he said, and then, "but a husband may be as fond as a father, and to yield up your—
your—"

"Jewel of virtue?" Désirée laughed at him. "That is
lost already."

Suddenly Philip understood why Désirée had been
so obliging as to accompany Jeannine. No doubt if he
had not been available, Georges would have brought
along a friend, perhaps a different one each time. . . .
Well, if that were true, there was no need to deny himself, Philip thought. He drew her into his arms again,
kissing her, opening a way between her teeth with his
tongue. The fashions of the times being what they
were, he did not need to undress Désirée to get at her
breasts. She seemed surprised, almost impatient, when
he began to caress them, although she soon sighed and
began to press his head more tightly into her bosom.

Delicately Philip began to unhook her dress. Unable to wait, she pulled loose and removed it herself.
Philip was startled and slightly repelled. The sensation did not increase but became mixed with lust when
he realized she was not wearing anything underneath.
Her pelisse had concealed her before they entered the
house, and he had been too troubled to notice once he
had met Jeannine's "aunt." It was a nice enough body,
although coarser than Meg's, but it was flaunted like
the commonest whore's. Without more ado Philip
stripped, but he was disturbed. This girl might not be
a virgin, but she was not experienced—of that he was
sure. He turned toward her, trying to think of a way
to explain that there was no need to behave crudely,
that a little delicacy was more exciting to a man than
blatancy.

Philip never spoke, however. The avidity in Désirée's eyes as she stared at his genitals struck him mute. It was exciting and disgusting at the same time. Not that Philip thought it indecent for a woman to admire his sexual organs. Meg had praised him and patted him, even spoke directly to the "redheaded soldier standing to attention"—but that was in fun, teasing and laughing. That was not all Meg saw in him. To Désirée, on the other hand, he was not a man with thoughts and feelings; he was no more than an upstanding penis.

It was purposeless to worry about the fact that her father had been kind to him. If it was not he who shafted her, it would be someone else. There was no need, either, for him to wonder whether she would grieve when he was gone. The only thing Désirée would grieve over was the length and breadth of his rod if the next man she found was less well endowed. Least of all was there any need for gentleness, for sweet words or loving looks. Philip, who had always taken time to praise and admire his whores so that they should feel valued, simply walked into the bedchamber of the suite, pulled back the covers, and waited for Désirée to lie down.

It was an exhausting afternoon, although Philip did not need to waste time or energy restraining himself until his partner should be satisfied. She came to climax almost as soon as he entered her and twice more before he was himself finished—and he took no long time about it. However, she did not compliment him or even remark on her own enjoyment. Philip could not help remembering Meg's praise and the way she clung to him when they had finished making love. Désirée tipped him off her as soon as he stopped moving, before he had caught his breath.

Instinctively Philip began to say how pretty she was. It was his habit to speak a few words at least. He

had been cautioned by his father about the cruelty and
crudity of simply turning his back and going to sleep
when he was finished with a woman.

Désirée looked a little surprised. "Are you ready
again?" she asked.

Philip choked. "No, not quite yet. I only meant to—
to—"

"Is there something you want me to do to make you
ready?" she wanted to know.

He laughed. It was impossible not to do so, but he
was even more repelled. Meg could rouse him by the
merest look or touch. In fact, the simple knowledge
that she desired him, without any action or words,
acted as an aphrodisiac. Yet he sincerely pitied Désirée
at the same time. If she continued to act this way, no
man would ever really desire her even though she was
quite pretty—a small, dark piquant face, large-eyed
and small-chinned with a tiny pouting-lipped mouth
and good skin.

"Different men like different things, Désirée," he
said. "I like to talk a little, to tell a woman that I find
her charming, that I enjoy her."

"But you do not need to bother with that with me,"
she replied. "I am quite willing without that nonsense."

"It is not nonsense," Philip said sharply. "Most men
do not like to be regarded as—as animated penises."

Désirée's eyes opened wide with shock. She had probably never heard that word spoken by a man before,
but she knew what it meant.

"A man likes to think he has chosen a woman and
she has accepted him because she finds something of
value in him."

"But that is love," Désirée protested. "I do not want
love. I love Papa. I do not want to leave him. What
would he do without me? Do you not see that it would
be wrong in me to allow a man to think I cared for
him?"

Although Philip realized that Désirée wanted to eat her cake and have it too, he was moved by her honesty. He told her how to handle him, and soon enough he was ready for her. He also suggested that she ride him. That way he could hold off longer, and she could do what would best satisfy her. Indeed, Philip sincerely hoped she would exhaust herself so thoroughly that she would leave him in peace until it was time to go. To forward that purpose he lay with closed eyes, earnestly trying to think of a way to leave Boulogne.

It was not surprising that he did not find a solution to his problem, but he did manage to delay his orgasm until Désirée collapsed into stillness, sobbing with exhaustion. Then he turned her over to satisfy himself. He was quite annoyed when she tried to push him away before he was finished. It was easy enough to ignore her protest and hold her still until he came to climax, but Philip was thoroughly disgusted again. He had never met anyone so completely selfish and self-centered as Désirée—except his own mother. It was not honesty that had spoken, he thought cynically—although the words were couched in terms of her father's need and a putative lover's feelings—Désirée simply did not wish to be inconvenienced by the responsibilities of marriage or the importunities of a man who hoped to win her.

This was it, Philip decided angrily. He would rather have his virility questioned than serve as a stud again to a woman who was not even willing to allow him to satisfy himself, not to mention pretending a wish to please him. Without a word he rose from the bed and went into the other room to dress. Désirée had not made a sound after the angry protest he had ignored. He assumed she had dropped off to sleep. He felt in urgent need of a little repose himself, but was more than content to stretch out as far as he could on a sofa that was more elegant than comfortable.

He thought again of Meg, of the peace and sweetness of lying beside her when their lovemaking was ended. That was truly making love. He had been a fool to yield to a physical need and a sense of curiosity. It was no longer true for him, he realized, that all cats look alike in the dark. Now he could really understand why his father never seemed to want any woman other than Leonie. Then he grinned briefly because, of course, Leonie was jealous as a cat. She looked like one too, her yellow eyes gleaming with rage, ready to spit and scratch if she suspected her husband's attention might have wandered. Philip had defended Roger to her once, and she had shrugged her shapely shoulders.

"So he is innocent this time, but—*du vrai,* he is too handsome that devil, and too adventurous. It does no harm to remind him that I am not a complacent wife— not I!"

And truly it did no harm. His father was a little upset and indignant when Leonie flew into a jealous rage, but he was flattered also. With a pang Philip wondered whether Meg would be jealous. He missed her acutely. The longing for her, now untainted by sexual need, was so urgent as to come near to physical pain. And each time he thought of Meg he was made more uneasy by remembering what she did. It was not safe—no matter how careful she was. He had to stop her from smuggling. Pierre could find another partner. Philip grew more and more worried each time he thought of Meg surrounded by those rough men. And was he really sure Black Bart would stay away from her?

He must leave Boulogne! But now he was worried that Désirée might want to use him again. He felt sick at the thought, but she was just the type to be spiteful and accuse him of something if she thought he was trying to escape her. It was infuriating that he could not think of a good reason to leave, but his mind

would not work and his eyelids felt weighted with
lead.

The next thing Philip knew he was being shaken
awake. He had a moment's confusion and another
brief sensation of near horror when he recognized
Désirée, but before he could betray himself he saw
that she was also fully dressed.

"It is nearly time to go," she said. "You will have
to come here alone tomorrow, and I will meet you.
Georges will not be able to get leave two days together, and I do not trust anyone but Jeannine."

Philip opened his mouth to refuse. He was really
infuriated by the girl's calm assumption that he was
a sexual machine that would function at her order and
—assuming his story to be true—had nothing better to
do on his vacation than service her. However, he remembered in time his last thought before sleeping,
that she was likely to be a spiteful bitch, and instead
of refusing outright he shook his head as if he were
not yet completely awake.

"What?" he asked blurredly.

Désirée repeated herself in more detail, explaining
that she did not wish to bother finding another excuse
to take him with her in the carriage, particularly when
she had no female companion. He could ride out himself. She would forget her reticule. If he were waiting
for her inside, the coachman, who never came into the
house, would not know she had met him.

"It will not take us long," she said baldly. "I can
be out in half an hour or so, and it will cause no surprise that I should stay that long."

By the time she was finished, Philip had seen his
chance. He was furious, but he smiled as sweetly as
an angel and agreed to everything. He would leave
Boulogne at first light. Let her come and find that he
had not kept the appointment. Perhaps that would
make her understand that men were neither bulls nor

stallions and should be treated as human. He would
have liked to go back to Boulogne at once, but was
not given any choice in the matter. They moved on
about half a mile and had dinner with Madame Miallis, Jeannine's aunt.

It was not as unpleasant as Philip had feared.
Georges was a nice enough man, who jestingly railed
at Philip's pretended profession. Apparently Jeannine
had told him about Philip's finding the smugglers'
cache. "You had better watch your back," he said.
"There are those who are not fond of Customs in
these parts, especially of strangers who intrude into
what they consider their private affairs." Then he
smiled. "And I do not know how we poor soldiers are
to clothe our wives if you gentlemen really stop im-
ports from England."

Philip made some stuffy reply about Lyons silk
being better and cheaper and that smugglers should
be in the navy where their maritime skills would be
of use. He had a little difficulty getting these pious
sentiments out, aware that he sounded like a prig, but
fortunately Georges took the whole thing as a joke,
laughing loudly and winking as if to say he understood that Philip could not afford to say anything else.

That avenue of conversation being closed, to
Philip's great relief, another opened concerning the
doings in the camps Bonaparte had established around
Boulogne. Georges was a very junior officer and did
not know much, but what he told Philip served to
confirm the information he had gleaned from listening to Bonaparte's conversation with the men who
had accompanied him the previous day. The men were
being taught to swim so that fewer should be lost by
drowning if boats were upset during the landing. All
the talk was of currents and roadsteads, about wind
and anchorage. In Georges's opinion, at least, there
were no doubts as to the success of the enterprise. He
assumed they would move in the spring, when they

would have 150,000 men trained, but claimed in ring-
ing tones that he was ready to leave on the morrow.

Philip was afraid even so poor an observer as
Georges would notice how spurious his enthusiasm
was. Fortunately the lack was taken to be envy because
Philip, desk-bound as he was, would not share in the
glory and the spoils of the conquest. Philip gratefully
accepted the excuse and even mumbled something
about considering changing his service. The talk
ground along, and finally it was time to go. Georges
kissed his wife. He said nothing about when he would
see her again. Philip assumed either it was already
arranged, or perhaps Désirée acted as go-between so
that she could provide for her own liaisons.

The carriage was waiting when they came to the
door. The two girls kissed Madame Miallis, and Philip
bowed politely and thanked her for allowing him to
visit. Then, at last, they were on their way. This time
Désirée made no objection to Philip taking the forward seat. He was well enough pleased to do so, having no inclination to have Désirée in his lap again. In
fact he could hardly bear to talk to her. He closed his
eyes and pretended fatigue, not caring whether or not
the girls would giggle about it. Actually they were also
quiet after a few sentences exchanged. The carriage
rolled on over the rutted road, bumping more than it
had on the way up to Ambleteuse. The moon was
bright and full, but it was still harder for the coachman to see than in full daylight and the horses were
moving a little faster on the downhill slope.

Philip opened his eyes cautiously and sighed softly
with relief. In spite of the bumping, the girls seemed
to be asleep. He would not have minded following
their example, except that a bad lurch might throw
him onto them. Just as he thought it, there was a
very bad bump. However, instead of Philip pitching
forward, it was Désirée and Jeannine who slid off
their seats because of the slope of the road. Philip

put out his hands to catch them. In that instant a pistol went off, the coachman shouted with alarm, and the carriage came to a jolting halt in response to a loud voice, which ordered them to "stand and deliver."

Chapter 15

Just as he heard the shot Philip had grabbed the girls. Instead of bracing them back into their seats, he pulled them roughly to the floor of the coach. Both screamed shrilly. Ignoring their shrieks of pain and protest, Philip put a knee into Désirée's back and pressed down hard with his left hand on Jeannine's head. He could not hear what was being said to the coachman because of the cacophony of screams, but he had his gun out and cocked. Cuffing Jeannine hard, he snarled an order to be quiet unless she wanted to be shot.

Then his left hand was free and he could lower both windows. He was barely in time. A shadow fell along the road at the right side of the carriage. Philip leaned out and fired. There was a bellow of surprise, but it did not come from the man Philip had aimed at. He was now one with his shadow, flat on the road. The female shrieks that had quieted a bit after Philip's order to Jeannine began anew.

The second man came up fast, more cautiously, squeezed against the other side of the carriage, but Philip had not waited. He had opened the door and leapt to the ground on the same side as the man he had shot. There was one on horseback, too, his guns trained on the coachman. It was fortunate that Monsieur Fresnoy's horses were placid animals, for the way the reins trembled would have sent a high-spirited pair plunging ahead at a gallop. Philip was afraid even these horses would bolt, but he had no choice. Raising the long-barreled Lorenzoni, he aimed and fired. The man on horseback screamed and fired his own gun, but he was already falling forward, clutching with a weakening hand at his horse's mane.

Philip sprang back from the carriage as the horses, unnerved by the noise and the twitching reins, finally bolted ahead. He worked the reload mechanism of his gun frantically, knowing he would be completely exposed on the open road. However, he did not need to fire again. The man who had been pressed against the side of the carriage had not been expecting it to move. He had been knocked down when the horses bolted, and a rear wheel had passed over his legs. He was screaming in agony, but Philip wasted no time on him. Instead he ran to catch the horse of the mounted man, which had not been able to get up any speed because the dead rider had fallen with his arm tangled in the reins and the beast could not free its head.

Philip worked at untangling the rider in frantic haste, flung himself into the saddle, and rode off after the carriage. He had a vision of certain curves in the road that came dangerously close to the edge of the cliff. If that idiot coachman should faint or be unable to get his horses under control, the equipage might plunge right off into the sea below. Just what he could do to prevent this, Philip was not sure. Luckily his inventiveness was not put to the test. When he came in sight of the carriage, he saw that it was moving fast but certainly not out of control.

As soon as Philip was sure that the coachman could manage his team, he slackened the speed of his own mount. There was no way he could identify himself without coming very close, and to pursue the carriage too hard might make the coachman think he was another highwayman out to revenge his fellows. Philip followed just out of sight, judging by the creaks and bangs the carriage made how far ahead the girls were. After a little while he began to laugh, realizing that those selfish little bitches had abandoned him without a thought. It made him think of Meg again, riding to his rescue with blazing pistols and then nearly fainting—but only after she knew he was safe—because she had actually shot someone.

Just outside of Boulogne he caught up with the carriage. The coachman babbled excuses as Philip rode alongside. He had wanted to stop, but the ladies were so hysterical they would not hear of it. Philip assured him that he did not blame him. It was necessary, of course, to get the young ladies to safety. Philip got the direction of the police station from the man and rode off to make a report as soon as he had seen the carriage safe to Monsieur Fresnoy's door. The Chief of police was summoned from his home, men were sent out to see whether the bodies and injured man were still on the road, and the chief himself accompanied Philip back to Monsieur Fresnoy's house.

There both girls, still sobbing intermittently with shock and fear—and perhaps a little for dramatic effect —threw themselves at him, hailing him as their savior. Nothing could be done in their presence, because they shrieked every time Monsieur Fresnoy or the police chief asked a sensible question or Philip tried to answer. Nor would they consent to being left alone. Fortunately Monsieur Fresnoy had had the good sense to send for Jeannine's parents. Her mother took charge of the shrieking "maidens" and the men were left in peace.

Everyone was exceedingly shocked at what had happened. There was the trouble with the thieves, of course, but that had subsided considerably after Bona-

parte's severities in the Vendée. Moreover, they were
rebels who operated in larger groups and were not
known to attack carriages on the road. Usually their
raids were directed against well-to-do farmers or busi-
nesses whose owners were known to support the government. As for common highwaymen—it was most
peculiar that they should be on the road to Ambleteuse, which was not heavily traveled and would be,
in a general way, slim pickings.

Since Philip did not dare mention the kind of
establishment they had been visiting, he kept his
mouth shut at first, although he knew it was common
enough for a "madame" to work with a gang of
thieves. Then another common connection of those
who kept bawdy houses leapt into Philip's mind.
Surely here on the coast such a place would be in
league with smugglers. No "madame" in her right
mind would pay the tax on the wine she served, and
the clinging, transparent Indian muslins were just
the kind of thing a procuress would use to clothe her
girls. True, Philip had not seen any "girls" at the
house, but it was logical they would be kept out of
the way when the place was used for an assignation.
Thank God, there was his reason for leaving Boulogne. Philip assumed a worried frown.

"Gentlemen," he said, "I am afraid that I might be
the cause of this attack. Monsieur Fresnoy knows that,
by accident, I came across and exposed a smuggler's
cache. Could it be that this was an attempt of the gang
I discommoded to punish me? I did not speak of it
before because I had no proof and did not wish to
seem like a nervous fool, but when I came to dinner
in this house yesterday, I had the distinct impression
that I was followed from my lodging."

This proposal became a matter for lively argument
and speculation, Philip adding this and that remark,
trying to encourage the notion without seeming to do

so. In fact the idea did not seem so farfetched to him as the discussion went forward. He remembered that Désirée had told his story to the First Consul in the dockyards in full hearing of at least half a dozen workmen and probably a great many others who had found a reason to pass close by in order to see Bonaparte. Eventually everyone seemed convinced that Philip's suggestion was the likeliest explanation.

"I do not wish to seem a coward," he remarked then, "but I begin to think that the wisest thing I could do is return to Paris. I have only a few days more of leave in any case, and these men seem to be quite without scruples. Mesdemoiselles Désirée and Jeannine could have been injured in this stupid attempt."

As he said it Philip realized that, if he had not resisted, there would have been little danger to the women. Obviously the men had not expected him to be armed. That first one had approached without the slightest caution. Perhaps if they were smugglers they would have pulled him out of the carriage and beaten him or killed him as a lesson. The women would have been permitted to continue on unhurt, although they might have been robbed.

However, Philip was certainly not going to voice this idea, and, if it occurred to anyone else, he did not mention it either. The two fathers in particular fell on his suggestion with joy. His continued presence in Boulogne could only cause them either embarrassment or danger. No doubt their daughters would insist on entertaining the "hero." To refuse would be churlish; to agree might draw unwelcome notice to them from the smugglers, who did not seem to stop at violence. The Chief of Police hesitated fractionally, wondering whether Philip might be useful as bait, but actually he was not eager to tangle with the smugglers either. It was not impossible that too-close investigation would reveal things he did not wish to know. Soon all were in agreement that the interests of peace and safety would best be served by Philip's departure.

He spoke his regrets with an appearance of sincerity that was all the more convincing because of his passionate relief. He was ready, he said, to leave at once. He hoped they would be so eager to be rid of him that they would agree. No one could doubt his courage or think he was running away to save himself—not after the men the police chief had sent out returned with the two dead bodies. The man with broken legs was gone; they had not sought him in the dark. For that Philip was grateful. If the man had confessed that the group were simply highwaymen, his opportunity to depart would have been ruined. As it was, they would not hear of his going in the dark, and Philip had to wait until morning.

To his disgust the police chief insisted on having him guarded and escorted out of town. Philip tried to protest that he could take care of himself. This was acknowledged as true, with some laughter and head-shaking, but the police chief said he hoped another attempt would be made so that they could capture some of the men. Philip's methods of self-defense were too permanent. He was spared taking leave of Désirée and Jeannine, however. Their fathers felt it would be too harrowing for the girls to be reminded of their horrifying experience, and Philip agreed with most insincere regrets.

Fortunately the road to Paris and the road to Brittany were identical as far as Abbeville, and his escort only accompanied him as far as Montreuil. Philip had no more difficulty returning to Monsieur Luroec's farm than he had had getting to Boulogne. It was a shame, he thought more than once as he rode through the peaceful countryside, that Bonaparte could not be satisfied to rule France without wishing to swallow up the rest of the world. He had done enormous good for the country in the few years he had dominated it.

Philip was a little concerned that his presence at the farm would be noticed, since he was supposed to be in Paris at his desk and a good many people in the area knew him now. However, his luck remained good. Pierre was actually in his own house when Philip arrived. That was not as much luck as it seemed, although Pierre did not confess it to Philip; he had made only one trip after bringing Philip to France. After that he had sat home and worried. It was a greater relief to Pierre than to Philip when the young man was guided safely through the dark without anyone but Monsieur Luroec and his daughter knowing anything about it.

The reunion was all the more joyful because of Pierre's past fears. All he had thought about for several weeks was that something would go wrong and he would have the unenviable task of telling Roger that his son was dead. Now he could really listen to what Philip had done and how he had done it and enjoy the adventure without feeling a sick anxiety under his encouraging exterior. He took such a delight in Philip's cleverness that he insisted on hearing every detail, including how he had made out with Monsieur Fresnoy's daughter.

On this subject Philip was relatively reticent, but his expression and the things he did *not* say, coupled with his description of Jeannine's "aunt's" establishment, which he had to give to make the story of the smugglers/highwaymen comprehensible, told the whole tale clearly enough. Pierre laughed his head off, pooh-poohing Philip's slightly nervous feeling that things were going entirely too well and that when the penny dropped, it would go right through the floor. Luck, Pierre insisted, was made by cleverness and care, by foresight and planning. And even when chance threw misfortune in one's way, skill and a cool head could save the day.

This latter remark was put severely to the test when they set sail for England a few days later. It was a fine, calm day with just enough wind to make good headway, and they crossed the Channel in excellent time. Here, however, misfortune was thrown in their way. Some alarm must have alerted the British fleet. It seemed, just when they were too far to put safely back to France, that every ship in the navy was scouring the Channel. Not that they were looking for the *Bonne Lucie,* but they were looking. Pierre flipped the *Pretty Lucy* signboards over the French name and ran up the Union Jack, but they really could not afford to be stopped and questioned—not with a crew of Frenchmen and a hold full of brandy and tobacco. They spent the night running and dodging, and between their speed and skill escaped challenge.

Philip would almost have preferred that they were captured to what actually happened. He had the papers that would identify him and free Pierre, and they probably would have been brought to shore at Falmouth. As it was, they dodged about all the following day, and by night they were much too far east to make a signal to the cliff house for Meg in the allotted time. To add to their troubles a brisk westerly sprang up, which grew fiercer and fiercer until it was clear that they could not make port either in Lamorna Cove or at The Mousehole. It was too dangerous to thread the rock-fanged Cornish coast in the dark with such a wind blowing.

It was also too dangerous to idle about all the next day where such a concentration of naval vessels was patrolling. Pierre gave up and allowed his ship to run before the wind. It was hoped that, if the navy was concentrating off the Cornish coast for some reason, the Kentish coast would be free. Philip knew he should be glad of Pierre's decision. It would permit him to bring his information to the Foreign Office a full week sooner. Nonetheless he could have wept with frustration. He had been looking forward so much to seeing Meg, even if it was only for a few hours. He did not care whether they had time to make love. He just wanted to see her, to smile at her and have her smile at him, to tell her he was safe and would soon be back to make her his own for good.

The settled fixity of that purpose both startled Philip and soothed him. Ever since Falmouth he had intended to make his relationship with Meg permanent, but the idea had been vague and nebulous, something to be considered seriously only after he was back from France. Now he was back, and his brief experience with Désirée had clarified and reinforced his desire for Meg. The trouble was that the unformed notion that he "would manage something" evaporated with the other vagueness.

Philip had no time for more than a bare glimpse of the complexities involved in arranging such a relationship. Maneuvers such as Pierre had carried out to avoid the ships they had sighted required every hand, and Philip had been as busy and as exhausted as any other member of the crew before they made a safe haven at Kingsdown. There Pierre had paused no longer than necessary to set Philip ashore. He would beat back across the narrow strait to the French side, he told Philip, and wait in safety until whatever emergency had made the navy as thick as flies over bad meat subsided.

"If I am not there before you, when you get back to Cornwall, tell Meg I am safe in England and I will come to her as soon as I can finish my business" were Philip's last words as they parted.

However, after he had got to Stour, where Leonie and his father should be established for a few weeks at this season of the year, any hope of preceding Pierre to Cornwall faded. He found only Leonie in residence.

At first this did not surprise him. As Roger's involvement with the government of the nation at large had
become deeper and had taken more and more of his
time, Leonie had assumed the management of their
estates. There were, of course, bailiffs and estate factors, but Leonie had seen too vividly the results of
absentee ownership in her native France. She not only
checked the accounts herself but personally made the
rounds of the tenant farmers to be sure there was no
discrepancy between the bailiff's reports and the
actuality.

The violence of Leonie's joy in greeting gave Philip
a hint that there was more to the separation than he
originally thought. And when Leonie immediately
made ready to accompany him back to London, Philip
realized that their anxiety over him had been so acute
that his father and stepmother had, probably for the
first time in their married lives, been more comfortable apart than together. Not that Philip thought
either blamed the other for allowing him to go; only
together they could not leave the subject alone, and
each infected and reinfected the other with fear.

Philip was aware, of course, of how dearly he was
loved by his father and stepmother, but this new evidence brought their devotion into renewed sharp
focus and added to the problem of his relationship
with Meg. The one deep sorrow of his father's and
stepmother's marriage was that Leonie was apparently barren. The situation had been eased by his
presence and by the recovery, soon after Leonie and
Roger were married, of her Uncle Joseph's younger
daughter, Sabrina. But Sabrina was God-knew-where
with her diplomat husband, and she was a worry also.
Philip had guessed that Leonie was not as happy
with Sabrina's marriage as she should be.

William, Sabrina's husband, was the best of good
fellows, but perhaps he was a bit too good-looking,

and Philip knew William had been rather heavily into the petticoat line. Since Philip had been oriented in the same direction, he could not afford to criticize William—only William preferred the excitement of an "affair" to the simpler satisfaction of buying his pleasure. After he had declared himself to Sabrina, that had stopped, naturally. It was obvious enough that William couldn't look at anyone else once he'd seen her. But now that he had her . . .

Was William finding marriage too tame? Mindful of painful and embarrassing entanglements, Philip (except for one experience) had confined his dalliance to paid companions, but William seemed actually to take pleasure in the alarms and excursions of illicit love affairs. Probably that was what worried Leonie. Of course, if Sabrina never knew . . . Anyway, Philip wished most sincerely that Sabrina would get with child and stop traipsing around with her husband. That would solve a lot of problems. What she didn't know couldn't hurt her, and Leonie would be so concentrated on the forthcoming child that, with luck, she wouldn't worry about him.

Even as the thought went through his mind, Philip knew it was ridiculous. Leonie's heart was bigger than her whole body. There was room for everyone in it, and unfortunately fear is proportional to love. It wasn't her concern for him that Philip was trying to deflect; it was the desire she had, and his father too—although neither had ever said a word about it—for him to produce children. Meg's children? Philip felt sick. How could he present the children of a maid-servant, a female smuggler, to the St. Eyres and the daughter of the Earl of Stour?

All the way to London that unpalatable question rattled around in Philip's head. Various expedients passed through his mind. Some disgusted him; some he knew Meg could not or would not accept. It was an enormous relief to be plunged, hardly half an hour after his father's ecstatic greeting, into a whirlwind of reports and questions.

It took over a week and about ten different people had a go at him, including the past Prime Minister, Mr. Pitt, who, it was thought, might soon be back in office. Philip felt as if his brain had been picked apart, but a good deal more was found in it than he had realized was there, so he could not complain. Besides, everyone was so happy, so complimentary; he was not actually called the savior of his nation, but no one hid the fact that the information he had brought back—directly from the source—was as important as it was unpalatable. Moreover, when the extensive probing was finished and all departments felt they had drained him dry, Lord Hawkesbury handed him a draft on the Bank of England that struck him mute.

This was fortunate, because if Philip had had the use of his tongue, he would have protested and handed it back. He had never thought of himself as a paid spy. As it was, Hawkesbury, who did understand what he felt and for once knew that talking would only make the situation more uncomfortable, gently shoved him out of the office. Philip then voiced his protest to his father, at whose town house he had been staying for convenience. Roger laughed at him.

"I am paid for my services. Lord Nelson is paid for his. So is everyone, down to the drummer boys. You have performed a service, a most necessary one, and have done it well."

"Very well," Philip agreed, after a moment's thought. "I can return Leonie's money, then."

"Don't you dare, you idiot," Roger exclaimed. "You'll hurt her feelings. You could buy her a pretty trinket. She'd like that—but not too expensive. That would worry her. By the way, do you remember that letter you sent about Jean de Tréport?"

"Yes."

Philip did remember it, but it seemed very far in the past now, and all he really remembered vividly was Meg trembling in his arms after the fight was over. Meg should never have been involved in such a thing. Again he was flooded by anxiety for her. How could he have left her so lightheartedly? He had to get back and get her out of this smuggling business. It was an effort to wrench his mind from that to what his father was saying.

"Naturally we started an investigation as soon as I reported. It is still continuing, although not much has been discovered. Either de Tréport was operating individually, reporting only to one man who was clever about not being seen with him, or he covered his tracks very carefully. However, one odd thing turned up. Henri d'Onival, who was known to spend a lot of time with the young men who worked at the Horse Guards, was found murdered in Hyde Park a few days after your letter arrived. He wasn't a known associate of de Tréport, but they did know each other."

"You think d'Onival was involved too?"

"I think so—yes. He hadn't been seen in London during the entire period in which de Tréport was missing, and neither of them was at any of the country houses they were known to frequent either."

"But that would have made three—"

"No," Roger interrupted. "There's virtually no chance that the man you shot outside of Exeter was actually a French agent. He may have been hired to kill or rob you, but equally likely he was just an ordinary rank rider on the high toby." Roger laughed at the expression on Philip's face. "Don't bother to feel guilty. You just exterminated some vermin. He was well known in the area and badly wanted. You saved the country the cost of a trial and a hanging by killing him."

Philip was silent, staring into space.

"You mustn't worry so," Roger urged, clapping his son gently on the shoulder.

"I was not thinking of that, sir, only wondering how Jean got on my trail. You cannot really believe that he was skulking outside Lord Hawkesbury's house."

"By God, I know he wasn't!" Roger exclaimed. "He came here not an hour after you left, asking about you. He said you had a dinner engagement for the previous night and you hadn't met him—did you?"

Philip thought back and shook his head. "I do not think so, but I cannot swear to it. But, sir, if I had not come to dinner, why did he not come in the morning to ask about me? Why wait until nearly two o'clock?"

Roger stared at his son, going pale. "Fool that I am," he breathed. "I could have killed you with my stupidity! It never occurred to me. I could—"

"Now, sir, that is not kind," Philip said, laughing. "You should not make it so clear that you think me a helpless idiot who cannot take care of himself."

"I think nothing of the sort," Roger protested. "What you set out to do was dangerous enough without my stupidity complicating it. But there's no sense in worrying about that now. I take your point. Considering our drive home and the time you took to make ready, plus the lapse of time before de Tréport called here—someone heard of what went on in Hawkesbury's office within two hours of our leaving there. That's too soon for Hawkesbury to have blabbed the thing. . . . No! Actually, it's not. I believe he went to the Foreign Office immediately after we left him, and his head was full of your mission. I wonder if it will be possible to find out to whom he spoke."

"Good God, sir, that is nearly two months ago. No one would remember—and it is barely possible that he met someone in a corridor or in some other office so that it would not be in his appointment book."

"I don't think he's that much of a blabbermouth. I wish I could think of a—a tactful way to ask, but the government is so shaky now and there are so many attacks on Addington that any questions are regarded as implying distrust."

"Yes, well, I do not think it would be a mark of confidence to ask if the Minister of Foreign Affairs had just happened to confide the details of a secret mission to the nearest French agent less than an hour after—"

"Idiot!" Roger laughed. "That was not precisely the question I was going to raise."

"No, I suppose not, but it is not impossible. After being shown around the installations at Boulogne by Bonaparte himself, I could believe almost anything." Philip hesitated, then went on suddenly, "Sir, there is a simple answer that does not presuppose Lord Hawkesbury to be a fool. There was another person present beside you and myself. Could d'Ursine not be what he seems?"

Roger bit his lip. "It crossed my mind—yes, but I cannot believe it. Really, it is unthinkable. He suffered very severely in the Revolution. I believe his father was executed and his wife and children died under brutal circumstances."

"He went back," Philip remarked tentatively. "Leonie would not go back. She did not even want you to try to reclaim her estate."

Doubt filled Roger's eyes. "Well, it was easy enough for her. That was so insignificant in comparison with the Stour lands. And you know she felt it would be wrong to reclaim the lands when she could not live on them. Her father gave her a horror of being an absentee landlord. I have had a devil of a time convincing her not to sell the Irish properties because she cannot be there to make sure they are fairly administered. It is a very different thing for d'Ursine, who is virtually a pauper. I don't believe he has any income at all, except what he is paid by Hawkesbury.

Naturally, he would be eager to reclaim his French property which, I believe, was extensive."

"I suppose you are right, sir, but there is something so—so theatrical in his hate for Bonaparte. . . . Leonie never—I mean, she does not wish to go back, but she does not foam at the mouth when France is mentioned."

"You mean to imply the hatred is assumed?" Roger mused. "It's not impossible, of course, but you mustn't judge other people by Leonie's moderation. She's a woman of quite exceptional generosity—not a hater by nature—and also she . . . Well, Philip, you know she was always afraid to express herself for fear she would instill hatred in you and Sabrina. That wouldn't be fair. Sooner or later this war will end and we must deal with the French in peace."

"Yes. But it is not my problem anymore," Philip said lightly.

Roger frowned. "That's not quite true. It's everyone's problem. What I said about d'Ursine I believe to be the truth, but that isn't going to stop me from digging around to be sure. I don't dare accuse him, Philip. As I said, what he has from Hawkesbury is all he has in the world, and an unfounded accusation could ruin him, which would be dreadfully unfair. It's terribly hard to prove you *aren't* a spy. And it isn't as if he were at the War Office or the Admiralty. It's the exception rather than the rule that a mission like yours goes through the Foreign Office. Still, it could do no harm for you to dig around too, from the other end."

"But d'Ursine does not mix with my friends."

Philip was horrified. His light abandonment of the subject of who had set de Tréport on his trail was preparatory to informing Roger he intended to go back to Cornwall. He had come no closer to an answer to his problem of what to do about Meg, but he knew he had to stop her from smuggling as soon as possible. This, of course, could not be accomplished from London. He had not bothered to think of any particularly good excuse for returning. If his father had asked at all, he intended to say that he had left his horse there and that he found the Moretons congenial and the area interesting. Now, obviously, such a slight purpose was not sufficient.

"I didn't mean that you should ask questions about d'Ursine but about d'Onival and de Tréport," Roger said, burying even the faint hope Philip had of escaping his duty. "You can innocently ask what happened to de Tréport, since he isn't in his usual haunts. Then you can ask who were his friends, those you didn't know—and you can ask those for further references. You will need to think of a fairly pressing reason—you lent him money? A horse? He cut you out with a woman?—But you must seem good humored about it, not really angry."

"Yes."

Philip was doing his best to conceal his bitter disappointment. He realized that what his father was asking him to do was of importance; he was the one known associate of de Tréport whose loyalty to England could not be questioned. Since inquiries from the outside had revealed nothing, it was necessary for him at least to try. Nonetheless he could not work up the smallest enthusiasm for the task. All he wanted was to see Meg and make sure she was safe. After that he would be glad to hunt spies or do anything else required of him.

"Sooner or later I am sure someone will mention d'Onival to you," Roger continued blithely, completely misunderstanding Philip's rather bleak expression. He assumed it was distasteful to his son to act a part among his own friends, some of whom might be involved in Jean's and Henri's treasonous activities. That was reasonable. Roger was sympathetic to Philip's distaste but knew his son would not shirk his duty simply because it was unpleasant.

"Yes, I am sure someone will," Philip agreed, "but first I had better think of a good reason for disappearing myself, and, secondly, I had better find out how deep I am in everyone's black books for missing my engagements. I shall toddle along to White's a bit later and see if anyone beside us is in Town. Will you tell Leonie I will not be in for dinner?"

Roger agreed and left Philip to puzzle over what could have caused his disappearance. In spite of having half his mind filled with violet eyes and dark red hair, he found a solution to the easy problem. It was compounded by his desire to travel west and his father's remark about Leonie's Irish estates. It would be easy enough to say that Roger had sent him there, ostensibly to check on the land, but really to separate him from the drinking and gambling that filled the hours left empty by hunting on the country estates to which he had been invited. Naturally Philip would have been sullen under the circumstances and not in a mood to write and explain he had been sent away to sit in the corner like a naughty little boy.

The excuse was so good that Philip was almost cheered up. However, he never got a chance to use it. There was no one at White's with whom he was closely enough acquainted to know he had been gone, and at the gambling halls he visited after dinner—places to which de Tréport had introduced him—such questions were not asked. It was assumed that an answer to them would be embarrassing. No one had seen de Tréport, which Philip accepted as a natural thing, since he was likely to be staying in the country at this time of year. Philip collected the names of several houses at which Jean might be a guest and—since he did not need the money at all—won heavily at both places he stopped. He also drank heavily. It was impossible for him to avoid doing so and remain in character.

It was also impossible, because he kept winning, to break away, and it was five o'clock in the morning before he was able to roll into bed. Philip, therefore, greeted with something less than enthusiasm his valet's attempts to rouse him some four hours later. In fact he rejected the idea so violently that Sorel retreated in disorder, holding a handkerchief to his bleeding nose. The next move was thus up to Leonie, who was waiting in the corridor with a message that she would not entrust to anyone.

Leonie was quite annoyed with Lord Hawkesbury for sending a note superscribed "The Foreign Office—Urgent" directly to Philip instead of addressing it to Roger, who had innocent reasons in plenty for receiving such notes and was better fitted to wake a powerful and furious young man with a bad hangover. Nonetheless, if it was urgent government business, it could not wait until Philip had slept off his head. Leonie had never lacked courage. Resolutely she marched into Philip's bedchamber, picked up his evening walking stick, and prodded him with it.

Chapter 16

Although Megaera did not strike Rose when she was gently shaken at almost the same time, she was nearly as unwilling as Philip to wake up. Not that Megaera had a hangover from drink; she was sick at heart. Two nights earlier Pierre had finally made his long-delayed call into Lamorna Cove, and the previous night Megaera had ridden to The Mousehole to pay him and to arrange his next visit. Pierre had been in bubbling good humor, and the first words out of his mouth had been, "Philip is home safe."

Relief had made Megaera mute one moment too long. Full of his own cleverness in arranging so good a cover and Philip's cleverness in using it so brilliantly, Pierre told the whole story, except that he disguised Philip's purpose. Thus he did not say anything about the meeting with Bonaparte but made the main direction of Philip's effort an attempt to find a safe way to dispose directly of luxury goods to the army officers and rich shipbuilders in and around Boulogne. Philip's adventure made excellent sense from that point of view. It was logical that Philip should plant smuggled goods to test the numbers, honesty, and efficiency of the customs officers. It was also reasonable for him to approach the harbor master. If he could make a deal with him, it might not be necessary to land secretly by night in a cove.

Somehow the harbor master's daughter got mentioned. Pierre, who had never extended his cleverness to the delicate management of women, remembered in the same instant he mentioned Désirée that something, possibly far more serious, was brewing between Meg and Philip. Because he had not cared enough in many years to lie to one woman about another, Pierre made a basic mistake. He paused, looked uncomfortable, and shifted the subject.

Until that awkwardness Megaera had been listening with bated breath, horrified and delighted at the same time. She could not help but admire Philip's bold deftness, but his skill at deception troubled her. It smacked too much of the cully-catcher, and the sly use of cleverness against the innocent and unsuspecting. Like Pierre, Megaera did not really believe smuggling was dishonest. It cheated no one except the government—at least, the way she and Pierre ran the business—and the government was a faraway thing Megaera had a hard time relating to herself.

The simple mention of the harbor master's daughter would have passed right over Megaera's head if Pierre had not become so self-conscious about it. It had not occurred to her to doubt Philip's sincerity, but Pierre's obvious embarrassment coupled with the impression she had received of Philip taking advantage of the gullible officials in Boulogne brought a horrible doubt to her mind. Was she simply another cully to be "catched" for what she was worth by an artful sharper? A passion of loss shook her. Tears welled in her eyes and tightened her throat. Pride followed swiftly behind, lashing her for credulity and demanding that no one— least of all Pierre—know of her foolishness and her pain.

Thus, instead of flying into a rage and demanding

more information, Megaera pretended she had not noticed the halting, overquick end of the story and the shift to a safer subject. It was very dark in The Mousehole, and Pierre was talking hard and fast to cover his blunder, so Megaera was able to hide her distress. The smuggler, thinking he had gotten away with his coverup, decided to leave before he put his foot in his mouth again. He arranged the date and signals for his next trip, but Megaera understood that these were now tentative, depending on the more and more uncertain weather. She would wait for his signal for several hours two nights running. If he did not come, she would try again the same day the following week, unless a storm was raging. In that case she would wait one day after the storm was over, and begin the pattern again.

Just before they left the inn, Pierre asked about Black Bart. Megaera merely said that she had neither seen nor heard any sign of him—and that was the truth, but not all of it. At any other time she would have confided to Pierre that Tom Helston, who gathered the men and brought them from the Treen area, had remarked to her that he had had to drop four men because they were constantly grumbling and causing dissatisfaction. They did not like the long walk to Lamorna Cove; they did not like being cut out of the distribution end with the perquisites of a little robbery and, perhaps, a rape of a servant girl if they could catch one.

The older men, those with families, preferred Megaera's system. The dangers of distributing nearly the entire shipment on the one night, which was Black Bart's method because he had no really safe storage place—were far greater. They were less interested in pilfering and rape than in getting home safely to their wives and children. The younger men, however, had been inclined to listen to the agitators. They were less afraid of being caught because they had no responsibilities and also because youth was adventurous. To them a stolen piglet or hen had the lure of something for nothing, and a soft servant girl, even if she wasn't willing, was exciting.

Megaera was worried. She knew perfectly well that cutting the men out was not sufficient. It was absolutely necessary to punish them also. If they were not lessoned sharply, and soon, her authority over the men would be shaken. She had intended to ask Pierre's advice—actually she had a faint hope that he would offer to use his crewmen to take care of the matter for her. However, the shock and grief of hearing of Philip's "unfaithfulness" had overwhelmed her. She could think of nothing except his "betrayal" and, even when Pierre's question about Black Bart brought the problem of the disaffected men to mind, Megaera could not bear to discuss anything. All she wanted was to get home to her bed where she could cry in peace and privacy.

She had taken full advantage of her bed for that purpose, only the more she wept over Philip's falseness in the big, empty bed, the more she wanted him. She realized he had not meant to abandon her completely. After all, he had told Pierre to assure her he would come as soon as he could. She found herself making a million excuses for him. In fact, before she knew what she was about, she found she was angrier with Pierre for telling her than with Philip for having betrayed her.

From there it was an easy step to begin wondering whether Pierre had told her on purpose. Could he object to his son's relationship with her? Could he fear that Philip would wish to settle down in Cornwall and no longer be willing to play his father's game? Perhaps there was no harbor master's daughter, and Pierre had made up the whole thing just to separate her from Philip.

At this point Megaera checked her overactive imagination. She knew she was twisting the facts to ease her sore heart. If Pierre wished to keep Philip and her apart, surely he must have more effective means at his disposal than the casual mention of a girl and an awkward and embarrassing shifting of the subject. Rage and shame returned all the more intense for her desire to excuse her lover at any cost. She was just another doxy in Philip's stable. No wonder he was so charming, so thoughtful, always doing and saying the right thing—he had plenty of practice.

Exhaustion finally sent Megaera asleep despite her disordered and wavering mind and heart, but it was nearly dawn by then and she roused most unwillingly when her maid came to wake her. Rose examined her mistress with distress. Her lady had been worried and nervous for over a month now, but this was the worst of all. Rose had no doubt that her lady's lover had betrayed her. Perhaps he had said he would be away for a week or two; perhaps yesterday was the day he had fixed to return, and he had not done so; perhaps her lady had heard yesterday that he had taken a new love—or been killed in a duel.

Rose thrilled to the romantic tragedy, but it soon became clear that it was betrayal, not death, her lady was suffering. Her eyes might be heavy and swollen with tears and lack of sleep, but they flashed with controlled rage under their long lashes. What was more, grief for a dead lover did not send one to examining all the invitations in the last week's post or ordering that all one's dresses be laid out for refurbishment.

Of course, Rose was sorry that her lady had been disappointed in love, but the kind of love that required sneaking out of the house to a secret rendezvous was not very satisfactory in the long run. Rose was romantic, but she knew that sort of thing could only lead to trouble. In a way she was glad it was over, and even gladder that in her hurt and disappointment her mistress finally seemed ready to do what Rose had been urging (when she dared) ever since the strict period of mourning for Mr. Devoran had ended. Her lady was so beautiful. Rose was sure that if she had accepted the invitations she received to balls and other social events, she would soon be married again.

Rose understood why her lady did not seem interested in men. A husband like Mr. Devoran could easily cure such an interest. Most of the servants had guessed that the marriage was not happy, and Rose knew more of the truth than the others. Nonetheless it seemed ridiculous to the maid that her lady would not go to parties or even more decorous evening engagements like musicales. It almost seemed as if, horrid as he had been, her lady were mourning her husband.

Megaera was fond of Rose and, to a degree, trusted her. She was sure Rose would conceal any love affair or any other romantic peccadillo. However, when Rose was frightened by something she did not understand, she could not be trusted to hold her tongue for long. If she had known about her mistress's smuggling activities, sooner or later she would have gone to someone in the household or even to Dr. Partridge for comfort and assurance. Thus Megaera had been very careful that Rose should not know. And, of course, that she had to be out so many nights making deliveries kept her from accepting invitations to evening affairs. Even if she was not delivering on the night of a party, Megaera was in such desperate need of sleep that her bed was far more inviting to her than the most brilliant ball in the world.

Philip's betrayal had changed that. Megaera was more than willing to give up her sleep—or even a few deliveries—to salve her pride and prove to herself that she would still be attractive to men other than a smuggler's bastard. Perhaps she was even attractive enough to snare someone who would make her activities as a smuggler unnecessary. Just because Edward and Philip did not find her worth being faithful to was no reason why she should not try again. Perhaps this time *she* would not be faithful.

Filled with bitter thoughts, Megaera dashed off three acceptances: one for a musicale at the Levallises', one for an informal party to celebrate a birth at the vicarage, and the third for a masked ball—a very grand affair—at Moreton Place. Although she went in a spirit of bitterness and rage, Megaera enjoyed herself very much. She knew she was a favorite with Mrs. Levallis, but everyone was flatteringly delighted to see her, not least the Levallises' eldest son and heir, who was a recent widower. Megaera could not bring herself to respond to him, not because she did not like him but because she liked him too well. Gilly had always been kind to her. She could not repay kindness by allowing him to take on the debts still saddling Bolliet.

Other men paid court at the vicar's party, and Megaera was delighted. She did not repulse any advances, but she certainly did not encourage them either. For each man there was an appropriate excuse: One was too young, another too old, a third did not have sufficient income to help rescue Bolliet, a fourth spoke with a sneer of her father (this was manufactured out of a decent inquiry about Lord Bolliet's health), for a fifth—Perce Moreton, it was—she simply did not like blond men. There was no way Megaera was going to admit that all faces faded into insignificance beside her memory of Philip's dark but vivid intensity.

Nonetheless all the attention was delightful, and Megaera promised herself that she would shift deliveries or try letting John go alone to the places he had been most frequently so that she could reestablish a social life beyond the afternoon visiting and tea parties among ladies, which was all she had permitted herself for more than a year. There was now the masked ball to look forward to. Instead of donning riding clothes and going to see whether the new tenant farmer in the high valley had plowed over the fallow field and left the fields she had pointed out to lie fallow, Megaera began a careful inspection of her ball gowns. At a masked ball part of the fun was not being recognized. All of her gowns had been worn too often, and she and Rose conferred earnestly over how to turn several of the old into something new.

It was ridiculous, of course. Rose knew that one glimpse of her lady's hair or eyes would give her away, but she was too happy to see Megaera interested in something feminine to protest. Between them they devised a breathtaking confection of white spider gauze embroidered with acorns of silver (from Megaera's wedding dress, which she had never worn again) over an underslip of blue-violet that matched her eyes. Harbor master's daughter indeed, Meg thought, looking at herself in the long, oval mirror. Even she had to believe she was lovely. Well, Philip had said he was returning. She would give him something to regret before telling him she never wanted to see him again.

In happy ignorance of Megaera's intentions, Philip was joyfully making ready to leave for Cornwall at the very moment Megaera was planning just what cruel things she would say to him. Despite his intense eagerness to return to Meg, he had not been quite as happy several days earlier when the proposition from the Foreign Office had first been broached to him. This had nothing to do with the proposition itself, but was owing to the fact that Philip was not at all convinced he would live long enough to accept the mission. Never before had he had the experience of listening to a convoluted political plot while enduring a hangover of really titanic proportions.

Hangovers were not exactly a new experience for Philip, although he had not had one for nearly two months, which possibly added to the horror of this one. However, he had never had the misfortune of being unable to sleep off the worst of the effects of overindulgence previously. Thus, when his valet persisted in trying to wake him after he had mumbled, "Go 'way. *Laisse-moi tranquille*," Philip had struck out at him. He had only meant to push Sorel away sharply, but the push had struck the valet, who was leaning over the bed, in the nose with rather more force than Philip intended. Not that he knew anything about it then. He had sunk back into a blessed unconsciousness—but not for long.

Being prodded with a cane was also something totally outside Philip's experience—with or without a hangover. Naturally, being recalled to his misery did nothing to reduce the indignity. Philip let out a bellow of rage, which was a terrible mistake. The agony that followed, of course, enraged him even more, but he was saved from further painful reaction by a trill of feminine laughter that filled the gasping, agonized silence following his roar of fury.

For one moment Philip was paralyzed with shock. Could he have brought a whore home with him to his father's house? He had been living with Roger and Leonie since his return from France, partly because it did not seem to him worthwhile to open his own rooms for the short time before he left for Cornwall and partly because it was easier to conceal his trips to the Foreign Office if he slipped into Roger's carriage. Indeed, he looked enough like his father in height and body shape and unconsciously copied mannerisms that, if his face were not clearly seen, he could be mistaken for Roger.

In the next moment a spate of French had relieved his mind on that score. The intruder, the poker with canes, was Leonie. This was so astounding—Philip had not been of an age when his father and Leonie married that encouraged visits from a very young stepmother to his bedchamber, and he could never remember Leonie entering his room before—that

Philip sat up. Naturally, he was then so taken up with the agony in his head and the urgent need not to retch that he did not understand a word she said to him. For a woman who had little experience of drunken men, Leonie had great patience and sympathy with Philip's condition. She repeated twice, but more softly, that he had a letter marked "Urgent" from the Foreign Office.

"Read it to me," Philip groaned.

"It says 'Urgent,'" Leonie reminded him, unwilling to intrude on state secrets.

"All the more reason," Philip sighed, holding his head. "Do you think I can see to read?"

Shrugging her shoulders, Leonie broke the seal, but there was nothing she should not see in the note. It merely summoned Philip to a conference at eleven o'clock that morning.

"No," Philip moaned, "I cannot. He has found someone else to ask me a million stupid questions. I cannot, really, I cannot, Leonie."

"Now, now," Leonie soothed, "you will feel much better when you are washed and dressed. I will send Sorel back, but you must promise, Philippe, not to beat him again."

"Beat him? I have never laid a hand on Sorel in my life—oh, anyway not since I was a baby and he tried to dress me in those velvet and lace confections my mother fancied, but—"

"I do not think he bloodied his own nose," Leonie interrupted severely. Then she softened her tone. "No doubt you did not mean to do it, but I think you should ask his pardon."

Since Philip was obviously in no condition to argue, she did not wait for an answer, and she was kind enough to smother her laughter until she was out of the room. She explained Philip's pitiable state to his valet—who needed no explanation and blamed Leonie rather than his master for the pain and indignity he

had suffered. Leonie had not, of course, explained to
Sorel the need for Philip to be wakened, only insisted that he should be, and the valet assumed it was
some purpose of her own for which she was inflicting
this suffering on his master.

By the time Philip reached the Foreign Office he
was capable of concealing his misery, although it was
still acute. They did not, to Philip's surprise, remain
in Lord Hawkesbury's office. Instead he was subjected
to another half hour of agony, increased by being
jolted over cobblestones and then a rutted private
lane. The resentment built up in Philip, but even
his headache and nausea were quelled—the resentment
permanently and the physical discomfort temporarily
—by his surprise at the end of the journey. In an
elegant room, more French than English, he was introduced to Charles Philippe, Comte d'Artois, the
brother of the current (exiled) King of France.

Philip was asked to repeat yet again his meeting
with Bonaparte and his estimate of the climate of
public opinion in France. It was apparent that his
recitation was not at all to the liking of his auditor.
Sharp, arrogant questions followed, replete with insinuations concerning Philip's prejudice and inability,
since he was merely English, to understand the
French.

"If you mean the fine points of the language,
monseigneur," Philip snapped, "it is my first language,
spoken from infancy. My mother was Solange Amelie
Marie de Honimarceau, fourth daughter of the Comte
de Langres. French is the common language of my
home even at present, my stepmother being the eldest
daughter and heiress of the late Earl of Stour but
born in the château de Saulieu on the lands of her
mother, Marie Victoire Leonie de Conyers. If you
mean I lack understanding of Frenchmen, only an
idiot, French or English, *could* have misunderstood.
The country is at peace and is prosperous. I was in

Brittany, Normandy, and the Pas de Calais, where the most bitter resentment could be expected against Bonaparte for the brutal suppression of uprisings. There were, indeed, individuals who hate him, those who were directly affected by the cruelty of General Brune, but most of them blame Brune rather than Bonaparte, and anyway, that was in 1800. Most have changed their minds. There is law in the land, most officials are just and honest, and most of all there is work and food for all. Between fear of an army devoted to and completely in the control of the First Consul and the good things his rule has brought, there will be no uprising in France in the immediate future."

"Yet we have had information exactly to the contrary," Hawkesbury put in hastily.

Although he concealed it well, Hawkesbury was considerably amused by the shock displayed in d'Artois's face. Surrounded as he was largely by sycophantic émigré courtiers, who lived by the dead rules of Versailles and whose livelihood in many cases depended on what the comte could give them, the noble Charles was not accustomed to the blunt truth, especially not delivered in a voice made irritable by an aching head.

Philip shrugged. "I do not know from whom the information came or what part of the country he was describing, but if it was an émigré he might be self-deceived, my lord. I, as you know, have nothing to gain or to lose. I tell you what I saw and heard. In the future, when the drain of men and the pinch of war touch them—or if there are military reverses—the people may think differently. At present I could not see any reason to hope that France wishes to be free of her master."

"I do not think Méhée de la Touche is the kind of man to be self-deceived," d'Artois said frostily.

"Then you give me no choice but to wonder

whether he is in Bonaparte's pay," Philip replied
with deliberation.

There was a brief, appalled silence before d'Artois
broke out, "That is nonsense! Do you think a man—
even such a lunatic as this upstart Corsican—would
pay someone to start a plot against himself?"

"Bonaparte is no lunatic. Do not for a moment
deceive yourself with that pleasant notion. He may
be a monomaniac, but he is astute, brilliant, in
his comprehension of the *possible*. He does not dream
vague dreams made up of vapors. He puts thousands
of men to work and hundreds of thousands to train
and builds a fleet and an army that will give reality—
if he is not stopped—to his mania."

"Be that as it may," d'Artois riposted, "you are
ignoring the question of starting a plot against oneself."

"But that must be obvious," Philip hesitated, restraining the words *even to you*. "You start a plot
against yourself, when you are sufficiently secure, to
smoke out any traitors you suspect who are close to
you and concealing their dissatisfaction. I said that the
bourgeois and the lower orders were satisfied. I can
imagine, however, that other ambitious generals, who
have seen what Bonaparte has accomplished, might
think they were better fitted for his exalted position
than 'the little corporal,' as he is called. Moreover,
there would always be the chance that some or all of
the remaining house of Bourbon could be lured into
his grasp."

This time the silence lasted so long that Philip
looked from one face to another, then closed his eyes.
Apparently he had hit a tender nerve with that last,
wild guess. Lord Hawkesbury said something that
Philip could safely ignore, since it was addressed to
the Comte d'Artois. Quite suddenly his headache and
nausea had flooded back, made more intense by his

distaste for the comte. If Bonaparte had not demon-
strated so clearly his unalterable intention of destroy-
ing "perfidious Albion," Philip would have preferred
him infinitely to the haughty, stupid, self-important
Bourbon.

Fortunately he was not required to continue the
conversation. In a few minutes, as the worst of the
effects of his hangover receded again, he realized that
Lord Hawkesbury was taking leave. Philip managed
a civil if unembellished farewell, and they were back
in the carriage. This time, however, Philip was not
allowed to suffer in silence. Lord Hawkesbury em-
barked on the full tale of the results of Méhée de la
Touche's information.

The man, well known to the Comte d'Artois, had
arrived in February with a most convincing tale: The
Republicans were much alarmed by the cavalier behavior of Bonaparte. He had reestablished religion,
emasculated or suppressed the elected, and appointed
bodies designed to help him govern, extinguished the
free press, induced the emasculated Senate to offer
him a life tenure as First Consul, and established a
Legion of Honor, which many felt to be a monarchial
institution. In fact, the Republicans felt that the First
Consul meant to make himself king. They were ready
to rid France of this incubus. If they must have a
king, they would prefer the rightful monarch so long
as he would rule by constitutional right rather than
divine privilege.

The Royalists, whom Bonaparte had granted amnesty and invited back into France, did not love him
any the better for that, Méhée de la Touche also
pointed out. They had been promised far more than
they had received. Bonaparte had refused to return
lands purchased from the state during the Revolution. Even when the lands were still vacant, he had
only permitted the recovery of a small part of what
had previously been theirs. What was more, all their

ancient privileges over canals and highways and other public institutions had been withheld. They were scarcely better off than when they had been in exile. They, too, desired the return of the rightful king.

For the first time, Méhée de la Touche said, the Royalists and Republicans were ready to compromise. Both ardently desired the removal of Bonaparte. The Royalists were now willing to accept a constitutional government if the rightful king headed it; the Republicans were willing to accept the king if he headed a constitutional government. Both groups were convinced that they could rouse the parts of the country in sympathy with them against the foreign upstart, who had seized power because of a few victories really won by other generals who had been deprived of the honors owing to them.

Some of the events of early 1803 seemed to support de la Touche's claims. The need to pass a law to conscript 120,000 in March implied that Frenchmen were not volunteering to enter the army. The sale of the Louisiana Territory to the United States in April implied a desperate need for money on the part of the French government—which was Bonaparte, of course—and a despair with regard to the power to keep the overseas colonies. With such encouragement the British government had decided to support the plot to overthrow the rule of the First Consul, particularly after war had been redeclared between England and France in May.

In August a British cutter had landed Georges Cadoudal, one of the chief commanders of the Vendéan uprising of 1799, in France carrying drafts for a million francs to finance the uprisings that were planned in Paris, the Vendée, and Provence. Since that time various reports had cast considerable doubt on the real probability of such rebellions actually taking place.

"You aren't the first to tell us that de la Touche's

hopes were oversanguine, Philip," Hawkesbury finished, "that is, if they weren't deliberate lies. However, as with the business of the invasion, it was very difficult to sift out the truth. Likely you are right. Some were paid to lie, some were sincere and self-deceived. However, we are virtually certain now that there will be no rebellion, just as you said."

"I gather d'Artois does not agree with you even now," Philip said.

"It doesn't matter whether he agrees or not," Hawkesbury snapped. "We will have no more to do with the matter. If anyone else wishes to involve himself, it will be without the assistance of this government. However, Georges Cadoudal is, in some sense, our responsibility. It is necessary to inform him that no further help will be forthcoming and to offer him a way back to England if he desires to return here. There was also—er—a promise that a 'prince' would come to lead the uprisings when the moment was ripe. This is now out of the question."

"I see," Philip said, and now he understood why he had been brought to speak to the Comte d'Artois.

"Yes, well." Hawkesbury cleared his throat awkwardly and Philip looked at him with surprise.

"Yes, my lord?"

"We need someone we can rely on to deliver our message and to—to assist Cadoudal to return," Hawkesbury went on, "Very frankly we are—there have been several leaks, aside from the trouble you reported. . . ."

"From your private office, my lord?" Philip asked sharply.

"No! No, indeed!" Hawkesbury replied, looking affronted. "There has never been any problem—you are not accusing poor Jacques, are you?"

"I am not accusing anyone, my lord," Philip assured him. "I was only trying to pinpoint the place."

"I promise you we are working on that, and particular care will be taken—very particular care—if you are willing to accept this charge."

"Me?" Philip gasped inelegantly, and then felt stupid.

Whatever the purpose for bringing him to d'Artois, Hawkesbury would not have told him that long story unless he needed to know it. Because he was still in the throes of pounding head and heaving stomach, Philip had somehow just accepted resignedly that Hawkesbury was talking to hear his own voice. Now he realized that, however much the Minister of Foreign Affairs enjoyed his own conversation, he would scarcely have chosen for pleasure a subject that showed his own organization in so poor a light.

"We were most pleased with your speed and ingenuity, and even more with your ability to gather extraneous information, Philip. And then there is the matter of a contact to bring Cadoudal back to England. It is so very difficult to arrange for a British ship to call for him. We hope that you will not need to engage in any particularly hazardous—"

"Oh, forgive me, my lord," Philip interrupted, "I did not mean to sound unwilling. I will be delighted to go. I was only surprised because I thought someone with more authority would be necessary. I do not know Monsieur Cadoudal. Will he believe me? I mean—"

"I am afraid you will have to carry letters that would be rather incriminating if you were caught. . . ." Lord Hawkesbury's voice drifted away and he had the grace to look a little embarrassed after his somewhat less than candid remark about the lack of hazard.

Philip laughed and was immediately sorry he had done so. He raised a hand to his head and massaged a throbbing temple. "That does not matter, only please do not tell my father. He worries, you know."

"Wouldn't he worry more if you simply disappeared?" Hawkesbury asked.

This time Philip restrained himself to a smile; laughter was too painful. "I did not mean not to tell him I was going to France again. I will have to do that, of course. I meant about the papers. And, my lord, now that we speak of papers, I never returned the pass—"

"Keep it by all means. It may be useful and I am sure it will not be misused," Hawkesbury interrupted. "I am very glad you are willing to do this, but I'm afraid it will mean getting to Paris in something of a hurry."

"It makes no difference—" Philip began.

"Well, I thought we could have you put ashore at a more convenient spot."

"Good God, no!" Philip exclaimed.

His violent rejection of Hawkesbury's proposal was not owing to any suspicion but because it would rob him of the opportunity of seeing Meg before he left for France. He could scarcely say this to Hawkesbury, however, and it was absolutely necessary to respond in some way to the surprised question in the Foreign Minister's face. In view of their past conversation, it was not difficult.

"If you do not mind, my lord, I prefer to find my own way into France. I know you said speed was important, but I deem it far more important that I *get* there and that no one is waiting to pick me up when I arrive." Then, in spite of his still throbbing head, Philip's mind really came to grips with what he had been saying just as an excuse. "However, I will need new identity papers. I do not like to use the same ones twice."

"Yes, of course, that is already arranged."

Philip nodded with satisfaction. He had no intention at all of using those papers, and they would serve very nicely to confuse his trail if there was a leak from Hawkesbury's office. Pierre would provide him with a new identity, or he could go back to being a customs official, this time one who was stationed in the provinces and had come to Paris to visit relations.

"And one thing more, my lord. You were so good as to warn me that there may be a—a source of information coming from the Foreign Office. Since my life will hang on this, would you do me the favor of writing whatever is to be carried to Cadoudal with your *own* hand and not permitting anyone at all—none of the secretaries nor even your assistants to see it?"

"You are suspicious of Jacques!"

"I am suspicious of *myself*, of everyone and everything, my lord. However, it would make my mind easier if nothing were written that was not essential and that no one except you and I know where, when, and how I am to meet Georges Cadoudal. In fact, I will not discuss that either in your office or in your home. We can do it now, in the carriage, or take a walk on a later day."

"I assure you that Jacques has been thoroughly investigated," Hawkesbury said angrily.

"I am sure he has been," Philip agreed. "And very likely your faith in him is completely justified. However, it is *my* life that hangs in the balance."

That was, of course, a telling truth. Hawkesbury frowned. "But I don't have the seals and forms that are necessary to preparing identity papers. To tell the truth, I haven't the faintest idea—"

"No, no. Those can go through the normal channels. France is settled and peaceful now. There is not much chance I will be asked to show my papers. I rode all along the north coast without being questioned once."

That was natural enough, since most of the time Philip had been in uniform, but he did not mention that. Plainly Lord Hawkesbury was much annoyed by Philip's lack of trust in his secretary, but he agreed at last that no one should know the contents of the

letter or to whom it was to be delivered, or even that
he had ever written such a letter. All the reports could
be made *after* Philip's mission was completed. He
pointed out, after he agreed, that there were already
a number of high-level officials who knew a good deal
about the plot.

"As long as they do not know the time and place of
my leaving or arriving or meeting with Cadoudal, I
do not care," Philip said calmly.

He did not imagine any part of the plot was a secret
from the French. It seemed to Philip that there was
more chance that Méhée de la Touche had been sent
to England with the tale he told than that the man
was self-deceived. However much Philip disliked
d'Artois, he did not believe the prince would not recognize utter stupidity in an informant, and to Philip's
mind only utter stupidity could misread public opinion in France. None of that would affect him, Philip
decided. It was plain from what Lord Hawkesbury
had said that part of the plot (the French plot, not
the English) rested on a Bourbon coming to France.
That meant that the conspirators would not be accused or arrested until d'Artois or some other Bourbon
close to the throne arrived—or until it was certain
none would ever arrive. Thus if no one knew the contents of the message Philip carried or to whom he was
bringing it, there should be virtually no danger, particularly if d'Ursine—or whoever else was the double
agent—had mistaken information about the identity
Philip would be using.

By evening, when he was explaining all of this to
his father and stepmother, Philip was nearly euphoric.
"*Ce sera très amusant,*" he said enthusiastically. "This
time there cannot be anything to worry about. I am
not seeking information nor is it even necessary for
me ever to meet Cadoudal, as I understand. I will
have a token, which will be meaningless to anyone

except him." Philip uttered that final lie blithely. It was in a most excellent cause.

"If it is necessary, it is necessary," Leonie said with apparent calm, but her golden eyes were dark.

"It's better than the West Indies," Roger agreed with a wry smile. "You wouldn't like some company, would you? My French is pretty good."

"We will make a family party, then," Leonie remarked brightly. "Yes, why not?"

"No!" Roger and Philip roared in chorus.

"Petit chou," Leonie said, eyeing Roger determinedly, "without me, you do not go. You like French women too much. Two French wives. Next you will bring home—"

"I don't like French women!" Roger exclaimed.

"Then why did you marry me?" Leonie asked, pretending affront.

"Because like *un âne,* I promised your father I would take care of you."

"Then you cannot leave me to languish alone in a foreign country . . ."

Philip smiled benignly at them and addressed himself to his dinner. Having had no appetite for most of the day, he was now ravenous. There had never been anything serious in his father's offer to go, although Leonie might very well have meant what she said. Roger was too deeply involved in the government now to disappear on an unnecessary venture. He had spoken only out of the feeling of frustration that chokes a man of action when he is tied to a desk. The half-laughing squabbling between Roger and Leonie, the teasing references to precious shared experiences were an anodyne to fear. They had lived through worse dangers than Philip would face, they were telling each other. Surely he would be safe and escape as they had done.

Chapter 17

As Megaera prepared her gown for the masked ball and planned cutting things to say to her "faithless" lover, Philip at last freed himself from London traffic and sprang his horses in the direction of Cornwall. He was making no effort to conceal the fact that he was leaving this time. He intended to outdistance rather than elude pursuers. Thus he drove his own light, racing curricle with his groom sitting beside him, and he whipped his horses to the best speed they could make. Under these conditions Philip could not expect to get much mileage out of each team, but that did not trouble him. He was prepared to change horses every time those he was driving began to flag. It was a very expensive way to travel, but it was fast.

Waking early and driving until it was too dark to see, Philip arrived in Moreton Place on the morning of the fourth day after he had set out. This time Perce was expecting him, Philip having sent a letter express as soon as he arrived home after speaking to Lord Hawkesbury. Perce raised one fair eyebrow as Philip came up the steps to shake his hand.

"Not in any hurry, I see," he remarked, looking at the steaming, trembling horses. "Your groom looks like something you dug up and reanimated. Have a pleasant trip, Pajou?"

The groom, who looked almost as exhausted as the horses, shuddered. "M'sieu drive, like you say, to the inch," he sighed loyally.

"Um, yes—to within an inch of your life, I think." Philip laughed. "I *was* in a hurry, rather. Pajou, take the horses round to the stable. Tomorrow morning you can drive the curricle back to Dymchurch House by easy stages. I won't need you out here. These roads are better for horses than for carriages. Spite is still here, is he not?" he asked Perce.

The groom muttered something under his breath that made Philip laugh again. "He doesn't think much of your Cornish highways," he said.

"I don't know that I'd care much for them myself at the pace you must have been going. Do you know your letter only came yesterday? Yes, Spite's still here. I've exercised him a bit, but his gait—ugh! I'll tell you something else. Don't be surprised if Fa kisses you on both cheeks or kneels down and salaams. I don't know what you did, but it must have been interesting."

"It is no secret now—at least, not from you, but I did not do anything. It was—er—someone else's idea, and the rest was all luck. Look, I will tell you the whole later, but I must go out now for a little while."

"Go out?" Perce walked to the long window of the library, to which he had led Philip, and looked out. "There's going to be a beauty of a storm. I'd say it was going to snow. M'mother will have the vapors. We've got a masked ball tomorrow night."

"Masked ball?" Philip sounded horrified. He had hoped to be with Meg the following night.

"Yes, and you're on the dinner list. Unless it will cause a genuine national emergency, you had better be here."

"Yes, of course."

The Moretons had been too kind for Philip to distress his hostess by disrupting her dinner arrangements. It might be very difficult, in the limited society
available to her, to find another single man if Philip
did not appear. A moment later Philip smiled more
genuinely. He could slip away from the masked ball.
All he need do was to tell Meg he would be at the cave
late—after midnight.

"Yes, I will surely attend," he repeated, "but I *must*
go out now. I must leave word for my friend."

"Philip, don't be daft!" Perce exclaimed. "If your
friend comes by ship, he isn't going to come tonight.
If you nearly killed yourself and your horses to meet
a boat, I assure you it was useless. No ship will make
harbor in any of the smaller coves for several days.
I know Cornish waters."

Philip smiled. He was not sorry to learn that Pierre
could not possibly show up for several days. He had
been killing his horses to arrive well before Tuesday
so that he could have a few days with Meg, but he
knew it was possible that Pierre's day had been
changed. If, by accident, it coincided with his arrival,
he would have had no time with her at all.

"No, I did not expect to meet a ship tonight or
tomorrow, but I must leave word that when it comes
it should wait for me. Also, there is something else I
may need to do that will necessitate going to Falmouth
—not before your mother's party. I know it is dreadfully rag-mannered to use your home as a way station,
but—"

"Don't think of it. I told you Fa's delighted. You
can have anything you want here, anything at all.
Mother thinks you're a little odd, but she blames
your unhappy childhood. Tell me—no, go ahead
and leave your message, and if you're drowned on the
way, don't blame me."

Philip was not quite drowned, but he was soaked
through by the time he returned from the cave. He

had been praying that Meg, by some twist of fate, would be there, although he knew perfectly well that she almost never was during the day. Fate was not kind, and Philip could only leave a note full of joy and love and longing. Even as he wrote it near the edge of the cave for light, the rain broke, falling in torrents. Philip cursed, but he knew Meg would not deliver in such a downpour. That meant there would be no point in returning that night. Since she couldn't know he was back, she would have no reason to come to the cave. The best he could do was tell her he would come, despite hell or high water, the next night after midnight and each night thereafter by eight o'clock.

Despite his regret at not being with Meg, the time did not drag. Each time Philip had told his story, he had to edit it carefully. He did not, for example, think the incident with Désirée suitable for Leonie's or Lord Hawkesbury's ears (although he would have told Roger if he could have gotten him alone long enough), and he had modified other adventures so that his father would not get the idea that he was reckless. With Perce he could tell the whole thing just as it happened.

"It was all luck," he ended. "Someone is cheering for our side. I mean, what I did was right and should have worked, but all the extras—Bonaparte at the dockyard and the rank-riders or smugglers on the way home from that bordello—that was just luck."

"Not to mention Désirée herself—"

"No," Philip said, wrinkling his nose with distaste. "I meant about as much to her as a dildo. My only advantage over it was that I moved by myself."

"You didn't used to be so fine," Perce remarked. "Is there so much difference between being a dildo and a pocketbook? If I had a choice, I suppose I'd rather be 'loved' for my rod than my gold." Then he began to laugh. "It just goes to prove that the specialist has it all over the dilettante."

"I do not specialize in—"

"Oh, but you did, Philip m'boy. You spent a hell of a lot of time and money in Corinth's or with convenients while I was wasting my time at Almack's. Lucky I didn't get caught, fooling around the marriage mart like that. But you'd better be careful, Phil. You sound like a man ripe for settling down."

There had been the slightest hesitation in Perce's voice over that phrase "Lucky I didn't get caught." Philip suddenly remembered that he had thought at one time that Perce was really interested in Sabrina, but she always seemed to treat him exactly as she treated Philip, and nothing had come of it. In any case, that was nearly a year ago, and Sabrina was married now.

"Maybe," Philip said, pushing Perce's problem, which was completely insoluble, if it were real, out of the way. His own was bad enough. "But I've got a devilish problem. I met—"

The door opened and Philip broke off. He could not discuss Meg in the presence of anyone else, particularly not Perce's mother and sisters, who joined them. No other opportunity presented itself, even after the ladies went up to bed at night, because Lord Moreton made some delicate inquiries that led to still another expurgated version of Philip's adventures. The next day did not provide any opportunity for private conversation either. Both Perce and Philip were kept well employed by the female members of the household, running errands in preparation for the ball.

The weather had improved—at least for land travelers. It was no longer raining bucketsful. Instead the wind was howling with such ferocity that the ornamental trees in the garden were bowed almost to the earth. This did not distress Lady Moreton and her

daughters, however, since it would not prevent her
guests from traveling. Inside their closed carriages,
with fur rugs and heated bricks to keep them warm,
the gentry would not be dissuaded from attending a
ball by a little wind. If the coachmen, footmen, and
horses had had any say in the matter, the decision
might have been different, but they did not and the
ladies of Moreton Place felt no dissatisfaction about
the weather. They hardly paused in their arrangements of the decorations and other details to tell their
brother/son and his guest not to be such complainers
when they came in nearly blown to pieces from fetching something from the village or some other errand.

Philip could only hope the tempest would die
down a little. If it did not, Meg might not go to the
cave and would not get his note and he would not see
her until the following day. This was drawing things
a bit fine, since he needed to buy a cargo—or at least
some items of cargo—for Pierre that would be suitable
for public sale at a port from which the road to Paris
was short. This meant going to Falmouth, and Philip
could hardly bear to think of going alone, not to
mention that he would need the support of a good
English "wife." Anti-invasion hysteria was no calmer,
in spite of the news Philip had brought, and a man
with a French accent trying to buy what might be
thought supplies for the army or navy might be misunderstood. It was much less likely that an émigré
with an English wife would be suspect.

With regard to the weather Philip got his wish,
although Perce warned him that the eye of the storm
was passing and it would start up again. This did not
trouble him, but he was beginning to worry about
whether he would be able to slip away before the ball
was over. On this second visit Lady Moreton seemed
to have put aside her attempt to treat Philip as the
adult acquaintance of her adult son. He was again, as
he had been when they were at school, Perce's little

friend—never mind that he towered head and shoulders over the small, plump matron—and was being treated very much as a convenient second son in the household. He could see that Lady Moreton planned to use him as ruthlessly as she used Perce to be sure that no wallflowers would exist at her ball.

This dismal prognostication became horribly true as the dinner guests—those who had to travel twenty miles or more and would be accommodated overnight at Moreton Place—began to arrive. Philip and Perce were sternly ordered to make themselves pleasant to the blushing maidens who accompanied their parents, and Philip was seated between two sweet and simpering misses whom he labored (with, unfortunately, great success) to entertain. He knew he was successful because of the approving looks he received from his hostess, although he might not have guessed from the behavior of his dinner partners, who did little besides blush and giggle, no matter what subject he introduced.

Philip had begun to think that marriage to Meg—which would exclude him from polite society altogether—might be a salvation rather than a damnation. This idea took firmer hold after the party had gone up, changed into their ball clothes, and assumed their masks, after which he was shooed into the ballroom to keep the young ladies occupied until the guests invited only for the ball, who were now arriving, should pass the receiving line and the dancing could begin.

Rebelliously Philip went instead to join a group of young bucks, but he was wrenched away from a conversation about the speed with which he had arrived in Cornwall (specially to attend this affair, he said) by the start of the first dance. Here it was his pleasant duty to lead out the eldest of Perce's unmarried sisters. As she was neither muffin-faced nor simpering and was safely engaged to one of the youngest captains in

the navy, Philip had a breather and enjoyed himself.
In fact, to his surprise, he continued to enjoy himself.
The donning of masks seemed to release the inhibi-
tions of the young ladies to a very great extent. Philip
thought it was silly; he recognized each girl he had
met previously, and he was reasonably sure they recognized him. Nonetheless, with part of their faces covered they were willing to talk and laugh in a much
more natural fashion.

For the first hour of the ball Philip was too busy
doing his duty among the shy, awkward, or ill-dressed
girls to look around at those who were more popular
and did not need his assistance. On his way back from
fetching one of his least attractive but nicest partners a
glass of orgeat to quench the thirst engendered by a
particularly energetic country dance, Philip's eyes
were drawn to a group of men all earnestly soliciting
a lady's attention. Curious, Philip slowed down to
catch a glimpse of the haughty beauty, thinking that
the advantage of squiring the less attractive ladies was
that one's attentions were at least received with gratitude.

The lady must have made her decision at that moment, because there were laughing cries of protest
while the circle of men broke up to let her pass.
Philip's heart stopped. Meg! Surely it was Meg! It
was her hair, her sweet mouth, her little round chin
so delicate and so determined at the same time.

She passed without seeing him or without recognizing him in his eighteenth-century finery and mask.
Whatever made her do it, he wondered? She was mad
to take such a chance! She would slip and give herself
away, be shown out with cold, haughty sneers, perhaps publicly embarrassed, scolded . . . *I will kill
them*, Philip thought, then realized he was being ridiculous. He was fond of the Moretons, and Meg should
not have done such a thing.

Nonetheless Philip could not bear the thought of

Meg being hurt or shamed, no matter how foolish she had been. He had to get her away before the unmasking, before anyone realized she had somehow got into the party without being invited. He could not get to her at that moment because she was dancing with the man she had accepted, a vision of loveliness and gaiety, graceful, light as a bird, sure enough of her steps to talk with freedom while she danced. Philip delivered the orgeat and excused himself. He was aware of his partner's disappointment and sorry for it, but he could barely say what was civil. His mind, his heart, his whole being was following Meg around the floor.

As soon as he was free he began to follow in fact as well as in fancy, moving as inconspicuously as possible around the floor in pursuit of the dancers. When the dance ended, however, he still had no opportunity to approach her. Apparently her next partner had been watching, as Philip was, and came across to claim her before she could be led to the sidelines. Philip had to go, he had a partner waiting himself. That dance was not a success. Biting his lips with worry, Philip watched every move Meg made and tried to determine from her partner's expression whether he had noticed anything odd. There was no evidence of it that Philip could see, yet to his terrified mind it seemed suspicious that, as soon as the dance ended, her partner headed quickly toward Lady Moreton.

If Philip had not been so frantic, it might have occurred to him that the gentleman wanted to find out who the vision of loveliness was. However, in the state he was in, Philip was sure Meg had been recognized as an intruder. Even if he had thought of the other reason, it would not have altered his actions, since he was sure that to call Meg to Lady Moreton's attention would also result in her immediate expulsion. Thus he threw caution to the wind and rid himself of his partner rather abruptly as soon as the dance

ended. Then he rushed up to Meg, as if to pass out
of the room hurriedly, and instead bumped her hard.

Since Philip was prepared for the results of his
action, he had no trouble catching Meg in his arms
and swinging her around, well away from her new
partner. "I am sorry, so sorry," he cried aloud, and
whispered fiercely in her ear as he seemed to be steady-
ing her on her feet, "It is Philip, Meg. Come away,
quickly."

Philip's shock, which had been bad enough when
he first saw her, was nothing compared to Megaera's.
Hers was compounded by the physical blow, which
had nearly knocked her down, being seized in the
arms of a strange man, who suddenly spoke in Philip's
voice, and then recognizing that it *was* Philip. Philip
here! The betrayer, the cully-catcher, who had doubtless insinuated himself among her friends to seduce
another innocent woman or to fleece them by some
dishonest dealing. Not only Meg's heart but her mind
stopped too. She stood absolutely frozen, staring
blankly, fighting with all her strength not to faint.

"Are you drunk?" Megaera's partner asked furiously, pushing himself between her and Philip, and
then, "Mrs. Devoran, are you all right?"

"Quite all right," Megaera said, amazed at the fact
that her voice came out quite clear and unshaken.

Gaining courage from that, she was able to think
so far as to recognize the first move necessary. That
was to convince Philip she was *not* Red Meg. She had
never wanted him to know, but now it was of major
importance that he should not know. Cheat, betrayer
that he was, he would surely blackmail her if he ever
gained a hold on her. She smiled at her partner.

"You are not supposed to have recognized me," she
said, playfully scolding. "I am not the only redhead in
the neighborhood." Then, coldly, she curtsied to
Philip. "You will excuse us, sir, I hope. Allow me to
suggest that you do not visit the punchbowl quite so

often—or, even better, that you simply stay in its neighborhood, for you are clearly quite incapable of dancing."

The voice was not Meg's! Philip gulped with combined disbelief and relief as he bowed and backed away, still apologizing. The high, nasal, haughty tones were not those of his Meg. Philip's bewildered eyes were still fixed on her, not seeing the surprise on her partner's face that suggested he did not recognize the voice either. Meanwhile Perce had come across the floor to see what the disturbance was. He had heard the comment Meg's partner had made and, although he had not seen Philip drink more than the minimum socially necessary, he remembered vividly how often his friend had overindulged in the recent past. It was clear as soon as he looked at Philip, however, that he was not drunk.

"What the devil's wrong?" Perce asked softly. "Seen a ghost?"

"Yes—sort of," Philip replied, taking a deep breath. "I—I thought I recognized someone, the woman with red hair. But it was not the person I thought—at least . . ."

"Which woman with red hair? There are five here, although three are wigs."

"Not the wigs. There, the one who is going out toward the refreshment room. Do you know who she is?"

"Oh, Mrs. Devoran, yes. I wouldn't have recognized her myself except that my mother made such a fuss when she came in. Her husband died—" Perce hesitated, but it hardly seemed the right time or place to explain how and why Edward had been murdered. "He died about a year and a half ago, and she's been—well, not a recluse but not going to any social events except afternoon teas."

Then it was not Meg. Philip made no connection between the nighttime deliveries and the afternoon tea parties. Oddly, he did not feel in the least attracted to the woman either, although she still looked so much like Meg—what he could see of her face—that he was amazed. He noted that her body was different. She carried herself very stiffly, too proudly erect, no longer graceful as she had been when she was dancing. A real puzzle, Philip thought, but Lady Moreton claimed him just then to rescue another maiden in distress, and Philip had to put the matter aside to be decently attentive and polite.

The stiff carriage Meg had assumed was not any attempt to deceive Philip but only a defense against shaking all over with shock and terror. She had no idea what she said to her partner, who guided her solicitously into the refreshment room and begged her to take some wine to restore herself. Desiring only to be rid of him, Megaera agreed. She would have been glad to take poison to gain a moment's quiet in which to regain control over herself. He seated her on a settee some distance from the tables and left her.

Megaera's first impulse was to run away, simply to slip out of the house and find her coachman and order him to take her home. She knew even as the desire racked her that it was not possible. Almost certainly the carriage was a long way off; possibly the horses had been unhitched and placed in a sheltered area. The coachman was probably down in the servants' hall or in the quarters of Lord Moreton's coachman, enjoying a "heavy wet" and a lively exchange of opinions with the other men of his ilk. Those were not places where Mrs. Edward Devoran could intrude. A footman must be sent to order her horses put to and to summon her coachman. Even so simple a matter as finding her own cloak was not possible without the intervention of a maid or footman. And to be so rude as to run away without taking leave of Lady Moreton and thanking her—no, that was impossible for Mrs. Edward Devoran.

Nonetheless, Megaera *had* to leave before the un-

masking at midnight. She might have fooled Philip for
the moment; he had retreated looking puzzled, but
when her face was fully exposed no alteration in voice
or manner would continue to fool him. Yet she could
not leave without explaining why to Lady Moreton.
For one instant Megaera's sense of humor loosened
the bonds of terror that held her. She had a vision of
Lady Moreton's face as she said, "I'm sorry to go, but
I've just run into my smuggling partner's bastard. I
must leave before he recognizes me. No, he can't be
mistaken. He knows me too well because he's been
my lover."

Tears came into her eyes instead of laughter when
she realized Philip would be her lover no longer.
Never again would she caress his smooth, dark skin
with its triangular mat of black hair, harsh and curly
on his chest, silken smooth on his belly, tight curled
and springy around his manhood. Never again feel
his lips, hot and hard, passing over her body or hear
his voice husky with passion telling her that each time
he saw her she was more beautiful than before.

"My dear Mrs. Devoran," her partner murmured,
bending over her, "that fool must have hurt you."

"Yes," Megaera whispered, then caught her breath.

"Did he tread on your foot? Bruise your shoulder?"

The anxious questions, so far removed from what
Megaera was thinking, recalled her to reality and
provided a solution to her problem. She shook her
head and smiled "bravely."

"I must have twisted myself somehow when we
bumped. I didn't feel it at all at first, but now . . . If
you could find Lady Moreton . . ."

He was off at once, which provided the double
benefit of allowing Megaera to remain hidden in her
quiet corner and of giving her another few moments
to work on her story. She had been afraid at first that
Philip would follow her into the refreshment room,
but even if that happened, she would prefer to con-

front him alone. Philip had missed her partner's look
of surprise when she changed her voice, but Megaera
had not. Since her escort had said nothing, she assumed he put it down to her being so startled or
perhaps hurt; however, she didn't wish to need to use
that false voice again in his presence.

She didn't need to do so. Philip was still engaged
with the graceless girl Lady Moreton had wished on
him when Megaera was begging to be excused and to
have her coachman called to take her home. At first
Lady Moreton would not hear of it. Megaera must
come above and lie down. Dr. Partridge would be
summoned to her at once. She must stay the night. It
was unthinkable that she should be jolted over the
rough roads in the dark when she was hurt.

"Papa," Megaera said, "I cannot leave him for too
long. If I should not be there in the morning . . ."

She allowed her voice to drift away. Everyone local
knew her father's problem. Lady Moreton could not
guess exactly what Megaera meant her father would do
if he found himself unsupervised, but she felt it would
be a disaster. Megaera didn't know what she meant
either, since Lord Bolliet was no longer capable of
getting out of bed until well after noon. However,
Lady Moreton began to waver and Megaera sprang in
with assurances that she would rest quietly in Lady
Moreton's dressing room until her carriage was ready
and that she would send for Dr. Partridge as soon as
she arrived. He would come to Bolliet quicker, Megaera pointed out, since he was closer to the manor.

At last, seeing that Megaera's color was returning
and her voice sounded strong and sure, Lady Moreton
agreed. It did not seem that Megaera was badly hurt,
but if she had sprained herself, she would not be able
to dance and, really, it was very dull to need to sit out
all the dances. Megaera was helped tenderly up the
stairs and tucked into a luxurious chaise longue with
Lady Moreton's maid in attendance until the coach

and horses could be readied. Lady Moreton had
offered herself or her daughters to sit with Megaera,
but she civilly refused, saying, quite truthfully, that
as long as she did not move much she had no pain at
all. Of course, she had no pain when she moved violently either—but no one asked about that so she did
not need to tell any lies.

The half hour's quiet that Megaera procured while
preparations for her departure were made did not do
her any good. Her mind seemed unable to get beyond
the need to flee. After that it was blank. No Philip,
never again Philip—and no other man either. Now
that she had seen him again all the others became
nothing, pale shadows without substance, unable to
raise a flicker of response in her. That pain was so
fierce that she could not fix her attention on anything
but getting away, hiding where she could express her
grief and despair.

Once ensconced in her coach Megaera noted that
the wind had risen again but was coming from a different quarter. In the back of her mind she knew that
the storm would be renewed in full force before
morning. Slowly that thought made its way forward
through her misery and connected with it so that
Pierre came into her mind. Pierre had said Philip
would come "as soon as he could," but Philip had not
come to her. Had Pierre misunderstood him? Was
Pierre false also? Had he sent Philip to find a new
partner? But that was going too far. Even in her disordered state Megaera knew it was ridiculous. One
did not go to a masked ball at the Justice of Peace's
estate to seek out a prospective smuggler.

Then there must be a cully-catching game afoot.
Philip must intend to defraud some unsuspecting individual in some way. She had to stop him. He would
be caught. Lord Moreton was no fool. But how was
she to reach him? He had not tried—or had he? Suddenly Megaera straightened from the agonized huddle

in which she had been sitting. Pierre was no fool either. If Philip had not intended to see her again, Pierre would not have mentioned him. She tried to remember exactly what Pierre had said, but the words had been swallowed up into her rage and shame. Philip had no way to reach her either, except by coming to the cave—and she had not been there for several days. Was there a message at the cave? Did he think she had abandoned him?

Now Megaera leaned forward as if her tense position could drive the horses faster, but she managed to subdue the urge to scream at the coachman. She knew the man was moving the carriage as fast as he could with safety. The moon had been out, the winds having blown away the rain of the previous night, but new clouds had formed and intermittently obscured the moonlight. The drive seemed interminable, but ended at last. Then Megaera had to deal with Rose, who could not understand why her mistress was home so early. Finally, after pretending to take some laudanum to soothe the nonexistent pain in her back, she was free.

Beyond caution, Megaera leapt out of bed as soon as Rose had left the room and locked the door. Ordinarily she waited until she was sure the maid was asleep. She knew it would offend Rose, who would feel obliged to peep in at her mistress to be sure all was well before she went to bed herself, but Megaera could not wait. She could soothe Rose tomorrow.

Slipping through the door to Edward's dressing room, she pulled off her nightdress, threw it into his wardrobe, and pulled on the clothing she wore for smuggling. She had only to lock Edward's door behind her and no one could say she had ever been out of her bed. Megaera shivered a little as she entered the passage to the cave. This was the first time that John had not preceded her with a lantern. Sometimes she made the trip back from the cave alone, if John were still

moving kegs, but there was light and warmth to welcome her return. Somehow it was disturbing to go
toward the empty black immensity of the cave by
herself.

At least she did not need to go in the dark. Lanterns
and flint and tinder waited ready in the passage just
by the door. Trembling with cold and nervousness,
Megaera had to try three times before she struck a
light. With each tiny failure her heart fell. As the
sparks died they seemed a symbol that nothing would
go right ever again. It seemed a warning for her to go
back, that worse trouble waited for her. Still, pride—
and a tiny, forlorn hope—would not let her give up.
The third flame flickered, held, and Megaera went
forward into the dark.

Chapter 18

The first thing Megaera saw was the folded square of white on the table. The light from her lantern had seemed useless, swallowed up in the blackness, hardly piercing the dark enough for her to see to walk. But the letter leapt into her vision, beckoning to her in a dimness where nothing else was visible. Megaera uttered a cry of joy and ran forward. She stumbled against a chair and nearly fell, and the brief pain and shock dampened her spirits a little. It may be only to say he is *not* coming, she told herself severely, but she could not believe that was true.

Megaera was not disappointed. She had never had a love letter before. She read it, then reread it, then cried bitterly with joy, then read it still again. All she had absorbed from the three readings, however, was the first part—that Philip loved her, missed her, needed desperately to see her, that he would come "despite hell or high water." She sat contemplating that miracle until she was shaking with cold. Her heart might be light and warm now, but the cave was freezing. Naturally her next thought was of returning to her warm bed.

It was then that she finally paid attention to the

last sentence: "Tomorrow, after midnight," the letter said. That meant Philip had come to the cave only yesterday and he would return *tonight*—of course, he must leave the ball before the unmasking so he would be here "after midnight." Megaera felt for her watch, but in her haste she had not put it in her pocket. She did not dare go back to the house for fear she would miss Philip. Then she remembered the rising wind and ran to the mouth of the cave. Already the moon was obscured and the wind was much worse. There was just enough light for Megaera to see the leafless bushes near the cave entrance tossed and whipped about. Soon—too soon—the rain would begin, and it would be a heavy rain. Her heart sank. Philip would not come.

Yet she could not force herself to go back to the house. Instead, she lit the braziers that she had brought to the cave so long ago to try to convince the smuggling gang that she lived there. The charcoal was damp from its long wait, but tending it gave her something to do and at last the wide, shallow pans began to burn steadily and give off some heat. Megaera hung over them, warming her hands and face. This far back in the cave one could scarcely hear the wind. For a time she tried to convince herself this meant the weather had improved, but she knew it was not likely.

Against her will she was drawn to the entrance. It was bitterly cold away from the braziers, but it was not the cold that made Megaera shudder. Even if Philip wanted to come, he could not, she told herself. He would not be able to see in the driving rain that was half ice. It must be after midnight now; she had been a fool to wait. Slowly she started to the back of the cave again. She wouldn't wait any longer. It was ridiculous to do so. In fact she was a fool to believe that letter. All those sweet words—they did not wipe out the harbor master's daughter, and a cully-catcher must be a master of sweet, soothing words.

She snatched the letter from the table where she had laid it so that it should not get soiled while she worked over the charcoal. She would throw it on the fire; let it burn! But instead she opened it and looked hungrily at the words: "My love, my darling—at last I am here. I cannot wait to hold you in my arms again. . . ." Like a mesmerized bird, she could not pull her eyes away. Still reading, she sank down on the bed that had never been used and pulled the tattered blankets over her. Always short on rest, and exhausted by her own emotions, Megaera slipped asleep, still holding her letter.

She dreamed of Philip and was light and warm and full of joy, but then she turned and he was gone. Before desolation could overcome her, she heard his voice far away. She ran, she reached out, but there was only his voice and fear tightened her throat and her body jerked with her effort to run faster—jerked her awake, but she still heard Philip calling.

"Meg? Meg darling?"

"I'm here," she cried, struggling to throw off the blankets.

"May I bring Spite in? It is dreadful out, and I do not think I can find—"

"Yes. Yes."

She was free, running toward him, then she gasped with shock as he disappeared. In the next instant she was laughing, realizing it was only that he had turned to pull Spite into the entrance and his black cloak and hat had blended into the dark. He drew the horse in, holding one hand outstretched to keep Megaera away.

"Do not touch me, love," he said, "I am all ice. Let me take off my cloak."

But by the time the words were out he had flung the garment to the ground and seized Meg in his arms, kissing her and squeezing her so hard that she gasped with pain. For a few minutes both were too

immersed in their greeting to be disturbed by anything, but the gusts of wind and rain were whipping
in through the entrance and Spite, being at a loss for
what to do, nuzzled his master affectionately and
lipped at his hair. Philip pulled his head away, which
broke the kiss, and Megaera realized the wet from his
clothing was soaking hers.

"You are soaked through," she cried.

"I must dry Spite," Philip said simultaneously.

"I'll get some hay."

Megaera recognized the need to care for the animal,
and she went carefully to the left, feeling her way in
the dark, to where hay for the ponies was stored. Between deliveries the ponies were kept distributed in
various barns, from which John fetched them during
the day before a pickup or delivery was made. The hay
was kept in case Pierre should be delayed, so that the
animals would have something to eat and John would
not have to take them back to their barns. Philip had
Spite's saddle off and the bit out of his mouth by the
time Megaera had dragged a bundle of hay over. Some
they spread on the floor and some they used in hand-
fuls to wipe the horse down. Finally Megaera got one
blanket from the bed, and they threw that over him
and tied him well away from the windy entrance.

At first Megaera had been so enraptured by Philip's
greeting and by the fact that he had come through
such terrible weather to see her that she could think
of nothing else. As she helped make Spite comfortable,
however, questions began to rise in her mind. Was it
so noble of Philip to come? Where else did he have to
go? Obviously he could not stay at Moreton Place
after the unmasking. Was she no more than a convenience? A body to warm his cold bed until he should
move on?

The activity of drying Spite had kept them both
relatively warm, but now Megaera shuddered. Philip

turned to her at once. "Go back where it is warmer, my love," he said. "I am nearly finished. I will come in a minute."

Ordinarily Megaera would have protested that he must be as cold or colder than she. Her thoughts were so depressing, however, that she retreated to the braziers, aware suddenly that she still had not *seen* Philip nor he her, except as a dark blur. Would his first memory on seeing her be of the masked woman at Moreton Place? Perhaps he had put the encounter out of his mind, believing that he had not really remembered how she looked. If so . . . She had to think of something! She could not let a cully-catcher, a smuggler's bastard . . . Bastard! That was it! Her story, full and complete, sprang into her mind.

The moment Philip walked into the lamplight, it sprang right out again. He was blue and shaking with cold. She pushed him toward the brazier, and he stretched his hands to it, unable to speak because he had his teeth clenched to keep them from chattering. As Megaera urged him closer to the heat, she remembered how wet he was.

"You will have to take off all your clothes," she said, "and I will dry them."

"I will freeze," he protested. "I am freezing now, but naked—"

"You can get into the bed," Megaera urged, pointing past the glow of light.

He had forgotten. He looked toward it, grinning broadly, his eyes alight. Without a word more he ripped off his coat and began to unbutton his shirt. What he thought was so obvious that Megaera flew into a rage, its intensity in direct proportion to her own violent desire to do just what Philip believed she had suggested.

"You, not I," she exclaimed explosively.

Philip paused in his unbuttoning, but it was too

cold to stop and he finished undressing in haste, got into bed, and drew the remaining blankets around him before he spoke.

"I am sorry to be so importunate, Meg," he said, but his eyes were still laughing. He clearly thought she was offended because he seemed to enjoy the fact that she had been indelicate.

In fact that was a good part of Megaera's fury, until she recalled that she really had something to be angry about. "If that is what you want," she spat, "you should have stayed in France with the harbor master's daughter."

"Harbor master's daughter?" Philip echoed.

"Don't you dare pretend innocence to me," Megaera shrieked. "You cully-catcher! Well, I am no silly Meg for your catching. I would not see a dog freeze in weather like this, but I wouldn't get into bed with it to warm it either."

At the moment Philip had echoed Megaera's phrase, he honestly had not known what she meant. In the next moment, of course, everything was quite clear. That idiot Pierre must have told her about Désirée! But he had said virtually nothing about Désirée to Pierre. And why was he being called a cully-catcher? But that hardly mattered. Philip recognized the sparkling eyes, the flushed face, the lips drawn back in a feral snarl. He had seen them all before. Meg was jealous! She loved him!

"But Meg—" he said, making his face solemn with an effort.

"Are you going to deny you slept with that slut?" Megaera raged.

"No."

"What?" Megaera screamed. "You don't even deny it?"

"No," Philip repeated quietly. "I would be a fool to lie to you, whom I love, about something so unimportant."

"Unimportant?" Megaera gasped.

The wind had been taken out of her sails not only by Philip's admission but by his manner. He was quite unembarrassed. Nonetheless he did not look as if it were because he did not care what she thought. His expression was both eager and concerned.

"Perhaps that is the wrong word," he said before she could work up a rage again. "It was very important at the time. I dared not behave out of character." He paused and cocked an eyebrow at her. "Would you rather have me pure and dead or sullied and alive?"

"I don't believe you," Megaera cried. "That's only a story. You aren't Don Juan. You don't need to seduce a girl to remain in character."

"But I did not seduce her! The idea never entered my mind." That was not the complete truth. Philip had at one time considered seducing Désirée, but not after his plan to penetrate the dockyards had worked so well. "How should a young, newly appointed officer of the *Douane* dare try to seduce the harbor master's daughter?" Philip went on convincingly. "Think, Meg. I was there for business, not for playing around with girls."

"Some men find that always to be their main business," Megaera snapped resentfully.

"Well, I do not!" Philip snapped right back. "And you should know it. I would have given years off my life to stay here with you in November, but I have my—business." Philip had nearly said duty and had stopped, forgetting that he had already used that word to Meg in Falmouth.

Megaera only noticed the hesitation, and it sparked her anger again. "Are you telling me," she asked sardonically, "that the girl seduced *you*?"

"No," Philip replied and laughed. "A seduction it was not." Then, involuntarily, he shuddered. "It was

really dreadful, Meg, all at the same time funny, piti-
ful, and disgusting."

Although the lamplight did not reach the low bed,
it was full on Philip's face as he sat up. Megaera
stared at him. The amusement was gone from his eyes.
He was not trying to convince her of anything right
now; he was remembering—and it was not with pleasure. She came toward him and put a hand on his
shoulder. He looked up at her.

"It was dreadful," he repeated. "She was younger
than you, I think, no more than a girl and—and she
had nothing, no feeling at all. I could have been a
hunchback or a drooling idiot. So long as what was
between my legs was the right size and shape. . . . I
was not a man to her, only a—a thing to provide a
physical sensation. There is a shameful name for it,
but I do not think you would even know the word,
my darling."

Unthinking, Megaera sat down beside him on the
bed. He took her hand, but there was nothing sensual
in the gesture. It was a seeking for comfort and re-
assurance.

"God knows," he went on, "I am not pure. I have
paid many women for physical pleasure, but even so
I—I was aware of them as women. And I have never
been ashamed. There was nothing of which to be
ashamed. I enjoyed my partners and I tried to be
sure that they enjoyed me. We talked and laughed.
Perhaps there was no deep feeling between us—well,
there could not be when I knew the girls would do
the same with another man the next night—or even
as soon as I left them. . . ." He sighed. "I should not
be talking to you about such things, Meg."

"I know they exist," Megaera said quietly, "and I
never thought you were a—a virgin. It's odd to say that
about a man, but it must be true at some time in his
life."

"Not for long in mine," Philip admitted, smiling

wryly. Then he shook his head. "But I have never had an experience like that—never!"

"I don't understand."

So, although Philip was not in general a man who kissed and told, he did describe to Megaera the whole episode with Désirée, ending, "It was completely outside my experience, and that is not small. She did not know how to kiss; she did not want me to caress her or tell her she was pretty or that she had pleased me; she did not wish to please me! Of course, it might have been my fault. She might have sensed somehow that I was not really willing—"

"Now that's going too far," Megaera interrupted. She was convinced of the truth of Philip's tale, and as her jealousy washed away her sense of humor was restored. "Now you are just pandering to my vanity to make me forgive you."

Philip's startled expression was proof enough that he had not even been thinking of that. Megaera was flattered. Whether it had been true at the time or not, Philip honestly now thought that he had been unwilling. Then he grinned at her.

"Oh, my body was willing. Be reasonable, Meg. I had not looked at a woman since I left you. Well, I am not used to so much—to such restraint. I was, in fact, hard up. I am now, too," he added plaintively. "I have been a model of faithful celibacy since my—my rape by that repulsive girl." He did not say he had been too busy and too tired to think of women; that would not have been politic.

"Have you?" Megaera's voice quivered—a little laughter, a little desire, a little doubt.

"One look at me will prove it," Philip said naughtily, and lifted her hands to kiss and nibble the fingertips.

Megaera pulled her hands away. "They're filthy, Philip."

"And cold, too. You found the cure for me. I am

warm enough now. Come to me, Meg." He had been
smiling, but his face changed suddenly to deep seriousness. "There have been many women, but never
before one I loved. Meg, I love you, truly I do. I cannot bear to think we could ever be parted for long.
We must—"

She put a hand over his mouth, her eyes suddenly
full of tears. What right had she to be jealous? And
was she any better than the harbor master's daughter? Was she not using Philip nearly in the same way?
She had no intention of sharing her life with him.
How could a Bolliet share a life with a smuggler's
bastard? As much to silence him as because she desired
him, Megaera began to undress. Perhaps, if she had
time, she could think of some kind reason why she
could not be his forever. Perhaps he would be diverted
and forget what he had been saying.

Certainly if Megaera's purpose had really been to
think, she made the wrong move. The moment she
slipped in beside Philip, all thought was suspended.
The warmth of his body was like a foretaste of heaven,
and the full dinner was soon served. Although Philip
tried to restrain himself, it was apparent from the
urgency of his caresses, the frantic play of hands and
lips, and the involuntary thrusts of his hips that he
had spoken the truth about being in physical need.
Fortunately Megaera was just so inclined—even more
so; there had been no male Désirée to release her
tensions.

Philip could sense her desire, and, excited as he
was, he feared to fail her. Perhaps because they had
been talking of Désirée the expedient he had used
then came into Philip's mind. Instead of mounting
Megaera, he pulled her atop him. She was confused
at first, but perfectly willing to try something new
that would give her lover pleasure. It was a revelation
to her to regulate her own speed and angle of movement. Moreover, the position made her breasts and

throat more easily available to Philip's hands and lips, since he did not need to support himself.

The device produced all and more than Philip hoped. In a very short time Meg was crying out so loudly that he reached up and pulled her head down to close her mouth with his. He barely had strength and control for it, however. Megaera's plunging, twitching climax threw him almost immediately into his own, and his groans mingled with the last of her sighs and whispers. She lay limp above him—and that, too, was delightful. It was the closest and warmest they could be, and Megaera's weight was no problem to Philip, as his would have been to her.

Meg's yielding had not really diverted Philip. He was more, not less, determined to make their union permanent. There was so marked a difference between this lovemaking and the last, crude coupling with Désirée that his need always to have Meg was deeply underscored. But in the quiet that followed their mating he felt no urgency to mention that problem to which he still had no solution. Instead, he touched her hair and kissed her little round chin. He began to say again that she was more beautiful than ever, but he was suddenly reminded of that other beauty whose hair and chin were, as far as he could remember, identical with Meg's.

"I had the oddest experience earlier tonight," he said lazily. "I was at a masked ball at Moreton Place—" He stopped abruptly because Megaera's body had tensed all over. "What is it love?" he asked.

"What were you doing at Moreton Place?" Megaera challenged. She needed to divert him from asking about their meeting. Although she had her story ready, she did not want to lie to Philip. In addition, the mention of Moreton Place had recalled his cully-catching activities to her mind.

"I am a guest there," Philip said, laughing.

"You are cully-catching there!" Megaera contradicted. "Oh, Philip, don't. Please don't. Lord Moreton is no fool. You will be caught. Please! I can't bear the thought of you cheating, tricking the innocent. Surely you make enough on the smuggling lay. Surely you don't need to—to gull the unwary."

Philip had been about to confess all, to tell Meg that he had been a schoolmate of Perce Moreton's, when she had interrupted him. He hesitated, wondering whether she would believe him or whether she would think it was another lie tied in with whatever unsavory scheme she believed him to be hatching. At once he realized that the hesitation had precluded his telling the truth. If he had burst out with it at once, she might have sensed the spontaneity. Now if he spoke she would only be more convinced he was lying. Still, he did not want her to think him a "sharp."

"I am not!" he said forcefully. "I do not gull the unwary."

Megaera slipped to the side. She had meant to move away, but it was too cold and she pressed herself against Philip, shivering a little from the chill of the unwarmed portion of the bed.

"Don't play with words," she begged. "Whatever you call what you're doing at Moreton Place—stop, please—for my sake if not for your own."

Philip opened his mouth to protest innocence again, and then, realizing she would never believe him, decided to make a virtue of a necessity. Let her think she had turned him away from crime. It would make her feel good and do no harm. He shrugged his shoulders.

"Very well. It was not what you think, Meg, but if you do not like me to stay there, I will move back to the house on the cliff. I must go back to France with Pierre again, darling, but this time it should not be for long. When will he be back, love?"

"Not this week. The weather is too bad. I will

watch for him again next Tuesday. But you cannot live in the cliff house in this weather, Philip."

"I suppose I could stay here," he said without enthusiasm. The cave was not a very attractive place of residence.

"Oh, no!" Megaera exclaimed.

It was her immediate reaction to the fact that Philip would inevitably learn of the passage to Bolliet if he lived in the cave. Although she was pleased and touched by Philip's willingness to give up his present dishonest enterprise, whatever it was, his agreement had fixed in her mind that there had been something dishonest afoot. This made her too fearful to expose herself to him. Half her mind said: *He loves me; he would never betray me.* The other half cautioned: *Now he loves you, but a cully-catcher finds weak prey irresistible; be safe, not sorry.*

A little devil tickled Philip, and he said most seriously, "If I promise not to do anything of which you would disapprove, Meg, why shouldn't I stay at Moreton Place? I can slip out after dark each night and come here to meet you."

The question confirmed Megaera's worst fears. "Can a cully-catcher keep a promise?" she asked coldly.

"I said I was not," Philip replied sharply, but not as angrily as he might have. Something in the voice and phrasing of that sentence of Meg's reminded him again of the haughty Mrs. Edward Devoran. "Never mind," he continued before Meg could respond to his protest. "Tell me instead why I saw a woman who I could have sworn was you at that masked ball."

"You should not need to ask such a question," Megaera replied, her voice trembling. There was no hope of diverting him again. If she tried to sidestep the question, he would begin to investigate and soon discover the truth. She would have to tell her story. "And you should have been more of a gentleman than to do so."

"What the devil do you mean?" Philip asked, drawing back so he could see Meg's face. It was flushed, and she would not meet his eyes.

That ended her last hope of not saying the lying words outright. "She is my sister," Megaera whispered, and then louder, defiantly, "My *half* sister."

"My God," Philip gasped, "you mean you are Mrs. Devoran's natural sister?"

"Very natural," Megaera confirmed.

The lie had been hard to get out. Philip always seemed to know when she was lying, and she had been very much afraid that he would laugh at her and then insist on the truth. His ready acceptance was such a relief that it sparked a devil of mischief in Megaera and gave a fillip of enjoyment to her pretense.

"Are you judging only on looks," Philip asked, "or were you—recognized."

The question supplied the answer to a number of things Megaera knew she would need to explain as soon as Philip began seriously to consider her background, and she determined to play her hand for all it was worth. This time the cully would catch the catcher.

"Oh, yes. I was brought up in the household. I am a year the elder. My father married soon after I was born, but he did not abandon me. My sister and I were raised together, educated together—"

"I see." Philip thought he did see. "My love," he went on gently, "I know it is galling to be eldest and yet not—not first. Still, it is very wrong of you to engage in such a venture as smuggling. If it becomes known, you would bring great shame on your house. Sweet, give it up. I will explain to Pierre—"

"Do you think I have become a smuggler to spite my sister?" Megaera laughed. "Don't be silly! I'm smuggling to save Bolliet from the gull-gropers. My father is a gambler and a drunkard, and my stupid sister allowed him to marry her to one of his own ilk.

Between them Edward and my father sank the lands under huge mortgages. All that idiot sister of mine could think of was to sell her mother's jewels—oh, well, she meant it for the best, but she's too proud by half. She's a real grande dame."

"Yes, I know, I met her—"

"But you needn't think you can make anything out of knowing who I am. She would just disown me and throw me out, so—"

Megaera's voice checked. The look on Philip's face had silenced her. She was so frightened that for the moment she was paralyzed and mute. Without a word he threw back the covers and began to get out of bed. She knew that he was so bitterly hurt, so blazingly angry that if he got away she would never see him again. She flung herself forward and caught him, crying, "Forgive me! Philip, forgive me! I am so afraid all the time. Don't leave me. Don't be so angry!"

He turned stiffly, not even shivering in the cold. "How could you bed me and think such a thing?" he choked.

"I'm afraid. I'm afraid. I'm sorry. I'm sorry."

She began to cry bitterly, clinging to him. After a moment his body relaxed, and he got back into the bed and took her heaving body into his arms. It was unfair to be angry with poor Meg. He could understand, now that his own initial fury had subsided, why she was so desperate to hide who she was from everyone, and it was natural that she should be defensive, should strike out to protect herself even from him now that she was exposed. It was still hurtful that she should have been suspicious, but Philip realized he was hiding many things from her also and she must sense that.

"Do not cry, Meg," he said softly after a while. "You need not be afraid of me. I will never do anything to hurt you, I swear it. Do not cry, love." The frantic sobbing diminished and the desperate clutch on him relaxed a little. Philip patted her consolingly. "But Meg, darling, do you not see it is not your problem? Why do you not let Mrs. Devoran worry about the estate, since it will undoubtedly belong to her some day."

Megaera stared at him for one terrified instant. She had been wrong to lie, and now she was caught up in the lie. If she told Philip the truth now, he would leave her; he would never forgive her for her distrust. She had to answer as if the stupid pastiche of truth and lies were real.

"Because she wouldn't do anything," Megaera said softly, her voice still somewhat broken by lingering sobs. "She would just let it all go and wring her hands. We would all be thrown out. Maybe she could marry again, but there wouldn't be any dowry for me. . . . Not that that matters, but she couldn't take my father with her. He's—he's pretty far gone. Anyone would insist on locking him up and . . . Maybe he hasn't been much of a father, but he loves me . . . as much as he can. I couldn't . . ."

Philip's mind had been working frantically throughout this not-too-lucid explanation. From his point of view things were even worse. He had thought all he need do was offer Meg security and she would give up the smuggling. Now he found she was struggling to save an encumbered estate that was not even hers. It would have been bad enough to need to explain to his parents that he was making a permanent arrangement that would preclude marriage. Philip knew Meg would not stand for his marriage no matter how he tried to explain that it was only for the purpose of providing grandchildren for his parents—and she would be right. Unless he had the misfortune to marry a monster like his own mother, years of avowed and approved relationship strengthened by the bond of children was sure to damage, if not destroy, an illicit love, no matter how strong.

Besides, now an irregular relationship was not to be thought of. Although she was illegitimate, Meg was acknowledged to belong to a decent family. It would have to be marriage. Philip shuddered at the thought of the pain he would inflict on his father and Leonie. How would he ever explain that he intended to marry the bastard of a drunken sot who had gambled away his estate so that his daughter started smuggling to . . . No! And yet Meg herself was so fine, so good. Perhaps if they met her first . . .

Even so, could he force Meg to leave her father and sister to destruction? He doubted it. The estate he would inherit from his father was adequate rather than handsome. Of course, it was growing considerably as Roger added to it from income derived from his practice as a barrister and his government work. Still, he did not think his father would permit him to pledge it to save lands on which he would never have a claim. And he did not know how great the encumbrance was.

"How much is owed?" he asked, when Meg's voice finally trailed away. He was wondering whether he could manage to pay the interest, at least, so that the lands would not be forfeit and Meg could quit the dangerous game she was playing.

Although she had no notion of most of Philip's thoughts, Megaera understood what was behind his question immediately. She felt even more guilty for having deceived him. Obviously Philip intended to try to get the money for her, but she could not permit that. He could have no idea of the sum involved, and he might do something desperately dangerous when he found out.

"I—I don't know," she stammered, never having expected this contingency and having no better answer.

"What do you mean, you do not know?" Philip said, pushing her away a little to look at her face.

"I—I never asked. It—it didn't matter, did it? I knew it would take years and years to pay back, so—"

"You little, loving idiot!" Philip exclaimed, torn between surprise at her goodness and irritation at her trustfulness. "You mean you just hand over the money? How do you know what your sister is doing with it?"

"She wouldn't cheat. She wouldn't!" Megaera gasped, caught between the devil that was her lie and the deep blue sea of Philip's desire to help her.

"I did not mean to imply that your sister is deliberately dishonest, only that she may be using the money for other things that she feels are equally necessary. And those things might be more necessary to her than to you. That gown she was wearing tonight, for example. It was not inexpensive."

"She didn't spend money on that. I know she didn't," Megaera protested. "I helped her make it. Let it go, Philip, please."

"No, because I think I could help."

"My sister wouldn't hear of it. She doesn't know you exist."

"She knows now," Philip pointed out. "I accosted her at the ball and called her Meg."

"I can explain that, but—"

"You find out what that debt is," Philip ordered. "And do not take any 'no's' from her, you little ninny. I know you have been made to believe that she must always come first and have her own way, but that *must* end now. As I told you, I must go to France again, but when I come back this time I intend to take you away with me."

"Oh, Philip, I couldn't," Megaera wailed.

"Yes, you can! Now listen to me. Find out what the full sum is and what the quarterly interest is. Maybe I can find a way to pay part of the interest. The rest can be made up from the rents. Probably there would not be much left over, but your father and sister could continue to live here until she marries again. Then—"

"No! No, I can't let you. Don't do anything rash. It's my problem, Philip, not yours."

Philip lifted her chin and stopped her lips. "Your problems are my problems, Meg. Love is like that. Now stop being such a goose. There isn't any sense in our arguing about this until I know what the figures are, but if your smuggling is paying the piper, I might be able to swing it. We would have to live close, no luxuries, but we could be together without the customs men breathing down our necks."

Even as he said it Philip began to wonder whether he was doing the right thing at the wrong time. He had no doubts about wanting Meg, but it might not be wise to take her away, because it was not really likely they could be together. He was reasonably sure this would not be the last time he would be sent to France or even farther afield. Would it be fair to her to force her on his parents and then leave her alone? Roger and Leonie would not be unkind, but Meg might well guess how little welcome she and her expensive troubles would be to them. And to face the snide remarks and nasty insinuations of the *ton*— those who would receive her for the sake of the Stours and the St. Eyres—all alone, that would be cruel.

In any case there was no time to marry her before he left for France again. In London or Kent he could have obtained a special license and married her the next day, but he knew no bishop in Cornwall and the thought of explaining this situation to Lord Moreton —who might or might not know of Meg's existence— was more than Philip could face. Perce's father would certainly try to dissuade him from what he would consider (and Philip himself considered, except that he loved Meg too much to give her up) a disastrous action. Perce would undoubtedly agree with his father.

Philip knew he would lose his temper, which would not convince anyone of Meg's sweetness, only of her hold on him. No!

Then an idea struck Philip. Perhaps he could work the deal from the other direction and protect Meg from her vampire sister and father through Pierre. It was the winter season anyway, and the long passage between Brittany and Cornwall could only be made at very irregular intervals. Philip believed he could convince Pierre not to make a run until he himself returned. Even better, perhaps he could convince Pierre to go back to his old base in Belgium and run lace and Dutch brandy if he could not obtain French wine. That would keep Meg out of trouble, not do Pierre's business any harm, and, in the short run, keep Pierre closer to Paris until he finished this job.

Megaera had not said anything when Philip said he would take her away. She was aware that it was not a proposal of marriage; perhaps Philip, like his father, did not believe in marriage. Nonetheless she recognized his deep seriousness. All she could do was bury her face in his shoulder and struggle with her tears. He was so good. Imagine him being willing to take on such a burden only to have her. What was she to do? Every cell in her body cried out to belong to Philip forever, but how could she? Even if the debts could somehow be settled or staved off, there was the stupid lie she had told between them and, even worse, how could a Bolliet live openly with a smuggler's bastard?

Chapter 19

Jacques d'Ursine did not learn of Philip's new mission until several days after he had left London. Although Lord Hawkesbury could not believe the suspicions cast on his secretary, he had given his word that this matter should not be discussed with *anyone* except the Prime Minister or the Minister for War or others at that level of government—and it was not. There is a limit, however, to what can be kept from a confidential secretary who wishes to pry. Putting two and two together, and then looking in the places in which the "four" might be filed, put Jacques in possession of all the facts, except one, within three days.

Because the original plot was no secret from d'Ursine—he had provided the clues that made Méhée de la Touche's story fit British desires and expectations so perfectly—he did not need the names of the conspirators or the outlines of the plot itself. From the files he had pried into, he discovered that "Baptiste Sevalis," a Parisian merchant, had papers that permitted him to trade in Paris, and that those papers had been given to Philip St. Eyre.

It was highly unlikely that Philip was expected to

stay in France for any length of time, so the purpose
could not be to insinuate himself into a responsible
position—as d'Ursine had done. Moreover, there were
no military secrets that could be ferreted out quickly
in Paris. Then Philip was going as a messenger. It was
possible that he was merely picking up information
from spies there, but not likely. It would be ridiculous
to risk a young nobleman with Philip's abilities and
family influence as a simple messenger boy. Thus the
message was crucial and Philip's special qualifications
were needed.

Logic then told d'Ursine that Philip was going to
meet Cadoudal. Obviously, then, Philip must be
carrying the name of the "prince" who was coming
to lead the uprisings, and the time and place of his
arrival· so that Cadoudal and his fellow conspirators
could meet him. Unfortunately, something had gone
wrong and Hawkesbury had not asked Jacques to prepare the message. Jacques felt a flicker of fear. Was
he suspected? It did not seem so from Lord Hawkesbury's manner, but who could tell anything from the
English who, glad or sad, furious or joyful, even when
making love, no doubt, had all the animation of
dead fish. Then he shrugged. Lord Hawkesbury would
not be in office much longer. If there was any danger,
d'Ursine would simply slip away and François Charon
would arrange for his passage back to France, where
he could claim his reward.

Since d'Ursine had no entrée into the Admiralty, it
was not possible for him to find out whether a naval
cutter would land Philip in Normandy or the Pas de
Calais or whether Philip would make his own arrangements as he had before. Nor did Jacques intend to
use amateurs again. The debacle caused by Jean and
Henri was more than he liked to consider. He was
reasonably sure he had managed to silence Henri
before his tongue wagged—imagine that fool trying to
blackmail him—but he was not taking any more

chances with self-important idiots who had neither experience nor understanding. Philip St. Eyre was more of an opponent than he had believed originally.

Expending more care than usual, d'Ursine went to a shop that dealt with old manuscripts and foreign books. The owner welcomed him with restrained enthusiasm and told him he had something special in his line. They went together into the private showroom. In a few minutes another man joined them. He had not come through the shop. François Charon and Alexander Hilliers were slick and believable—and both had families in France supported, protected, and *watched* by Joseph Fouché. There was no chance either would betray his purpose or d'Ursine, no matter what the circumstances, and both knew several routes to France. Each carried, after d'Ursine left, full information about Philip himself, the message d'Ursine believed he was bringing to France, and the recommendation that Philip should be killed, as he was dangerously adept at spying, quite ruthless, and had already brought to England information very detrimental to France's war.

Later that day François Charon told his English assistant that he was going to Scotland to obtain several manuscripts that had become available. The assistant accepted the information without surprise. Mr. Charon did a great deal of traveling and never gave him more than a day's warning. Needless to say, Charon traveled south rather than north. His task was to take the information d'Ursine had brought directly to Fouché by the quickest route available. Usually he did not go himself, but this news was of crucial importance. Once a Bourbon was discovered in a plot against Bonaparte, the family could be discredited and the First Consul could take the next step in his program and found a hereditary dynasty.

Alexander Hilliers did not need to make excuses to anybody. He rented a chaise not more than half

an hour after he left Charon's bookshop and set out
to stop Philip in England if he could find him. This
was not impossible, since d'Ursine knew that Philip
met a smuggler in Cornwall somewhere not far from
Penzance. Jacques had learned that much from Henri
before the conversation had degenerated into threats
and murder. Unfortunately, Henri had not remembered the exact name of the place—that was one of
the causes of the degeneration of the conversation—
so he could not tell d'Ursine. Hilliers grunted irritably
that there were ten thousand places near Penzance
where cargo could be landed; however, he did not
refuse to try. His own best contact was in Polperro,
and that smuggler might know who ran a route near
Penzance or where the ship lay to.

Although Hilliers did not equal Philip's feat in the
speed with which he traveled, he made excellent time
to Cornwall. He arrived in Polperro three days before
Pierre was due at Lamorna Cove and just one day
after Philip and Megaera finished buying goods in
Falmouth. The agent's contact was not in at the time,
and the inn he usually stayed at in Polperro had
changed hands, so that he was eyed with suspicion.
He rode inland then, to the Punch Bowl in Lanreath,
where he was well known as "safe," and he found
many tongues there willing to wag at the glint of a
coin. Unfortunately they did not know much, only
that there was a regular run from somewhere in Brittany. If he wanted more information, the innkeeper
said, he might get it at The Mousehole.

Across the room a thin, ragged, half-drunk man
lifted his head. Black Bart had not done well since
he fled from the battle at The Mousehole. The money
he had carried away had not lasted long, of course,
and no one was in the least impressed by him. In
Treen he had built his power with the backing of his
bullyboys. Here in the Polperro area the bully bucks
already had leaders, and his bluster, unsupported by

any good connection with a smuggler, was regarded with contempt. He had found occasional work unloading ships and helping with large deliveries, but only as a "last and least" hired hand, and his grumbling and whining had made him so unpopular that he had left the port and come to Lanreath.

The name "Mousehole" had drawn his attention, and he listened blearily to the short remainder of the talk between Hilliers and the landlord. Somehow he got the impression that the man was carrying a large sum of money. What was more, there was something about him that reminded Black Bart of the two sheep turds who had queered his chance to get that bitch Red Meg. It occurred to Bart that here was a chance to get everything back to where it had been before the gentry mixed in and fouled the pitch.

More than a month had passed since the shooting at The Mousehole, and not a rumor of it had come to Polperro or Lanreath. No word had been passed that he was wanted. Likely Meg had kept the whole thing quiet, thinking she had scared him off for good. She had never been one for mixing up with the beaks. If he hushed that fancy cull with the funny way of saying words, there would be money, a horse, decent togs. That would make him look as if he were up in the world. Black Bart snarled softly as he remembered how far from the truth that was. But no more. He knew now there was no sense in running. A man had to be in his own place. He wasn't really afraid of the law. When he had done Meg, he would have the money from the smuggling operation to pay them off. Then they would dance to his piping rather than hers.

Mumbling to himself, Bart got up and staggered out. No one paid any heed to him. He was regarded as bigmouthed and pot-valiant when drunk, but of no danger to anyone. Even if his purpose had been guessed, no one would have said anything. Each man was expected to watch out for himself, and, to speak the truth, Hilliers was known to be deadly and capable and not pleased with those who minded his business.

It was the total idiocy of the action, the total improbability of it that made it succeed. Looking around for a suitable spot for attack, Bart paused to piss in a dark area near the gate in the wall that cut off the stable yard from the main entrance of the inn. Just as he finished, the door of the inn opened, the stranger stood silhouetted against the light for an instant, and then came directly toward Bart. As he passed Bart simply took one step forward and stabbed him in the back.

The only part of the whole thing that was not dumb luck was the knife stroke. That was a skill learned so well that even drunkenness did not affect it. Hilliers did utter a cry, but Bart's hand was over his mouth already, and he was dead too fast to make another sound. Then Bart pulled him back into the darkest place, somewhat alarmed, although he was too full of brandy to be really frightened. Still, he knew the grounds of the Punch Bowl were "safe." That is, the landlord and the men who used it were agreed that no violence (except what was necessary to quell obstreperous drunks) was permitted there. Men who violated the rule did not do so more than once.

Quickly Bart rifled the agent's pockets. Then he clapped the man's hat on his head and drew on his greatcoat. There was a slit in the back, but most of the blood had been absorbed by the shirt, waistcoat, and coat he wore beneath. Still uplifted by the brandy in his belly, Bart drew the hat low over his face, raised the collar of the coat, and shouted for "his" horse.

It was cold. The ostler glanced at the garments, recognized the "swell" who had come in, and led out the horse. Remembering by a miracle who he was supposed to be, Bart flipped a coin. His drunkenness favored him again. He was unable to throw the coin straight and the ostler missed his catch. With a curse the man turned and bent to scrabble for his tip. Meanwhile, Bart mounted and rode out of the yard. The dead man was not discovered for some time. By then it was far too late to wonder who had committed the crime. The body was stripped of everything that could be of the smallest value. A little blood on things was not going to bother anyone who frequented the Punch Bowl. A quiet spot was found, and one more French agent disappeared without a sign.

Not being perfectly sober at the moment, Bart had ridden straight out on the road in front of the inn. He was too drunk—and growing too frightened—to remember he must turn right or left to go along the main road. The track he followed led nowhere, and he found himself in open country. He would probably have fallen into the spreading pools of the West Looes, had he not stumbled on a shepherd's hut. He took the horse in with him for warmth and simply curled up and went to sleep.

It was the best thing he could have done. In the morning he was sober, if thickheaded. For a time he regarded his surroundings and the horse with blank amazement. Then slowly it all came back. First he plunged into a morass of despair, realizing he was finished in the Polperro area too. Then his drunken reason for what he had done began to take hold of him again. It was useless to keep running. He must have a reckoning with the red bitch. If he won, he would have the good life again. If he lost, he would have nothing to worry about anymore.

In this mood of reckless despair Black Bart began to examine what he had taken from the man he had killed. At first he was bitterly disappointed. There was some money, but no extraordinary sum, which was natural. Hilliers had only to pay for his travel (which money had been spent already), food, lodging, and passage. After that, English money would not be necessary. In France there were funds ready for him. In his fury Bart began to tear apart the saddlebags. From between the back seams, papers fell. Bart seized them eagerly and then cursed viciously, disappointed again. They were all in French. Growling, he threw them into the fire he had started in the primitive hearth.

That act of destruction, which he would have undone if he could, checked his rising rage and made him consider what he had found in the saddlebags more seriously. Two good pistols, plenty of ammunition, clothing. Again he thought of the idea that had induced the murder, and it did not seem so farfetched now. If he went back to Treen dressed like a swell and able to fling money around for a day or two (there was enough for that), he could get some of the men back on his side. And those men, unlike the ones Red Meg favored, wouldn't mind a little extra, even if they had to put a few others including the red bitch to bed with a shovel to get it.

Three days later when Black Bart rode into Treen, he found he would have been welcomed even without the money and clothing. His men, the ones who had run the gang under his supervision, had all been cut out by Meg. Without a leader to direct their resentment they had done nothing, but now they welcomed Bart with open arms and spouted wild plans for revenge. Bart was so uplifted by this fawning attitude that he actually stopped to think before rushing out to bash.

Having discovered when Pierre had last delivered a cargo—and that could not be kept secret, for most of the men in the village were employed in beaching it—Bart had a reasonable idea of when the smuggler might come again. He gestured his men closer and began to outline a plan. Basically it was the same as his original idea. They had to get Meg after the cargo was delivered and before she went to pay Pierre. They could invade the cave, kill John, and seize Meg.

After that they could have their fun with her. That might convince her she had better play the game their way. If it did not, she could be convinced by more forceful methods than rape to show them where the kegs were stored and to disclose all of her customers. They would have the money, the routes, and the kegs. If Pierre would deal with them, they would pay him; if not, they would have time to induce another smuggler to make Treen or Lamorna Cove his port of call.

In the joy of having Philip back and the excitement of another buying trip to Falmouth, Megaera forgot all about the problem of the disaffected members of the gang. If they had caused trouble, Tom Helston would have left a message at the cave, and that would have reminded her. The arrival of Black Bart, however, had forestalled any desire on their parts to be taken back into the gang. Had Helston been a cleverer man, the quiet would have made him suspicious. As it was, he accepted the peace as a gift from God and did not question it.

For Megaera it had been both a dreadful and a wonderful week. She nearly went mad finding devices and excuses to avoid telling Philip the full sum of the mortgages on Bolliet and the quarterly interest. She would never have succeeded, except for two things. The trip to Falmouth gave her three days of grace; if she was there, she could ask her "sister" no questions. The second thing was that Philip was not really determined to discover the answer right then. Since there was nothing he could do about paying either interest or debt until he returned from France, it did not seem worth quarreling about with Meg.

It was too complex and too delicate a matter to try to explain to his father in a letter. Besides, Philip had

now decided that Roger and Leonie must meet Meg
before he told them her troubles. Once they had seen
her, good, sweet, and beautiful as she was, they would
help him find a solution. If he told them the tale first,
they would be sure she was some kind of harpy that
had got her talons into him. The idea of Meg as a
harpy was comical. She resisted his attempt to give
her anything, except the warmth of his body and his
love.

Thus, in a way, Megaera won the battle of wills.
On the night that the *Bonne Lucie* lay to in Lamorna
Cove and the kegs of wine and tobacco were brought
ashore, Philip still did not know how much or to
whom the money was owed. He did not go back to
Moreton Place that last night. He stayed in the cave,
but he did not waste his time that night or the next
day—the last hours he would spend with Meg until
he could get back to Cornwall—asking questions he
knew she did not wish to answer. To the best of his
ability—without betraying his mission which was, after
all, a state secret—he explained what he was going to
do. He said he had to go to Paris to make some
arrangements; he did not say for whom, knowing Meg
would assume it was for Pierre. She in turn promised
she would be extra careful, and that she had not forgotten the letters he had given her and would use
them if trouble should find her despite her care.

About that, Philip said nothing. He had determined
to stop Meg's smuggling without her permission by
inducing Pierre to change his port of call. At any
rate he was not too worried about her this time. Just
before dusk Meg sent John away on an errand that
would take about an hour. On his way back he was
to pick up two ponies, one for Meg and one for
Philip—Spite had been left at Moreton Place again,
where Philip had said his adieux the previous afternoon. They would ride over to The Mousehole and

there they would part, but they would not think of
that yet.

They made love gently, lingeringly, without the
frantic heat that had marked their first parting. Philip
spent a long time just stroking Meg from shoulder to
thigh, following the path of his hands with his lips.
He was relaxed, certain of his purpose although he
was not certain of how he would accomplish it. There
was, nonetheless, no need for him to get as much of
Meg as he could. He was sure this time he would be
back to take her home with him in a few weeks.

Megaera, on the other hand, kept telling herself
this was the end, that she must break with Philip, that
she could not deceive him any longer. She should
have been completely miserable; in fact, she was not
sad at all. Something inside her simply would not
accept the facts as her mind stated them. Against all
reason, against all denial, there was a sure expectation
of continued joy and love.

Their mutual climax—a thing they did not often
achieve—was an additional blessing. If it was less explosive than other times, bringing sighs rather than
groans, it was sweeter. They lay locked together as
the long, soft thrills slowly faded. Then it was time to
dress. They had taken so long over their foreplay that
it was full dark and John might be back at any time.
Still, neither was inclined to light the lamp, fearing
that the peace and fulfillment each felt might not be
reflected in the other's expression. Better, then, to
dress by the dim red glow of the braziers. They were
not going to a ball. It would not matter if Meg's hair
was tousled under her woolen cap or if Philip had not
shaved.

This love and concern for each other, the unwill-
ingness to show a face of joy or make too casual a remark and unwittingly hurt a less peaceful partner,
saved their lives. Dressing quietly, silently, they heard

the hiss of a whisper, the crunch of a step on a pebble that gritted on the stone floor. Into each mind leapt the same question and answer: John? No! John's foot might crunch on a pebble, but to whisper was beyond him.

Philip's gun was in his hand, loaded and cocked, before another crunch confirmed the invasion. He did not wait or question, but darted around the screen and fired at the sound. There was very little chance that he would hit any target. It was utterly black in the cave, except for the faintest gray luminousness at the opening, and his movement spoiled his impression of where the sound had originated. What he hoped was that the fear generated by his shot would unbalance whoever had come into the cave.

The noise itself would be a shock, and it would show that he was aware of the intrusion. This alone might drive away any single, unarmed person who had come to steal a keg or some tobacco. If there were more than one and they were armed, Philip's loosing off a shot might be considered a panic reaction. The intruders probably thought Meg was alone and might believe she would need time to reload and might try to rush her. At worst, seeing his gun spit fire one of them might try to hit him by aiming at the sparks.

It was the last that happened. As he fired Philip crouched, working his reload mechanism. Before he had completed his loading, a gun barked. Philip slammed home the lever and returned the fire, aiming as the other had done at the powder spark. A shriek followed, and Philip smiled grimly, moving sideways again as someone shouted, "That's both her pops. We can take her now."

Two more shots went off simultaneously—Philip's third and Meg's first—both aimed at the voice, but unfortunately that was a less sure guide than powder sparks and neither hit. A string of curses greeted the double shot as the intruders shouted warnings to each other to be careful, that the dummy was armed. It was a reasonable conclusion, since the men did not know that Philip was back. It was also a dangerous conclusion. Four shots had been fired, so four guns must be empty.

The only things that saved Philip and Meg from a concerted rush, which might well have overpowered them, were the men's fear of coming to grips with John, and Black Bart's terror of the cave itself. He had come in a little way past the entrance, the dark inside not being much greater than that outside near the opening, but he could not go forward another inch. It had been he who had shouted that Meg should be taken. Had he been able to rush forward—he still had an unfired gun in each hand—the three unhurt men would have followed. But Bart's terror of the echoing black immensity facing him held him fast.

The other three could not quite decide on their approach. If they delayed, presumably Red Meg and the dummy would have time to reload. If they rushed forward, the dummy might catch one of them and squeeze the life out of him. None would have minded much if it happened to one of the others; it would be a good thing because it would provide an opportunity to rush up to the screams and shoot the dummy in the head. Unfortunately, each was as reluctant to be the victim as he was indifferent to the victimization of the others.

Philip, of course, was already reloaded, ears straining for a sound, but it was his eyes that gave the clue. Periodically his glance went to the cave opening, still faintly lighter than the interior. He had no idea whether John had been waylaid or whether he would suddenly appear. If so, Philip wanted to warn him. But how could one warn a man who could not hear a shout? Nonetheless he looked at the cave entrance. Suddenly there was a flicker of a blacker shadow there. He fired at it before he thought and, before he could hate himself for having hurt John when he had just been thinking about him, a scream responded followed by gasping moans. Philip sighed with relief. That could not be John.

Two men had been hit, but Philip had no idea whether they had been put out of action permanently —or how many more there were. An outburst of obscenities came from the right of the cave entrance. To Philip's left Meg's pistol barked. The obscenities cut off abruptly as the bullet whined in ricochet. Philip could hear Meg sobbing softly and fumbling behind the screen, then the tiny scratch of paper tearing. Good girl! She might cry, but she didn't lose her head. She was opening a cartridge to reload. Philip's own gun was ready, but he had no target. He stared hopelessly into the blackness, feeling the approach of a dozen men, although he knew there could not be so many close; he would have heard their breathing.

Then, as his eyes swept back and forth, he saw a faint gilding of the lesser darkness that marked the cave entrance. John? Reinforcements for the attackers? No, it must be John. The intruders would not show a light. It was maddening not to be able to warn the man. All Philip could think of was to fire his gun when John was fully in the entrance. Perhaps the deaf-mute would see the powder flash. But would he know what it meant? John was not exactly quick in his thinking.

It would never work. The gilding grew brighter. Probably the intruders had not yet noticed it since they were looking in toward the back of the cave, but the light would soon be strong enough to draw their attention. Philip started to edge forward. He could not let John walk into the cave carrying a lantern in his hand. They would shoot him down at once at point-blank range because the big man would be blind to anything outside the small circle of light and, at the same time, the light would make him a perfect target.

Between one step and another, Philip hesitated. Would he be leaving Meg to be caught if he went to warn John? And then there was no time for decision. Everything happened at once. Someone saw the light and shouted, turning suddenly, feet grating on the stone floor. Philip fired at the sound, quite close to him, too good a target to miss. A shriek and more grating, a thud, proved his aim had been true. Simultaneously the cave was full of light! Philip was temporarily blinded. Two guns went off, but there was no response and Philip did not know whether the shots had missed or, although hit, John could not scream.

As his sight adjusted Philip realized that the lantern had been dropped, spilling its oil across the floor. That had ignited, furnishing the sudden blaze of light. Although blind, Philip had reloaded the Lorenzoni, but he never had a chance to use it. John had just come to his full height after he had fallen or crouched. He opened his mouth, perhaps to scream, but no sound came out, not even his usual distressed gobbling. Philip had to glance away to look around the cave for enemies. When he looked back, he saw John lurching to the side, heard a man scream—a high, thin shriek of mindless terror that stopped abruptly on a creaking noise that ended in a small, sharp snap.

As both men fell, two others ran—one limping and the other staggering, both whimpering—out of the cave. Philip sent a bullet after them on principle, but he did not think they would be back immediately. He hurried over to where John lay, and gasped. The light from the burning oil was dying down, most having been consumed and there being nothing else to burn on the floor, but there was enough light to see the blood, a huge pool of it. Philip could not imagine how so much blood could pour out of a man in so

short a time. Both were dead. John had been hit at
close range. How he could have stood up and—Philip
shuddered and looked away. He had twisted the other
man's head right around. Although the body lay on
its stomach, the face, horribly contorted, eyes bulging,
stared right at Philip.

He stood and turned, holding out a hand to warn
Meg away, but Meg was not coming. Then Philip
screamed! In the last of the light he saw her lying
on the ground, her face covered with blood. He was
beside her in a moment, cradling her in his arms, too
frozen with grief and loss to cry. His utter silence,
breath held in horror, was the source of his relief.
He realized that she was not dead, that the low,
whispery moan was his beloved drawing breath.

Then he became frantically busy, carrying her to
the bed, covering her warmly, lighting the lamp, pouring water from the pitcher to sponge her face. He was
trembling with terror. He had no idea how long she
had been unconscious, but if it was really long . . .
Half mad with fear, Philip sponged her face, her hair,
but blood was still flowing. At last he found the place
of the wound.

Just above the temple on the right the bullet had
struck, but it had not entered. There was a horrid
gash showing white bone under the welling blood and
matted hair. Philip nearly fainted. He had been sad-
dened by the pool of blood that marked John's death,
but not even that really bothered him. He had tough-
ened since he shot that first highwayman. Only, this
was Meg! His Meg—and he did not know what to do
for her.

Turned idiot with fear, Philip could think of nothing but Pierre. Pierre would know what to do. He
wrapped Meg in her cloak and then in both blankets
and carried her out. Mounting was a nightmare, but
fortunately the sturdy ponies were shorter than horses

and very placid. Holding Meg against him with one arm, he got his foot in the stirrup. He nearly dislocated his arm, but he managed to haul her up with him as he rose. Then they were off. If Philip had not envisioned what would happen to Meg if they took a spill, he would have whipped the beast into a gallop. As it was they went far too fast, but the pony was surefooted as well as sturdy.

Aeons of fear and despair passed, perhaps twenty minutes in real time. Philip would have gone mad except that Meg moaned every so often, so that he knew she was alive. Still, he was shouting at the top of his lungs for help and for Pierre by name by the time he was fifty yards from The Mousehole. Several men came running from the inn, pistols drawn. That mistake was quickly rectified, but all Philip could do was to keep repeating, "Meg's hurt. Meg's hurt."

"Give 'er to me, you fool!" Pierre bellowed, tugging at the blanketed form.

At last Philip released his precious burden and slid from the saddle, running to catch up with Pierre. "Her head," he cried. "It's her head."

"I am not blind," Pierre snarled, but his hands were very gentle as he laid her on a table and lifted her blood-soaked hair. Seeing the injury, he sighed with relief. Philip bent to kiss her, crying now. Pierre pushed him away. "Out of my light," he ordered. "Paul," he called to the landlord, "give me a tankard of brandy to wash this out with, the strongest, and bring a lamp over 'ere. Then take away this fool!"

"No," Philip choked.

Pierre looked up. "She is not badly hurt. You can see the bone is not broken or dented. You are too much moved. I must sew this up. Do you wish to watch?"

"No," Philip gasped, and turned away.

One of the men, he never knew which, put an arm around him and led him across the room to Pierre's

corner. He sank onto a seat, resting his elbows on the
table, his hands over his face. He could hear muted
voices and hurried footsteps. Time stretched again so
that Philip could not guess whether it was seconds,
minutes, or hours that passed. Someone pulled at his
hand, thrust a tankard into it. He sipped, coughed,
then pushed it away, whispering, "Meg does not like
me to drink brandy."

"She won't know nothin' of it, cully, not for some
while. You knock that back and you'll feel better.
Yair, it's a shaker to see a dimber mort damaged."

Philip looked dazedly at the speaker. He knew the
man meant well and was trying to comfort him, but
all he could do was wonder how he had ever permitted
Meg to associate with such people. Why had he not
sent her to Leonie where she would have been safe
and protected?

"I should not have allowed her—" he muttered.

"Nah, nah! It's no use worritin' that. You can't
stop 'em. If a mort sets her head to summat, save yer
breath to blow yer porridge."

For all his anxiety Philip had to smile wanly. The
man had a point. It was ridiculous to think about
sending Meg—as if she were a package without voli-
tion. Meg . . . Fearfully he turned his head to look.
Pierre was just straightening up. He swung around
and caught Philip's eye. Philip jumped up, overturn-
ing his seat with a clatter, and rushed over.

"Not so bad," Pierre said as Philip bent over Meg.

Pierre had cut her hair away from the gash, but
not widely, and sewn the torn skin together quite
neatly. Now that most of the blood had been washed
from the area and the horrible gleam of bone was
gone, Philip could see that the wound was not large.
Meg looked terribly white, however, and was breathing very heavily, almost snoring. Philip looked at
Pierre, his eyes wide with fear.

"Her breathing," he whispered.

"She's drunk," Pierre said in French, with a wry smile. "I did not want her to come around, so we poured brandy down her. I tell you, she is not hurt much, although she may be dizzy for a day or two and she may not remember what happened. What did happen?"

"I do not know," Philip sighed, stroking Meg's face.

"You mean you found her like that?"

"No. No, I was at the cave—the place where the kegs are taken. We were—we were saying good-bye. Suddenly there were men in the cave."

"What men?"

"I have no idea. I only saw one." Philip swallowed and shuddered, then laughed a little hysterically. "His head was on backward, so I—I did not look long."

"His head was on backward!" Pierre echoed.

"John—oh, God! John is dead, but before he died . . ."

"Customs officers?" Pierre asked. He needed no further explanation after John was coupled with the backward head.

"I do not think so. Surely they would have called out when I fired."

"It is very strange," Pierre muttered. "Mademoiselle Meg said nothing to me of any trouble."

"She would not," Philip said, his voice shaking. "She is so brave. Not once did she cry out, and she used her pistols—"

"But on whom? Ah! The Black Bart?"

"I do not know," Philip repeated helplessly. "I never saw the man before, and Meg—" Philip swallowed convulsively. "I would not have let her look at what John did anyhow."

Privately Pierre thought Meg might be less affected than Philip. There was a hard core inside that delicate-looking woman that had permitted her to take on a dangerous trade and manage it with great efficiency. He said nothing of that, however, having learned through broken friendships and other sorrows that it was not wise to try to destroy the illusions of a man about the woman he loved. Besides, he did not think Philip's vision of Meg was all that illusory. For only the second time in his life Pierre regretted that he could not try to make a woman his own. The emotion was very brief. He was nearly old enough to be Meg's grandfather, not to mention her father, and he was comfortable enough without a woman who thought she owned him and would be forever telling him what to do.

Then suddenly Pierre blinked, realizing that he was, or at least should be, surprised to see Philip, a thing he had not had time to notice previously. "What are you doing here?" he asked.

Megaera made an indistinct sound and moved a little. Philip bent over her. Her eyes flicked open, her brow wrinkled, and she mumbled something. Philip kissed her gently, and her lips twitched toward a smile.

"All safe now," he murmured softly. "Go to sleep, darling."

Her eyes closed, and Philip sat back with a deep sigh. He finally believed she would be all right. He started to run a hand through his hair, then realized he was covered with dried blood and asked where he could wash. By the time he returned, he was pretty well back to normal. First he asked the landlord whether he knew where laudanum could be obtained. A golden guinea changed hands, and the landlord's son went out to ride to Penzance, where he could wake up an apothecary. Then Philip went back to Pierre and told his story, starting from his return to Kent.

"Eh, well," Pierre said when he was finished, "I will be glad to take you, and your idea about selling the woolens and shoes openly is good. We have time to talk about that, but what is to be done about Miss Meg?"

"She cannot be left here. For one thing, that sister of hers must not know about me. For another, I am afraid if I brought Meg to her house in this condition, her sister might refuse to receive her. I do not know who those men were, and now that John is dead, she has no one to protect her."

"The cargo?" Pierre asked.

"That is safe, and I think she has the money with her—"

"I did not ask for that reason," Pierre interrupted. "I was thinking that if you leave her here, she will try to deliver, and without the poor John . . ." He sighed. "The men will not like it, Philippe, for her to be on the ship. And also, that is not safe for many reasons."

"I think I will take her with me," Philip said slowly. "I do not believe what I have been sent to do is at all dangerous. Only to tell someone that 'it is all off, every man for himself!' It is an act of courtesy on the part of my government. They do not wish it to be said of them that they abandoned without warning or a hope of escape one to whom they made promises. However, the information must reach the man before the New Year, and it is already the second week in December. I cannot take Meg home, and I cannot leave her here; thus I must take her with me."

"But she has no French!"

"So?" Philip grinned. "I will be the envy of every man alive. I will have a wife beautiful, intelligent—and mute as a stone! We have the signs she used with John."

Pierre burst out laughing. "Wonderful! That is wonderful!" Then he frowned. "But do not say she is mute—only dumb, unable to make words. She might forget herself once or twice, and when you are alone you will not be able to stop her from speaking. If someone should hear, it will not be so suspicious. Let her tongue be in some way at fault. Perhaps let her even say a word or two, badly garbled, so that people will think she is ashamed to speak in public but, naturally, not to her husband in private."

Megaera stirred and moaned again. Philip looked at her anxiously, patted her shoulder, and whispered reassurances into her ear. Pierre assured him that she felt nothing, or at least she would remember nothing. When she had quieted, Pierre suggested that they move her to the ship.

"Yes, that would be best. We can put her in your bunk—you will not mind?"

"I did not intend to sling a hammock for her among the men."

Philip laughed. "No. Clearly my head is still not working quite right. But Pierre, I will have to stay ashore and come later. There are several dead men in the cave and a pony tied up outside. I cannot allow the poor beast to freeze or starve, and I cannot simply leave the bodies. John, at least, deserves a decent burial. And I had better leave a letter for Meg's sister—no, I think I will write to her father. He is not good for much, but she says he loves her, and he is still the head of the household."

"You will write—but what?"

"Um—I think that Meg has been invited to stay with Leonie and that she will herself write and explain everything as soon as she is settled. I will have to write to Leonie also. If I leave the letters with the landlord here, will he send them off?"

At that moment the boy who had gone for the laudanum came in and brought the bottle to Philip. He passed it to Pierre.

"You will see her safely to the ship? I must go and see that the pony is released and John and the others, whoever they are, are placed where someone will find them. If she becomes restless, give her some of the laudanum. She will be mad as fire that I have abducted her this way, but I cannot see anything better to do."

Chapter 20

Philip was absolutely correct about Megaera being furious when she discovered what he had done. He had kept her dosed with laudanum all the while she was aboard ship. That was not only because he wished to avoid argument. Philip also wanted to be sure both her hangover from the brandy Pierre had poured down her throat and the worst of the headache from the blow of the bullet on her skull would be over before she was fully conscious. Thus it was not until they were safely lodged at Monsieur Luroec's farm that Philip let her wake naturally.

She stared at him for a long moment, so long that Philip began to fear she did not recognize him. Then she said, "I've had some very queer dreams."

"They were not—at least not all of them—dreams," Philip said gently.

Megaera raised her brows, exclaimed wordlessly, and lifted a hand toward the healing wound. Philip caught the hand. "That part was not a dream then? My head did hurt. What happened?" she asked.

"You remember being at the cave?" Philip asked in turn. Pierre had warned him that people who were hit on the head sometimes did not remember what had happened just before the blow.

"The cave?" Megaera repeated. Then she looked around the room. "This isn't the . . . Philip, where are we?"

"Now, do not get all excited," Philip warned. "Let me tell you what happened."

He did not quite get through the tale without interruption, but he had the advantage that when Megaera began to scream at him, her head began to ache. She contented herself with glaring after that. Philip shrugged.

"I could not bring you home all bloody, with a bullet hole in your head. I do not even know exactly where Bolliet Manor is. For all I knew, you could have bled to death before I found the place."

"John would have taken me. What did you do with him?"

Philip hesitated, then said softly, "I am sorry. I tried to get to him in time to warn him, but I could not. I was behind the flames when the lamp spilled, and he may not have been able to see me. And it happened so fast. . . . He is dead, my love. I am so sorry."

Megaera's eyes filled with tears, but they did not fall. "Poor John," she whispered.

"I do not think he suffered," Philip lied, blanking the memory of John's open mouth, screaming soundlessly. He could see no reason to tell her that the deaf-mute had lived with that dreadful hole in him long enough to wring one enemy's neck. "It was so quick."

"Very well," she said, quietly now because the news of John's death had taken the edge off her anger. "But after Pierre had"—she touched the wound on her head gingerly—"had sewed me up, why did you carry me off to France, you idiot? Everyone will go mad worrying about me at home."

"Oh, no," Philip replied. "I am not stupid. I wrote a very polite letter to your father, purportedly from my stepmother, to say she had taken you to stay with her for a few weeks and that you would write later."

Megaera just stared. His stepmother? But Pierre was not married. Was there some cuckolded father who had married the woman Pierre. . . . No, that was far too complicated. Anyhow Philip's parentage was a side issue of far less importance than this stupid abduction. She protested again, but Philip kept repeating calmly that it was far too late to worry about it now, that Pierre was gone to get them false papers, and that he would not take her back to The Mousehole alone because there was no one to take care of her with John dead.

"This smuggling must end, sweetheart. It is too dangerous for you. Pierre agrees with me. He will find a new distributor or move his base back to Belgium so that he can trade from Kingsdown again. No, do not begin to worry about your precious sister and her home. I swear I will find a way to pay the interest, at least. My father's man of business will work it all out."

"Your father's man of business?" Megaera echoed faintly.

An adoptive father? But Philip was French—no, he had said he was English. It began to seem as if she had jumped to a wrong conclusion. Yet Pierre had called him *mon fils,* and she knew enough French to recognize that meant *my son.* Also, Pierre went to extraordinary lengths to oblige Philip and to protect him. But Philip gave her no time to think out the problem. He had changed the subject and was reminding her that he had to carry a message to Paris.

Megaera had accepted that without doubt when he first said it, but suddenly she realized she knew nothing, absolutely nothing, about Philip. Everything she believed she knew had been cast into doubt. "To whom? For what purpose?"

There was a hard suspicion in Megaera's eyes now. She might cheerfully defraud the government of taxes she felt they had no right to collect, but she was a loyal Englishwoman in any contest with the French. She had no intention of aiding and abetting a spy. What if the message he was carrying to Paris would in some way injure her country?

"Sweetheart," Philip began, and reached for her hands.

She snatched them away. "You have been using me," she whispered with horror.

"No!"

Philip had been about to tell her he could not answer her questions. After all, the plot to unseat Bonaparte was a state secret, and he really did not dare to mention the name Cadoudal. What Meg did not know could not slip out. However, he could see she would not accept a simple statement that he was a loyal Englishman. She must be reassured, and words alone would not do it. Philip pulled off his boot and pried open the glued leather, so that he could show her the pass signed and sealed by the Secretary for Foreign Affairs.

Megaera sighed with relief. In fact she was so impressed that she hardly noticed the different spelling of his name. Even if she had, it would not have meant anything to her. Because of her father's "little" weakness and her early marriage, Megaera had never had a London "Season." She had no acquaintance among the *ton,* and if the other families who did, like the Moretons, had ever mentioned the St. Eyres, it had passed over her head. She passed back the paper and watched Philip work it carefully into his boot again.

"But I will be the greatest danger to you," she protested. "My French is—is schoolgirl stuff, and I'm sure my accent would scream 'English' to anyone who heard me. How could you be so foolish as to drag me along with you?"

"I have answered that four times already," Philip said reprovingly, "but I will tell you once more. Because I love you. And I cannot see why you should be a danger to me. Since married men are not called up for conscription, you are a ready excuse why I am not in the army. Moreover, Pierre and I together have thought of an excellent reason for you not to talk in public—you are afflicted of the tongue, not mute but unable to say words normally. We can use the hand signs we used with poor John. Think about it a few minutes, love, while I get some glue from Monsieur Luroec to fix this boot again."

By the time Philip returned, Megaera was not only reconciled but was bright and cheerful. She had at first been worried about the servants' reaction to her absence, but she realized that her father's valet would read any letter addressed to Lord Bolliet. Usually such letters were invitations, and Colson knew which to refuse outright and which to mention to his lordship. When he found the letter announced Megaera's visit to Leonie, he would inform Rose, the housekeeper, and the butler. It was a stroke of luck that Philip had taken such a dislike to Mrs. Edward Devoran. If he had addressed the letter to her, it would have lain unopened and the household would have been frantic.

With that worry off her mind Megaera realized that she was thrilled with this chance for adventure. She had got used to doing rather unusual things, and it seemed to her she might be of real use to Philip. Who would suspect a man traveling with a mute wife to be a spy? Spies did not customarily bring along their womenfolk. As to the muteness, it would be easier for her than for many because of the long hours she had spent working with John, to whom it was useless to speak. She would be able to do an excellent imitation of a person with a speech impediment. And if she could not speak, the chances were that people would believe she was sort of simple. That might be valuable.

The only thing that bothered Megaera was the lie she had told. It was tenderly amusing that Philip should be so fiercely protective and have taken her nonexistent sister in such aversion, but it would not be funny at all when he learned the truth. She could not forget that icy fury that had taken him when she had implied he might take unfair advantage of knowing who she was. This time would be even worse. He would be convinced that her apologies then had been all false. Megaera did not believe he would abandon her in France, but she could not bear the thought of his hurt and rage when he discovered she had not trusted him.

Why, oh why, had she not told the truth at once? Should she tell him now? Megaera shuddered. He would be so angry. Perhaps he would leave her here until his mission was finished. Perhaps he would be so upset that he would be thrown off balance and betray himself to the authorities. No, it was too late now. She would have to wait until they were back in England. There Philip would be safe and it would not matter as long as he was safe if he never spoke to her again.

To divert herself Megaera plunged into a discussion of how Philip's mission was to be accomplished when he returned to the room. He was a little surprised at her complete about-face, but put it down to sweetness of disposition and most willingly told her what he had outlined and Pierre had elaborated.

As soon as their papers were ready Philip and Megaera would travel by road to Paris. They would be *nouveaux mariés* on their *voyage de noces*. He would keep his old role as a customs officer, but now one stationed in the provinces who wished to show his new wife the great city of Paris. Meanwhile, Pierre would sail around to Dieppe. There he would linger, selling his legal and welcome cargo of leather, boots and shoes, heavy woolen cloth, and other such necessities. He could drag out negotiations for some time, seeming to be looking for the best price. If Philip and Meg had not arrived at Dieppe before he disposed of his cargo, he could pretend his crew was off on a spree, or do some fishing. Possibly the weather would oblige by being nasty. In any case he would return to Dieppe every evening or every other evening.

Exactly how Philip and Meg would come aboard ship had been left to the spur of the moment. Pierre had several plans ready. There would be no trouble about Philip finding the ship. Dieppe was not a naval base, and there was no reason why people should not walk the docks just to look at the vessels there. Philip knew the *Bonne Lucie* as well as he knew his own yacht.

Megaera had no quarrel with any of this, but she pointed out that Philip had snatched her away without so much as a change of linen and in boy's clothing. What was she to do about that? It had all been arranged, Philip said with a touch of pride. Monsieur Luroec's daughter had already gone to Rennes to procure suitable clothes and would be back tomorrow or the next day. Meanwhile, Megaera was to get back her strength. She laughed at him at first, saying she felt fine, but in fact she found when she got out of bed that she was shaky and tired easily. It took her all that day and part of the next to get the clotted blood out of her hair and find a style for it that would conceal the gash in her scalp.

In this endeavor Philip was no help at all. He was willing enough to assist in washing, drying, and combing her hair, but he looked at her with a perfectly fatuous expression each time she asked whether she had hidden the bare spot and said she was more beautiful—bare spot or no—than ever. This led Megaera

to ask tartly, but with laughing eyes, whether he was
hard up again. She expected to put him out but found
she had underestimated her lover. Philip merely
opened his dark eyes wide and said, "Always, when I
am with you. How could it be otherwise?" which made
her blush.

Active or idle, the two found great pleasure simply
being together. Pierre returned with the necessary
forged papers; Monsieur Luroec's daughter brought
clothing suitable to a new bride. If the style was a
little more flamboyant than Megaera herself would
have chosen, that was all to the good. It was truer to
what a girl of the class Megaera was pretending to be
would have chosen. Only the most minor alterations
were necessary, and Megaera was delighted with the
rich Lyons silks, which were not obtainable in England or brought prohibitive prices.

Neither Philip nor Megaera had ever stopped to
wonder how they would deal together over the long
run when their time was not filled with urgent tasks.
Their attraction to each other had been intense and
largely physical, and had been markedly heightened
by the feeling that they would soon be parted again.
During the five days it took them to reach Paris over
the muddy, rutted roads of winter, they had adequate
time to realize that they liked each other's company
even in dull and uncomfortable circumstances. They
barely made twenty miles a day, for the hours of
light were short and it poured icy rain.

However, they had no trouble aside from the condition of the roads and the weather. Philip was armed
to the teeth, remembering the attack on the road from
Ambleteuse, and Megaera now carried one of the
quick-loading Lorenzonis in her pocket and the muff
gun in her muff. There was not the slightest need. No
threat of any kind troubled them. Virtually no riders
appeared on the road; everyone who could not travel

in a sound carriage simply postponed business until the weather should improve. Even carriages were few and far between, and these were as tightly closed as Philip's, the drivers as indistinguishable as he was himself.

The dearth of travelers made Philip and Megaera particularly welcome in the inns at which they stopped. They had the best room, the best service, and every extra consideration the host or hostess could devise. Megaera's "affliction" seemed to increase the attentions they received. *La pauvre petite* had only to set her eyes on something to have it brought to her at once. No one seemed surprised that Philip had married her—so sweet her smiles, so beautiful as she was. Some of the men sighed and murmured that they wished they had thought of it themselves.

The first day or two Megaera found the enforced muteness a difficulty, but she made up for it in bed and in the carriage, only falling silent when someone passed them. As they traveled Philip debated with himself the wisdom of really explaining his mission to her. State secret or no state secret, she was already involved up to the eyes, and it was unfair that she should not know what they were to do. He had been very pleased by her restraint; she had asked no questions at all, and he had just about decided that he must tell her as they came down the low hills around Dreux and began the last thirty miles of their journey on the better roads and relatively flat land around Paris.

Megaera had been interested in the hilly countryside, mentally comparing what she could see of the farming practices with those of Cornwall, but she soon ceased to watch the gentler panorama. "We should be getting pretty near Paris now," she said.

"Tonight, if the road stays good, or early tomorrow. Are you very tired of traveling, my love?"

"No, not at all. I am dry and warm, but—Philip, I don't wish to pry, but is there something, some way I should or should not behave? Is there any way at all I can be of help to you?"

He turned his head away from the road to smile brilliantly at her. "We always think alike, sweetheart. I had just decided that I had better tell you the whole thing now. It is a state secret, you see—oh, do not look so troubled. All that means is that someone has behaved like an idiot and would rather that the whole world did not know of it. Those dunderheads at the Foreign Office—and for all I know at the War Office, too—allowed themselves to be convinced by their own desires and a man called Méhée de la Touche, who *I* suspect was sent by Bonaparte's government if not by him personally, that France was ready to rise against the 'foreign usurper' and welcome back the Bourbons."

"But, Philip, that's ridiculous," Megaera exclaimed. "Everything is so quiet, and even though winter is always a hard season, everyone seems—well, rather content. Oh, I know people were complaining about the taxes and this and that—my French is good enough to understand what they say—but . . ."

"Yes, but there was no bitterness in it. People always complain. Really, they are quite satisfied, and very proud of their 'little corporal.' One can see it in their faces. It was a trap, I think—de la Touche, I mean. Actually, it was a rather clever device for drawing the disaffected leaders back to France."

"It worked?"

"Oh, yes, it worked. In August our government landed a number of men—Georges Cadoudal is the most important—with a million francs in drafts to arrange an uprising."

"Good heavens!"

"Yes. Well, then other information began to come in—"

"Was that what you went for last time, Philip? Oh, I'm sorry, perhaps you can't tell me."

"No, no. I came to see whether there was an invasion fleet ready at Boulogne. There had been information both ways and the Foreign Office and the Admiralty did not know which to trust. So many émigrés have been 'inspired' by Bonaparte's victories and have changed sides, that one can never be sure for which side a spy is really working. The fear of invasion was tying up too much of our fleet in the Channel and the North Sea."

"You mean the threat of invasion is all false?"

Philip's lips tightened. "Far from it. If Bonaparte has his way, a hundred and fifty thousand men will pour over us—"

Megaera gasped, and Philip's grim expression relaxed.

"Only not this year, love, and if our fleet can catch the French and destroy them, it will never happen. That was the point, you see, to free our ships for a while to go farther away and seek out the French fleet."

"And you found this out?" Megaera's eyes were worshipful.

Philip laughed. "It was all luck. I tell you, Meg, that adventure made me very confident that we will triumph in the end. God surely had His hand over me."

He told her the whole story this time, and Megaera laughed heartily when she understood the role the harbor master's daughter had been designed to play. She said Philip had been rightly served for his evil intentions by having Désirée nearly eat him alive, as female spiders were said to do with their unfortunate mates. However, it was plain that she did not discount his skill, cleverness, and courage. Bonaparte's intervention was luck, perhaps, but only coolness and intelligence could have seized the opportunity.

"Well, I nearly did not," Philip confessed honestly. "That man is overpowering. When he looked at me, I felt he could see right through me."

"But he could not," Megaera pointed out proudly. "And so you were able to use him and get away."

"I had no choice, Meg, but I can see why he inspires devotion. I said we would triumph in the end, but to tell the truth I fear the end may be far away." He sighed. "It will be a bitter struggle."

Megaera slipped her hand out of the cocoon of carriage robes that kept her warm and dry and reached forward to squeeze Philip's arm. "You're doing your part, my darling. There's no sense in worrying about the rest."

Philip shrugged. "You are right, of course, but I cannot help wishing that Bonaparte could be content to rule France in peace and let the rest of the world alone. There is much to admire in him. He has brought the people justice and an honest administration—"

"I don't think Pierre would agree with you," Megaera giggled.

Irresistibly Philip burst out laughing, which broke his somber mood. "You are right again, my love. In any case, in getting to Boulogne I traveled through Brittany and Normandy and the Pas de Calais as well as other places. I told Lord Hawkesbury there was no unrest—"

"Gracious, Philip, was it because of your information—"

"Of course not! There had been many others who brought the same information. I was only one more pebble on the beach, perhaps a more trustworthy one. Hawkesbury may have been a fool, but at least he is not a *stubborn* fool. When he added up everything and understood that the situation was hopeless, it was decided that the British government would withdraw and give no further support to so mad an enterprise.

However, Cadoudal must be warned of this and provided with a way back to England, if he wants it. One
cannot abandon an ally."

"No, indeed," Megaera agreed with enthusiasm.
Then she frowned. "But will Mr. Cadoudal believe
you?"

"He must know the facts himself by now. Frankly,
I cannot understand why he did not return. From all
I have heard of him, he is an honest and honorable
man. I hope he has not been trapped already. However, whether he believes me or not is irrelevant. I
have an official letter for him from Hawkesbury."

Megaera was silent for a moment. "It is in your
other boot, I suppose," she said, "but how will you get
it out to give to him? You know, Philip, if what you
said about de la Touche is true, Cadoudal *must* still
be free—and carefully watched. You must do what you
think is right and best, but I don't believe it will be
possible to meet him secretly. Anyone who has private
contact with him will be watched and followed, probably stopped and questioned. I fear a torn boot—so
neatly torn—will make them look at the other."

So surprised was Philip by this perceptive statement
that he pulled up his horse so he could turn fully to
look at her. "Very clever. I did think he would be
watched, but I thought I could somehow tell him to
follow me to the jakes. Very well, I will have to
carry it—"

"A letter would make excellent bonnet stiffening,"
Megaera remarked. "Paper is often used. In fact, it is
used in my blue bonnet. I do not think an extra sheet
would be noticed. If you wore your uniform that day,
anyone could search us forever without finding anything once the letter was handed over. The only thing
we need consider is whether our papers are good
enough to endure a close scrutiny. Do you think they
are, Philip?" She hesitated as she took in the expression on Philip's face. "Have I said something stupid?"

"No, of course not! You are a heroine, my love, but I could not permit it. It is too dangerous for you—"

"Don't be silly, Philip," Megaera said impatiently. "You know it doesn't matter which one of us carries the letter. If you are caught, I am, too."

"Not at all. I had no intention of taking you with me to meet Cadoudal. You could—"

"Escape without you? Don't talk nonsense! Even if I could, I wouldn't—and I don't think it would be possible, since I would be suspect the moment I open my mouth. No! There's no use in arguing about such a stupid thing. If we do it my way, there won't be the slightest danger. Who would suspect a poor mute girl?"

Philip bit his lip and looked back at the road, slapping the reins on the horse's back to start it again. For quite a long time they drove on in silence. Megaera was clever enough to hold her tongue. The best method was to assume her proposal had been accepted. She was certain that if she tried to convince Philip, he would become more and more opposed to the idea. If she said nothing, he could accept it gracefully without seeming to have yielded to argument. After a while, when the road grew better rather than worse and it seemed certain they would reach Paris before dark, Megaera asked whether there was any place in particular they were to stay. Philip turned his head briefly and smiled easily.

"There is one place that we will *not* go—La Maison du Faucon on the rue François Miron. That is where Lord Hawkesbury suggested we stop. It is said to be a safe house, the landlord holding strong Royalist sentiments."

"Is Cadoudal there?"

"For his sake I hope not. I know there is a leak of information from the Foreign Office, and I think it is from Hawkesbury's secretary."

Megaera said nothing, but Philip heard her breath

suck in and he could feel her eyes on him. The horse was negotiating the edge of a wide, glutinous mud puddle, and for a minute or two Philip was fully engaged in making sure that avoiding the puddle would not send the carriage into the equally glutinous ditch at the edge of the road. When he was free, he turned his head toward Megaera again.

"You need not worry about us, love," he went on. "I have taken no chances. That is why Pierre obtained papers for us. I have others, from the Foreign Office, but I did not choose to provide the French Ministry of Police with prior notice as to who I was and what information I carried or my port of arrival—"

"But is he to be allowed to get away with this? You have taken precautions, but what about others?"

"I have done my best. After all, Meg, I have no proof. Perhaps I am wrong. It would mean d'Ursine's ruin. How does one prove one is *not* something. I have hinted my suspicions to Hawkesbury. Perhaps he will think twice about allowing d'Ursine to handle any really sensitive information about France."

"I see . . . yes, without proof . . . But what will we do about meeting Mr. Cadoudal if we cannot go where he is staying?"

"Arrangements have been made for that. He comes to the cafés situated in the Palais Royale most days between two and four o'clock. It is chancy, of course. We might miss each other for several days, but it is far safer than designating one particular place."

"But isn't that dangerous to him?" Meg asked. "Isn't he known to the police?"

"I assume he has changed his appearance in some way—grown a beard or shaved it off. He has been in Paris since September or October and I suppose has been doing this all along. But I cannot wear my uniform as you suggested. I must wear a black bow with my neckcloth. It is done here sometimes, though rather out of fashion, but for a rustic provincial it will not be thought exceptional. Then I must lay that walking stick I have been carrying around, the one with the leaping horse as its head, across the table—or make it obvious in some other way. He will come and ask whether I am not the son or nephew or brother, depending on what our relative ages are, of his old friend Monsieur Fidèle. I will then give him the name Honoré, which is the code reply."

"And then you must pass him the letter, I suppose," Megaera said thoughtfully.

"Yes."

"But it would be more natural if he sat down to talk awhile. Surely it would be very suspicious to watchers if he spoke a few words and you and he left together— or even separately. Yes, you must ask him to join us, that would be natural, and you will talk for a while, mentioning that I am a mute, perhaps. Then I will sign that I must go to the jakes. When I return I will sit down and my muff will slide off my lap. He will pick it up and give it to me. That way he can draw the folded letter out without anyone noticing, and you and he will never have been in any place private and it will be seen that you never passed anything to him. You can even tell him quite openly and innocently where we are staying. Then, if there is to be an answer or he wishes to discover how to leave France, after he reads Hawkesbury's bad news, he will know where to find us."

"And so will the Minister of Police."

"I fear he will know that the moment you exchange even one word with Cadoudal. I am sure they will follow anyone who speaks to him."

Philip considered that in silence. It really was a very good plan. The letter was, of course, on fine paper and folded small and in code. Cadoudal need only thrust his hand into Meg's muff for an instant, and that action would be screened by the feet and other people in the café, so long as he and Meg chose

a table carefully. Surely Cadoudal must stop and talk
to innocent bystanders from time to time to cover his
more purposeful conversations. Meg was right. They
were far better off being very open. That business
about giving Cadoudal their direction openly was a
clever idea too. It would certainly seem that they had
nothing to hide.

"I suppose anyone Cadoudal talks to must be
checked upon. Yes, and we can make the whole even
more innocent by staying right there. I had thought of
taking rooms at the Epée de Bois on the rue de Venise,
but it would be more natural for a young sight-seeing
couple to stay in the Palais Royale itself, and at this
season of the year we may find accommodation there
easily enough."

Philip was quite correct. Before dark, they were
comfortably situated in the Milles Colonnes. Philip
had explained Meg's problem to the landlord and
the servants while she smiled like an idiotic angel,
dropped her reticule, dropped her muff, and bumped
into a chair before he got her up to their room. That
night they were extra careful, Megaera speaking only
in whispers after they were in bed. About five o'clock
in the morning she transferred the letter from Philip's
boot to her blue bonnet by the light of the night
candle while Philip glued his boot together again and
put it back outside the door where the bootboy had
left the pair after cleaning.

The next day passed without incident. Megaera and
Philip visited various sights around Paris, and Megaera purchased several lengths of silk at remarkably
good prices. The vendors were touched by her disability and sympathetic to Philip, who was obviously
embarrassed by needing to bargain for her. Somewhere
along the way the bottle of glue Philip had used was
"lost." At two o'clock they went to the Café Foy,
where Philip explained again to a waiter who was
impatiently expecting Megaera to order. If he would

name the dishes slowly, she would sign what she wanted. They ate slowly; then, since no one had approached them by four o'clock and the sun was not quite set, they took a brisk walk around the square before they returned to their own establishment.

The second day was much like the first, except that they ate at the Café Carazza. Again Megaera's condition was explained and the complexities of sign language for ordering displayed. Megaera's muff slid from her lap twice while her hands were engaged in the signs, to be retrieved once by Philip and again by a waiter, but the careful preparations were useless. That night Megaera said to Philip just before they drifted off to sleep after making love that their friend had better find them soon or people would begin to notice how often she wore the blue bonnet.

The third day, to avoid that problem, Megaera and Philip dined at the Milles Colonnes. They were both dressed to go out after their meal. Megaera wore a fetching green bonnet with pale green trim, and her muff slid to the floor so often that Philip told her to put it on the chair next to her. At three-thirty they were about ready to give up when a gentleman entered the room and looked around for a moment before moving toward an empty table near them. Philip reached for the wine and his foot hit his walking stick, which had been prominently propped against the wall beside him, so that it toppled to the floor with a crash. The gentleman naturally looked at the cause of the noise—as did all the other diners—and then at Philip who was retrieving the stick.

"I beg your pardon, m'sieu," he said quietly but not secretively, "you have the very look of an old friend of mine, Monsieur Fidèle. Is it possible that you are related?"

"If you mean Honoré Fidèle," Philip replied, "I am his nephew."

"Indeed, dear Honoré. . . . Then you must be—"

"His sister's son, Philippe Saintaire, sir."

"And I am Monsieur Georges."

Philip got to his feet at once, exclaiming, "Monsieur Georges! Of course! I have heard my uncle speak of you many times. Will you not join us? This is my wife, Marguerite. Unfortunately she cannot speak, but . . . Marguerite, my love, take your muff off the chair so that Monsieur Georges may sit down."

Megaera's heart was beating like a hammer in her breast, but she moved her muff to her lap and smiled as naturally as she could. She realized then that she had never really believed this would happen. It had been like a story to her, exciting but unreal. Only it *was* real. She could only thank God that her French was so bad Philip had decided on the "mute" role for her. She knew she could never have controlled her voice. It would have squeaked or been too loud or come out in gasps.

Concurrently with that knowledge, her admiration for Philip rose. He was perfect, smooth and natural with a flow of small talk about his imaginary uncle and family. Well as she knew him, she could see nothing in his face other than simple pleasure. Now he was urging Monsieur Georges to order dinner, but Cadoudal refused, saying he had eaten already and had come to have coffee with a friend. Philip looked around and said that since the friend was late, Monsieur Georges should do them the honor to have coffee with them. It seemed to Megaera that Cadoudal was looking a trifle worried. They had better give him his message before he became alarmed and ran away. She touched Philip's arm and made the agreed on signs.

As she rose Cadoudal did so also, but Philip seized his arm and leaned a little closer as if to mention something "indelicate." What he said was, "Pick up my wife's muff when she drops it. There will be a message inside it." As he spoke, however, he twisted his lips in a slight leer, like a man who complains that

his woman "always" has her flux or has a weak blad-
der. It was clear to him that Cadoudal was in two
minds at once; one part believed he was in a trap,
and the other told him it was too late to run and if
there was a message, he must have it.

Philip could only hope that Meg would be quick
and that Cadoudal would not lose his nerve. It was
then, while he was quickly scanning the room to see
whether any new faces had appeared, that he saw
Meg's muff still lying on her chair where she had put
it automatically when she rose. Philip's heart sank.
Cadoudal had also seen it, and he looked at Philip
with a mingling of hatred and despair that made
Philip burst into a long, uninterruptible description
of his work as a customs officer.

Plainly Cadoudal believed Meg had gone to warn
the authorities of his presence and was only hesitating
because he did not know whether to try to make a run
through the kitchens or whether that had been foreseen. Just as Philip was sure Cadoudal was about to
try to escape, Meg appeared at the door, her cupped
hand with a handkerchief in it at her mouth masking
a cough.

Philip's heart had not been the only one that sank
when he saw the muff had been forgotten. As she set
her foot on the stairs to go to their room, Megaera
realized that in her excitement and nervousness she
had left the muff behind. For one instant she was
paralyzed, half turning to go back but knowing that
it would be too suspicious-looking if she went to get
a muff and carried it upstairs. She would just have to
conceal the message somehow and put it in the muff
when she came down.

At first, as she snipped the threads of her bonnet,
her mind was a terrified blank. Tears of fright came
to her eyes, and she snatched a handkerchief to dry
them, knowing that she dared not show red eyes. She
was still clutching the handkerchief in her ring finger

and little finger when she drew the letter out. It came to her instantly how she could conceal it and then, in a rush, that this was much better. Anyone who noticed her carrying the muff would have realized that was an odd thing to do and wondered why she should have taken it when she did not intend to go outside.

This happy accident restored Megaera's confidence so that when she came down she tripped happily across the room, picked up the muff so she could sit on the chair, and thrust her handkerchief into it. Cadoudal, who had started to say good-bye very firmly, abruptly changed to a compliment to Megaera and a question about something Philip had said. Megaera poured herself another cup of coffee and began to make signs to Philip. As she did so, her muff slid to the floor as it had done a hundred times in the past few days. Most politely, Cadoudal bent to pick it up. A few minutes later a new person entered. Cadoudal rose at once, saying his friend had arrived and, no doubt, he would see Philip again.

After the barest hesitation Philip said, "We are staying right here at the Mille Colonnes, but only until tomorrow. My wife has conceived a desire to see Versailles and insists, even though I have told her there is little open to the public worth seeing. And do not smile. She can be quite vehement, even in silence."

"At least stay one day longer so that we can dine together. I would like to give you a little present to take to your uncle."

Philip glanced at Megaera, and she nodded and smiled, but he was aware of a sudden stab of fear. It was not going to be so simple after all. He had assumed that, knowing the situation, Cadoudal would have returned to England already if he intended to return. Now he wondered whether the man had remained because he had no way out. If so, Philip was committed to help him, and that would be dangerous, very dangerous. What a fool he had been to bring Meg along.

Then he hoped that Cadoudal might think that a return message would be necessary. He should have guessed from what Philip said that none was expected; however, Philip now realized that Cadoudal might have something new to propose or some other message of his own that would take a longer time to transmit. There was no doubt in his mind that this second meeting would increase the danger of being associated with Cadoudal and, therefore, of being caught, and as he agreed with Cadoudal's proposal he began to seek some scheme to insure Meg's safety.

Chapter 21

That night a fierce argument raged in whispers. Philip wanted Megaera to pretend to be ill and let him go to "dinner" with Cadoudal alone. Megaera would not hear of it. She pointed out that she would inevitably be caught, either as soon as they—whoever "they" were—realized she was not with Philip or as soon as she tried to escape from Paris. In fact she would be in more danger alone. If anyone tried to arrest them when they were together, she could provide a diversion, which no one would expect from a mute woman, so that they could escape or fight their way free. Alone, she would be helpless.

Philip argued that she would have no problem getting to Dieppe. All she had to do was write her destination down. She had plenty of money, and everyone would pity a poor, mute girl. They certainly would, Megaera agreed, and that muteness would mark her trail so successfully that she could be followed no matter where she went. All that could be accomplished by her escape would be to lead the police agents to Pierre. This was a sufficiently cogent argument, added to Philip's reluctance to have Meg wandering around totally unprotected, to silence him. He had some hope

that they were unsuspected, too. He had been watching the room carefully and he had not seen anyone
enter except the man whom Cadoudal claimed as a
friend. Since they had left separately and Philip and
Megaera had not gone out at all, Philip had some
hope that Cadoudal's followers, if there were any,
would think he had come to meet that man and no
one else.

This hope showed Philip's ignorance of the way an
effective police-spy network functioned. It was true
that Cadoudal was discreetly followed by Fouché's
men, but they had no need to do anything so crude as
to trail their subject into a room, making their purpose obvious. Long ago, as far back as the days of the
Terror, Fouché had developed sources of information
in many of the cafés and hotels of Paris. When he
became Minister of Police, the network was elaborated
until there was hardly a single poor wineshop that
did not have an employee who would pass information
to Fouché's agents.

Thus, some time after Cadoudal had left Mille
Colonnes, a waiter responded to a signal, served wine,
and acknowledged credentials he recognized. Later he
met the man just outside, and acknowledged he had
seen Cadoudal, whom the agent described precisely. In
response to several perceptive questions the waiter
described the meeting between Cadoudal and Philip
quite accurately, and as much of the conversation
as he had heard, which fortunately was very little indeed. The agent, however, was not interested in the
conversation, which he knew would be perfectly innocent. Cadoudal made a practice of stopping to speak to
people who, after checking and rechecking, were found
to be totally clear of any disaffection.

What the agent wanted to know was whether Philip
had passed anything to Cadoudal or vice versa. This
the waiter answered in the negative. He was sure, he
said, that Monsieur Saintaire had not touched the

other man, except once to lay his hand on his shoulder, nor given him anything. He did not mention Megaera leaving the table nor the fact that her muff had fallen to the floor and Cadoudal had picked it up. In fact, he had not seen that happen, but even if he had, he would not have mentioned it. He himself had picked up Madame Saintaire's muff at least ten times. It was always slipping, and besides, of what interest could a woman's doings be to Monsieur Fouché?

The agent then listened to a description of the second man Cadoudal had met without much interest. They knew all about him. The agent was not terribly interested in Philip either. This seemed simply another case of Cadoudal's laying a false trail; however, men who worked for Monsieur Fouché did not trust too much to their own judgments and left no stone unturned. He asked whether the waiter knew anything at all about Philip besides his name.

"Yes, indeed, Monsieur Saintaire is staying here with his wife—ah, poor woman, she is dumb."

"Where are they now?"

"Above in their chamber."

"They went out after my man had left?"

"No. They had intended to do so, I think, but it started to rain again and they stayed within. They played cards together, laughing very much. Ah, yes, before your man left he asked their direction."

That, plus the change in plans might or might not be suspicious, the agent thought. He confirmed that Philip and Megaera were expected to stay, as far as the waiter knew, passed the agreed fee, and then decided to step inside again to ask the landlord some questions. He wanted to be sure that the waiter was right. If this couple suddenly decided to leave the next day, that would cast a different light on the matter.

What he learned made Philip seem even less likely as a suspect; a clerk in the *bureau de service* of the Customs with a commendation for finding a cache of

smuggled goods (Pierre's forger had made good use
of the letter Philip had received from the director at
Boulogne) , a young man obviously very much in love
with his afflicted wife, did not seem a good prospect
for a conspirator. Nonetheless he ordered the landlord
to delay them and to send a message to him if they
tried to leave early in the morning. Having taken what
he felt were sufficient precautions, he troubled no
more.

In any case, Saintaire was fixed for the night and
could not leave without notice. There was no emergency about communicating the information. The
morning, when he made his regular report on Cadoudal's activities, would do quite well. That next morning, however, Monsieur Fouché was very much occupied. It was becoming more and more obvious that the
First Consul would recall him to office as Minister of
Police, and he had many "unofficial" visits and conferences with members of the Council of State. That
morning the conference was with Consul Cambacérès,
the man most closely in sympathy with Bonaparte's
desires and deepest in his confidence. Such a meeting
could not be interrupted for a routine report on
Cadoudal's activities, even if there were a minor varia-
tion. Cadoudal had been in Paris for more than three
months, and the landlord had not reported any suspicious activity on the part of the Saintaires.

Only shortly before dinnertime did Fouché's agent
get to give his report. The white face was expression-
less, the frightening eyes masked by the white lashes
until the agent mentioned the name "Saintaire."
Joseph Fouché was not a man to use obscenity, but
he said *Merde!* with such force that his agent re-
coiled. Before the agent could catch his breath to speak
again, Fouché had regained his poise and his voice
was soft and pleasant when he assured the agent he
did not blame him.

"He is an English spy, this Saintaire, I am sure. I

had word of his coming from our agent in the British Foreign Office, but you say he is a customs officer with a young wife. Hmmmm. This is the second time I know of that d'Ursine has led us astray—just a little astray, just enough so that, had we not been especially watchful, we would have missed the man completely this time also. I wonder . . ."

"Pardon," the agent interrupted anxiously. "I left word to be warned if Saintaire intended to leave Paris, but I did not put a man to watch him. He could have met Cadoudal—"

"Calm, be calm. If he has, we will know of it through the man watching Cadoudal. If he has, then we will seize them both immediately, but they have gone to great lengths to make this meeting seem accidental. Thus they should try to make their next meeting, if there is to be one, a natural thing. I think they will meet for dinner—that would give the longest time for talk. Send at once to the Milles Colonnes to learn of Saintaire's activities."

The agent ran out to do so, and Fouché sat with steepled fingers, thinking. When his man returned, he asked, "If they meet for dinner, can you guess where?"

"Almost certainly at La Maison du Faucon. It is a nest of Royalists where Cadoudal conducts most of his business. But it does not matter, I sent a man to watch Saintaire and the one watching Cadoudal will send word if he goes out or meets anyone. That is arranged."

"Good. Three men should be enough. It must look as if the suspicion is directed only at Saintaire and that the search of Cadoudal is a mere formality because he was found in suspicious company. Saintaire is to be questioned first—by any means necessary—and then killed."

"What of the woman?"

"Kill her also, but not until the man has answered

all questions. We want to know what message he brought and, most important, which Bourbon is coming and where he will land. If direct persuasion cannot convince Saintaire to answer, try working on the woman where he can see and hear it. There are many men who cannot endure that, particularly when it is their fault that the woman is in difficulty. Even if they are not lovers, which they probably are, since they claim to be husband and wife rather than sister and brother, he may give information when she is hurt more quickly than he would to ease his own pain."

"I suppose since she is mute we cannot get information from her?"

"Why not? She may be able to write, but I do not think it worthwhile. She may well be a blind, picked up on the way. D'Ursine would not go so far as to fail to mention her if her presence had been planned in England. This Saintaire may have known her from before. He may have spent considerable time in France before we ever knew of him. You say he is a young man?"

"I did not see him myself, but there can be no doubt. The woman is young, and if he were older the waiter would have remarked on it."

"Yes. It must be the son. I met the father in 1792? 1793? He was a 'gunsmith' using the name Saintaire—funny how those men cling to their own name. I met him again in 1802 and learned he was an English barrister, St. Eyre by name. He said he had been trapped here during the Revolution, but I think he was always an English spy. He worked with a woman also. I think she was an aristocrat. Later he married her. Yes, from your description it must be the son. The looks are much the same, except the father's eyes were blue."

The agent sat silent, listening. It was not common for Monsieur Fouché to say more than what was necessary. Therefore, he expected the agent to use the information in some way, possibly during the questioning of the prisoner. He rang a bell, a secretary entered, and was directed to bring the file on d'Ursine. Fouché studied this for a time, and made a moue of distaste.

"It is time to make sure of d'Ursine. I am beginning to think he may be a double agent. In any case he has near outlived his usefulness. The administration is about to change in England. That means his employment with Hawkesbury will not place him in a position to send information of value. Doubtless he will use that as an excuse to come back to France."

Fouché looked into the distance. The agent, who knew how his mind worked—if any man knew how Fouché's mind worked—believed he was considering whether d'Ursine would be useful in France. False information could be sent to England through him if he was really a trusted double agent. Fouché did not voice those thoughts, but summoned his secretary again. He instructed the secretary to send a footman for François Charon, the spy who had brought d'Ursine's message to France first, and when that was done, to add a pass so that Charon could use government horses to take him to the coast at top speed.

Then Fouché himself wrote to d'Ursine. The letter was cold and brief. It stated that Philip Saintaire had been killed on d'Ursine's recommendation and that Fouché believed this to have been a grave error. "I feel," Fouché wrote, "that this was a most cruel and unnecessary waste of life. The young man was a scion of an honorable English family, as you must have known. He should, even if he were engaged in spying, have been taken prisoner and held for exchange." In the future, Fouché added, d'Ursine should transmit more accurate information, not instructions that, owing to ignorance, were bound to be incorrect.

It would be interesting, Fouché thought as he signed and sealed this missive, to see d'Ursine's reaction to this criticism. If he were sincerely with the French cause, he would redouble his efforts to redeem himself —and that would be useful. If he were a double agent, he would be far more careful about the information he sent. And if by some mischance the letter should fall into the wrong hands, it would clear Fouché of any suspicion of guilt in the death of an Englishman whose father might possibly have friends in high places. At the very worst, if d'Ursine should be clever enough to take fright because the letter was not in code and was signed and sealed by Fouché himself, it would save the trouble of having him killed when he came back to France.

When everything was ready, Fouché handed the parcel to the waiting agent. "François Charon is waiting in the antechamber. He is to be one of the men who raids La Maison du Faucon—or wherever you trap Cadoudal and Saintaire. If Cadoudal has given Saintaire a message to carry, lift the seal carefully, make a copy for me, and let Charon take the original to England. He can report the sad death of Saintaire and deliver Cadoudal's message, which will reassure the English as to his reliability, and he can pass my letter privately to d'Ursine."

While Fouché was writing his letter, Philip and Megaera were climbing the stairs to a private room in the Epée du Bois. That morning a ragged boy had delivered a note for Philip, inviting him to dinner at the Faucon. Since the boy had been instructed to wait for a reply, Philip had the opportunity to write that there was some reason to believe the Faucon "no longer served the kind of dinner we wished to eat." Could they meet instead at the Epée du Bois on the rue de Venise off the rue St. Martin? If so, no answer need be sent.

Although Philip was totally unaware that he was already suspect, he and Megaera went to the meeting armed and ready for trouble. Philip was very much afraid that this second meeting would mark them and that an attempt would be made to arrest them after they left Cadoudal or when they returned to their hotel. He was not even sure they should return to the hotel at all. Their baggage was still there, but that did not matter. They were warmly dressed and had all their money and their papers with them.

Cadoudal had changed overnight. He was gray with fatigue and grief and seized Philip's hand, apologizing for asking him to come. He looked with haunted eyes at Megaera. "Why did you bring her?" he whispered, as if her muteness rendered her hard-of-hearing also.

"Because I would not stay behind," she replied softly in English, smiling at him. "I'm 'mute' because I speak little French. Don't worry about me. I'm well able to take care of myself."

"Ah, the gallant English ladies," Cadoudal said. His expression lightened for a moment, although he did not really approve of such boldness in a female. This minor matter could not hold his mind, and he went grim again as he looked back at Philip. "I had to ask you to make this sacrifice because, although one hope is dead, another has risen in its place. We were fooled about the attitude of the people toward Bonaparte, but their satisfaction is not shared by many of his own high officials. They see now that he will not be content to rule within a constitution. He seeks to make himself even more absolute than the king."

Philip merely nodded. This was scarcely a surprise to him.

"Then we still have hope," Cadoudal continued earnestly. "If we can bring strong Republican leaders like General Moreau and Monsieur Carnot to listen to us, we can have a king, like yours, who is not above the law. I think the Republicans will prefer a constitutional monarch to a tyrannical emperor, and we who desire a king of the legitimate line will be glad that a foolish one will not be able to commit the follies and extravagances of the past."

"Very true," Philip remarked, "but I do not believe Bonaparte will step down just for the asking."

Cadoudal's face set like stone. "He must die, of course. That is not your part nor the part of your government. We French must deal in our own way with a tyrant and usurper."

Megaera's lips parted, but she swallowed and held her tongue. She saw from Philip's frown that he, too, was not at ease with what could only be an intention of assassinating the First Consul, but Cadoudal had said it was a matter for the French to deal with themselves, and there was a certain justice in that.

All Philip said was "Then what is my part?"

"To obtain the agreement of General Moreau is essential. He is an honorable man, a strict Republican and regards me as an enemy, knowing that I desire above all the restoration of the true king. Thus there is no way for me to approach him. However, General Pichegru, who is now in England, having fled after Bonaparte's coup d'état in Fructidor, is an old and dear friend of Moreau's. I am sure Moreau would listen to him. It is our last hope. It is also England's best hope for preventing a long bloodbath. This is why I asked you to come, even after I learned that de la Touche is probably a traitor and I—all unwitting—have probably marked all my friends for death."

He covered his face after these words, but recovered in a moment and continued, "I have written to Pichegru, to Lord Hawkesbury, and to the Comte d'Artois. Will you carry these letters for me?"

"Yes, of course," Philip replied at once, "but is it safe for you to remain here? I have a friend who will give you passage back—"

"I will disappear," Cadoudal interrupted. "I can. Whoever follows me is clever. Even though I knew

today there must be someone, I could see no sign—
but I have made it easy for them in the past. Now that
I know better—we know better—we will all disappear
tomorrow, after you are gone. Until then we will act
just as usual. I will go to the Palais Royale, a friend
will meet me there—all as usual. I hope this will be of
some help to you."

"Do not sacrifice your safety for ours," Philip urged.
"Meg and I are prepared to go now. We will need
only an hour or two to leave Paris. After that—"

"No, no." Cadoudal found a smile. "You are very
generous, but if I am bait, I am in no immediate danger. Only tell me if there is something you can think
of that will be of more help to you than my simply
acting as I have all along."

The agent who "shadowed" Cadoudal had seen the
boy who carried the note to Philip go and return, but
he had been instructed never to give Cadoudal any
reason to suspect he was watched. Thus the best he
could do when Cadoudal set out for the Epée du Bois
was to follow and send a message telling the new destination back to their informer where Cadoudal lived.
He did not hurry to do this, delaying until he was
sure Cadoudal intended to stay at the Epée. Often his
subject moved from place to place meeting different
people before he settled on a spot to dine.

Thus Philip and Cadoudal were almost finished
with their discussion when the messenger arrived at
the end of the street in which Cadoudal lodged. From
the corner house, with a glass, it was possible to see
without ever being seen oneself. The landlord of that
house, who also was in Fouché's pay, gestured the
messenger upstairs and signaled that he had better
hurry. He found Charon and the other, higher-level
agent waiting with impatience. They rushed out the
moment they knew where to go. It had been clear to
both of them that their master would not be pleased

if their quarry should escape. After a hurried conference to pass on Fouché's instructions, which were simple enough, Charon walked into the Epée du Bois and requested a private parlor to entertain two friends, who would arrive in a few minutes. They had already dined, he said, and chose several bottles of wine, which the landlord carried upstairs with him, since Charon said he did not wish to be interrupted by waiters. The three other agents entered as they started up. Two followed Charon and the landlord, the other went into the bar. At the door of the room Charon took the tray, the agent opened the door, and the three pretended to enter while watching the landlord descend the stairs again.

None of the agents had spoken, and the landlord had got out no more than, "This room, gentlemen—" before he was silenced by a frown. However, Philip had just been reaching for the door to open it for Megaera, and he heard. He paused, listening intently. Megaera, who had just put on her pelisse, stood stiffly beside the table, one hand inside her muff clutching the two-shot muff gun. Cadoudal, who had been sitting opposite her and had risen when she did, began to back away from the table to go to Philip's assistance.

The tableau held only for a moment. Realizing he had not heard the door of the room opposite shut, Philip thrust his hand into his greatcoat pocket to draw his gun, but before he could do so, the door slammed open, knocking him backward. Cadoudal leapt forward, but it was too late. All three men were in the room. Two brandished pistols, while the third stopped to turn the key in the lock of the door. Megaera uttered an inarticulate cry and toppled to the floor beside the table.

When he saw Megaera fall, Philip cried out also and started forward, only to be knocked down by a blow from the barrel of Charon's pistol. Disregarding the threat of the other agent's gun, which was leveled at him, Cadoudal rushed at him. He knew he would be executed anyway if he were taken—probably after extensive "questioning"—so he had little to lose in dying at once. The agent, who knew no harm must come to Cadoudal, naturally did not fire. He managed to sidestep the rush, and the third man, who had been pulling off his neckcloth to tie up Philip, grappled with Cadoudal.

No one gave a glance to the crumpled heap of garments that marked Megaera's position. Fouché's men had not given her a thought, assuming she would be equally harmless conscious and only glad that she had fainted because it kept her from screaming. But the heap of garments had not been still. With surprising alacrity it had wriggled past a chair and under the table.

When Philip had stiffened at the door, Megaera knew instantly that they were trapped. It never occurred to her that the people on the other side of the door could be innocent visitors to the inn. For a second or two she was so frightened that vision and hearing faded and she felt that she would faint. The weakness retreated as her heart pounded harder, pushing blood to her brain. Her next fear was that she would be a danger to Philip. She knew he might expose himself unnecessarily to protect her or that she could be used as a weapon against him if she were seized.

She had been holding the gun in her muff since she got to her feet. It was necessary to do so or it would fall out, being heavy. At first, in her terror, she only clutched it tighter, mindlessly, not understanding what she held. When her accelerated heart-rate and breathing had cleared her head, however, she remembered she was not helpless and defenseless. In the small room the little muff gun was as deadly as the more accurate long-barreled pistols Philip carried. All

she needed was a central position so that she would
not be too far from any part of the room.

As that idea came to her she realized she would
never be given time to cock and fire her gun. As soon
as she drew it from the muff, she would be either shot
or seized. Fear gripped her again, her head spun, and
all the thoughts jostled together. Out of the maelstrom
came a plan that seized on weakness and used it to
hide her strength. Thus, when the door shot open,
thrusting Philip backward, Megaera did just what a
proper lady should do and sank to the floor in a faint.

After that she was too busy for the next minute or
two to notice what happened to anybody but herself.
By the time she had wriggled herself under the table,
pulled the gun from her muff, and cocked it—all without anyone noticing—chaos had erupted in the room.
The noise was behind her, but Megaera did not turn
her head. Her gaze was fixed on Philip, lying on the
floor with blood running down his face. Without a
second thought Megaera lifted her pistol and shot
Charon in the back. He screamed and fell on top of
Philip, his gun exploding harmlessly into the air.

The other agent spun around, cursing, looking wildly for a target. His half-formed thought that another
man had been concealed in the room was not quite
finished when Megaera, swiveling around on her knees
under the table, shot him full in the chest. He did
not scream. Shock overrode pain. Even as he died he
could not believe that the woman who had fainted
with fright as they came in the door had changed into
a fury, with blazing purple eyes, pointing a gun. Had
he lived another minute, he would have told himself
that it was a small man in disguise, or that his eyes
had deceived him and a man had been hidden under
the table all along and shot from behind the woman
as she roused from her faint.

Death saved him the trouble of rationalizing reality

to fit his prejudices and from the further shock of
seeing Megaera busily crawl out from under the table
with a vicious expression on her normally sweet face.
It seemed as if the first man she had shot was struggling with Philip despite the widening stain of blood
on his coat. However, just as she got to her feet, firmly
clutching her empty gun with the intention of hitting
Philip's attacker on the head as hard as ever she
could, Philip rid himself of the corpse and rose also.

The man who had been grappling with Cadoudal
to restrain him was now trying desperately to get free,
but it was far too late. In the next instant Philip's
long-nosed Lorenzoni was pressed against his head. He
ceased to struggle, stammering a plea for mercy. Although he received no response, his terror diminished
somewhat when the neckcloth he had partially undone
was removed and used to bind his hands. Those
of his unfortunate comrades were then used to finish
the job and to blindfold and gag him also.

Megaera, who had controlled herself nobly while
there was still danger, now flew to Philip crying that
he was hurt. Cadoudal gaped at the two men lying
dead on the floor, looking from them to Megaera and
back again. Finally Philip broke off assuring her that
it was nothing, that even a small cut on the head was
a great bleeder, to laugh.

"You are getting hardened, love," he said softly,
kissing her carefully so as not to get blood on her.
"You were all upset when you shot Jean."

"Not after I knew he was after you. And that man
was going to shoot you too," Megaera replied, trying
to wipe the blood from his face with his handkerchief.
She shuddered once, and then said determinedly, "Do
you want me delicate and you dead?"

That made Philip laugh again; he knew Meg was
deliberately echoing the words he had used to excuse
his conduct with Désirée. Cadoudal was now looking

at her with mingled admiration and horror. She had
said she could take care of herself, but he had not
expected the proof of it to be two dead men. So delicate a lady . . .

"It is too quiet below," Philip said suddenly, in-
terrupting Cadoudal's thought and pulling away from
Megaera. "Surely the shots should have brought the
landlord up here. There must be more of them downstairs—or the landlord knew. . . ."

"Yes, but whoever is there must believe that we
were subdued," Cadoudal pointed out.

"I agree. Otherwise they would have come up to
lend a hand. That means we have a little time—I hope.
I cannot believe they came here just to kill us. That
one"—Philip gestured toward the bound man—"was
undoing his neckcloth, and that could only have been
to tie up someone."

He handed his gun to Cadoudal, in case there
should be another attempt at surprise, and began to
search the corpses. On the man shot in the chest he
found papers from both the Ministry of Police and
Fouché. On the man shot in the back he found a
wallet containing the passes Fouché's clerk had written out and a small-folded sheet sealed with an emblem
he did not recognize. He did not pause to examine
that; there would be time enough later, and he
did not wish to break the seal. Perhaps the message,
read and passed on, could be of use to trap a whole
ring of spies. On the living man was identification as
Fouché's agent, but nothing more.

Philip considered the harvest he had garnered, then
returned to Charon and searched him more thoroughly. Sewn inside the waistband of his trousers Philip
found English papers of identification somewhat like
his own but less sweeping in their protection. Charon
was a double agent! Now he began to search in
earnest. Putting aside the easily discovered belt under
his shirt, heavy with French and English gold, Philip

opened the man's boots, pried at the heels, ripped the lining and seams of every garment, but found nothing more.

While his hands had been busy, Philip's brain had been busy too. He looked up at Cadoudal, made a sign to him not to interfere, and struck the bound man on the head with the butt of Charon's gun to knock him senseless. "I am sorry about that," he said, "but he must not hear what I am about to say. Meg and I must leave at once. I am sure these men were to report back to Monsieur Fouché. I deduce they were to question me—that must have been the purpose for the neckcloth to tie me up—since it would be lunatic to question you. Although what they thought I could know . . . Well, that does not matter. If what I hope is true, Fouché cannot expect a report for some time, assuming we would resist questioning—so we will have time to escape Paris."

"We must get out of here first," Megaera said as steadily as she could. She was standing by the side of the window, where she could not be seen but where she could look out and avoid seeing the results of her determination to protect Philip.

"Yes, but we cannot leave this man or any others who may be belowstairs behind us."

"No, of course not, but I know how to solve that problem," Cadoudal assured him. "I have friends also. If we can overcome the men below and you can give me ten minutes to summon assistance, you can leave."

"Good enough," Philip agreed.

"Wait until I load my gun," Megaera protested, hurrying to the table where she had laid the weapon.

"You should have loaded it right away," Philip complained teasingly. "What good is an empty gun? And what an idiot you are to leave it lying around."

"I didn't have time to load it. I thought that man was going to strangle you. I was going to hit him on the head, and—"

"Adding insult to injury—yes, I see. But he could not have strangled me very hard with a bullet in him. It would have been more practical to load and shoot him in the head."

"One cannot think of everything in a moment of crisis," Megaera said reproachfully, and then burst out laughing.

Cadoudal made a strangled sound of distaste at the laughter and bantering and at Philip's seemingly callous attitude toward the woman. The English sang-froid was too much for him. Philip did not bother to explain; he did not care what Cadoudal thought. He was only glad that Meg's eyes were clear again, the lingering shadow of horror in them gone. His seemingly casual acceptance of what she had done—which now that he thought back on it turned his insides all fluid with pride and gratitude and love—had reduced the importance of the two deaths. To scold her for so minor a failing in a jocular manner almost made an everyday matter of the affair. Megaera still kept her eyes away from the bodies, but she was beginning to equate them with the vermin she would casually order killed on her estates.

"Do not hurry your loading," Philip said next, pulling off his greatcoat. "You will have time. I am going to wear this man's coat and hat while I go down and see with how many we have to contend."

A babble of protest broke out from Megaera and Cadoudal, to which Philip replied briefly as he untied the unconscious man's hands to remove his coat. When he was dressed, he took the Lorenzoni from Cadoudal and handed him the gun that had not been fired, as well as Charon's gun, which he had loaded quickly.

"Stop talking foolishly, both of you," he said sharply. "Meg, tie this man up again, good and tight. Monsieur Cadoudal, follow me to the head of the stairs and then come down slowly, unless you hear shots or other sounds of violence. Then do what you think best—but do it fast! Meg, when you have the prisoner secured, take my coat and hat and follow Monsieur Cadoudal."

He wanted to tell her to escape with the Frenchman, that Cadoudal could provide her with a guide who would take her to Dieppe, but he knew with both despair and an intense joy that he would be wasting his breath. If he ran into trouble, Meg would be right there beside him, fighting to her last breath to save him. Debt or no debt, bastard or no bastard, he would have her as his wife, even if it meant severing ties with his father and Leonie. That would hurt, but not nearly so much as losing Meg.

Chapter 22

The tense agony Megaera endured when Philip left the room was somewhat mitigated by the force with which she hit the third man when he groaned and twitched as she retied him. Cadoudal had not quite left the room. He winced at the *thonk* the blow made and muttered an involuntary prayer of thanksgiving that his association with this "sweet" English lady would soon come to an end. He hated to think what might happen if he inadvertently offended her, but worse than that, he had no idea how to deal with her. How and about what did one talk to a woman who swatted men like flies?

The period of doubt was very brief. In minutes Philip had called to Cadoudal to come down. Megaera was on his heels, her gun drawn. If the Frenchman thought her vicious, she thought him weak. Neither was correct, but the misunderstanding was not significant since their association was not to be renewed. They found Philip holding the last of the agents and the entire staff of the Epée, whom the agent had conveniently assembled in the kitchen. There had been no trouble at all. The agent had not even had his gun in hand. He did not need it. No more was needed to quell the staff of the Epée than to show his credentials and tell them that what happened was none of their business and was sanctioned by Monsieur Fouché.

All the male members of the staff were summarily bound, and Philip watched them while Cadoudal went out for the agreed ten minutes. Actually, the time stretched to twenty, and Megaera was frightened to death, thinking they had been abandoned. However, Cadoudal did return, and Megaera had spent the time usefully in removing all traces of blood from Philip's face, finding a clean shirt and neckcloth for him among the landlord's clothing, and in general removing any trace of the conflict from her own as well as Philip's outer garments.

They returned to the Milles Colonnes, told the landlord that they would stay another day since they had met friends, and walked out carrying only the small parcel of silks Megaera had purchased—which were wrapped around the breeches, shirt, and jacket she had been wearing when Philip abducted her. The garments had been cleaned while they were at Monsieur Luroec's farm and packed with Philip's clothing in case they should need to make a run for it. Over his arm Philip carried the greatcoat he had taken from the agent, which concealed Megaera's boots.

A fiacre took them to the stable where the horse and carriage that had brought them from Brittany were kept. Philip paid the bill (with Charon's money —he thought that a nice touch) and left two francs to reserve a place two days hence when, he said, he and his wife would return. So far, although both Philip and Megaera had been watching as carefully as they could without being obvious, they had seen no sign of anyone following them. However, the worst was yet to come. If word of the failure of his plan had come to Fouché, there had been time by now to have watchers at the gates.

Of the two, Megaera's appearance was the more distinctive. She did what she could, sitting as far back in the carriage as possible, exchanging her pelisse for the extra greatcoat, pinning her hair away from her face and covering it with the too-large hat. She also removed her shoes and put on the boots Philip had carried out. They took the road to Versailles, heading southwest toward Dreux, the road they had followed into Paris.

Since they were not stopped at the gate, Philip and Megaera assumed that Cadoudal had given them the few hours he had promised. Philip made the best of the time that he could, but he knew that pursuit could not be long delayed. When no report of what had happened came to Fouché, he would send to find out why. Even if the landlord claimed the agents had taken him, Cadoudal, and Megaera away to protect himself, Fouché would know something had gone wrong.

When the horse tired, Philip stopped at a posting house. Megaera removed the man's hat but continued to wear the overlarge greatcoat, which hung down right to her feet. Philip shepherded her tenderly into the inn and requested a private room with a good fire. His wife had caught a chill, he explained. He did not explain why he carried in a parcel, but that was not necessary. If it contained something valuable, he would not wish to leave it in the carriage. While Philip ordered something to eat—they had never had dinner with Cadoudal—Megaera changed into the men's clothing that had been hidden in the parcel of silk. The waiter who brought the food noticed no difference in her; she was sitting by the fire still huddled in the greatcoat. Since her face was turned away, he did not see the sweat beading it.

They ate as quickly as possible and left. The horse was not rested, but that did not matter, since Philip did not intend to drive him much farther. He took

the next crossroad leading north. Somewhere along
that road Philip lost his red-haired wife and acquired
a mute servant boy garbed in his master's castoffs.
Megaera quite willingly sacrificed her dark red mane;
it was Philip's eyes that were filled with tears as he
hacked off her hair with his knife. She laughed at him,
assuring him it would soon grow again, but he felt
to blame for her sacrifice.

Next Philip drove the carriage into a field, unhitched the horse, and bestrode it bareback with
Megaera behind him, her women's clothes now hidden in the parcel of silk. They rode to the next village. It was a small place. Here Philip dared show
Fouché's pass and order that François Charon be
supplied with horses. He said he had lost a wheel on
his carriage, paid for two horses, and made an exchange of the other for two saddles. The owners might
have made difficulties had Philip tried to make such
arrangements on his own, but Fouché's name was a
talisman. The former Minister of Police might not be
loved but, in or out of office, no one had any desire
to cross him. Everything was settled quickly, and
Philip and Megaera were off again.

They rode out of the village on the road, but it
soon curved west and they abandoned it, riding across
the barren, wintry fields as close to due north as they
could. They had hardly spoken to each other at all,
except for necessary questions and directions, but now
Philip looked across at Megaera, utterly ridiculous in
the too-large greatcoat and hat tied to her head with
a scarf to keep it from falling off and exposing her
hair.

"I must be insane," he said.

"Why?" Megaera asked anxiously. "Are we lost?"

"No, of course we are not lost. It has just occurred
to me that on some crazy pretense that I was protect-
ing you I have exposed you to hideous dangers, to

the discomforts of riding all over a foreign country in the dead of winter. . . ."

"I don't mind," Megaera said cheerfully. "In fact I'm rather enjoying myself. I do hope we won't be caught, though."

"You must be insane too!" Philip exclaimed.

Megaera glanced at him mischievously. "It is certainly best that we both be afflicted," she agreed. "Otherwise we would be constantly at odds with each other, and that would be a sad shame."

"Meg!" Philip sputtered, but he was still troubled and the laughter soon died. "Do you realize that I could have left you safe at Luroec's farm until Pierre—"

"Oh no you couldn't!" Megaera interrupted heatedly. "What do you think I am, a parcel that may be 'left until called for'? I told you that you were an idiot to drag me to France, but once you did that you were stuck with me. Why, are you regretting my presence?"

"Bitterly," Philip replied.

Megaera knew perfectly well that Philip was suffering pangs of conscience for not having foreseen that his task would not be quite as easy as he believed, but she chose to misunderstand. "I don't see that I've been such a burden to you up to now," she said huffily.

"Burden! I would be dead if not for you, my darling."

"Then isn't it fortunate that I am a little lacking in that modesty and delicacy which would make me miserable under these circumstances and instead—"

"You are a bold and bewitching wench," Philip finished. "Oh, Meg, I love you so. I wish—"

Megaera could see in his face that Philip was going to say something very serious, possibly explain why he could not propose marriage. What could she do?

She was beginning to suspect he was more than a smuggler's bastard, much more. If that were so, naturally he would not consider marrying her. She had said she was a bastard herself, and had slept with him without even a pretense of reluctance. She had already made herself ineligible to marry, she realized.

Nonetheless Megaera knew she would be furious if Philip offered her a carte blanche. Ridiculous as it was, she was hurt that he had accepted her story. She knew it was wrong but still felt he should have seen through the pretense, recognized her for what she was. She had not minded when he said he would "take her away with him" while she believed him to be Pierre's illegitimate son. A smuggler's bastard would not know any better. A gentleman, however, should know better, should recognize his own kind. Megaera could not bear to let him make the proposition. Desperately she tried to divert him.

"Not in a stubbly field in the middle of the winter!" she said.

"That was not what I was going to suggest," Philip protested, laughing.

"Liar," Megaera remarked succinctly.

"I am not!" Philip exclaimed. "I may be insane, but not insane enough to want to make love under those conditions."

Megaera shrugged. "Then you are a liar in another way," she said provocatively. "Didn't you tell me—not so long ago either—that you were always ready—hard up, you called it—when you were with me?"

Philip blinked. He knew perfectly well that Meg was teasing him, but he was not sure why. Was it just so that he would not go on blaming himself for exposing her to danger? He hardly knew how he replied because he suddenly wondered if he had been a fool. Did Meg want him to stop blathering on about how sorry he was he had brought her because he was frightening her? He studied her face, but there was no fear there. No, she must have stopped him because she did not want him to finish what he was saying. She didn't want him to marry her and take over her family's debts.

Damn it, she *was* insane, insisting on supporting that useless sister and father at the risk of her own life. Well, that was over. If he had to tie her down or blow up Pierre's ship, Meg's smuggling days were over. And that was as foolish as Meg's insistence on managing without help. She was no silly schoolgirl who could be ordered around. If he convinced Pierre to stop trading in Cornwall, that would only make matters worse. Nine chances out of ten Meg would just make contact with another smuggler—and that might be far more dangerous than leaving things alone.

Pierre really deserved the name generally bestowed on smugglers; he *was* a "gentleman," but most were not. Somehow Philip knew he would have to convince Meg to let him shoulder her burden, but he had no idea at the moment of how to go about it. All in all he was grateful to her for stopping him. If he had proposed, she would have felt obliged to refuse him, and that would only have complicated the situation. This was not the time and place anyway. After they were safe he would be able to concentrate properly.

Having come to this conclusion, Philip put Meg's personal problems out of his mind temporarily. The sun was pretty close to setting, and they needed to find a road before it grew dark. Fortunately this was not far to seek. Before they had traveled another fifteen minutes they saw the spire of a church. They were at Maule, Philip was told when he asked, and they were directed toward Mantes, where they could find a road going north to Abbeville. The farmer to whom they spoke did not seem surprised at their having lost their way. He thought they had come out of

Paris on the new road being built to Boulogne. This was unfinished in many places, and there were detours on which many came to grief.

Philip was delighted with this information, since Mantes was on the direct road to Dieppe. It was highly unlikely that Fouché's men could scour the countryside so thoroughly as to question this farmer. Nonetheless Philip was not taking even so remote a chance as to name their true destination. Their route out of Paris should direct their pursuers toward Brittany. If they should be traced this far, however, Philip's questions would imply that they were going to cross at the shortest point, probably from Calais, or make for the Belgian border.

In addition to information Philip obtained a loaf of bread, cheese, and sausage. They rode on, making better time along the road until the horses began to flag. Then they found a barn, warm enough with the heat of the cattle. They let the horses rest and lip over some hay while they themselves ate. Fortunately the barn was large and they stayed at the end farthest from the house. They intended to be quiet, of course, but they were both somewhat giddy with fatigue and the aftermath of extreme tension and they fell into giggles over the difficulties of eating in the dark.

Things were not so funny as the night wore on. They made their first change of horses without difficulty at Mantes, where Philip asked the way to Abbeville again. Since there was only one tired ostler and Philip wanted to be sure of good horses, he used Fouché's pass. The ostler could not read, but he recognized the seal and he made haste to lead out two excellent mounts. In fact he was so awed that he never stopped to wonder why the master helped him to transfer the saddles while the servant leaned wearily against the wall with closed eyes.

Megaera was reaching the limit of her endurance, but she managed to mount and stick to the saddle for a while longer. She could feel Philip looking at her with anxiety every few minutes, and second by second she clung to her horse until, at last, all her efforts could not retain wakefulness. The reins slipped from her hand and she sagged. If it had not been for Philip's watchfulness, she would have fallen. He caught her, brought the horses side by side, and with some feeble help from her took her up before him in the saddle.

"Sorry," she mumbled, "so sorry. . . ."

"Hush, beloved. Sleep."

Although he was not much better off than Megaera, Philip drove himself on. It was about forty miles to Rouen from Mantes, and Philip felt that the worst danger would be there. He was eager to enter the town early in the morning when there would be a crush of people coming in to sell produce and do business while an equally large number were going out, too. The numbers would be less in winter than at other times, but traffic was still heavier in the morning and evening. Within the town it probably would be safe to change horses for the final thirty-five miles to Dieppe.

Finally he could drive himself no farther. When the arm that held Meg became so numb that he nearly dropped her, Philip began to search the sides of the road. Before disaster struck, he made out a darker shadow against the slightly lustrous dark of the clouded sky. He shook Meg awake, hating to do so but promising her she could sleep again as soon as they got to shelter. It was necessary to dismount and lead the horses over a stone fence, but once again their luck held good. The darkness was a barn with a decently filled hayloft. Philip unsaddled the horses, shut them into the pen usually used for calves, which were absent at this season, and somehow got up the ladder to the loft. He never remembered lying down in the hay and pulling it over him.

It was the horrors of the previous day, plus Megaera's guilt over having failed, that saved them from oversleeping. For two hours she slept heavily, but after that bad dreams pursued her, the men she had shot, dripping blood, reaching to drag her from a horse that kept becoming insubstantial so that she slipped down toward those clutching hands. At last she jerked awake, crying out fearfully, to find that the barn was dimly visible around her. Now she shook Philip awake and he started up, his gun in his hand, staring around wildly.

"I think it's dawn, Philip," Meg said, pushing the barrel of the pistol down gently.

He uncocked the gun and struggled to his feet without answering, shoved the pistol back in his pocket, and made his way down the ladder. It was fortunate, he thought as he relieved himself, that the manure removed from a barn was seldom studied. The thought cheered him for some obscure reason, and he found a pail, pumped water into it, swilled it clean, pumped more water, and brought it in. If the sounds brought the farmer, he didn't care. Travelers had passed inns in the dark and taken shelter in barns from time immemorial. If a coin did not soothe the man, there was always the pistol.

No one came, however. Philip had the idea that someone had looked out the kitchen window when he was pumping water, come to just the conclusion he had expected, and decided not to inquire lest the traveler would want to be invited to breakfast. But they did not have that need since a good part of the bread, cheese, and sausage remained.

Megaera had relieved herself also by the time Philip brought the bucket in. He washed sketchily; she did not. It was the part of a servant to look dirty. Considering the temperature in the barn, Megaera did not envy Philip his cleanliness. She ate while he saddled the horses, and they were away again. They made good time but at the gates of Rouen realized they were no longer ahead of their pursuers. While they had slept in the barn, messengers had preceded them. However, either they were not the quarry being hunted or Fouché had no real information when he sent out to stop them. All carriages, particularly rented vehicles, were being stopped and searched, but no one gave more than a casual glance at the gentleman with a dirty servant in cast-off, too-large clothes.

In the jakes of the large, busy posting house where they stopped to eat and change horses for the third time, Philip destroyed François Charon's passes. He would not dare use them again, and they could be incriminating if he were stopped and searched. The sealed message Charon had been carrying was sewn into the hem of Philip's greatcoat—not the best hiding place, perhaps, but he had not dared to open his boot or purchase glue to seal it again.

Carriages were still being searched when they left Rouen, but riders were scarcely scrutinized. Fouché was still unaware of Meg's exploits, Philip thought as they cleared the gate and spurred their horses along the road to Dieppe, so he did not think her capable of riding a horse so far and so fast. Then he grinned. Monsieur Fouché also seemed to be convinced that English agents were gallant gentlemen who would not abandon their female partners.

If Philip had known Fouché better, he would have been even more flattered. Monsieur Fouché never generalized about people. He had no preconceived notions about Englishmen, Frenchmen, or any man or woman of whatever nationality. Each individual was studied and judged on his or her own. It was because Philip was Roger's son that Fouché was so sure he could not leave his woman behind. Fouché knew the whole story of Leonie's rescue from Chaumette's plot. Before he went to the guillotine, Chaumette had told the tale to Fouché. Chaumette had been still furious with Roger, still puzzled as to how Roger had found his wife, still convinced that if he had managed to get the dauphin into his hands he would never have been sent to the guillotine.

In any case, once again incomplete knowledge had deceived rather than enlightened. Fouché was correct that Philip would not under any circumstances leave his accomplice behind, but he lacked two essential pieces of information: Philip was not Roger; he did not have his father's overanxious sense of responsibility. Also, Philip's attitude toward Megaera was very different from Roger's to Leonie. Double Leonie's age when he met her and aware of her mistreatment, Roger always acted as if it were a miracle that his sturdy and courageous wife had sufficient strength to draw breath. Fouché had seen Roger with Leonie, had been told that Philip was obviously very much in love with his red-haired companion—and, for once, jumped to the wrong conclusion.

Philip and Megaera were equal in age and, he believed, considering the profession in which he found her employed, equal in daring. Although Philip knew Meg's physical strength was less than his own, he never felt that a harsh wind would knock her down or that she would dissolve in the rain. Actually, it was necessary for him to remind himself from time to time that it was wrong to lead a woman into the kind of scrape he enjoyed. He regarded Meg as the perfect companion—and so she had proved herself to be.

Entering and leaving Rouen had been no trouble, but Philip was worried about Dieppe. There, he knew, the scrutiny of those coming in would be more careful. Rouen was one town out of hundreds through which the fugitives might pass, but Dieppe was a seaport and one on a narrow section of the Channel. There were other seaports, of course, and many small villages and coves along the coast where a vessel might put a boat ashore. Philip's best hope was that Fouché would expect him to be picked up secretly by an English vessel so that the greatest attention would be paid to patrolling the coast.

This day there was a wan sun, and they stopped to rest the horses where a wall caught what warmth there was from the south. Megaera was asleep before Philip had lifted her down from her horse. He tethered the animals, then sat down and took her in his arms to give her what warmth he could. Gallantry suggested that he take off his own coat and put it around her, but practicality warned him not to be an idiot. The compromise worked well enough, although both were stiff and very cold when they woke. The sun was gone, but they rode on, Philip intending to enter Dieppe as they had entered Rouen, in the midst of the morning traffic.

Because they had started earlier and the distance was shorter, they were able to stop only a few miles from the town before midnight. Philip obtained this information at the inn where he stopped to buy food. He thought briefly of a bed, but dismissed the idea at once. There was no way he could take Meg into the room with him without drawing marked attention. One did not take dirty servant boys to bed, and obviously Meg could not bed down in the men's servant quarters.

Philip now realized he had another problem. Once in Dieppe they had to wait for Pierre if he was not there. In the country one could take refuge in a barn, but not in a town. It was too cold and they were too tired to walk the streets. An inn, as he had already realized, was impossible. He had not solved the problem when they found a suitable barn and slept too soundly to be troubled, but he woke with it in the morning.

Because Philip did not want Meg to feel she was a danger and a burden, he said nothing to her about the problem of where they could stay in Dieppe, but it made him rather silent. Megaera, on the other hand, had left the horror of her double murder behind, felt rested for the first time in two days, and was in bubbling good spirits. Philip had told her to be still while they were in the barn, with the excuse that someone might hear her speaking English, but when they were on the road again that would not serve. Her chatter receiving short answers, she finally asked whether they were in trouble.

"No more than before," Philip replied.

"Then what's wrong?" Megaera persisted.

"It will be dangerous for us to go to an inn," Philip said finally without specifying why.

As he had expected, Megaera accepted that as a general statement rather than something specifically connected with herself. She wrinkled her brow in thought for a while and then said, "I know, we must go to a bawdy house. In a seaport there must be several, and I have heard that Bonaparte is much against immorality and has been harsh with such people. They will do their best, I suppose, to disoblige him and, unless they are forced, will not give up a 'criminal' to the police. Do you think Fouché has explained why you are wanted?"

Philip gaped at her. It was, in fact, a brilliant idea and one that would work—although innocent Meg did not know why. He looked at the sweet features under the dirt on her face and whooped with laughter. In a seaport the vice he was thinking of was particularly prevalent.

Megaera raised her brows. "It isn't such a silly idea at that—" she began.

"No, no," Philip assured her. "It is not a silly idea at all. Not at all."

"But I will have to change to my woman's clothes," she said, frowning at the thought of undressing in some icy alley.

"Oh, no!" Philip exclaimed, beginning to laugh again.

"You monster!" Megaera snapped. "Do you think I'm going to sit in the stable with the horses while you disport yourself—"

"No," Philip choked. "No, I did not think that. I remembered that you were not at all understanding about the harbor master's daughter."

"But you wouldn't bring your servant into a bawdy house with you. That's ridiculous."

"You know nothing about it at all," Philip rejoined, his eyes dancing, "and you are not to be my servant, just a boy picked up in the streets."

"Very well, but I don't see that that can make any difference. Why the devil should a man bring a boy into such a place?"

"I do not think I will tell you," Philip replied. "It is very shocking, and not at all the sort of thing a nice girl should know."

That puzzled Megaera so much that she fell silent. From time to time Philip glanced at her and burst out laughing again, but though she teased him for an answer, he would not give it. Then, as they drew closer to the town and houses, horsemen, and carts became more frequent, she stopped speaking, as she knew she must. About half a mile from the gate there was a lane that Philip turned down. Not far along was a shed that screened them from the road. They both dismounted and Philip unsaddled Megaera's horse, tossed the saddle into the shed, removed the bit from the bridle.

"I am sorry, love, but you will have to walk the rest of the way. You are taking the horse to town. If they ask you where, mouth something indistinguishable and keep repeating it over and over and pointing. Do the same if they ask where you are from. Do not worry, I will be right near. If I have to shoot the

gate guards, let go of the horse and run. Turn left—
there is bound to be a huddle of houses near the wall.
Just run and hide. Then make your way to the water-
front. You can ask for Pierre—just say his name as
best you can and mumble anything else you can think
of. You have both guns—the little one and the Lorenzoni?"

She nodded. "Can't I—"

"No! For God's sake, do not try to help. Remember
I will be on horseback so I can get away easily. I will
find you down by the docks. Do not worry about me."

Philip sounded confident, but he hated to make
her trudge nearly a mile in the bitter cold. He could
not imagine what any other woman would have said
to him had he suggested such a thing. Far from feeling ill-used, Meg just asked what else she could do to
help. He could only pray that she would do as he
asked and escape if there were any trouble. Now
that she was in Dieppe, she could get safely away with
Pierre, even if he were taken—so long as she did not
try to save him. He dared say no more. The last thing
he wanted was for Meg to believe he expected trouble.

The plan went awry before they even reached the
mouth of the lane. From the road a grizzled farmer
driving two sheep hailed them and asked whether
they were going to Dieppe. Since there was nowhere
close enough that he knew, which he could claim as
their destination, Philip had to agree. However, since
he felt it was important that he and Meg not be seen
to be together, he added that he had an errand in the
other direction first and that he would overtake them.

"Well, then," the farmer said cheerfully, "I'll company the boy."

"He will not be much company," Philip said sourly.
"He can't talk much."

"Ah," the good-natured man replied, "poor child,
but I see he is well fed and warmly dressed. You're a
good man to be kind to the afflicted. Go, and don't

hurry. I'll see him safely through the gates. Does he know where he's to go after that?"

"Yes, of course." Philip could feel his lips stiff, but he managed a smile. "Where are you going?"

"To the market."

"Could he wait there with you?" Philip asked, seeing a new possibility. "I have an offer for the horse, but—well, I do not trust the man and he might take advantage of the boy if I were delayed and he brought the horse there himself."

"Gladly. Gladly. Come along, boy, there's nothing to fear. Jean Sabot will take care of you."

Philip had no choice now but to canter off down the road in the opposite direction. He went only until he was sure he was out of sight, then turned and sat chewing his lips, undecided whether he wanted to kiss or kill Jean Sabot. If the man was honest, he had solved most of Philip's problems—a guide for Meg, who could not ask questions, and a clear meeting place for them. If he was not what he seemed—and he was unusually friendly for a French peasant—they were in really deep trouble.

None of these worries touched Megaera. She assumed that if Philip had left her with Jean Sabot, he had reason to believe she would be safe with the man. She smiled at him sweetly and trustfully, and he smiled back and handed her a piece of cheese that he dug from his pocket. It was rather crumbly and sharper in flavor than Megaera liked, but she bit into it with goodwill, listening to a rather rambling monologue on the state of farming. To her surprise she understood nearly everything he said—her French had been enormously improved by this stay in the country—and twice barely stopped herself from asking questions about farming methods that were different from those used in Cornwall.

Fortunately they came to the gate before she gave herself away. Here her heart sank for the first time.

The guards were examining each person who passed. Megaera looked back down the road, but Philip was not yet in sight.

"What the devil do they think they're about?" the farmer asked.

Megaera gaped at him, wordless, hoping he would think she didn't understand, but fear must have shown in her eyes, for he patted her consolingly. Then Megaera was afraid to look back for Philip again. She knew he intended that they seem separate travelers. She wished she didn't feel so lost without him. Both guns were in her pockets at half cock, but she knew she would never be able to fire them. All she could do was rely on Philip's trust in the old farmer and hope for the best.

This decision was the safest she could have made. Old Jean, although friendlier than most, was a redoubtable opponent when crossed and, fortunately, he was well known at this gate, which he had used to enter and leave Dieppe for some fifty years. By the time they got to the guardpost, he was already annoyed by the delay. The sheep had broken away twice, and Meg had run after them, giving the horse to the old man to hold. Thus, when the guards asked him for his papers, he burst into loud abuse, calling them idiots and asking them whether they had become blind and deaf that they could not remember him from the previous day. Since of course they knew him quite well, the asking had been half a joke, even though it was in accordance with their orders.

Next, of course, was Megaera. She had papers, but could not show them since they were for a woman. When asked, she looked piteously at the old man and mumbled, "*Quoi? Quoi?*" Before he could answer, a guard had gripped Megaera's arm. She cried out, more actually in nervousness than in pain, but this roused Jean to a new fury. He called the guards several improbable things, interspersing the explanation that the boy's master was down the road and, obviously, would not entrust identity papers to a simpleminded creature who would lose them. To the order that the boy must then wait Jean suggested that they shoot *him*, since he was not going to wait and had promised to bring the boy to the market and care for him.

The crowd behind by this time was growing restive at the delay, and loud abuse began to rain on the guards. A few knew Jean Sabot, but most simply were opposed automatically to authority. So, when Jean put his hand on Megaera's back and pushed her past the guardpost, telling her to drive the sheep ahead, the guards glanced at one another, shrugged, and did nothing. They were looking for a man and a woman traveling together, not for a dirty, feeble-minded boy accompanying a farmer whom they had known for most of their lives.

The decision, although they were unaware of it, saved their lives. At the edge of the crowd Philip sat silently astride his horse with his pistol at full cock concealed by a flap of his overcoat. At that distance he could have picked off both men before either could have seized his weapon and returned fire. When Megaera passed through, Philip carefully eased his weapon back to half cock and waited his turn. If they stopped him, he could shoot one and strike the other unconscious with the discharged pistol—if they were close enough. If that did not work, there would be other opportunities.

However, the contretemps between the guards and Jean Sabot stood Philip in good stead also. He showed the papers that Hawkesbury had prepared for him in the Foreign Office. All d'Ursine had been able to discover about those were that they were for a Norman merchant. Norman merchants were thick in seaports. In any case the guards were looking for two people in a carriage, and now they were hurried by a larger and larger and more and more irritable crowd. There was no special reason to think the fugitives would come to Dieppe. They glanced at Philip's papers, all in order, and let him go.

It had not been difficult for Philip to discover the direction of the kind of bawdy house he wanted once he was in the marketplace. Later, after they had left the horses in a stable and he was drawing Meg down the street toward a place known for allowing "unnatural" practices, he began to laugh again. The question in Megaera's eyes was so clear that Philip laughed still harder and drew her forward more quickly.

"Poor little boy," he gasped. "You are about to suffer a fate worse than death."

Chapter 23

From the outside the house looked quite respectable, the paint fresh and everything clean and neat. And from the affronted expression on "Madame's" face, one might have thought her a bourgeoise mortally offended by Philip's suggestion. He knew better, however. French or English made no difference; there was a pattern stamped upon "Madame" that Philip recognized. What had offended the lady was not Philip's suggestion but Megaera's dirt. Philip had requested "class" with his perversion, and apparently the man who directed him had been correct.

The problem was speedily solved when Philip requested not only a room but that a bath be brought up to it. Then he spoke very plainly on the subject of spyholes and ears glued to the walls, outlining the shape of the pistols in his pockets to make his point very clear.

"That will be expensive," the woman said, although there was a bleakness in her expression that made it plain she had recognized that Philip was no chicken for plucking.

"I will pay what is reasonable," Philip said calmly. "Do not be a fool. You have no choice. I do not live in Dieppe, and you—under the First Consul's auspices —have no one to whom to complain. However, you have a good house in a good place. I would like to be able to come here again—often. I will pay what is fair."

He named a sum, obviously less than the woman had hoped to extract from him but more than she feared he would offer after the jibe about Bonaparte's "campaign" to purify France. The clear statement that Philip intended to return was also of value. Regular business at the price he offered, when he was bringing along his own "meat," would in the end be more profitable than a single fleecing.

"Is the boy willing?" she asked. "You don't live here—very well—but I do. If he complains . . ."

"He is willing, but even if he were not, he would not complain—"

"No killing!" Madame snapped. "I don't hold with that—at least, not in the house."

"I am not a murderer," Philip said, but his smile made the woman step back involuntarily. He shook his head and the smile twisted further. A bad reputation was as valuable as a good one in different circumstances. "The boy is—not mute—just unable to make words," he remarked softly, and for evidence he twisted Megaera's ear.

That part had been rehearsed. Megaera squalled wordlessly, and pulled away looking frightened and angry, although Philip had not hurt her at all. Before she could get free, he had an arm around her and was offering assurances that he would not hurt "his dear boy" again. Megaera made angry gobbling sounds but soon allowed herself to be soothed. Madame smiled warmly at Philip, a man right after her own heart who took no chances. Then she peered more closely at Megaera, noticing for the first time the beauty of the features under the filth.

Philip saw the look and had to repress a smile. He

knew Madame was mentally licking her chops, intending to hold on to Meg after he was gone. He pretended not to notice as he handed over more of Charon's gold. He paid for three days, and Madame drew a soft breath of pleasure. By that time the "boy" should be well broken in. She thought she would have no difficulty getting him to remain. Where else could the poor creature find such a comfortable haven? Probably he had never known there was so easy a way to come by warmth and good food. All she had to offer was that and, perhaps, some fancy clothing and she would have a valuable male whore—not too easy to come by.

Upstairs Philip insisted on a corner room with two outside walls and a bed with heavy curtains. He went over the inner walls from ceiling to floor and then the ceiling itself. Madame was not pleased when he found the spyholes and was even less pleased when he caused them to be blocked by a plug connected to a long, thin rod that would clatter down, giving warning if the plug was removed or tampered with. She yielded with good grace in the end, recognizing she was dealing with a man of experience who could not be cheated but did not intend to cheat her either.

During all this Megaera stood watching with eyes so wide that Philip almost expected them to fall out, and with mouth agape. Since the attitude was quite correct for a boy of the streets, Philip did nothing to hint she should act otherwise, but he nearly strangled keeping himself from laughing aloud. And when Madame was finally gone, the bath in place and filled, and the door locked behind the servants, he gave way and roared.

"What the devil is this all about?" Megaera whispered. "You rake! You seem to have *lived* in these places."

"Not quite," Philip replied in a low voice, but grinning from ear to ear, "but I am certainly well acquainted with them. However, I admit the ones I—er—frequented did not usually sport spyholes in the ceilings and walls."

Megaera goggled at him, catching her breath, before she hissed, "Have you no shame at all?"

"No, why should I?" Philip chuckled. "What did you expect me to do, go about seducing respectable young females?"

Gasping with outrage, yet reasonable enough to be unable to reject so simple and honest a reply, Megaera could only shift her attack to new grounds. "Why was that woman virtually licking her chops when she looked at me?"

"Because she thought you were a boy," Philip answered provocatively. "Although," he continued with a grave, judicial air, "I daresay she would have been interested even if she knew you were a woman. Of course, beautiful female whores are common enough. It is much harder to obtain boys."

He jumped out of the way as Megaera launched a kick at his shin. Her eyes were blazing, her face flushed with frustration, but she could not help laughing at the same time. Philip caught her in his arms and kissed her passionately. She struggled against him at first, but not for long. Soon her arms came up around him and her mouth opened under his. Little more could be accomplished until the layers of clothing were removed, and as soon as Philip released her mouth to untie the scarf that held her hat, Megaera was demanding explanations again.

"Don't be so mean, Philip. What in the world does that woman want with a boy, beautiful or not? Do women come to these places too? And even so, why didn't she seem in the least surprised that *you* should bring me here? What would a man want with a beautiful boy?"

"My love," Philip said, pulling off her hat and be-

ginning to unbutton her coat, "you would be very
shocked if I answered you."

"I would rather be shocked than ignorant," Megaera snapped, slapping his hands away from her coat.

"Do you not want a bath, sweetheart?" Philip
wheedled. "You certainly need one—although I love
you just as much when you stink."

"I can believe it!" she exclaimed spitefully.

"Oh, no," Philip protested, grinning again, "my
women were always the best class of whores—clean,
reasonably intelligent, quite handsome—"

"I'm surprised you bothered with me!"

The laughter left his face, and he touched her
gently. "I love you. Meg, I have never tried to hide
what I am. I am not ashamed of it. I did no decent
woman any harm and, I hope, was fair to those who
make their living from their bodies. That has nothing
to do with us. I love your body, Meg, it is very beautiful; but if—and God forbid it—anything should happen that made it impossible for me ever to couple
with you again, I would love you just as much. It is
you I love, not the act."

She stared at him, utterly silenced by his deep seriousness. Megaera was desperately unsure of what she
wanted. Everywhere she looked there were new difficulties. If Philip offered her a carte blanche, she must
reject it; but even if he should offer marriage, and it
was certain that he was not contemplating a casual
relationship, she did not think she could accept. His
family would be appalled—a widow dowered only with
a mountain of debt was sufficiently unappealing.
When the tale of her unhesitating surrender to Philip
and her smuggling activities was added, they would
disown him rather than accept her.

Philip had no notion of Megaera's thoughts, but
his—except for the question of the carte blanche,
which he had dismissed long ago—were roughly simi-

lar. He was not fearful of being disowned and cut off
without a penny. He did not misunderstand his father
and stepmother so widely as that, but he was deeply
concerned that he would give them pain in choosing a
woman of whom they "could not approve." This did
not cause any wavering in his determination to marry
Meg; it only made him wonder how he could cushion
the blow for his parents.

Megaera was so responsive to him in every way that
Philip felt she could read his mind. Because he had
intended to marry her for so long, it never occurred
to him that he had not mentioned this fact to her. He
slipped off his outer clothes and stood watching her
bathe, trying to decide whether he should take her directly to London, get a special license, and present
Roger and Leonie with a fait accompli. That would
save argument and permit him to live with Meg while
they got used to the idea. It would also prevent them
from hoping they could change his mind by gentle,
indirect persuasion.

On the other hand, it would hurt them bitterly that
he should marry a woman he had known for months
without even mentioning her to them. Also, it might
put a permanent strain on the relationship between
his family and Meg, and that would be dreadful. It
would be worth depriving himself of her sweet body—
although at the moment, watching her as he was, he
was not at all sure he would survive so painful a de-
privation—if he could induce his parents to accept
her gladly. The debt could not be concealed, but
perhaps . . .

The thought became irrelevant as Megaera prepared to rise from the tub. Philip came forward holding a towel in which to wrap her. His offer to be her
lady's maid was not refused. Megaera also wished to
drown her fears about the future in a sea of physical
sensation. Philip did not disappoint her and she
uttered no complaint, even though he was not nearly

as efficient as Rose. In fact some parts of her were just as wet when he was finished as they had been when she came out of the bath. Other parts, however, were treated much more thoroughly, and nothing Rose had ever done felt so good.

Between sighs and kisses Megaera returned the compliment and served as Philip's valet, ridding him of shirt, breeches, and underclothes. From his expression and reactions he also found her ministrations more interesting than those of his regular servant. In any case they did not spend too much time comparing notes over preliminaries. They had not touched, in the sense of lovemaking, since their last night in Paris, and both were eager.

Dropping the towel, Philip pulled off his shoes and stockings. Megaera had already disappeared between the curtains of the bed and he followed her without delay. He caught her in the act of climbing into the bed and grabbed her ankle. He kissed her toes, the sole of her foot, ignoring her gasps which were half laughter from being tickled and half increasing desire, then ran his lips up her calf to the bend of the knee. Her breath drew in sharply—and not because Philip was tickling her. Involuntarily her thighs opened. Philip kissed them, her buttocks, the small of her back.

Megaera tried to turn, but he held her as she was, pulled her back toward him so that she was kneeling on the bed, and took her that way. She gurgled with surprise when he entered, but Megaera was readily adaptable, particularly when each new device Philip tried furnished exquisite pleasure. This, like riding him, allowed her freedom of movement and made even more of her body available to his hands and lips. He kissed her in places she had not even imagined lips could reach during coupling so that all too soon she slid forward burying her face in the bedclothes to muffle her shrieks of pleasure.

"I'm sorry," she whispered to Philip when he, too,

was finished and she had helped him crawl into the bed beside her. "I hope my noise won't bring them all around our ears. But, really, Philip, the ideas you get!"

"The result of my misspent life," he said wickedly. "And believe me, screaming your head off would not raise an eyebrow in this house. I imagine from the way you were gaping at everything, Madame rather expected you would do some screaming."

"Why?"

"Because you were not familiar with such a place and would not expect what would happen." He had answered lazily, hardly thinking what he was saying, half asleep in the aftermath of a climax nearly as violent as Megaera's.

"What *are* you talking about?" she asked, then shook him. "Philip, stop teasing and tell me. First it was funny, but now—screaming—I would rather be shocked than imagine horrors. If it is so dreadful, why did you—"

"I? No, love, not I," he exclaimed. "Never! I swear it! But in a boys' school one hears and sees things, and it is particularly common among sailors, from their being cooped up with only men for such long periods of time. I know a good many sailors."

"*It*. But what *is* it?"

Philip shrugged. "There are other orifices in the body, Meg. A boy can be taken as you were, except—"

"Oh, my goodness!" She looked at him with wide eyes. "No wonder screams were expected. It must be horribly painful, and—and wouldn't it squeeze you—I mean the man doing it—dreadfully?"

Philip burst out laughing. "You are the most—most . . . Are you not even a little shocked, love?"

"I'm horrified," she replied honestly, "but—but it seems so unlikely. Are you roasting me, Philip?" He shook his head silently, and she saw he was telling the truth. "I simply cannot see what pleasure—"

"Neither can I, sweetheart," Philip assured her, "and I never could, so it is useless to ask me any more questions. All I can tell you is hearsay, but those who have a taste for it seem to enjoy it fully as much as you and I. It may be hard to believe . . ."

"It certainly is."

But Megaera's voice was rather absent, as Philip's had been before it had drifted away. He seemed more interested in the shape of her lips at the moment than in the words coming out of them. To be sure he had not forgotten their shape, because his mouth had been engaged in other activities previously, he pressed them with his. Megaera understood his problem and pressed back firmly to be certain the imprint would be clear. From there on they behaved far more conventionally but no less enjoyably. Afterward neither had strength for answers or questions. Both slept.

Philip woke some hours later, told Meg to stay quietly inside the curtains until he called her out, and rang for the servants to remove the bath and bring dinner. He noticed several curious looks directed toward the closed bedcurtains, but ignored them, refraining from smiling with an effort. A wardrobe in the room had furnished a dressing gown for him and, after the meal was brought and the door relocked, Philip found another for Megaera. There were women's robes also, but he preferred that she don the too-large man's gown.

By now, for all he knew, new peepholes might have been opened. If Madame should come to suspect they were wanted by the police, which she might if she realized Megaera was concealing her sex, she might turn them in to curry favor. They had discussed this problem in low voices before Philip got out of bed, so Megaera knew just what to do. They ate quickly, and when Megaera was finished, she snatched her clothes and went to hide behind the bedcurtains to dress. Philip pretended to try to tempt her out, but she resisted his blandishments and only emerged completely clothed.

A good part of what Philip had been saying were promises to buy the "boy" presents. When Megaera came out from behind the curtains, she refused to allow Philip to kiss her, pretending that she wanted her "presents" first. Whether or not they were watched, Philip was taking no chances. They maintained the pretense consistently, and soon both donned coats and hats to go out. Madame was at the foot of the stairs when they came down, to ask what the trouble was and to suggest, if Philip was through with the boy, that he be left with her.

"An excellent idea," Philip agreed. "I would hate to think of him back on the streets again, and it would be lovely to know he would be here when I return. However, I am not yet ready to part with him. I am only taking him out to buy him a trinket."

The woman smiled significantly. "Don't spoil him," she warned.

But they didn't turn in the direction of the shops once they were out of sight. Instead they made for the docks, where, in the last of the daylight, they saw the *Bonne Lucie*. Both stopped dead. Megaera started to shake. Now, with safety so close, she began to fear they could not achieve it. They had just started forward again when a burly form cannoned into Philip, nearly sending him sprawling on the filthy, fishgut-laden street. Philip uttered an angry-seeming oath, but permitted his arm to be seized and listened to Pierre's voice offering a drunken-sounding apology and urging him to come have a drink as a "settler."

Megaera's fears evaporated, and so did the difficulties. Philip never found out what story Pierre had told the keeper of the wineshop. He was careful not to ask after he saw the leer the man gave him. What was important was that he looked the other way while all three disappeared into a back room from which only two men, both garbed as seamen and both seeming past middle age, emerged. Between them the men carried a barrel of cordage. At the dock a guard glanced at their identification perfunctorily, kicked the barrel, which did not slosh and thus could not be liquor on which the tax had not been paid, and let them go.

In Pierre's tiny cabin they all embraced. Megaera wept a little with joy and relief, and Philip gave a brief summary of their adventures. "The only thing I regret," he said, "was that we had to leave that parcel of silk with Meg's clothing."

"It doesn't matter," she said.

"But why ees eet necessary?" Pierre asked. "Where deed you leave them?"

"With the saddle at the stable where we left the horses. I would not say they were necessary, only I hate to bring Meg ashore in England dressed as a boy. There will be talk. . . ."

"Tell me what the package looks like, and Mademoiselle Meg weell 'ave eet," Pierre said, smiling at her fondly. "And do you want to do sometheeng about the 'orses?"

"No, they will be all right. The owner will sell them after a while to pay for the feed and, in the meantime, they will get a good rest. Poor beasts, they deserve it."

"If the horses are all right," Megaera protested, "it's stupid to go for the clothes. What do I care about talk in Kent or Sussex?"

"Well, I care," Philip said. "I live in Kent!"

Megaera was hurt, but neither man noticed. Pierre remarked that he had to speak to the harbor master about leaving port, so he might as well pick up Meg's parcel anyway. Megaera promptly forgot her hurt in fear for Pierre.

"Don't let him," she begged Philip.

"It will be no trouble for him, love," Philip soothed. "He feels left out. We have had all the adventures.

And you might as well have the silks." He looked sternly at her. "You will not be seeing so much of Pierre, so he cannot bring you others. I have not changed my mind. No more smuggling for you." He kissed the scar on her scalp, where the hair was just beginning to grow in around the thin line that marked her wound.

"You cannot assume the debt for Bolliet," she said faintly.

"Since I still do not know how much it is," Philip pointed out dryly, "I do not know whether I can or not, but I told you not to worry about that anymore. Something will be arranged. Now, I must go first to London to deliver Cadoudal's letters and the papers we took from Charon. Most likely they will keep me for several days asking all kinds of questions—mostly irrelevant. But after that, my love, I will escort you back to Cornwall and *I* will speak to this precious sister of yours. If she is too proud to accept my help, then she must 'dree her ane weird,' as it is said. She cannot batten on you any longer."

"But Philip—"

"Do not 'but Philip' me," he snapped angrily. "I will see that your father comes to no hurt. Perhaps he can be established in a wing of Dymchurch House if you desire that he be near you—"

"Philip—"

"I will not listen! This is ridiculous! I cannot bear to see you so worried. I tell you that if your sister were worth one hair on your head, she would never have permitted you to endure such dangers for her. Did she ever—"

"There *is* no sister," Megaera cried desperately, and burst into tears.

Philip gathered her into his arms. She cried so seldom; she had passed through such horrible dangers without crying. "Do not cry, love," he pleaded. "Do not cry. If she is so precious to you, I will learn to love her. We will see. . . ." His voice stopped as the sense of Megaera's words came to him. He had been reacting only to her pain. "What did you say?" he asked.

"I said there is no sister," Megaera sobbed. "*I* am Megaera Devoran, Mrs. Edward Devoran."

There was a rather long silence, during which Megaera clung to Philip while his arms gradually released their hold on her. Finally he gently undid her grip on him and moved back a step. "Did I hear you aright?" he asked. "Was that story all a lie?"

"Not the debt. Only—only who I was," Megaera whispered.

"But why?" Philip breathed. "Why did you lie to me?"

"I was afraid," she confessed, wiping her eyes with the back of her hand like a child.

"After what was between us you still thought I would betray you or blackmail you?" Philip's voice was cold.

"You don't understand! When I saw you at the Moretons' I couldn't think what you were doing there. I believed then that you were Pierre's natural. What could I guess but that you were cully-catching?"

"Even so," Philip said, "what had that to do with you and me? Does a man, even a cully-catcher, gull the woman he loves?"

"But I thought—"

Unfortunately Philip did not allow her to finish. If he had let Megaera go on, she would have mentioned Désirée and he would have understood that fear and jealousy had combined to unbalance her judgment. Instead he chose to leave the cabin, to walk the deck and fume until Pierre returned with the package and with permission to sail with the tide. He, asking innocently whether Meg was asleep, was treated to a full, furious recitation on women's deviousness and lack of faith. Pierre looked at Philip blankly, then smiled.

"That is to be compared with your honesty and openness, no doubt," he remarked. "Exactly what have you told *her*? Does the poor girl even know your name?"

"Of course she knows my name," Philip shouted. Then he stopped and wondered, *Did she?* What had he told Meg about himself? "I must have . . ." he began, but his voice drifted away when Pierre raised his brows quizzically. "But I did not lie," he bristled.

Pierre laughed. "Perhaps not in words." He thrust the package of silks and clothing into Philip's arms. "Here, take this. It is a good excuse to go down. Possibly you can make your peace with her before she realizes you are no better than she. Tell her, if she asks, that I have duties on the ship, which is true enough."

However, it was too late. For a while after Philip left, Megaera was desolate. She had known he would be furious when the truth came out. Then she began to feel ill-used and to tell herself that if he could discard her for a little white lie, told out of fear, she did not need such a man. And she could not have him anyway, she told herself. His parents would never accept her. It was better to save herself the shame of such a rejection and, more important, save Philip from an open break with his family. It was easier to put it that way, much easier, than to face the fear that Philip did not wish to marry her, had realized after she identified herself that a carte blanche was no longer possible, and had seized on her confession as a way out. Thus, when he knocked she would not admit him nor answer his pleas to be forgiven. At last he left the package and retreated.

It was just as well that they set sail very soon. Pierre managed to keep Philip busy helping to work the ship. It was a short passage, although bitter cold, and Pierre sailed boldly into Newhaven. It took some hours before anyone high enough in authority could be found to accept Philip's credentials and free the *Bonne Lucie*. Philip was necessarily deeply engaged in these negotiations and had no time to spare for Megaera. She was a deep anxiety at the back of his mind, but Pierre's freedom was his first responsibility. Until he was sure of that, he could do no more than arrange a room for her at the best inn in the town.

A deep depression lit by small flickers of resentment—which Megaera repressed by reminding herself that she deserved what she was getting for her abandonment of propriety and morality—sent her to bed numb and silent. By the time Philip had been successful in arranging permission for Pierre to sail again, it was two o'clock in the morning. Exhaustion had conquered Megaera's depression, and she slept. Philip tapped softly at her door when he returned from seeing Pierre off, but he was really grateful that there was no reply. He went to bed and to sleep, too tired to worry.

Chapter 24

Megaera and Philip were wakened at first light as Philip had requested. It was a long drive to London, even going post in the luxurious carriage Philip had ordered to be sent round from Brighton nine miles away. The start of the day was not auspicious. A nasty, cold rain was falling, and Megaera's mood was in perfect accord with the weather. Before Philip could speak, she demanded that he send her back to Cornwall at once.

"I do not have enough money," he replied, paling slightly. "Meg, please try to understand. It is my duty to get to London as quickly as possible with the information I am carrying, so I cannot accompany you, and I simply do not have enough money with me to pay for another carriage, horses, outriders—"

"Don't be ridiculous," Megaera snapped. "Do you think I've more hair than wit? Give me enough to pay my passage on the Mail—"

"No," Philip interrupted. "I cannot allow you to travel that way. I know you are angry with me. I do not blame you, but if you would let me explain—"

"I don't want your explanations! I want to go home."

The only explanation Megaera could think of that would make her angry was an exposition on why Philip could not ask her to marry him, and she certainly did not wish to listen to that. Philip looked as if she had slapped him, but he tried again.

"Meg, listen to reason—"

"It is always I who must listen to reason. Was it reasonable for you to drag me off to France? Why is it more reasonable for me to go all the way to London before starting for home than—"

"Because I can provide more comfort for you that way. Perhaps I have not always done the right thing or been reasonable, but I have not been as silly as you are right now," Philip snapped.

That ended the conversation. Each consumed very little breakfast in a haughty silence, during which time the horses were put to the carriage. After a punctilious and totally unnecessary question as to whether Megaera was finished eating (she had not touched anything for ten minutes), Philip escorted her formally to the carriage, made sure the bricks for warming her feet were hot enough, the rug tucked securely enough around her, the picnic basket properly stocked and where she could reach it. Then he told the postillion that he would drive, which caused the man to gape at him as if he were a lunatic. It was very rare that a toff drove a post chaise; it was unheard of for one to drive in such weather.

However, he did not drive long. In a few minutes there was a tap on the glass. Philip turned his head and saw Megaera urgently beckoning to him. He pulled up the horses, got down, and opened the door. "What do you want?" he asked.

"Do not be such a fool, Philip," Megaera said quietly. "You will be soaked and frozen. Let the postillion drive."

Philip looked at her, but she would not meet his eyes. He turned away from the door, not really sure himself what he was going to do, but the curve of her cheek was so lovely and her mouth was so sad . . . Philip told the postillion to drive on, and swung himself into the carriage. There were a few moments of silence while he shook the wet off his hat and took off his gloves to blow on his fingers. Megaera stared out the window, and Philip stared at her. Color began to rise in her face. Philip's lips twitched.

"Sweetheart," he said softly, "do not be so angry. I realize that I seemed to be blaming you for lack of confidence in me, while I was withholding my own confidence from you, but it is not true. You will think me an idiot, but Meg, I just *forgot* to tell you who I am."

"Forgot?" Megaera was so surprised that she was momentarily distracted from her pain.

Philip laughed. "We were so close. I never remembered that we had not been—been properly introduced. Let me make it good. I am Philip Joseph Guillaume St. Eyre, only son of Roger St. Eyre of Castle Stour, Kent. My uncle is Sir Arthur George Joseph St. Eyre, Bart. of Stonar Magna, Kent. When we reach London, I can present bona fides for myself, but the Moretons know me. I was staying as a guest—not a cully-catcher—and I went to Eton with Perce, Lord Kevern. They will vouch for me, I am sure."

"Ah, that's easy enough to say when we are so far from Moreton Place," Megaera remarked wickedly. She had almost forgotten, in her amusement at the formal way he introduced himself, that endless misery was waiting to swallow her. She couldn't help teasing him in revenge for that remark about cully-catching. Then she laughed at him for looking taken aback. "Never mind," she said, "I don't need bona fides, and I'm sorry I hurt you, but—"

He didn't want explanations and interrupted eagerly, "Am I forgiven?"

"Am I?"

The answer to that took some time and eliminated any need for explanations. Emerging from an embrace that was growing far too passionate for their cramped quarters, Megaera sighed.

"What is it, love?" Philip asked tenderly. "You are not still worried about those stupid debts, are you? There can be no problem at all now that the lands will be yours someday. Leonie can buy up the mortgages if my father has not quite enough to cover them, and—"

The kiss was sweet and the concern for her worries kind, but Megaera had not heard the one thing she wanted to hear. Philip still said nothing of marriage —and now a woman's name, familiarly spoken with a note of tenderness had come out. "Who is Leonie?" Megaera interrupted sharply.

"Oh, you jealous little cat," Philip chuckled. "Do you think I ask my wealthy mistresses to . . . No, no, love, do not lose your temper all over again. Leonie is my stepmother—and as far from the wicked kind as it is possible to get."

"I don't see why it should make any difference whether the lands will be mine or not," Megaera said. "Why should your stepmother be willing to buy up the mortgages? If I cannot make money smuggling, it will take forever to pay them off."

"But my dear Meg, Leonie would think it highly improper for her daughter-in-law to be involved in smuggling," Philip said gravely, but with laughing eyes.

"Daughter-in-law?" Megaera echoed. "Are you married?" she shrieked.

"Married?" Philip repeated, totally confused. "Of course I am not married. What are you talking about?"

"Then who is Leonie's daughter-in-law? Didn't you say—oh, you mean Leonie's son's wife. But what has her smuggling got to do with my estates?"

Philip just sat staring at Meg with his mouth open.

He had lost control over the conversation completely. In fact he seemed to have lost contact with reality. "Do you think everyone casually takes up smuggling?" he asked. Then, before Megaera could answer, he shook his head sharply. "We do not seem to be speaking the same language. Perhaps I had better go back to the beginning. Leonie has no son—unless you mean me—and her daughter-in-law is you."

"You mean you are going to tell your family that we are married?"

Megaera was completely confused by Philip's use of the present tense rather than the future. Instead of recognizing that he had long considered himself married to her, she thought he intended to lie about it to remain free while his stepmother bought out the mortgages. She did not know whether to be hurt by his desire to avoid marrying her, revolted by the sneaking device, or touched by his concern for her safety.

"But Philip," she said faintly, "I don't see . . . I mean, that isn't right. Surely they will ask for proof before they . . . I know there are legal arrangements. . . ."

"Yes, and they take a damned long time, too," Philip said aggrievedly, concentrating on his own thoughts, so that Megaera's broken sentences did not quite penetrate. "I did think of marrying you by special license, but I am afraid it would hurt my father's feelings—"

"You mean you wish to marry me?" Megaera asked. If his concern was for his parents rather than that he himself thought her unworthy of marriage, it would be easier to bear.

Philip looked at her with abstracted eyes. "I am not sure—"

"What do you mean, you aren't sure?" Megaera shrieked, bitterly hurt.

He jumped with surprise at the ferocity and anguish in her voice. "I did not mean to hurt you, love.

Of course we will do just as you like. If you want St. George's at Hanover Square, that is what you will have. I only thought of a special license because I—because I want to be with you, and if we wait for the settlements to be arranged—"

"Do you or do you not want to marry me?" Megaera asked, shaking him in exasperation.

Enlightenment came to Philip. His eyes opened wide and he drew in his breath, torn between amusement and apprehension. "Good God," he murmured, "do not murder me, Meg, please do not. I—I guess I forgot to ask you."

There was a brief, breath-held silence while Megaera tried to decide whether to burst out laughing or slap Philip's face. He watched her anxiously, but with just a glint of laughter in his eyes.

"But Meg," he wheedled, "I never intended anything else. I thought you knew. It would be most—"

"If you say it would be most improper not to marry me after what you have done, I *will* murder you," she spluttered. "A remark like that would be insulting rather than—"

Naturally she was not allowed to finish. "It will have to be a special license," Philip sighed after he freed his lips to catch his breath. "I do not think I will survive months of lawyers fiddling about with settlements."

"Or I either," Megaera agreed frankly, "but we must. You cannot distress your parents by doing something you know they would dislike, especially when the woman you wish to marry will not be at all . . . Oh, Philip, perhaps we had better not. I could not bear to be the cause of an estrangement between you and your family."

"Do not be foolish. I would marry you even if no one in the world would ever speak to me again, but there will not be any estrangement. My father and Leonie are not that kind." Philip's voice was firm, but his eyes were worried. "Perhaps we could say nothing to them about—"

"No. No, Philip, you—or I—must tell them everything as soon as possible. It cannot be concealed. Too many of our memories are tied up with what I have done, and as soon as Pierre sees your father . . . No. For them to hear from anyone but you or me would be terrible."

"Yes."

They reached the end of the first stage before either spoke again. Philip asked if Megaera wanted to have some tea or stretch her legs, but she merely shook her head. Now that she realized Philip had never scorned or undervalued her, she was racked by guilt. She had enough good sense, however, to realize there could be no question now of running away or refusing marriage. It was a good thing that she had had only a few hours of sleep the previous night and none at all the night before that. Soon after the carriage started off again, sleep overcame her.

When he was sure Megaera was well and truly asleep, Philip took over the reins again. The rain had stopped, and the Brighton to London road was particularly good because it was traveled so often by the Prince Regent and his court. Philip was a far better whip than the hired man, so that the ride was smooth and swift, but Philip need not have worried about Megaera. Emotion and physical fatigue had combined to form a powerful soporific drug.

Megaera was roused finally by the frequent stops and starts of London traffic and the loud clatter of wheels over cobblestones. By now she was too accustomed to being in strange places to be alarmed, but she wondered for a frightened minute or two whether she had dreamed the escape and they were back in Paris. Then as sleep receded she realized the unintelligible cries of the street vendors were only a coarse accent new to her. The words were English. The houses went on and on. Megaera shuddered. They were in London already. She sat upright and tried to straighten her crumpled bonnet. It was hopeless.

Tears rose into Megaera's eyes. She would certainly begin on the wrong foot with Philip's family. She was wrinkled and dirty, her hair shorn raggedly and looking worse than it should because the bonnet had been chosen to sit over the heavy coils of her long hair. She had no baggage, not even clean underlinen. It must be obvious to anyone that she was Philip's mistress, traveling with him without even a maid. But perhaps he would not take her directly to his parents' house.

Where else could he take her? No decent hotel would permit her to cross the threshold in the condition she was in, no matter how clever the story Philip told. And if the manager could be convinced, it would only make matters worse. The story would be all over town in no time. Suddenly Megaera peered anxiously out of the window. Surely he would not take her to a bawdy house again! Although her fear was not immediately relieved, she could see that the streets were getting wider, the houses neater and better cared for. They were moving into a better part of the city—but Madame's house in Dieppe had been on quite an elegant street.

The doubt could not linger. The houses changed from good to elegant and then to grand. Megaera shivered again. She had no idea that Philip's father was so wealthy. From what Philip said, Roger was a younger son of a baronet, since his uncle was a Sir Arthur. As the carriage pulled up before a veritable mansion, Megaera shrank back farther in the carriage, so terrified that for a moment she really considered opening the far door of the vehicle and running away. Only the hard fact that she had no purse, no acquaintance, and nowhere to go held her in place.

The door opened very promptly to Philip's knock, giving immediate evidence of how precious a member of the family he was. The butler, clearly a well-trained and august personage, was so relieved and pleased to see Philip that his dignity broke, and he exclaimed, "Master Philip! Thank God!"

"Yes, here is the bad penny again," Philip said cheerfully, shaking the servant's hand fondly. "Is Lady Leonie at home?"

"Yes, indeed, sir, and, if I may say so, she will be very, very happy to see you again."

"Well, I—" Philip looked anxiously back at the carriage, unsure of whether to go in and prepare Leonie for Meg or bring Meg in with him.

The choice was not left to him. Leonie had heard a carriage stop and had looked out the window. At the sight of a hired vehicle hope sprang up unbidden. She knew perfectly well that it might be any of Roger's numerous half-brothers or -sisters—the luxury of the vehicle implied that it was a woman traveling. Nonetheless Leonie could not help running out into the corridor—as she had been doing like a fool since Philip left. But this time hope was confirmed when she heard the butler utter Philip's name. She flew down the stairs and into his arms, hugging and kissing him, careless alike of the cold, the butler's smile (soon hidden), and the shock on the face of a passerby.

"*Cher, cher Philippe, tu en es revenu sain et sauf!*"

"*Bien sûr, Leonie, ne sois pas si sotte.* But listen, I have someone with me. Her name is Megaera Devoran, and she is the daughter of Lord Bolliet of Bolliet, Cornwall, but—"

Megaera bit her lips hard to keep back her tears at the knowing look that flashed across Leonie's face, but what she said was a complete surprise. "*Bête!*" she cried, "the girl of whom you wrote. I know what you have done. You have led the poor girl into mischief, and now she is afraid to come in."

"But I want to marry her," Philip said.

"*Bien sûr,*" Leonie agreed. "Would you bring to me

a girl you did *not* wish to marry?" She advanced on the carriage and opened the door while Philip let down the step. "Come in, my dear, come in. That Philippe is a fool the most extraordinary. Did you hear him announcing to the whole street that he wishes to marry you? He has no reserve, that one."

Megaera swallowed hard. It did not seem to her that Leonie had much reserve either, but she did not dare laugh, and her eyes were enormous with nervousness. It was Leonie who laughed.

"You must think me mad," she said, "but I have been so worried. That Philippe, he takes no care. Everything he does he says is not dangerous. If he were to take it into his head to fly off a mountain, he would explain how it does birds no harm and, therefore, must be safe. Come, my dear, you must be very stiff and cold."

Knowing she could delay no longer—Leonie was shivering—Megaera struggled out of the carriage. She was not cold but was, indeed, so stiff that if Philip had not caught her, she would have fallen. Leonie cried out with concern, and Philip picked Megaera up and carried her into the house. He turned toward one of the drawing rooms, but Leonie waved her hands at him.

"Upstairs, upstairs," she ordered. "After such a trip Megaera will want to rest, and the maids must see to her clothes."

"I have none," Megaera whispered.

"*Zut!*" Leonie remarked with unimpaired cheerfulness, to Megaera's intense surprise. "Like father, like son! Always they cause such upheavals that a woman must come away just as she is. Roger is bad enough, but with Philippe I am surprised you are not in your bare skin. Never mind. We will find something. I am too big, but Sabrina's gowns may fit you with a little touch here or there. She is a blonde, unfortunately— but we will find something. The blue room, Philippe,"

she called after them, "I must send a footman to tell
Roger you are home."

"Put me down," Megaera said at the top of the
stairs, "I think I can walk now."

"Nonsense," Philip whispered, squeezing her. "This
is the last chance I will have to hold you until those
damned lawyers get finished haggling."

He got the door open and deposited Megaera on an
exquisite white-brocade chaise longue. She bounced
up instantly with a cry of horror, fearing her filthy
pelisse would soil the fabric. Philip laughed at her,
but realized she was upset by more than dirtying the
white chair.

"What is it, love?" he asked.

"I had no idea you were so rich," Megaera said
honestly.

"I am not," Philip replied. "This is Leonie's. She
is the heiress of the Earls of Stour." He kissed her
forehead. "Do not let it frighten you. You see, Leonie
is not at all a grande dame. However, I do not mean
to say that I am poor either."

"Philip, perhaps—"

But he would not let her finish and closed her
mouth with his. From the doorway Leonie smiled
approvingly, then stepped aside before they saw her
and called out, quite unnecessarily, to the butler.
Megaera pushed convulsively at Philip, and he released her reluctantly, turning his head to grin over
his shoulder at Leonie, who had reappeared in the
open doorway.

"Go away, bad boy," she said. "Sorel is having a
bath brought to your room. You have already filled
the whole house with the smell of fish, from which I
suppose you came on the *Bonne Lucie*. How is
Pierre?"

"Very well, and we should be seeing more of him
now. I think I have convinced him to trade at Kingsdown again."

"Ah, good—unless—will it be more dangerous? But no! This we can speak of later. Go! Bathe! And tell Sorel to *burn* those things you are wearing."

"*Oui, madame.*" Philip bowed deeply, formally, and scurried out of range, promising to relay Leonie's message to Sorel as she reached out to twist his ear.

Megaera stood frozen, barely able to restrain herself from running after him. She knew Leonie's kind playfulness in Philip's presence could be a mask drawn on for his benefit. She tried to brace herself for a new, colder, face and voice. It was ridiculous, she told herself, to be so terrified; there was nothing Leonie could do to her. But Leonie did not try to do anything. She was less animated with Philip gone, but just as pleasant. She talked gently to Megaera, encouraged her to take off her soiled pelisse and bonnet, and opened the wardrobes in the adjoining dressing room to display a full range of women's clothing. There was a tap on the door, which opened at Leonie's call to show menservants lugging a tub and buckets of hot water.

"I am so sorry, Megaera," Leonie exclaimed a moment later. "I should have left it to you to give permission to enter. You forgive?"

"Oh yes, indeed. Please—"

"It is Sabrina's room, you see, my cousin, but I have raised her and, like a mama, I have no courtesy when I am here. I thought if you would not mind staying here it would save the maids carrying the clothing back and forth until you decided what you wanted to wear. You do not mind?"

"No, but would Sabrina . . . I mean Miss—"

"Lady Elvan. Sabrina is married to William, Lord Elvan."

Did a flicker of a frown cross Leonie's placid face, Megaera wondered? If so, it was gone before Megaera could be sure and was replaced by a smile.

"This is Katie," Leonie continued, gesturing at a young maid, who dropped a curtsy. "She will wait on you. And this is Annie." An older woman also dropped a curtsy. "She is very clever with her needle. Just pick anything you like to wear, my dear, and Annie will fix it to fit you while you bathe. Do not give a thought to Sabrina. She would give it all to you, if she thought that would give Philippe a minute's pleasure." There was a short pause, and Leonie sighed. "Really, I would like best to stay and hear all about your adventure, but that would be very wrong, I know."

"I will tell you anything you want to know," Megaera said, trying to keep her voice steady.

"I know you would, *petite,* but it would be unkind of me when you are so tired and, I can see, still frightened. Roger would be angry. . . . Well, no, he is never angry with me, but he would think it cruel. Later, Megaera—ah, perhaps I should have called you Miss Devoran, but because you are Philippe's affianced . . ."

"Please, Megaera or even Meg, but—but it's *Mrs.* Devoran."

Leonie looked startled. "A widow. . . . Should I say I am sorry, my dear?"

"No!" Megaera exclaimed with so much force that Leonie's eyes widened.

"Did you—" she began, then clapped her hand over her mouth.

Megaera felt frozen again. It was plain that Leonie did not like the notion that she was a widow. She hardly felt Katie unbuttoning and removing her clothes and only came to with a start when the soft, Irish-burred voice of the maid asked if the peignoir she was holding would be satisfactory. Megaera agreed before she really saw it, but it was a lovely thing. Next Katie displayed two morning dresses and an evening gown.

"I don't think Annie could do more until tomorrow," Katie said shyly.

"No, and in any case I cannot make free with Lady Elvan's wardrobe."

But she hardly knew what she said. She could not imagine what Leonie had been about to ask before she stopped herself. In a way she was sorry for the restraint Philip's stepmother had shown. The warm welcome had been so unexpected and so wonderful. Philip had been right when he said that Leonie was a kind person and would want to love and be loved by her prospective daughter-in-law, that she would be willing to overlook certain deviations from the accepted code of good behavior. However, Leonie had already shown dismay on hearing that Megaera was a widow. How, then, would she react to the tale of smuggling, the huge debts on Bolliet, and living with Philip openly? Those were scarcely to be classed in the same order as losing one's wardrobe.

It would be all the more painful when coldness replaced warmth, Megaera knew. She tried desperately to think of some way of describing the situation so that it did not sound quite so dreadful. No matter how she turned it, however, it sounded worse and worse. She was hardly aware of being bathed and dried, wrapped in another, equally elegant, peignoir, led to the chaise to rest. She was only aware of the hours passing, of the fact that she had not been called to make a part of the family party that was no doubt hashing out her future without permitting her to say a word in her own defense.

She surfaced briefly when Katie urged her to sit up, inserted her into undergarments every bit as lovely as the special ones bought for her trousseau, and rewrapped her in a dressing gown so that the hairdresser might come in and attend to her. If she had not been so depressed, he would have made her laugh, a furiously voluble little man who clucked and groaned and said dreadful things under his breath about whoever had cut her hair. He made the best of it, although it seemed to take him a very long time.

When Megaera became aware of the immediate
present again, she was being asked anxiously if she
felt strong enough to be dressed and go down for supper or if she would prefer to go to bed. So, she thought,
the jury has come to its decision and the accused is
being brought before the judge to hear sentence. She
had one advantage; she could delay judgment by a
few hours. But Megaera was not really tempted. She
knew that indecision was always more unendurable
than pain. However, a real hope that Leonie was
on her side was born when she saw herself. She had
been dressed in a delightful confection of sea green
with tiny puffed sleeves and a deeply flounced hem.
Her hair was trimmed neatly and curled so enchant-
ingly that she did not miss the heavy knot with its
hanging curls. Surely if Leonie directed that she be
made to look beautiful, she did not mean to try to
turn Philip against her.

The enormous improvement in her appearance gave
her sufficient courage to go downstairs, but her knees
were shaking so much that she had to cling to the
banister. It was very odd, she thought, but she was far
more frightened now than she had been when Fouché's
men had nearly captured them. The door was invit-
ingly open, but she was the last to enter the room.
Leonie, Philip, and a man who resembled Philip so
closely that it had to be his father, were already
grouped near the tea table. Their voices came to her,
and when she heard the subject of conversation, she
felt a dreadful fool.

It seemed to her as if no one had been judging her
or even thinking about her. All the hours she had
spent primping and selfishly worrying about herself,
poor Philip had probably been making reports and
delivering the letters Cadoudal had sent with him.
Philip's father was saying, "I don't know what Addington will decide. He doesn't seem to be able to decide

anything these days, but I don't think it matters, either. If Pichegru wants to go, go he will. I think that matter is well and truly out of our hands."

"Yes," Philip replied, "and I am just as glad that it is. I do not like the thought of shooting a man in the head or the back by surprise. You would think the French had had enough of government by assassination during the Terror and the Directories."

"Ah," Roger laughed, "but that was legal—or semi-legal—assassination, if you can call anything done by the insane laws they had then legal. Now they are ready to try illegal assassination and see if that works better."

Leonie shuddered. "Me, I do not see that that is funny, Roger."

"No, my dear, it is not. I laugh because I am helpless—and furious—and whichever way I look I only see more bloodshed."

"Well, at least it will be a little less of ours now that d'Ursine is exposed," Leonie said with satisfaction.

"Yes, but the exposure of Charon was equally important. His shop was a center for spying. It is being watched very discreetly, and will be for some time. When we have all the information we can get that way, we will have a little gathering of the guilty."

Megaera had stood clinging to the doorway, listening. Her first relief had melted into dire apprehension. Perhaps the tender care she had received was because Philip had been too busy to tell her story. Now she would have to do it herself. At that moment Mr. St. Eyre looked in her direction. He had the bluest eyes Megaera had ever seen. Megaera tried to step forward, but couldn't. Now they would think she had been eavesdropping.

"My dear," Roger exclaimed, hurrying toward her and taking her hand, "you should not have come down. You should be in bed after the exertions of this past week. I have never been so furious with that hare-brained boy in my life. To drag you—"

"Do not be silly, Roger," Leonie said. "Megaera is not tired. She is frightened to death of you and me. Is it not so, *petite*? Come, sit with me, and Philippe will bring you a cup of tea. There is no need to be frightened."

"Yes, but I think there is," Megaera said, "for I am afraid that I am not at all the kind of person you would have wished your son to marry."

"Now that is what I call taking the bull by the horns," Philip remarked. "Meg, my love, tact is not your strong suit."

"There is no way to be tactful about the things I have done," Megaera snapped, quite revived by her fury at Philip's casual attitude.

This was reasonable, as she could not know that Leonie had laughed her head off at Megaera's direct attack on the subject of debts by smuggling to pay them off. Roger had clicked his tongue sadly over the silliness of women, pointing out that if she had gone to the creditors and explained her problem—or, rather, had a solicitor do it for her—very likely the payments could have been adjusted to the income of the estate and the whole enterprise would have been unnecessary. No comment at all had been made about the physical relationship; Roger and Leonie could not afford to be "holier than thou" on *that* subject. Now Leonie cocked her head at Megaera's statement.

"Why, what more have you done than Philippe has told us?" Leonie asked with an interested expression. "Did you murder your husband?"

"Leonie!" Roger roared.

Leonie shrugged, and winked at him. "No, one can see from poor Megaera's face that not only did she not do it but she never would have thought of such a thing."

"That's true," Megaera agreed, but added defiantly, "but I was *glad*. And I didn't turn in his murderer."

"That, I think, was not wise," Roger remarked judicially.

"It certainly wasn't," Philip laughed, "since he wasn't grateful at all. He turned around and tried to murder Meg twice."

"But he must have been a horrible man," Leonie pointed out, her golden eyes bright with what Megaera was shocked to see was approval.

"The murderer or the husband?" Philip asked teasingly.

"The murderer, too, no doubt, but I was thinking of the husband."

"Yes, he was," Megaera said, "but that's not important now."

"You are wrong, *petite*," Leonie contradicted with a brilliant smile. "It is most important because Philippe, he needs to be loved with a whole heart. It is hard sometimes for a woman who has loved her first husband to give without reservation to the second."

Megaera blushed hotly. "I love him," she admitted. "Perhaps you will think I have loved him too well. I—"

"You shot two men to keep him alive," Roger interrupted. "I am not going to complain about how well you love Philip."

"No, you cannot afford to do that," Leonie put in mischievously. "That would be too much like the pot calling the kettle black." Then she took Megaera's hand. "*Petite*, do not distress yourself. Philippe has told us all we need to know. What is past is past. There is no need anymore to worry. All will be arranged. Philippe desires to marry very soon, but you must say what is your desire and all else can be left to the men of business."

"Oh, I want to marry soon too," Megaera cried, and then turned red as a beet while Philip laughed at her.

She looked back and forth from Roger to Leonie. "You—you don't mind? The smuggling? The debts?"

Roger just smiled at her. His smile was softer than Philip's, warming and reassuring.

"Poof!" Leonie gestured it all away. "The land will pay back itself without trouble, and how can we, whose dearest friend has been a smuggler all his life, speak ill of it? No, there is only one thing you will have to do—"

"My father? But he can stay—"

"Not that, Meg." Philip came forward and took her hand. His mouth was laughing, but his eyes were full of love. "Leonie is jealous of your ability as a shot."

"Yes!" Leonie exclaimed. "For me it was necessary to put the gun right to the head of the beast. That is very inconvenient. You will teach me, *n'est-ce pas, petite*? Roger and Philippe only laugh at me, but you will have patience and teach me well."

Leonie paused and watched approvingly as Philip pulled Megaera to her feet and kissed her passionately. "But I think I will have to learn fast, before the little ones come," she murmured.

Author's Note

In the eighteenth and the very beginning of the nine-
teenth centuries, smuggling was a way of life in Cornwall. Everyone was involved to some extent; to stave
off starvation or obtain an occasional luxury, the common folk were happy to aid the smugglers or to "watch
the wall" while the "gentlemen" went by. The gentry
bought the goods and also "looked the other way."
However, for the gentry a marked gulf existed between
drinking untaxed liquor or smoking untaxed tobacco
and actually making money out of smuggling. To be
exposed as engaging in the unsavory trade for profit
could bring severe social penalties, even if one escaped
the legal consequences; one would become déclassé
and be ostracized.

As in *The English Heiress,* every attempt has been
made to maintain historical accuracy. Although the
central characters of the book are fictional, as are the
adventures in which they are engaged, the general
events are real. England did fear an invasion and
Bonaparte was indeed in Boulogne in November 1803,
going about the workshops and camps and encouraging the men to greater efforts. However, it should be
noted that it was not possible for the author to dis-

cover certain facts, like the real name of the *Chef du port maritime* of Boulogne in 1803 or whether he had a daughter. Since the result of Philip's spying was entirely negative—the invasion fleet, despite Bonaparte's efforts, was not ready until 1805 and in fact never was launched—the intrusion of a fictional spy does no violence to historical events.

In the same way, although Jacques d'Ursine, François Charon, and the other French agents are fictional, no distortion of reality results. The basic contention that some émigrés became spies for Bonaparte is true, as is the implication that some found their way into high places owing to their aristocratic connections before exile. Typical types are used: those who are totally unprincipled and those who are true patriots. It must be remembered, however, that only one side of the coin is shown in this book; in reality, as many émigrés were devoted to their adopted country and served England faithfully, and also there were plenty of Englishmen who betrayed their nation for money.

The final adventure is dealt with similarly. Georges Cadoudal and the plot to overthrow and later to assassinate Bonaparte are real. There is evidence that Méhée de la Touche and Joseph Fouché were involved as described. Logic demands some communication between the supporters of the plot in England and the activists in France. Again, no violence is done to history if the fictional characters take part in a way that "must have" happened.

It is my hope that this pastiche of reality and fantasy will bring life to history and be both enjoyable and informative. Any comments or corrections from readers will be gratefully received.

Roberta Gellis
Roslyn Heights, 1981

Author's Biography

A native New Yorker, Roberta Gellis has had a dual interest in science and historical literature since early childhood. She began her writing career twenty-one years ago as a diversion from new motherhood and has been writing historical fiction ever since. She has a B.S. in chemistry, an M.S. in biochemistry, and an M.A. in medieval literature. Some of her best-selling novels are *The Sword and the Swan, The Dragon and the Rose,* and *The Roselynde Chronicle.* Ms. Gellis presently lives with her artist-photographer husband, Charles, and her college-age son, Mark, in Roslyn Heights, New York. *The Cornish Heiress* is the second novel in the Heiress series. The series takes place in Europe from the time of the French Revolution through Napoleon's dynamic rise to power.

The English Heiress, the initial book in Roberta Gellis's passionate and intriguing Heiress series, introduces us for the first time to Roger St. Eyre and Leonie de Conyers.

In *The Kentish Heiress,* Book Three, we will follow Perce Moreton in his crucial role on the continent as Napoleon's dynamic rise to power begins to threaten all of Europe. And we see him meet and fall in love with the breathtakingly beautiful—but heartbreakingly unavailable—Sabrina.

Here is a glimpse of the romance and adventure that lies ahead in *The Kentish Heiress,* to be published by Dell next fall.

Sabrina had completed the leave-taking notes and was piling them together to be given to the

footmen to be delivered, when an incredible
uproar broke out on the floor below. She heard
a footman cry out in frightened protest and
then Perce's voice shouting her name. She flew
out of her sitting room and almost collided with
Perce, who was leaping up the stairs with his
greatcoat still on and a pistol in his hand. The
footmen, now recovered from their initial shock,
were pounding up the stairs behind him, determined to protect their "little mother" even at
the cost of their lives.

"Stop!" Sabrina shrieked at them.

They obeyed, but largely because they saw the
pistol drop to point at the ground the instant
Perce saw their mistress.

"Go. Go," she ordered. "You know well that
this is my dear friend and he would not harm
me." And then, turning to Perce, who was
clutching the bannister and gasping for breath,
"What's happened? Perce, what's wrong?"

"You're asking *me* what's wrong?" he choked.

"What are you doing with that gun?" she
cried.

He stared at her for a minute, until he caught
his breath. "What the devil did you expect when
you sent me a note saying, '*Something dreadful
has happened. Come at once*'—and then your
butler tells me you aren't receiving anyone. I
thought . . . I thought your husband was about
to murder you."

"Oh, heavens! Is that what I wrote? I—" She
grasped his arm and pulled him into her sitting
room. "I'm so sorry. I had no idea . . ."

He threw his greatcoat on a chair. "Sabrina,
what *has* happened?"

"Pitt's dead. William has been ordered home.
We must leave tomorrow." Sabrina was blushing furiously. "I only meant to tell you that we

were leaving. I can't imagine why I should have written anything so silly. I suppose—"

But there was no need for Sabrina to try to explain what she had done. Perce had taken two steps, caught her in his arms, and prevented her from speaking at all by kissing her. Surprise held her still for a moment, and then she was returning his embrace with passionate urgency, clinging fiercely to him when she felt his lips releasing hers. But he was not withdrawing, only lifting his mouth to whisper, "Darling, darling," before he kissed her feverishly again, pressing his lips to her ears and throat.

They were locked together, feeding on each other's passion. Sabrina slipped her arms under Perce's coat, the better to feel his body. He had worked one of her short sleeves off her shoulder and was kissing that and the tops of her breasts while she ran her lips up and down the back of his neck. One of his arms clutched her close, the other stroked her, picked at the tiny buttons on the back of her dress.

Neither heard the door open and then close softly almost at once. Katy stood with her back against it, a stunned expression on her face. She had begun to associate Sabrina's happiness with Lord Kevern's presence in St. Petersburg—but not for this reason!

The first novel in the spectacular new
Heiress series

The English Heiress

Roberta Gellis

Leonie De Conyers—beautiful, aristocratic, she lived in the
shadow of the guillotine, stripped of everything she held
dear. Roger St. Eyre—an English nobleman, he set out to save
Leonie in a world gone mad.

They would be kidnapped, denounced and brutally separated. Driven by passion, they would escape France, return
to England, fulfill their glorious destiny and seize a lofty
dream.

A Dell Book $2.50 (12141-8)

The continuation of
the exciting six-book series that
began with *The Exiles*

The SETTLERS

WILLIAM STUART LONG

Volume II of *The Australians*

Set against the turbulent epic of a nation's birth is
the unforgettable chronicle of fiery Jenny
Taggart—a woman whose life would be torn by
betrayal, flayed by tragedy, enflamed by love and
sustained by inconquerable determination

A Dell Book $2.95   (15923-7)

Dell Bestsellers